THE NEIGHBORHOOD WITCH

THE NEIGHBORHOOD SERIES
BOOK ONE

CHRISTOPHER M. MASON

The Neighborhood Witch © 2023 by Christopher M. Mason

Published by Candlestick Publishing, LLC.

Author's Website: https://www.christophermmason.com

First Edition

First Printing 2023

Library of Congress Control Number: 2023901469

ISBN 979-8-9874276-0-6 (Hardback)

ISBN 979-8-9874276-1-3 (Paperback)

ISBN 979-8-9874276-2-0 (eBook)

Cover Design by Fay Lane (http://www.faylane.com)

Edited by Nichole Heydenburg of Poisoned Ink Press

Book Blurb Edited by Kara Bernard of Bernard's Editorial Services

Animated Cover Design by Morgan Wright (@byMorganWright)

Character Art by Nicole Deal (@nicoledealart)

For those who have experienced loss.
It's okay to not be okay.

THE DARK NIGHT OF HUGO'S SOUL

Hugo Dodds sat at the L-shaped desk in the beige-striped wallpapered office of the funeral home director. The smell of carnations and lilies filled the air. Neatly formed stacks of paper littered the desk surface, but kept their distance from a solitary piece of paper in the center. Hugo slumped forward in the mahogany chair, shoulders drooping, his face inches from his wife's obituary. He scanned it, reading the lines over and over. His eyes labored with every word before continuing on to the next.

Elizabeth Patricia Dodds, age 37, of Newbury Grove, passed away March 30 after a courageous and lengthy battle with cancer. Elizabeth is survived by her husband, Hugo Dodds. She was born in Columbus, OH. A graduate of Newbury Grove High School, she followed her passion for teaching children by returning to Newbury Grove High School as a history teacher following college. Elizabeth was a beloved member of the community whose kind heart and caring soul brought much joy to Newbury Grove. She is preceded in death by her parents,

Joseph and Patricia Clark. Calling hours will be Wednesday from 4:00 to 8:00 p.m. at Hill Funeral Home. Funeral services will be held at St. Jude Church on Thursday at 1:00 p.m. Burial will follow at Newbury Grove Memorial Park.

This wasn't real to Hugo. It was nonsense. This was an alcohol-induced nightmare he'd wake up from at any moment to find her lying next to him in bed.

Elizabeth P Dodds... beloved member of the community.

Yes. A nightmare. A nightmare after having too much wine.

...A graduate of Newbury Grove High School...

Yet, he knew that wasn't true. This nightmare wasn't a dream. The piece of paper in front of him was all too real. He knew it because he lived it.

...passed away...

His hands cupped the underside of his knees. Hugo lightly tapped the chair bottom with his pinky fingers. His body shook as his foot twitched at a rapidly increasing pace.

The seat had no padding. The seat imprisoned him, torturing him to face reality. The seat had no padding. The armrests pinched Hugo's legs as he shifted to find a more comfortable position. He wanted to leave. Run away. The chair kept him in place, forcing him to confront the paper before him.

...preceded in death by her parents...

He had to escape.

...Burial will follow...

He had to break out.

Elizabeth Patricia Dodds, age 37...

He needed to flee.

...passed away...

The steady rhythm of the ticking clock broke the uncomfortable silence in the room. A cloud of liquid spray discharged from an air freshener, filling the room with the smell of fresh linen.

"Does everything look okay?" the funeral director asked.

Hugo turned his attention to the short, stocky man in front of him. Robert Hill, a third-generation funeral director who helped guide Hugo through these troubling times, awaited an answer. Hugo gave a slight nod and then dropped his icy blue eyes back toward the obituary.

...survived by her husband...

Robert grabbed the piece of paper and whisked it away into a manila folder. Hugo's eyes widened as the folder closed, further cementing this new reality. Hugo slumped back in his seat. Elizabeth's name was written on the folder tab in blue ink. He scratched his head, careful not to mess up his trimmed, combed brown hair. His hand worked down to rub his clean-shaven chin. He then pinched his black onyx wedding ring between his thumb and index finger, spinning it uncontrollably. He glanced over the room.

Flowers and pictures of Robert's family decorated a hutch behind Robert's desk. Pictures of a happy family from a happier time. Hugo fixed his gaze on a family portrait. Robert, his wife, son, and daughter all appeared happy, healthy, and having fun. Hugo focused on the manila folder and then the funeral director.

"What am I supposed to do now?" Hugo asked.

"Don't worry about a thing. We'll coordinate everything with the florist, the newspaper, and the cemetery. We'll make this as easy for you as possible."

"No, I mean, what am I supposed to do now that she's gone?"

Robert gasped and gawked wide-eyed at Hugo. "Umm..."

Robert's gaze dropped, and he shook his head back and forth as he scanned the desk in what Hugo assumed was the search for an answer. Any answer. The wait was excruciating. Robert turned back to Hugo. Robert's eyelids drew close together, but never touched. His lips pulled in tightly. He scratched his neatly trimmed black hair.

"I've.... I've never been asked that before," Robert replied.

Hugo slouched down, peering at where the obituary was moments earlier. He focused on the vacant space, searching for an answer. Nothing was coming to him. Hugo's mind was blank, his breathing labored, and his heart raced. He tried to speak, tried to think, but there was nothing. Hugo blankly sat there, lost, alone, and scared.

Hugo locked eyes with the funeral director, pleading for an answer on what to do next. Robert shifted his head, frantically searching around the room. He turned his attention to the photos behind his desk. Photos of Robert's family enjoying the happier moments of their lives. Hugo's stomach sank at the thought of his happy family moments stolen from him. Stolen by something he couldn't help fight. Elizabeth had to battle it on her own.

Robert slapped the edge of his desk, knocking a few pieces of paper off the piles. The slap startled Hugo.

"I've got it," Robert said as he leaned back in his chair. "A dog."

Hugo tilted his head slightly. "A dog?"

"Yeah, a dog." The funeral director raised his hands and shrugged. "Who doesn't love a dog?"

"We never really talked about getting a dog," Hugo replied.

"Sure. A dog. It will be perfect to keep you company. Trust me, it will keep you very busy."

Hugo raised his head higher. "A dog?"

"Yep, a dog. It's perfect for you."

Hugo grabbed the armrest and lifted himself up in the chair. He repositioned himself and sat upright. "Okay. I never considered a dog."

"Best thing you could do right now," Robert exclaimed. "I have to warn you, though; they can be a bit of a handful as a puppy, but totally worth it."

Hugo's Folk Victorian home was alive with well-wishers who stopped by to pay their respects. They held plates of food or drinks or both, laughing at anecdotes and stories from Elizabeth's past. Hugo attempted to navigate the crowded hallway to reach the closet door beneath the winding steps.

"Excuse me. I need to get in there." Hugo pointed toward the closet door, behind a couple of women talking.

"Oops, sorry," one woman exclaimed as she stepped to the side. "Beautiful service."

"Yes, beautiful service," the other complimented. "I'm so thankful the rain held off, and it was a beautiful day."

"Thank you. Me too," Hugo replied in a low voice as he opened the closet door.

He snatched a hanger and placed it inside his slim cut suit jacket. He hung up the jacket and closed the closet door.

"Thank you for coming," Hugo said as he continued to navigate down the hallway. He glanced into the living room and paused.

Well-wishers packed the room, laughing and reminiscing about old stories of Elizabeth. The sight emotionally suffocated Hugo. His body tightened. He wanted to continued past when he noticed a lone figure dressed in a black, long-sleeve, modest midi dress hovering near the fireplace mantel. A black wool hat covered her brunette hair. A black mesh veil lined the hat's brim that slightly covered her eyes. Hugo glanced down the hallway toward the kitchen and back into the living room. He took a deep breath and proceeded into the packed room.

The well-wishers acknowledged Hugo as he navigated a path through the crowd. He smiled and nodded at every "Sorry for your loss, Hugo" or "It was a beautiful service." He wanted to leave, but he had to keep going toward the lady in the black dress. Johanna Newes was a neighbor and close family friend, and Hugo suspected she was hurting as much as himself.

Johanna surveyed the pictures, picking up various frames to examine them closer before setting them back down. Her fingers were white-knuckled as she gripped one particular photo. Hugo stood next to her as they both examined the picture. Elizabeth beamed at something out of frame. Her wavy, auburn colored hair tucked behind her shoulders matched the brilliance of the golden yellow leaves in the background. Elizabeth's hazel eyes widened with excitement. Her smile shined brighter by the optimism of her head tilt. A memory of a happier time. A better time.

"I loved her," proclaimed Johanna.

"I know," responded Hugo.

"She was the only one who treated me with kindness. She always made me feel welcomed. She always made sure I had homemade cookies for Christmas. I'll never forget her. Don't you ever forget her, Hugo. Stay loyal to her forever. I know I will," Johanna said as she traced the outline of a ring-shaped cloak clasp pinned below her left shoulder like a brooch.

Her fingers followed along the ornate filigree lines that criss-crossed the inner ring. Its illustrious silver shine was worn away with age. Weathered from time. She continually circled her fingers around the jewelry as she examined the photo.

Hugo peered at the photo and then toward Johanna. Her eyes filled with a sadness that only Hugo could understand. "You can keep that one."

Johanna broke her gaze from the photo as she clutched the frame against her chest. Her eyes welled up. Her lips tightly drew in as if they were the only thing preventing a flood of tears. She wiped away a small tear that rolled down her check.

"Thank you. You don't know how much this means."

Hugo gave her a hug. "I need to go make sure Mrs. Raskin hasn't completely rearranged the kitchen." Hugo turned back toward the crowd.

"I should be going." Johanna wiped away another tear. "Never forget her, Hugo. Never."

"How could I?" Hugo returned to the hallway and continued to the kitchen.

Half-full silver aluminum pans of food covered almost every surface in the small kitchen. Carol Raskin, a short, older woman with a dyed black perm, directed her husband, Oliver, to remove a new pan from the oven and place it on top of the stove.

"There is no room," he said. He tried to squeeze the pan into the small space.

"There's too much food," Hugo offered support.

"See," Oliver said. "He agrees with me." Oliver Raskin was an older gentleman with thinning gray hair and a slightly bulkier frame. Oliver and Carol Raskin were owners of Raskin's Neighborhood Market, a local independent grocery that served the small town of Newbury Grove, Ohio.

"Nonsense," Carol exclaimed. She scooped scalloped potatoes from one pan into another. "See, plenty of room for more."

"Hugo will be eating all this food for weeks," Oliver explained.

"Oh no," Hugo replied. "You're taking some of this home."

"Don't you dare take any of this home," she threatened Oliver with her plastic, potato covered serving spoon. She turned her attention back to Hugo. "Hugo, honey, this is for you."

"At least let me pay for all this food." Hugo pulled out his wallet.

"Your money is no good," Carol said. He returned it to his pocket.

"We wouldn't dare take anything," Oliver said. "Elizabeth was like a daughter to us. I can still remember when she first started working at the store."

"All she talked about was wanting to be a teacher," Carol said. "That, and she wouldn't stop talking about you, either."

Hugo's head dropped to his chest, and he examined the floor. He pinched his black onyx wedding ring and twisted it back and forth. After a moment, he gave a slight smile. Carol set the scoop down and wrapped her arms around Hugo. The aromatic smell of her perfume overpowered his nose. He hugged her back.

"If you ever need anything, you just let us know," she offered.

"Thank you."

∽

THE EVENING BECAME NIGHT. Hugo thanked everyone who stopped by the house to pay their respects. The house slowly thinned out and fell into silence, as only Hugo remained. The echo of Hugo's steps across the hardwood flooring broke the silence as he entered the kitchen and opened the refrigerator door.

Carol had neatly packed in all the remaining food, each tray labeled in marker. Hugo snared a greenish-black bottle of wine between two fingers and yanked it from a crammed door shelf. He shut the door and searched through cabinet drawers for a bottle opener. The corkscrew twisted. He grabbed the handles and popped the cork from the bottle. Hugo took a wineglass from the overhead cabinet and poured the dark, purplish-red wine into it.

He headed back into the living room, holding the wineglass in his palm. The stem secured between his middle and ring fingers. The cozy living room had a center rug that protected the hardwood floors, a fireplace, a TV stand, a couch, and an armchair. Books and family pictures of Elizabeth and Hugo, from happier times, filled shelves built into the walls next to the fireplace. Not a single speck of dust lay on the mantel, pictures, or furniture.

The couch and chair had various colorful throw pillows strewn about from the guests. Hugo repositioned each one to its proper place. He grabbed a long stem lighter from the fireplace mantle and lit a few candles around the room. He set the lighter down and turned off all the lights. The flickering candles lit the room.

He kicked his shoes off as he plopped into the armchair. The light from the candle flames danced on the darkened walls. He took a sip of wine. The acidic grape flavor burned his lips and throat. A small droplet of wine rolled down his clean-shaven chin. Hugo brushed it aside with the back of his hand.

"Why did you have to leave me?" Hugo asked the empty room.

There was only silence.

He took another sip. He sloshed the liquid in his mouth, covering every taste bud possible. The strong hints of fruit and dirt washed over his tongue before gulping it down. "What am I supposed to do now?" He paused and waited.

There was no response. The overpowering smells of the funeral carnations and lilies scattered throughout the house filled the room.

"Please tell me," he pleaded once more.

Hugo Dodds sat in the darkness, in the silence, as he sipped his wine, waiting for an answer. There was nothing—only the silence of the half-empty house.

SAMHAIN

A Time of Remembrance

CHAPTER 1
SATURDAY MOURNING

A thick blanket of light and dark gray clouds hung oppressively low in the October sky. The air was crisp. A slight breeze bustled the dried and decaying leaves in a whirlwind as they moved across the dust covered trail of wilderness on the outskirts of Newbury Grove. Those leaves that had yet to fall painted a tapestry of rich orange, yellow, and red amongst the trees of Wildgrove Park.

The less fortunate trees, those now completely barren, stood as a reminder to those who lost everything. Their bare limbs stretched into the sky for a respite from the loss of foliage. They stood waiting for happier times.

A golden retriever enthusiastically pulled Hugo Dodds as they rounded a trail corner winding through the park. The dog pulled and yanked Hugo as she hurried to a new spot on the trail. She stopped and lingered to take in smells. She quickly marked the ground as her territory. Her nose twinged, and she focused on a new target. Hugo knew what was to follow. She took off at a quickened pace.

"Slow down," said Hugo, but the command went ignored. "Max, stop."

The dog got lower to the ground. Her upper body strength now overpowered Hugo as he tried to pull back on the leash. The resistance only fueled her desire. She was like a sled dog, determined to pull her passenger forward to the next destination.

Hugo stumbled over a rut in the trail. He relinquished his grip on the leash before being pulled to the ground. Now free, Max ran toward her new target. She rubbed her nose against the dirt to get the new smell.

Hugo collected himself and pointed to the ground next to him. "Maxine, come here now!"

Maxine pulled her nose away from the alluring odors. Her head was low, ears pulled back, and she dragged the leash behind her as Max returned to Hugo. She circled around Hugo's legs before sitting down next to him. She glanced up, tail wagging in the dirt, wide-eyed as if to beg for forgiveness.

"Good girl," Hugo assured her as he rubbed her head. He gripped lower on the leash, closer to Max's collar, and wrapped it around his hand to give him more leverage. "Now. Easy walk."

They continued down the path at a steady pace. Max hesitated for a moment to look at the spot of her mysterious smell, but continued forward next to Hugo.

The nature trail morphed into civilized concrete as Hugo and Maxine emerged from Wildgrove Park. They turned down the sidewalk toward the center of town. A white, wooden semi-circle sign with green lettering in the center median of the street greeted them. *Welcome to Newbury Grove, Est 1892.* On a small rectangular sign beneath was the town motto, *Welcome to the Neighborhood.* Hugo gave a passing glance to it and continued on.

Guarding the entrance to the town center was a stone cathedral with brightly colored stained glass windows. Streaks of white and grime weathered the gray stones of the facade. Hugo paused. His eyes drifted up the stone steps to the two large wooden doors of St. Jude Church, where he married Elizabeth—and where he buried her six months ago.

"ARE YOU READY?" Oliver asked in a low, hushed tone.

"As ready as I'm going to be, I guess," Hugo replied.

Hugo had sequestered himself in a church storage room, not yet ready to grasp his new reality. He focused on his hand movements in a mirror. Hugo tugged and pulled at his necktie, undoing the knot and ripping the tail of the tie back through. He repeated the choreographed dance once again, not stopping until the tie and knot were the correct length.

"Are you doing okay?"

"Yeah," Hugo replied, never looking away from the mirror. His gaze was unrelenting. Focused. "I'm fine." He gave the tie a few more tugs out of frustration. Tears welled in his bloodshot eyes, and his nostrils flared.

"Take your time." He patted Hugo on the shoulder and exited the room.

Hugo was now alone. A tear rolled down his cheek. He ripped the mirror off the wall, smashing it into a hundred little pieces, and threw what was left across the small storage room. Hugo picked up a heavy-duty plastic classroom chair and flung it at the window. The window glass splintered as the plastic and metal smashed against it. The block cement wall prevented the window from completely shattering as it caught most of the chair's blow. Hugo's nose snarled. His fists clenched. He hunched over and let out a soul splitting, agonizing, barbaric yawp.

There was a knock on the door.

"Hugo, it's time," the priest's voice entered the room.

Hugo snapped back into focus. His heart raced with adrenaline. His breath labored between rapid and short bursts. He glared into the mirror. His hands were still fiddling with his tie. It was all a dream. His outburst. Just a dream. A not so wondrous dream for his new nightmare.

Hugo wiped away the tears and brushed wayward strands of hair back into place. He checked on the plastic chair next to him to make sure it was still there. His eyes snapped to the splinterless window. His labored breathing relaxed.

Hugo took a deep breath and said, "I'm ready."

HUGO JERKED BACK to reality as Max tugged on her leash. A rush of dizziness overcame Hugo before he caught his bearings.

"Yeah. Yeah. We're going," Hugo assured the dog.

She took the lead, and they continued down the sidewalk toward the center of the town.

The town center was a bustling place of commerce. The old brick facades with brightly colored awnings, built right before the turn of the twentieth century, appeared well-kept and clean for their age. Hugo passed by a local bank branch, a pub, a barbershop, a bakery, and places of business that sold other items, such as jewelry and gifts. He stopped beneath a red, green, and white awning.

He focused on the gold lettering for *Antonio's Italian Ristorante* on the door leading into the rectangular building. He glanced over at the small, round table in the window's corner. That was their table —Hugo and Elizabeth's table. This was their favorite restaurant, where they spent many date nights over the years.

SWEAT ROLLED down Hugo's back. *Why did I wear the sweater?* Hugo thought.

He shifted back and forth in his seat, trying to pull up his pant leg. *These pants are way too tight. I'm going to rip them. Why didn't I get bigger pants?*

"How's the lasagna?" Elizabeth asked with her trademark radiant smile.

"Excellent, as always," Hugo replied. He set his fork down and took a sip of wine. "How's the ravioli?"

"There has never been a bad meal at Antonio's," she replied before taking a bite.

Hugo peered outside from their table in the corner. The full moon peeked from behind the clouds to illuminate the night sky. *The rain held off. Good.* He put his hand into the black leather jacket pocket.

His fingers traced the small felt box within. His thumb prodded the seam, opening it without Elizabeth noticing. He slipped his thumb and index finger inside, rubbing the metal ring to verify it was still there. He withdrew his fingers slowly, not wanting the lid to make a sound.

"Everything okay?" Elizabeth asked.

"Yeah. Things are great. Only going to get better," he replied with a smile. Hugo paused. "I was thinking. Let's take a stroll down to Wildgrove Park."

"At night?"

"Yeah. Beautiful night. Beautiful moon. Beautiful girl. It'll be a night to remember."

She lowered her eyes to her nearly finished plate, blushing and smiling with delight. When her eyes met Hugo's, she gave him a wink.

He raised his glass in a toast. "To a beautiful evening."

She raised hers. "To a beautiful life."

They clanked their glasses and took a sip.

MAX's loud and piercing bark snapped Hugo out of his daze. She had to make her presence known to people strolling across the street.

"Max! Stop that," Hugo commanded. "Sit."

Max did as instructed. Hugo pulled out a small dog biscuit from his jacket pocket and gave it to Max.

"No barking."

They continued down the sidewalk. As they passed the towns-folk of Newbury Grove, some people recognized the pair.

"Hey Hugo," a voice shouted.

"Hi," he politely replied.

"How you doing, Hugo?" others asked.

"I'm fine," he replied, not wanting to make small talk.

He hurried from the town center and turned down a side street. Folk Victorian homes lined both sides of the street. As Hugo journeyed past, the white, yellow, and beige houses all blended together. Leaves from the trees littered the sidewalk. They crunched as the pair continued home.

More voices shouted, "How you doing, Hugo?"

"I'm fine," he replied. "Just fine." His shoulders slumped, and he directed his eyes down on the leaves to avoid eye contact with anyone.

"Hugo!" a man shouted. "Hold up a sec."

Hugo stopped. He closed his eyes with enough force to will him home, but alas, he was still standing on that sidewalk. When he opened his eyes, an older gentleman ambled down his gray wooden steps, joined by his wife.

"Hi, George," Hugo responded with a dejected voice. "Hi, Julia."

"How are you doing?" Julia asked.

"I'm fine," he responded with the same monotone answer as before.

"I wanted to let you know that, well, that Elizabeth is greatly missed at school this year," George said as he hugged his wife. "It's... It's not the same without her. She brought so much joy to the students and us teachers. Her students are taking it pretty hard. We're all taking it pretty hard. We're going to miss her."

"How do you think I feel? Every day. Day after day. I'm home alone, waiting for her to walk through that door. This has been one long, horrible nightmare," Hugo shouted. "I want to see her smile again. Hear her laugh. See the brightness in her eyes. But nothing happens. I'm reminded of it daily. I don't need some jackass to do it for me. As far as Elizabeth's concerned, just stop. Stop asking how I'm doing. Stop talking about her. JUST STOP."

Hugo hunched over, fists clenched. He let out another barbaric, soul shattering yawp. His heart raced as George and Julia stood there in shock. Tears welled in Hugo's eyes as he fixated on their horrified expressions. Hugo broke eye contact.

He sighed and noticed George and Julia smiling at him. He wanted to say those words to everyone who ever asked how he was doing. Hugo slumped his shoulders in defeat. He attempted a half smile.

"Thank you," he replied in a sad, monotone voice. "She touched so many people and will be missed."

"If you ever need anything," Julia began. "Please. Please don't hesitate to ask."

Please stop asking me how I'm doing, Hugo thought before replying with a simple, "Thank you."

Hugo and Max continued their journey home. They turned down one more side street. They passed a few more houses before arriving at 1691 Ravenhill Dr.—a white, Folk Victorian home trimmed in dark green. Rectangular with tall, pointed gabled roofing. The paint was peeling from the siding, and the windows were dirty. Bushes on the side of the house were unkept and had grown wild over the summer. Elizabeth was the gardener, not Hugo.

An expansive porch spanned the entire front of the house. Stairs led up to a green door. Hugo and Max started up the stairs when someone from across the street called, "Hugo!"

Hugo stopped. *I just want to go inside.* He turned around to see Johanna Newes marching down the porch of 1692 Ravenhill Drive. Hugo relaxed, knowing Johanna would never ask *that question.*

"Look at this." Johanna pointed to the house next door. "Look what the new neighbors did."

Hugo followed Johanna's pointing to his right toward 1693 Ravenhill Dr. The once beige house was now a dark purple outlined with black trim. The front gazebo like porch was a dark shade of gray. The front door was as black as the trim.

"The house sold? When did that happen?"

"Two days ago," Johanna replied. "Look what they did to it."

"It's purple. Was it purple this morning?"

"No. I've been home all day, and I never saw anyone paint that house."

"I kind of like it."

"How can you like—" her voice trailed off. She tugged at her muted gray button up sweater. "It's an abomination."

"It's not that bad," Hugo assured her. "It brings character to the neighborhood."

"We're a simple town. We don't need any funny business."

"It's fine."

"It's not!" responded Johanna.

Max nestled against her leg, trying to get Johanna to scratch her head.

"You can pet her," Hugo said.

Johanna timidly pet Max's head twice before looking back at Hugo. "We live in a quiet neighborhood. If people are allowed to paint their houses purple, then next thing you know, the whole place changes. I don't want the neighborhood to change. I like it as it is!" Her fingers twice tapped the silver cloak clasp pinned to the lapel of her sweater.

"Tell you what," Hugo replied. "When I see the new neighbor, I'll mention something."

"Thank you," Johanna responded and peered down at Max. "You're a good girl." She gave Max a few more pats on the head before returning home.

Hugo and Max finally approached the front door. Hugo waved his phone over the lock. A gear moved on the other side to unlock the door.

He opened the door and shouted into the house, "Computer, I'm home."

Lights turned on immediately as they entered. He closed the door behind them. He removed Max's leash and hung it on a coat rack. She ran wildly throughout the house.

Collapsing piles of mail littered the dining room table. Clumps of dog fur balled together on the hardwood floor. The furniture tops were dusty.

Hugo entered the kitchen and grabbed Max's water bowl. He filled it from the tap and placed it back on the mat next to her food bowl. An empty pizza box spread across a garbage can and the dog food container. He moved the box to the side and opened the container. Only a few pieces of food lined the bottom. He closed his eyes and gave an extended, drawn-out sigh. He shut the lid and moved over to the refrigerator.

The fridge was nearly barren. A couple of water bottles, a bottle of ketchup, a take-out container, and a couple of bottles of wine was all that Hugo found. He pulled out the container and examined the contents inside. His dinner from a week ago. It didn't look very appetizing, so he threw the container in the trash. He grabbed his car keys from a hook next to the back door.

"Max," Hugo shouted. "Come get your water."

Max ran down the hallway, squeaking her favorite toy in her mouth. She dropped the stuffed green and yellow mallard duck and lapped up the water from the bowl. Water splashed all over the floor —most into the rubber mat, and some onto the hardwood.

Hugo opened the back door. "Computer," Hugo shouted. He waited for the familiar ping to reply. "I'm leaving."

"Setting away mode," a female voice echoed through the house.

The front door lock buzzed, and the lights turned off.

"Be a good girl while I'm gone," Hugo said.

Max glanced up; the bowl was almost empty. Hugo shut the door, and the buzz of a gear locked it.

CHAPTER 2
THE NEIGHBORHOOD MARKET

Located beyond the center of town was Raskin's Neighborhood Market—a white building with its name written in black cursive lettering above a matching awning that stretched across its rectangular facade. A banner tied to the side of the building read, *Serving the Neighborhood for over 50 Years!*

A small crowd of people exited the market, pushing carts of newly acquired groceries. Another group filed in. Raskin's Neighborhood Market was the place to be on a Saturday afternoon in this small town. Hugo pulled his car into the lot and parked in his usual spot, the furthest one away from everyone else. He exited the car and headed inside.

The overwhelming smell of flowers from the florist greeted Hugo as he entered. The place bustled with activity as shoppers searched for their goods. Three checkout lines jam-packed with waiting customers. The teenage cashiers, some working their first jobs, turned away from scanning items to greet anyone who entered.

Should have grabbed a hat. His body tightened; his shoulders arched up as he tried to bury his head in his jacket. He grabbed a shopping cart and darted down the nearest aisle. He relaxed his shoulders once he had a little more privacy from gawking eyes.

Hugo was tactical in his approach, trying to minimize the time he was visible in the public setting. First, he went down the snack aisle to grab a few bags of chips. Then he grabbed a few cans of chili and various soups.

Hugo hurried through the market. *Bread, wine, then deli, then milk. Also, cheese,* Hugo recited his grocery list.

He zipped around other shoppers, keeping his head down to avoid eye contact. He passed the shelves of bread and grabbed a loaf without looking, casually tossing it into his cart. *Dog food,* he thought. *Can't forget the dog food.*

Hugo backtracked to the pet section. Being a small-town grocery, the choice of dog food wasn't extensive, but Max didn't mind. Food was food. Hugo bent down to grab a large, blue bag of "Cheesy Chewies," a generic brand of dog food that specialized in mixed meats in a processed cheese flavor. He struggled to lift the bag from the bottom shelf. The heavy bag wouldn't slide. Hugo gave it a few more tugs before it broke free. He repositioned his hands around the bag and slid it onto the bottom shelf of the grocery cart.

When he stood up, his eyes caught a box of dog treats. *I can't forget those.* He placed the box in his cart. *Wine, then deli. Then you have to talk to the Raskins, or else you'll never hear the end of it.*

Rows and rows of wine filled the back corner of the market. Reds, Merlots, Chardonnays, Pinot Noirs, Cabernet Sauvignon, and every other type of wine filled the shelves. Everything from the cheapest wines to very pricy ones. The Raskins kept the expensive ones behind a glass case—not because they feared someone stealing the bottles —but because the Raskins didn't want them breaking. A small-town grocery never had the widest selection of food choices like larger chains, but the owners of Raskin's Neighborhood Market prided themselves on having the largest selection of wine in the area. People drove to Newbury Grove from Columbus and the surrounding areas to browse their selections.

Hugo's pace slowed as he perused the wines. He methodically scanned every label, looking for anything that caught his interest. Each label elicited a unique response to tantalize his senses. Some labels were ornate in their design to convey a sense of high status. Others added a fanciful sense of wonder as they invoked the mystical with images of moons or candles or dark lettering over gray smoke. Hugo grabbed a selection of different wines—some he tried before, and others that were new. Time slowed as he lingered on each label.

"I'LL MAKE a wine connoisseur out of you yet, Hugo Dodds," Elizabeth said as she placed a bottle of chardonnay into the cart.

"Wine is wine," he retorted. "Just pick one with a fancy label. It's all the same."

"How dare you?" she replied with a sly smile. "There is more to wine than just a label."

"It's all grapes. What difference does it make?"

"Difference? It's all about the soil and texture and the notes and the aging," Elizabeth answered. "Not to mention the food pairings."

Hugo grabbed the front of the cart and leaned closer toward her on the other side. A smirk on his face. "You just smash the grapes and then poof, like magic, you have wine. It's not as extensive as bourbon making. Now there's a real drink."

Elizabeth leaned closer to Hugo. "If you want me to be Mrs. Elizabeth Dodds, well then, you better get used to lots and lots of wine." She raised her left hand and presented her new engagement ring.

Hugo grabbed halfway up the cart and bent over to look closer at the ring. The metal rim of the cart dug into his stomach, but he didn't care. He leaned closer. His eyes lingered on the diamond ring. "Well, I guess we had a good run," Hugo responded with a smile. "They'll ask, 'Why did you break up?' Well, because bourbon will always be superior to wine in every way."

Elizabeth frowned and pouted her lips. She gave the cart a little push, jabbing Hugo in the stomach.

"Ow!" Hugo responded with a shocked expression.

"Fine." She smiled. "But I'm keeping the ring, though."

"Okay, okay. I give." Hugo went around the cart to hug her. "Wine is better than bourbon. However, I only say this under protest because my life is being threatened by a shopping cart."

Elizabeth gazed up at Hugo and said, "I knew you'd see it my way."

Hugo smiled and leaned in to kiss her.

"Excuse me," someone said behind Hugo, breaking his trance. "I need to grab that." A woman grabbed a bottle of wine off the shelf behind him.

"Pardon me," Hugo said as he moved the cart out of the way.

It took him a moment to regain his bearings. The world spun around him. His breath was shallow and hurried. He clutched the cart handle and closed his eyes. His knuckles turned white as his grip tightened. A rush of emotions flooded Hugo. He paused and took deep breaths until his breathing slowed. He opened his eyes. The menagerie of wine bottles slowly came back into focus.

Hugo stood in front of the red wine blends section. One brand caught his attention. The Raskins give the brand prominent placement, taking over an entire section of the shelves. Its label was a diagonal black and gray, checkerboard pattern. Written across the top in elegant, white, cursive lettering was the name *Red-Hearted Queen*.

A gold, multi-pointed crown sat in the center of the label, surrounded by the four playing card suits. There was a heart on top. The club pointed away on its side to the right. An upside-down spade was on the bottom, and a diamond turned sideways to the left. A white, curved edge rectangle, which invoked the image of a playing card, framed the four suits. Positioned in offsetting corners to further play into this aesthetic, were two red, capitalized Qs, with the bottom one flipped upside down.

"It's new," a familiar voice said from behind him. "I haven't tried it myself, but I've heard it's highly recommended. They gave us a great deal if we featured it."

Hugo turned around to see Carol Raskin standing behind him, waiting for their customary greeting hug.

"I'll give it a try." Hugo placed it in the cart beside the other bottles, then hugged Carol.

"How are you doing?" Carol asked. There were only two people in the world allowed to ask Hugo that question, and both of them had the last name of Raskin.

"Today's a not so good day," Hugo replied.

"You need to stop torturing yourself," she said.

"I know."

"Let me guess, the same walking path?"

"Yeah." Hugo averted his eyes as if he'd done something wrong.

Carol lightly guided his chin back to face her and pleaded, "Take a different route tomorrow. For me. Please."

"Sure. For you." Hugo forced a smile.

"Thank you," she said as tears welled in her eyes. "Come on, go say hello to Oliver."

Carol led Hugo to the deli counter where Oliver was holding court. He struck up conversations with people as they waited for their deli orders. A few workers hurried to prepare the orders as fast as possible.

"I have something for you," Oliver said as soon as he noticed Hugo. He bent down behind the counter to grab two neatly wrapped steaks.

"You don't need to give me anything," Hugo responded.

"They're not for you. They're for Max." Oliver pulled out a brown package. "Ask her if you can have one."

"I doubt she'd even let me have a taste," Hugo replied as he took them. "Thank you."

"Any time, sweetie," Carol said.

"Oh, the new neighbor moved in," Hugo said. "Pretty fast too. I didn't see a moving van or anything. And Johanna isn't happy. They painted the house purple."

"We know," Carol replied.

"We met her," Oliver chimed in.

"She placed a large order for grapes," Carol said. "Bought all the ones we had in stock and then some. My distributor flipped when I told her the size of the order."

"She has some pretty wild hair, and she's quite the looker too," Oliver added.

Hugo raised an eyebrow. "No one uses the term 'looker' anymore."

"Well, she is," Oliver replied. "You're quite the looker too if you put yourself out there."

"We talked about this," Hugo was quick to respond. "I'm not looking or wanting to date anyone. Not right now."

"We're not asking you to marry the poor girl," Oliver said.

"We think it will do you some good to get out of the house and mingle with people," Carol said. "You can't stay cooped up in your house forever. You need to actually talk to someone."

"I have plenty of people to talk to. I have the two of you and Max—"

"Max can't talk back," Carol interrupted.

"That's what I like about her. Besides, I have Johanna complaining about something all the time. It's perfect for me."

"You can't shut yourself away forever," Carol pleaded.

"I'm trying to," Hugo responded. Carol scrunched her face into a frown. Her eyes glistened as if she were about to cry. He knew he had overstepped this time. "Okay, I can't just go up to her and say, 'Welcome to the neighborhood. Hey, want to go on a date?' when I finally meet her."

"What? No, not her," Carol replied. "We know someone else."

"She's really great and sweet," Oliver said. "Divorced. No kids. She used to work in our store. You might have met her once."

Hugo sighed. "One dinner. That's it. Nothing fancy."

Carol smiled, then pulled a piece of paper from her pocket and handed it to Hugo. "Her name is Sarah."

"Wrapped steaks. Name and phone number in your pocket. Am I that predictable?" Hugo asked.

"You're in here every other day," Oliver said. "You can buy more than a few groceries at one time."

"But then what excuse will I have to stop in?" Hugo asked. "Besides, Max would eat everything, anyway."

"The next time you come in, you can tell us how things went," Carol replied before giving Hugo a hug.

"Have fun, Hugo," Oliver said. "You might enjoy yourself."

CHAPTER 3
BLINDSIDED

Hugo stood with his back to the warm glow coming from Antonio's Italian Ristorante. Hugo shivered from the chilled night air as he fiddled with his tie one more time before sticking his hands into his black leather jacket pockets. He carefully scanned the town center as a handful of cars drove down the street. People strolled behind Hugo, some entering Antonio's, while others continued on with their nighttime activities. Hugo inched closer to the curb to avoid anyone bumping into him, or having to talk to anyone who recognized him.

Ornate streetlamps lined the town center. Dark green and intricately carved to look like vines crawling up the posts toward two lamps, a mixture of glass and elegant twisted metal. The lights flickered inside to give the impression of old Victorian streetlamps from which they took their inspiration. Wreathes of orange, yellow, and brown leaves decorated each lamp to celebrate fall. Hugo leaned against the closest streetlamp and glanced up to the giant banner stretching across the street promoting the "Newbury Grove Fall Festival." He checked his watch and scanned the street again.

Please cancel, Hugo thought as each car passed. A silver sedan slowed down and pulled into a space across the street. *Please don't be her. Please don't be her. Don't be her.* The car door opened, and he briefly considered running.

The words of Oliver entered his mind, 'You might enjoy yourself.' He straightened his posture and removed his hands from his pockets.

A woman with dark hair wearing a black jacket, red blouse, gray pants, and black ankle strap pumps hurried across the street. She noticed Hugo waiting, gave a smile, and waved.

Damn it, Hugo thought before giving a forced smile and nodding. He extended his right hand and greeted her. "Sarah? Nice to meet you. I'm Hugo."

"Nice to meet you," she replied as she shook his hand.

Hugo led her toward Antonio's.

"I haven't been here in years."

"This is the best restaurant in all of Newbury Grove. As a matter of fact, it might be the only restaurant in Newbury Grove," Hugo joked as he opened and held the wood door. "After you."

"A gentleman," Sarah complimented as she stepped through the doorway. "I like that."

"Well, I try to be. Most of the time." Hugo entered the restaurant after her.

Antonio's Italian Ristorante was intimate. Round tables filled the black and white checkerboard tiled floors. Tables for two were up front, while larger tables and booths were in the back. The staff meticulously decorated each table with white linen sheets, glassware, silverware, and a glass tea light candle holder of either red, white, or green.

Dim lighting attempted to hide the other patrons to create a sense of intimacy for the diners. Soft music from crooners muffled the conversations of patrons at the tables. Aromas of recipes brought from old world Italy permeated through the restaurant.

They approached a host standing behind his podium. "Reservation for two under Dodds," Hugo said.

The host checked his schedule and map of the restaurant tables, then made eye contact with Hugo. "Right this way, Mr. Dodds. We saved your usual table."

Hugo peered over at the front corner. The empty table for two sat prepared and waiting. Hugo's breathing increased. He clenched his left fist.

"Umm, not tonight. Do you have something with more"—Hugo struggled to find the right words—"umm... privacy."

"Absolutely," the host said, as he grabbed two menus. "Right this way."

"More privacy, huh?" Sarah smiled.

"Well, I thought it's best to stay away from prying eyes," Hugo said.

The host guided them to a table for four near the back. He placed two menus next to each other and said, "enjoy" before returning to his podium. Hugo pulled out the chair facing the front of the restaurant for Sarah, but she pulled out the other for herself. A brief thought of moving entered Hugo's mind, but he didn't want to appear rude. He removed his jacket and hung it on the back of the wood chair before taking his seat.

"What do you recommend?"

"Well, you can't go wrong with any of the homemade pastas. The meatballs are world famous," Hugo replied.

A waitress approached the table. "Welcome to Antonio's," she said, addressing Sarah more than Hugo. "My name is Amanda, and I'll be your waitress tonight. Can I start you off with some drinks?"

"I'd like to see a wine menu," Sarah replied.

Amanda flipped the menu over to the back. "Our wine selection is very extensive."

Sarah scanned the list. "Wow, so much to choose from. What do you recommend, Hugo?"

"Well, umm, I usually get one of the blends."

"I'll take that," Sarah answered.

"Perfect. Two regulars?" Amanda asked Hugo, holding up two fingers.

"Uh, just make it one. I'll take a water," he quickly replied.

"I'll be right back," Amanda said and moved toward the kitchen.

"So, you're on a regular drink basis with the staff?" Sarah chuckled.

"I may have visited here more than once."

"I love the intimate feel of the place," Sarah said as she scrutinized the restaurant. "It's nice and cozy."

Amanda returned holding a tray. She placed the glass of wine in front of Sarah, a wine goblet full of water in front of Hugo, and a basket of complimentary breadsticks in between them. "Have you decided what you want?"

"I'm still deciding." Sarah glanced back at the menu. "You go first."

"The usual for me," Hugo said.

"That sounds good. I'll take that," Sarah quickly chimed in.

"You don't even know what my usual is."

"I'm sure it's perfect," she replied.

"Two usuals," Amanda said before leaving.

"Carol talked highly of you," Sarah said.

"She tends to exaggerate. Hopefully, she didn't spill all of my secrets."

"She didn't say that much. Where would the fun be in that?"

"Yep. Fun," Hugo said with a chuckle and a hint of sarcasm. "Since you know a little about me, what about you?"

"I'm recently divorced, but we've been separated for a while."

"I'm sorry," Hugo responded.

"Don't be. It probably lasted a few years longer than it should have. It was amicable. We had no kids. No pets. So other than a few years of stress, it was for the best."

Hugo offered Sarah a breadstick before taking one for himself. He then unfurled the napkin from the silverware and placed it on his lap. He bit off a piece of the breadstick and reached for the glass of water with his left hand. Sarah's eyes locked onto his wedding ring as he gripped the glass.

"I thought Carol said you weren't married?"

"I was married," he replied.

"Divorced?"

"Widower."

"I'm so, so sorry," she pleaded. "I didn't know. Carol didn't mention anything."

"Don't worry about it."

"How are you doing? It must be hard on you."

"I'm fine. Just fine."

"So, why do you still wear the ring? It gives off the wrong impression if you're looking to meet someone."

Hugo took another sip of water and placed the glass behind his plate, stalling to find the right words. He cupped his right hand around his left. He held the ring between his index finger and thumb, rotating the black onyx band.

"The ring has never left my hand since I put it on," Hugo replied as he focused on the ring. "I... I can't bring myself to take it off. We knew each other since we were kids. We went to college together. If I take it off, then that means it's over."

"I can't even begin to imagine what you're going through."

Hugo glared at the empty table in the corner at the front of the restaurant. "No one does."

"Do you have any kids?"

"Just a dog."

"I don't even want to think about what it would be like if you had kids involved," Sarah said, trying to reassure Hugo.

Hugo's eyes fixated on their usual table. The dim lighting attempted to obscure it, but his eyes found it. He fought against the vision. Each moment he fixated on the table drew out the ghosts of the second worst night of his life.

∼

"I WAS THINKING we could try again, since it's been six months since your last treatment." Hugo smiled at Elizabeth. "Wouldn't it be nice to finally have a little Max or Maxine running around the house?"

Elizabeth gave Hugo a half smile before concentrating on her plate. The hair from her auburn wig fell in front of her face to shield her from his gaze. She pushed the fist-sized meatball and spaghetti noodles around her plate. His smile slowly receded into terror. His face turned pale. He extended his arms across the table and placed his hands over hers.

"Is everything okay? Did I say something wrong?"

Elizabeth placed the fork down and brushed the frizzy hair back behind her ears. She slowly raised her head and locked eyes with Hugo. Her eyes watered. The white of her eyes turned a pinkish red color. A single tear escaped and left a trail down her face. "I wasn't going to say anything until later."

"Oh, God," Hugo blurted out as he fell back in his chair. His heart skipped a beat. He forced himself to take a breath as his throat tightened.

"I wanted one more meal," Elizabeth explained, "where it felt normal."

"No. No. No," Hugo pleaded.

"I wasn't feeling well, so I called the doctor—"

Hugo shook his head in disbelief.

"They—" her voice trailed off as she failed to find the next words.

Hugo leapt from his chair. The chair rocked and fell over. She buried her head into his chest as Hugo wrapped his arms around her. Hugo squeezed her tightly, trying to let her know it would be okay. He loosened his hold to avoid hurting her. She squeezed his torso as hard as possible, but he didn't care. He kissed her on the forehead, then rested his forehead against hers.

"It'll be okay," Hugo assured her. "It'll be okay."

"They want to start again as soon as possible."

"It'll be okay. We beat it once before. We can do it again. Together."

"I love you, Hugo," she mustered through the tears.

"I love you too, Elizabeth."

"Two orders of spaghetti and my world famous meatballs," a man with a thick Italian accent said from behind Hugo as he placed the plates on the table. "They're world famous because people in Italy know about 'em."

The room spun. Hugo's head throbbed, and sweat rolled down his back. A hot wave pulsated through his body. His eyes watered, but he wiped them before any tears could flow. It took Hugo a moment to regain his bearings.

"Everything okay?" Sarah asked.

"Fine. I'm fine," Hugo responded. "It's just been a long day."

Antonio was an older gentleman in his late 60s. Short, slightly overweight, and balding on top with longish black and gray hair on the sides and back. The smell of cheap cologne overpowered Hugo's nose. Antonio always had a smile on his face and wore a nice suit.

He patted Hugo on the back and said, "How you doin', buddy boy?"

Hugo had been around Antonio long enough to know that's how he greeted everyone: "How you doin'," followed by either "buddy boy" or "buddy sis."

"I'm doing good, Antonio," Hugo replied.

"I heard you were here with a pretty date, so I thought I'd deliver these personally." Antonio turned his attention to Hugo's date. "Antonio Moretti. A pleasure to meet you. Hugo here is the best guy I know, and I know a lot of people."

"I'm Sarah," she replied. "Pleased to meet you."

"Don't let him fool ya. Hugo Dodds can be quite the scoundrel, if you know what I mean." Antonio patted him on the back with his thick hands.

"I look forward to getting to know more about Mr. Dodds." Sarah leaned forward and turned her attention back to Hugo.

Hugo blushed. His eyes lingered on the empty table across the room before looking at the food in front of him.

"I'll leave you two alone," Antonio said. "And enjoy some free cannolis, compliments of the house."

"You don't have to—" was all Hugo could say before Antonio left the table. "Looks like we get free desert."

Hugo held the door open as they exited the restaurant. The full moon rose and provided a bluish hue to the clear night sky. Hugo shivered as the air grew colder. It was quieter and less populated through the town center.

"Thank you for a lovely evening," Sarah said as they headed toward the crosswalk.

"My pleasure," Hugo responded.

"Where are you parked?"

"Oh, I walked," he replied. "I live not too far from here. I can escort you to your car."

They checked both ways before crossing to the other side together.

"A lot of people care about you," Sarah said.

"I know," he responded. "I'm really thankful for it."

They stopped in front of her silver sedan. Sarah withdrew her keys from her purse. She focused on Hugo's eyes. "You seemed distracted tonight. Everything okay?"

Hugo cringed at the question. He placed his hands in his jacket pocket. "Fine. I'm fine," he replied.

"Did I say something wrong? I hope I didn't make you feel uncomfortable."

"No. No. It's just that well"—his gaze dropped to the ground, stalling to find the right words—"it's been a while since I've been out with anyone. It's usually just me and the pup. It was good to get out of the house."

"Good. I was worried I upset you."

"You didn't."

"It'll get better. I didn't realize that until some time after my divorce. It's hard, but it does get better."

Hugo tilted his head up at her and gave a half smile. "Thanks."

"Do you want a ride home?"

"That's okay. It's not far. I enjoy the chilly night air, anyway."

"Take care of yourself, Hugo."

"You too." He turned around and strolled down the sidewalk as the headlights of her car illuminated.

CHAPTER 4
THE WITCHING HOUR

Max's high-pitched moan, a mixture of agony and commanding attention, broke the silence. She was tall enough to rest her head on the edge of the bed without jumping up. Her tail swayed back and forth as she awaited a response. Hugo laid under a billowing dark comforter; his head buried in a pillow facing away from the demanding pup. She moaned again in a higher, distressed pitch.

Hugo rustled under the bedcovers. She let out a third moan.

"No," Hugo's muffled response emerged from beneath the comforter.

Max plowed her head as far forward as she could to get closer to Hugo.

"I said no," he reiterated.

Max's bark pierced through Hugo's ears and directly into his soul. He begrudgingly flipped the covers off and rolled over.

The yellow glow of the alarm clock resting atop the nightstand came into focus. 3:30 a.m. Max's tail wagged back and forth. Her manipulative, sad, brown eyes begged for Hugo's attention.

"It's only a few more hours," Hugo exclaimed. He rolled and, in one motion, flung the covers back over his head. "Go back to sleep."

Max jumped onto the bed with a single leap. She trampled around the bed, her body leaning against Hugo's. He emerged from under the covers to see her nose inches from his face. He could feel her warm breath with every panting. She whined once more.

"Fine," he agreed to her request. "Make it quick."

Max jumped around the mattress before leaping down from the bed.

Hugo rolled back over and swung his legs over the edge. He sat there, wiping the sleep from his eyes. "It's your turn to let her out," Hugo said to the other side of the king-sized bed.

His eyes locked onto a small indentation in the mattress, now vacant. He slowly rotated his black onyx ring. Another bark echoed through the bedroom.

"I'm coming. I'm coming," Hugo replied. "Quit being bossy."

Hugo tossed the covers about the bed without care—they hadn't been properly tucked or made in weeks. The headboard collected a small layer of dust. Two nightstands stood watch over the room like silent guardians—one with an alarm clock, the other with a small lamp. Hugo's side wiped clean, not with a rag, but with a wipe of his hand. The far nightstand remained untouched with a layer of dust like freshly fallen snow. Once full of warmth, joy, and love, the bedroom was a disheveled mess.

Hugo moved toward the door. The dark hardwood floor was cold to his bare feet. He dodged piles of dirty clothes that needed his attention scattered in front of a long dresser. He tucked his arms close as he passed by to avoid knocking over the stacks of papers and other oddities collected on top of the dresser. Max focused on the bedroom door with a burning intensity, as if she was trying to will it open. Hugo grabbed and turned the antique brass doorknob.

Max burst through the open door, running down the hall, and clattered down the stairs. Hugo struggled to find the light switch in the dark. With a flick of the switch, Hugo became temporarily blinded as the hallway illuminated. He rubbed his eyes, and his sight was quick to return. Pictures of happier times lined the hallway. Their frames crooked and disoriented from being bumped and never corrected. Max whined from the base of the stairs as she waited.

"I'm coming," Hugo yelled.

The hallway led past the bathroom and other bedrooms to a balcony railing that overlooked the winding stairs. Hugo braced himself between the railing and the wall, still getting his bearings and wanting to make sure he wouldn't trip over his pajama pant legs as he descended the stairs. His hand left streaks in the dust as it slid down the banister.

Max ran through the kitchen to the back door. Hugo retrieved his shoes at the base of the steps, slipped them on, and joined her. She twirled around in a circle as Hugo gripped the doorknob. She slipped through as soon as the opening was big enough for her slender frame.

A staircase emerged from the back door with paint chipped off the railing. The wood showed signs of rot and decay from being exposed to the elements. A single lawn chair and grill occupied a space next to the steps. A few trees towered over the yard from the surrounding houses. The glow of the full moon struggled to shine through the remaining foliage to illuminate the entire yard. The empty tree branches cast a shadow like gnarled fingers clawing out into the darkness.

The backyard was small, desolate, and unwelcoming. A picketed privacy fence enclosed the space, and a locked gate was the only point of exit. A small tool shed occupied a back corner. Wild, unkempt bushes lined the back fence. The decaying remains of leaves covered the yard.

Max sprinted down the stairs and explored the yard. She trounced around, rustling the fallen leaves, searching for that one perfect spot. Smelling every square inch, she hunted for intruders to her yard along the picket fence. She stopped to smell under the tool shed before continuing on her journey.

Hugo traipsed down the stairs and waited for her to complete her exploration. The air was crisp. Every exhale produced a diminutive, puffy white cloud. Hugo's teeth chattered. He buried his hands under the sleeves of his black T-shirt. Hugo paced, trying to make the vibration of his jaw stop.

"Hurry up," he commanded in a low whisper.

Max wasn't paying attention. She continued on her crusade, stopping momentarily to sniff the ground, only to run off to explore a new spot.

Hugo gazed up at the night sky. It was clear, only a few clouds. The stars shined brighter in the moon's glow. Hugo exhaled and watched as the white cloud of fog danced in the nighttime air before dissipating.

"I can still make a bigger cloud than you," Hugo said to an unseen figure. He closed his eyes and drew out his exhale, creating a much larger cloud of fog.

"I win," Hugo whispered, and then paused. "I miss you so much. Please. Please, tell me what to do."

He focused on the moon, keeping his eyes closed for a moment before opening them. A dark shadow flew past and disappeared behind a tree. Hugo struggled to see exactly what it was.

What was that? Hugo thought. *It was too big to be an airplane. An owl? No. It was moving too fast to be an owl.*

Hugo listened for any hint of sounds. He scanned the sky for any signs of movement. There was only silence.

Max's bark cut through the silence. Hugo snapped his attention over to where she was standing. She barked again.

"Max!" Hugo yelled. "Knock it off."

Max stood her ground, defending her yard from all intruders. Her barks echoed throughout the night sky. A cat moved along the tall privacy fence. Max rushed to the fence to defend her yard. The cat jumped off into a neighboring one.

"Stop barking!" Hugo commanded in a hushed tone.

A light turned on in an upstairs room of the newly painted purple house. The light caught Hugo's attention. He snapped quickly back toward Max with an angered face.

"See what you did?" He pointed to the window. "You woke the neighbors. Get inside."

Max blankly stared back at Hugo. She wagged her tail before plopping into a downward dog position.

"Get inside," Hugo commanded again as he moved closer.

Max sprung up and ran circles around the yard.

"Max, this is not playtime," his voice grew louder. "Come here, girl." He let out a low whistle.

She ran around the yard. Hugo kept a wide base, feet spread shoulder width apart, in anticipation of which way Max would run. A futile attempt to catch her. She juked toward the center of the yard. Hugo tripped as one of his pajama pant legs caught under the sole of his shoe. She escaped to be chased once again.

"Max! Come here!" Hugo yelled, no longer in a hushed voice.

"You won't catch her," a voice came from behind Hugo.

"I'm sorry," he replied. "My dog is being stubborn at the moment."

Hugo turned to see who was talking. A woman's face framed by a brimmed black hat peered over the top of the fence.

"You won't catch her by chasing her. Come here." She summoned him to the fence. "She'll come to you in time."

Hugo moved toward the mysterious woman.

"Keep your back to her. She'll be over in a moment. Just wait," she commanded.

Max stopped running and laid down on a bed of leaves.

"I'm sorry... She's not usually like this," Hugo explained. "She saw a cat and got all excited."

"Hopefully, that poor little kitty cat wasn't too mean to your dog," she replied with a slight smile. "I'm Alice, by the way. Alice Primrose." She extended her arm over the fence. Her hand emerged from inside the sleeve of her black jacket.

Hugo took her hand. It was cold to the touch, as if she had been outside in the crisp fall air for a few hours.

"Hugo Dodds," he replied as they shook hands. "I hope we didn't wake you."

"Not at all. I was already up. I never miss a beautiful moon."

"You moved in pretty fast. I never saw a moving truck. I like what you did with the house color, by the way. It's.... different."

"Yeah, it's more my style now." She nodded approvingly at the house. Hugo glimpsed what could be purple hair in the moonlight. She focused back on Hugo. "I hope that's not a problem."

"Umm, yeah. No. Umm," Hugo paused. "I'm sorry. I meant—I didn't see anyone paint it."

"My house painting methods are very... efficient."

"Very," Hugo replied. "I like it. It's an excellent color."

"Good," Alice gleefully replied. "I was worried it would scare some people away. But you have to be who you are, right? Even if it makes people uncomfortable."

"Right, although there are a few neighbors who might complain. One in particular."

Alice chuckled. "I told you it would work."

Max trotted over to Hugo, using her nose to nudge his left hand into position around her ears for scratching. She sat down, her tail brushing aside any fallen leaves. The dog glared at Hugo with her manipulative, brown puppy-dog eyes, smiling, tail wagging, waiting for him to scratch her. Hugo immediately grabbed Max's pink canvas collar, not wanting her to escape again.

"Thank you," Hugo said, with a hint of relief in his voice.

"You're welcome. Give her some slack; she's still young. Just needs a little training," Alice replied with a wink toward Max. "Does she aggravate Mrs. Dodds, or is she the favorite parent?"

"Umm..." Hugo paused. He pinched his ring. The black onyx band was cold to the touch. "There is no Mrs. Dodds. Not anymore."

"Oh, I'm sorry. I saw the ring and assumed—"

"That's okay. She—" Hugo hesitated. "She passed a few months ago."

"Oh!" Alice replied with a horrified expression. "I'm... I'm so sorry."

"That's okay," Hugo reassured Alice. "I'm fine, by the way."

"Fine?"

"That's the first thing someone always asks me. *How I'm doing*," Hugo explained sarcastically. "Fine. That's always my default answer. Just.... fine."

"I wasn't going to ask," Alice replied. Hugo raised an eyebrow. "Losing someone is... Any loss is tough. You're never fine. You never will be."

"*Right*," Hugo enthusiastically replied. "Everyone wants me to act like it's no big deal—"

"But you can't," Alice finished his thought.

"Exactly!" A sense of relief rushed over Hugo.

"It's as if the world wants you to move on. To forget. Like it never happened."

"But you can't. You can't erase everything like it never happened. Like *oh well. That's over. What's next?*"

"Well, Hugo Dodds, I'll make you this promise. I'll never ask you how you're doing. Deal?" Alice spit in her hand and extended it again over the fence.

Hugo stepped back; he furrowed his brow as he focused on the outstretched hand.

"A deal this important requires more than a pinky swear," Alice explained. "The order goes: Pinky Swear, Spit Swear, and then Blood Oath. I can go get my ritual tools, and we can agree to this in blood if you prefer, but I thought it would be less messy this way."

Hugo's face went vacant, unsure how to reply.

"I'm joking, by the way." Alice giggled.

Hugo laughed. He spit into his hand and shook hers. "I'll take that deal."

"A deal sealed with a kiss," she exclaimed.

"Excuse me?" Hugo yanked his hand away.

"My spit touched your spit. It's like we kissed," Alice replied with a wink and a smile.

"Well"—Hugo blushed—"That's one way of looking at it."

"You need to learn the history of the spit swear, Hugo Dodds."

"That sounds like something Elizabeth would have said," he replied with a smile.

"I like her already. Well, Hugo Dodds, take excellent care of that dog. She's a good girl, regardless of what you say." Alice locked onto Max. "Who's a good girl? You're a good girl." Alice raised the pitch in her voice.

Max wagged her tail and gave out a bark that pierced through their ears and directly into their souls.

"That woke up the neighborhood," Alice said as she slid behind the fence. "Have a good night, Hugo. It was nice to meet you."

"You too, Alice Primrose." He bowed his head, smiling. He gazed back up at the full moon one last time before turning his attention toward Max.

"Next time you come when called," he commanded. "Come on, let's go get a biscuit." He led Max back up the wooden staircase. Hugo held open the door as Max entered.

Hugo paused before shooting a glance back at the purple house. He smiled—a smile unlike any he's had in a long time. *Finally. Finally, someone who gets me.* His eyes dropped to his black onyx ring. He bit his lip to quell the smile, but it lingered. His smile wouldn't let Hugo dismiss his moment of joy. He once more glanced toward the purple house, nodded, and then joined Max inside.

CHAPTER 5
ALICE'S REFLECTION

Alice Primrose sat on the pillowed cushion of her dining room window nook sipping tea. Her long legs stretched almost the full length. She wore black leggings and a dark gray hooded sweatshirt that contrasted her brightly colored purple hair and matching lipstick. She stretched her bare toes back and forth.

She leaned against the wood frame, resting her shoulders in the corner where the wood met the window. The chilled fall air gave her goosebumps as she leaned against the glass. Her vantage point was high enough to see over Hugo's privacy fence. She shifted slightly to get a better view of the comedic show that transpired in his backyard. Alice clutched a black and orange mug with both hands.

He had to have seen me last night. He had to, Alice thought as she took a long sip of the steaming tea. *And he didn't say anything.*

Hugo was playing ball with Max, although Alice considered it more of a game of chase rather than fetch. Hugo reared back and underhand tossed the ball high into the sky. Max ran around the yard, judging the correct spot where the ball would fall back down to earth. She bent forward; her shoulders clenched and tightened. Her tail wagged. Eyes focused. Waiting.

The ball achieved its apex. It hung in the air for a moment, spinning, teasing the waiting dog below. *I should hold it there a little longer. Just to see what he'd do.* She smirked, but took another sip of her tea.

Max's eyes traced the ball as it fell to the ground and bounced back up. She jumped with her mouth wide open. The springing tension and her exuberance caused her to overshoot the target. Max tried to stab at the ball, rather than simply catch it. Her youthful inexperience betrayed her.

The ball ricocheted off her mouth and bounced to the other side of the yard. She ran after it. She scooped up the ball with her mouth, but the momentum of her body pushed her forward as she tumbled over a few times. Her eyes were wide as she had flipped over. She stood up, smiled, and wagged her tail over her retrieved item.

Alice heard his muffled commands through the window.

"Bring the ball back," Hugo said. "Bring the ball here, Max." Max ran in circles around the yard. "Max! Bring it here."

Alice chuckled as Hugo ran after the impish golden retriever.

A knock at the front door broke the silence in the room. The dining room was a rectangular space, large enough for an elongated table and multiple chairs. It was mostly empty, except for a square folding table and two collapsible chairs. Another mug sat waiting on the black padded table. Alice got up from her spot and placed her mug on the opposite side. She hurried down the barren hallway to the black front door.

A sheer, black veil covered the window set in the center of the top half of the door. Alice saw the shadow of someone on the other side. The sounds of wood hitting wood came from up the winding Victorian staircase. The staircase was a dark brownish-black stain. Detailed rectangular wainscoting traversed the walls as it followed the angular winding path of the stairs.

"It's okay," Alice shouted up the staircase.

There was another knock at the front door. The noise from upstairs intensified at a quickened pace. It reverberated off the walls, causing them to shake.

"It's Ez. Knock it off!"

The clamoring stopped. Alice gripped the ornate, diamond shaped vintage knob and opened the door.

"This day has already been ruined," a boisterous Esmeralda proclaimed as she entered the house, holding a purse in one hand and removing her overcoat with the other. "On the drive over here, they had the audacity to mention *the* Scottish play on the radio. It set me off."

"Nice to see you too, Ez," Alice said as she closed the door.

Esmerelda Honeydew—or Ez, as her friends called her—was an inch under five feet tall with slip-on shoes that added an extra inch or two. A woman of short stature, but larger-than-life personality. She styled her dyed blonde hair up into a beehive. Her knee-length dress was a brightly colored, sparkly green that commanded attention from across the room. A kaleidoscope of colored rings adorned each finger. Foundation makeup caked her face to hide any appearance of wrinkles on her aged skin. Her cheeks red from rouge. High arched, brown eyebrows drawn above light blue eyeshadow that highlighted her silvery blue eyes. She tried to give off a more youthful appearance for someone in their late 60s.

"A curse upon that bard and that godforsaken play," she proclaimed as she stood in the hallway to finish removing her coat. "A CURSE!"

"You take it way too personal." Alice took the coat and placed it on a highly detailed, carved staircase newel post.

"He knew what he did," Ez retorted. "He knew what he *stole*."

"You weren't even there," Alice said.

"Still..." her voice trailed off as she plopped her oversized purse down on the hardwood flooring. She grinned and opened her arms, waiting for a hug. "How are you doing, kiddo?"

"I'm good," Alice replied as she hugged Ez, whose head barely touched Alice's shoulders. "It would be better if I had all my stuff."

"We'll get to that. We'll get to that," Ez assured her. "What was all the racket? It sounded like the house was coming apart."

"That"—Alice responded with a hint of disdain, pointing upstairs—"was the overprotective one."

"Good," Ez replied. "He's doing his job. Why are you keeping him up there?"

"Because if he was down here, he'd be following me all over the place. I can't even step outside without him trying to follow," Alice answered. "You want a flying broomstick following me in broad daylight?"

"Good point," Ez said. She went to the wall and tapped three times, waiting for the response.

After a brief pause, three loud knocks echoed from upstairs.

"Good to see you too, old buddy!" Ez shouted upstairs before turning her attention back to Alice. "Now. Down to business."

They headed down the hallway to the folding table. Ez took a seat, while Alice grabbed the teapot. She poured for both of them, topping off her cup.

"Thank you, kiddo." Ez picked up the mug. She used her index finger to swirl the air above the steaming tea. The tea swished back and forth in the mug, following the same clockwise pattern as her finger, commanded by an unseen force. She took a sip. "Perfect. Absolutely perfect."

"My stuff?" Alice asked.

"It should be here in a day or two," Ez replied. "I have my best people working on it. We had to move it around, you know, to be safe."

"Any word on those who tried to attack me?"

"Nothing," Ez said before taking another sip of tea. "The trail went cold. We can't find Sam, either. Whoever Sam told about your little secret has gone so far underground that my contacts can't even find them."

Alice buried her head in her hands to hide her frustration. She took a few breaths before looking back at Ez with a solemn, stoic expression. "Am I safe?"

"There is no way anyone could track your movements. I personally made sure of it. You have my guarantee. As long as you stay here and keep low, you'll be safe."

Alice smiled. "Well, that's a relief."

"I like the color of the house, but don't you think it's a bit much? Could draw attention to yourself."

"If I have to move here, I'm going to at least put some of my style on this place," Alice replied.

"I think your hair would already attract enough attention without adding a matching house."

Alice brushed her purple hair behind her ears. "It's who I am, and no amount of running or hiding will change it."

"Well, at least you picked a great color," Ez said before taking another sip. "How is everything going so far? Any troubles getting set up?"

"The house is... cozy, even if it feels a bit too much," Alice said. "I have everything set up downstairs. I placed the order, but it's a small grocery, so it'll take longer to get that much in."

"That's fine. That's fine," Ez responded. "Do you think you can double the order?"

"I'll have to order more, but yeah."

"Perfect!"

Alice took another sip. "I'm sorry I got you involved in this mess. I'm sorry you had to give up everything because of me."

Esmerelda placed her cup on the table. She stretched across for Alice's hands and held them tightly. "Kiddo, you did nothing wrong. This is not your fault. Do you understand?"

Alice shook her head in agreement.

"That old club was just a place. Clubs can always be moved and rebuilt. You... you mean more to me than any club ever could. I'm glad you're safe now."

"Thank you." Alice smiled. "How is the new club coming along?"

"Slow. Too slow. Delays and delays and more delays," Ez responded as she let go of Alice's hands. "It would have gone much faster if I did it myself. You'll have to stop by when things calm down a bit. I'll give you a tour."

"Think of a name yet?" Alice asked.

"Thinking of keeping it simple. Maybe *The Coven Club*," she responded with a wink.

"A little on the nose, don't you think?"

"It'll be a private club, so we can control who comes in and out." Ez paused and turned her attention to the window.

Alice turned to see what drew Ez's attention. Hugo threw the ball, and Max chased after it.

"Interesting view."

"Don't worry. He can't see us. I have all the protection spells in place. I sat there watching him, and he never knew," Alice said. "Besides, he's harmless."

"Sam was harmless... at first." Ez turned her attention back to Alice. "Now look at you."

Alice closed her eyes at the utterance of that name. "He's not like Sam."

"Are you sure?"

Alice's eyes dropped to her drink. She gazed at a few pieces of torn tea leaves floating atop the brownish water. She took a sip. "I think he saw me last night."

"Saw you?"

"I was out enjoying the moonlight—" Alice started.

"I thought we talked about this."

"It was the witching hour. The moon was full, and I didn't think anyone would be watching."

"You need to be more careful. I've called in every favor I had to get you here. To get you away. I can't do it again."

Alice closed her eyes, slumped her shoulders, and lowered her head. "I wanted to feel like myself again," Alice said. She opened them and focused on Esmerelda. Her eyes watered. "I just wanted to be who I am."

Esmerelda set her mug down and once more took Alice's hands across the table. Esmerelda peered into Alice's emerald green eyes. "Kiddo, I know it can be difficult. The best thing you can do right now is maintain a low profile. Put on your big girl boots, and keep moving forward. It will be okay. I promise."

A tear slowly fell down Alice's face. Esmerelda let go, and Alice wiped away the tear.

"He liked the color of my house," Alice said.

"Oh, he liked it, did he?"

"He said it was an excellent color." Alice smiled.

"Well, at least he didn't go running for the hills," Esmerelda said. "You might as well keep it. I think it will draw too much attention if you change it. They'll ask what happened to the purple house, and then you'll really be in trouble."

They laughed and finished their tea.

"I have to say hi to my buddy before I go," Esmerelda said as she got up from the table.

LATER THAT EVENING, Alice stood alone in her bathroom. Her hands rested on the white porcelain sink pedestal. Steam rose from the sink as it filled with water. Bubbles swished around the porcelain like waves crashing along a coastline. They struggled to remain in the sink, but eventually slipped over the side onto the black and white checkerboard tile floor. Alice snapped her fingers, and the water stopped.

She grabbed a washcloth from a nearby shelf and submerged it into the water, churning the cloth, trying to soak up as much as possible. She bent over, carefully keeping a distance from the edge of the sink to not get her lavender robe wet. The warm, wet cloth soothed her face. She held it in place for a moment before scrubbing in circular patterns to remove all traces of makeup from the day.

She raised her head. A thin layer of condensation covered the oval-shaped mirror. An ornate gold filigree framed the outer edges of the mirror. She snapped her fingers again. Two candles suspended in the air moved behind her to provide more light. Other candles floated around the room. Shadows danced along the walls as their lights flickered.

Alice grabbed a dry washcloth and wiped away the condensation from the mirror. She meticulously rotated her face to examine it for any missed spots.

"Missed some right there," her mirror image said, pointing to a spot on Alice's left cheek.

"Thank you." Alice rubbed the spot.

"I think you got it," Alice's mirror image replied.

"Good?" Alice asked.

The image gave a confident nod.

The rag slowly descended into the murky depths as Alice tossed it back into the sink. She untied her robe and sauntered over to the white, claw-footed bathtub. The robe hovered in the air behind Alice after she removed it. With a snap of her fingers, the robe floated over to a hook on the wall.

Alice braced herself along the side and slowly stepped into the warm water. She slid down the angled back of the tub, stopping with her head above the bubbles. The water smelled of soap, rosemary, and rose petals. Alice leaned back, closed her eyes, and let out a deep, long sigh of relief, in pure bliss.

"She's right, you know," the mirror image proclaimed.

Alice opened her left eye to look at the mirror before closing it again. "About what?"

"That you need to lay low," the reflection responded. She smelled the luxuriously plush bathrobe she was wearing. "Adding lavender in the wash was a pleasant touch, by the way."

"Of course you would take her side," Alice replied. "And thank you."

The image leaned against a wall out of sight, tilted her head, and surveyed the room. "You don't want a repeat of Sam, do you?"

"Don't mention *her* name," Alice said as she sloshed around in the bubble bath.

"Still..." the image's voice trailed off. "It was fun."

"Debatable," Alice retorted.

"Sure, you had that whole incident at the end, but even you have to admit, overall, it was fun."

Alice glared at the mirror and sat up slightly. With a whisk of her hand, a wineglass descended from above, followed by an unlabeled wine bottle. The bottle poured the wine into the glass, knowing the perfect moment to stop. Alice grabbed the glass and took a sip.

"If, and that's a big *if*, you overlook what happened, there were moments—fleeting moments—where it was... fun," Alice said.

The mirror image gave a Cheshire Cat like smirk, grinning from ear to ear. "The nights were fun," she added.

Alice scowled at the image before looking down and taking another sip of wine. "The nights were fun," Alice admitted in a hushed tone.

"So, we had fun nights, fleeting moments, and one teeny-tiny incident. What's the problem?" the image asked. "Call up Sam. Let's get this thing back on."

"It's not that simple," Alice responded.

"Why not?"

"Sam betrayed me. I revealed the one thing I thought I could trust her with, and Sam betrayed me," Alice said in a raised voice.

The water sloshed back and forth as she swung her other arm around. "Now look. Moving around from place to place, like I was the one who did something wrong. Having to hide out. All of my friends gone, like I never existed. I'm trapped here. And on top of it all, I don't even have my stuff." She smacked the water. More bubbles slipped over the side and onto the floor.

"So, why do you want to risk it again?" the mirror asked. "Why take that chance? Because he liked your purple hair? Your purple house?"

Alice set the wineglass down on an invisible shelf above the tub. She leaned back, sinking further down into the water. The bubbles were now up to her chin. She rubbed her eyes before running her fingers through her hair. "He saw me," Alice responded. "He saw me flying around and didn't say anything."

"So? It's not like he would have brought it up in conversation. 'Hey, did you see the witch flying around on the broomstick?' Even I think I sound crazy saying it."

"Maybe I want to feel some sense of normalcy," Alice said. "Maybe I wanna be myself."

"You will," the mirror assured her. "In time. But right now, the best thing to do is lay low."

"Easy for you to say," Alice responded.

"It is easy for me," the mirror replied. "I'll be hanging around here all day."

"Hardy har har," Alice retorted.

"Come on. Cheer up. I can play you some music," the mirror said. "Do you want your SAD GIRL IS SAD playlist or the LOVESICK PUPPY one?"

Alice gave the mirror the finger and descended below the bubbles.

CHAPTER 6
A NEIGHBORHOOD WELCOME

A lice Primrose stepped with a stride of confidence; shoulders pulled back, her pert nose and emerald green eyes tilted toward the bright afternoon sky. An amethyst necklace jostled around with every springy step. She wore a brimmed, black wool hat where the top slightly curved backward into a point. Vibrant, wavy, purple hair emerged from underneath the brim and flowed below her shoulders. She had a sly smile, hiding a secret only she knew, with dark purple lipstick to match.

She wore all black—outside of a gray blouse—that contrasted with her pale complexion. A hooded modern take on the long-sleeved Victorian style tailcoat disguised Alice's tall, slightly curvy frame. The coat's pleated skirt, resting below her hips, swayed with every moment. It encircled her long legs, leading to the calf-length tails in back that exposed the purple inner lining matching Alice's hair.

A black hood bounced on Alice's shoulders with every step. Her thumbs kept her hands from fully slipping into the coat pockets as she jaunted down the sidewalk. Leather leggings tucked neatly into her thick-soled black boots. Alice loved being a witch. Even though she couldn't openly proclaim it to the world, she was determined to dress the part.

The town center bustled with activity. Shoppers went as they pleased, not a care in the world. Few stopped and acknowledged Alice as she passed. Some greeted her with a smile. Others greeted her with uncomfortable glances. Alice only returned a smirk and a nod. Some glances lingered. Some gawked—Alice assumed from prior experience—as if they wondered why someone would actively walk around in broad daylight, looking as if they were going to a costume party. Alice continued her journey, paying no attention. She knew who she was, and she was damn proud of it.

The enticing aroma of pumpkin spice leeched into her nostrils. Unmistakable hints of cinnamon and nutmeg. The ecstasy of the sweet pastry's siren smell compelled Alice inside the bakery. She stopped. Her necklace bounced a few times before coming to a rest. She surveyed through the bakery window, craving the freshly baked pumpkin spice scones sitting inside the glass counter. She had to have one. The cravings turned into near lust.

The bakery was a flurry of activity. Employees rushed to fill orders. A glass display case stretched across one of the longer side walls. The case was filled with a plethora of multi-colored treats that delighted the eyes. Freshly baked bread. Brightly colored cakes. Glistening cinnamon rolls. Festive orange and yellow iced cake pops neatly arranged in a display carousel. Brownies bigger than Alice's hand. Far too many choices to order in one visit. The enticing smells lingered in the air. The object of Alice's desire rested in the corner closest to the bakery window—the pumpkin spice scones.

She paid no attention to the odd glances and looks as she approached the display case. Alice turned her attention to a little sign that read *EAT ME* next to a serving tray resting atop the case. Sample-sized cupcake liners covered the tray. She picked up one and removed the golden-yellow cookie inside. Alice's taste buds exploded from the sensory overload of sweet and buttery flavors. She savored the cookie, contemplating grabbing another one.

"How can I help you?" a woman behind the display case asked.

Alice rushed to finish the sample. "Those are some good cookies," Alice responded, covering her mouth to not spill any onto the floor.

"Baked fresh daily," the bakery employee responded. "Would you like some?"

"A dozen, please. Also, a couple of those pumpkin scones."

The bakery employee grabbed two brown boxes along the back wall. She packed up the items and carefully placed them into a paper bag. "Twenty dollars," she said, handing the bag to Alice.

Alice gladly handed over the money, retrieving her prizes.

"Love the costume, by the way," the bakery employee complimented Alice. "Are you going to a Halloween party?"

"No."

"Getting into the Halloween spirit?"

"No. Just out shopping," Alice replied. A half smile held back any emotions she felt in that moment.

"Oh," was the only word the bakery employee could produce. A befuddled expression crossed her face. "Well, it looks fantastic."

"Thank you," Alice replied before leaving.

She peered into her bag, while grabbing the door, and collided with a man trying to enter the bakery. Their bodies spun around in the entryway.

"I'm sorry," Alice offered. "I wasn't paying attention."

"No worries," he assured her before continuing inside the bakery.

Alice steadied herself and stepped outside. The sight of a red knit hat covering blonde hair was unmistakable. She only caught a glimpse before it disappeared into a silver luxury car across the busy street. Her face was no longer full of giddy glee, but terror.

Alice held her breath. Her eyes widened, and her body tensed. The world slowed. Every emotion from the past three months came rushing back in a blurring display of anxiety and loneliness and heartache. *It can't be. It can't be. How did she find me?*

Alice rushed in between the parked cars facing the sidewalk. Her progress was impeded by the crisscrossing traffic going down the street. She paused, not wanting to meet a car head on. She had her opportunity and took it. The bag of baked goods flapped in the air as she ran across the street.

The silver car headed away from the town center. Alice arrived to the other side of the street and continued her pursuit. She wove in and out of the crowd. Many gave confused glances as she ran after the car.

Disable the car. You have to stop it. They can't know you're here. She raised her hand to the air, thumb and middle finger poised to produce the necessary component for her arcane powers. Her better judgement prevented her from putting on a magical display in the middle of the crowded square. Alice watched as the car sped away.

She squatted down, touching her hands to her shoulders. She buried her face in her arms. Her hat shielded her from the outside world. *How did Sam find me?* The name raced through her mind. Her breathing intensified in rhythmic gasps of air. She felt trapped in her self-contained bubble, trying to shut off the outside world for what felt like an eternity. She tapped her shoulders in rapid, alternating succession.

Ten... nine... eight... seven... It's only a red hat, she thought as her mind raced. *Six... five... There are lots of blonde people with red hats... Four... three... It's okay... Two... one... It's not Sam. It wasn't Sam.* She slowly lifted her head. Her eyes were bloodshot. A wet trail of sadness descended her face. She regained control of her breathing.

"Are you okay?" An older gentleman stopped to help Alice.

"I'm fine." Alice wiped the tears with her black polyester sleeve. "I'm fine. I thought I saw a ghost from the past."

He chuckled, offering his hand to help her up. "A witch afraid of a ghost?"

Alice gave a small laugh. She took his hand and stood up. "It does sound silly, doesn't it?"

"I love the costume," he tried to cheer her up.

"It's not a costume, but how—" Alice's voice trailed off. She wanted to defend her fashion tastes, but couldn't muster the strength in that moment. "Thanks."

"Well, keep an eye out for those ghosts, and try to avoid them," he said, walking away.

Alice stood for a moment to gather her composure. She picked up her bag of goodies. She checked off in the distance, trying to find any sign of the silver car. It was gone. She tilted her head, defeated.

"I should have drove," Alice muttered as her shoulders slumped. She picked up her bag of goodies and continued her journey.

As Alice approached, the doors of Raskin's Neighborhood Market opened. The blast of air inside the entryway attempted to knock off her hat, if not for her quick reaction to hold it in place. Happy hour activity was abundant at the store. Shoppers gathered their items before heading home for the day. Alice pulled her hat down over her eyes and slipped down an aisle to avoid any further unwanted attention.

She weaved in and out, avoiding eye contact with anyone who gave an odd stare at her appearance. Her winding twists and turns resulted in her appearing in the wine section. She stopped. The dark green hues mesmerized Alice as they glistened under the store lights. Her eyes soaked in the kaleidoscope of label colors. The brightly colored foils enveloped the corks hidden inside the bottle stems.

She grazed her fingers over the bottles, tracing their shapes as she lingered past. She longed to have her own wine brand on the aisle shelves. To be accepted by the public as a winemaker and not hidden away in clandestine clubs. She remembered her first big wine order.

PATRONS ENJOYING the night's revelry filled the smoky, dimly lit room. Soft jazz music played from musical instruments floating on a stage. Arcane invisible hands guided the instruments toward the next notes. Alice sat at the bar counter, taking in the atmosphere. She adjusted her form fitting, black dress as it rode up her backside. She snatched up a glass of wine sitting on the counter and took a drink. Her face contorted and shivered from the bitter taste washing over her tongue. She gave a final "blah" before shoving the glass back across the bar counter.

A petite woman with blonde beehive hair approached a bartender from behind the bar. The bartender, dressed in a white shirt and tartan style vest, scooped ice from a tray and filled three glasses in front of him.

"Is this her?" she asked. She waved her hand around in a grand gesture before pointing toward Alice with her lit cigarette, like a conductor's wand guiding his attention.

The bartender finished filling the glasses and nodded. The woman continued on to Alice waiting at the end of the bar.

"The name's Esmerelda Honeydew, but most people call me Ez," she introduced herself. Her eyes focused on the wineglass in front of her and then on Alice's purple hair. "Love the hair."

"Thank you."

Ez reached for an ashtray from across the bar counter.

"Here, use this. It might improve the wine." Alice handed her the wineglass.

Esmerelda took the glass and knocked the cigarette ash into the purplish-red liquid. She glanced back at Alice with a sly smile. "Take it you're not a fan?"

"I've had better. By better, I mean like every other wine out there," Alice replied. "That is horrible." She pointed at the glass before pulling her fingers away from the cursed wine.

"I've heard you're good."

"I'm getting better."

"I'm not looking for getting better," Ez quickly responded. Her words challenged Alice.

"Mine is the best you'll ever have," Alice stated.

Ez grabbed an empty rocks glass from behind the bar. She slammed it down on the counter and offered Alice the chance to prove her prowess. Alice produced a small silver flask from her purse. She unscrewed the top and poured the purplish-red contents into the glass.

Ez picked it up, swirling the contents inside. She took a sniff to smell the flavors of the wine. Alice crafted the wine to give off hints of vanilla and cedar. She took a sip. She swished the liquid around her mouth as if to savor every drop.

"You made this?" Ez wiped away the excess wine on her lips.

"I take it I passed," Alice inferred.

"Can you mass produce, say, one hundred bottles?"

"Shouldn't be a problem. I have an extensive list of varieties that I can make. That one was just plain, regular old wine."

"That was one hell of a plain, regular old wine." Esmerelda finished the glass without hesitation. "You're hired, kiddo. Go around back and talk to Sam."

THAT NAME JOLTED Alice back to reality. Sweat rolled down her back. Her body tensed, and her head throbbed. *I've had enough of Sam for today, thank you.* She scanned the aisle and found herself still alone. Alice continued, but a large display caught her attention.

Her fingers hovered over the label of an unfamiliar brand, *Red-Hearted Queen*. She picked up the bottle, examining it further. Her thumb traced the four suits. A minor detail, something that only a wine expert like herself would catch, drew her attention. Down in the lower right corner was a solitary, capitalized *A+* opposite the 13% alcohol by volume disclosure. Alice pondered its meaning. She had never seen a marker or indicator like that. She examined another bottle. It had a *B* in its corner.

Alice picked up yet another bottle, but immediately placed it back down. A figure appeared in the corner of her eye and pulled her attention away from the greenish bottles. She knew instantly who it was. That unmistakable coifed hair. The beard. The same black leather jacket playing ball with his dog in the backyard the day before.

She held her breath, unable to think of anything to say should he look her way. Alice froze as Hugo Dodds placed a bottle of wine in his basket. He moved on without looking down the aisle. Alice followed, leering behind the shelves to stay hidden. She grabbed a bottle of wine, pretending to examine it, but kept a keen ear to the conversation.

Hugo approached Oliver Raskin, who was behind the meat counter.

"Hugo, I have something for you. Pork chops," Oliver shouted as he produced a neatly wrapped package from inside the meat counter.

"Maybe she'll actually share with me this time," Hugo said as he placed the package of chops into his basket.

"Don't be stealing too much from her," Carol said as she approached the pair. Hugo wrapped his free arm around Carol Raskin as she hugged his side. "How are you doing? How did the date go?"

Hugo grimaced. "Well, let's say she wasn't my type."

"So, you have a type?" Carol asked.

"You know my type." Hugo avoided eye contact.

"And that's exactly why I'm trying to help," Carol pleaded.

"I met the new neighbor the other night," Hugo said, changing the subject of the conversation.

Alice's eyes widened as she focused on Hugo.

"And..." Carol egged him on.

"Max got me up in the middle of the night. We went outside and..." Hugo's words seemed to trail off to Alice.

Alice gingerly placed the bottle back on the shelf, not wanting to make a sound. *He did see me flying. How could you be so careless? He's going to tell them.* Her grip tightened around the paper bag handle. She shifted her weight, ready to make a hasty exit. She glanced down the aisle; it was clear.

"I think Max woke her up. She acted like she was already up, but I'm sure Max woke her. Max barks all the time," Hugo finished.

Alice let out a sigh of relief. Her grip loosened.

"You should ask her out," Oliver added.

A tantalizing jolt pulsed through Alice's body at the thought.

"I'm not going to ask her out," Hugo said.

The jolt of excitement turned into disappointment at those remarks. Alice peered around the corner of the aisle to get a closer look. They all focused on Hugo.

"Why not?" Carol said.

"'Hi. Welcome to the neighborhood. Sorry my dog woke you up. By the way, since you're up, would you like to go out sometime?'" Hugo said sarcastically.

"Ask who out?" Johanna questioned as she pushed her cart toward the deli counter. The black cart matched her buttoned up, long sleeve, three-quarters length jacket. Her brunette hair pulled back into a ponytail that dropped to the middle of her back. A burnt orange scarf draped around her neck and shoulders. The worn silver cloak clasp was pinned to her lapel.

"The usual?" Oliver asked Johanna.

"Yes, please," she replied.

He grabbed a few cuts of meat from the counter and took them to a packing station.

Hugo motioned with his head toward the Raskins. "They want me to ask out the new neighbor."

Johanna gave Hugo a discerning glance. Her eyes followed an invisible path from his eyes to the black onyx ring on his left hand.

"Ready to throw away the past, are you?" Johanna asked in a biting tone.

He shifted the basket to his left hand, pinched the ring with his right, and twisted. His face was pale, and all traces of a smile were gone.

"Well, I don't think he's throwing away the past." Carol patted him on the back.

"I apologize," Johanna said. "I didn't mean to say it like that. I meant to ask, are you ready to move on from Elizabeth?"

Discomfort flickered across Hugo's face at the mention of Elizabeth. Alice moved in closer.

"Hopefully, move on from this conversation. Besides, if you asked me, I might have said yes." Alice winked at Hugo.

Everyone turned their attention to the new participant. Head tilted. Her right hand placed on her hip. She stood poised, ready to guard Hugo from any more relationship questions. Alice extended her right hand toward Johanna.

"I don't think we've had the pleasure of meeting. I moved in across the street. Alice Primrose."

Johanna reeled back, covering the silver cloak clasp. She tapped it twice. "Johanna Newes," she greeted. She relinquished it and extended her hand, daintily shaking Alice's. "My! It seems some people take Halloween more seriously than others in this town."

"She's getting ready, even if it isn't for another two weeks," Hugo broke the tension.

"To me, every day is Halloween," Alice replied with a wink at Hugo.

"Well, I like it. You got to be you," Hugo said. Alice dipped her chin, so the brim of her hat hid her blushing and smiling face. "You'll have to forgive Johanna; she's not a big fan of the holiday."

"The holiday is rubbish. People knocking on doors. Begging for handouts. All in the name of what, monsters and ghosts and—" Johanna paused.

Alice raised her head and caught Johanna examining her from

her boots to the tip of her hat. "Witchcraft." She tapped her clasp twice more before grabbing her cart handle. She kept the cart between her and Alice.

"But, in Johanna's defense, you do look like Halloween walking," Hugo teased.

"I resent that, but thanks for the compliment." Alice smiled back. She turned her attention to Carol. "Have my grapes arrived yet?"

"I expect the first part of the shipment in a few days," Mrs. Raskin replied. "The distributor thought it was a typo when I asked for fifteen hundred pounds of grapes." She chuckled.

"That's a lot of grapes. Can you even eat that many before they spoil?" Hugo asked.

"The business of what I do with *my* grapes is of no concern to you," she replied to Hugo with a sly smirk as she turned her attention back to Mrs. Raskin. "I would like to place another order. The same amount. And if you can get them here before the next New Moon, that would be fantastic."

"I'll do my best, deary," Mrs. Raskin replied.

Oliver returned and handed the stack of meat, neatly wrapped in brown paper packaging, to Johanna. She thanked Oliver as she took the package and placed it in her cart.

Johanna turned her attention back toward Alice. "Any chance of you reconsidering the color of your house?"

"Well, a witch needs her place to reflect her personality," Alice replied, her words biting back against Johanna's. Alice turned her attention to Hugo.

"You already know my thoughts," Hugo replied, tilting his head to the side.

Johanna grabbed the plastic grip of the cart handle. "I thought not." She sighed as she wandered off.

CHAPTER 7
PERFECTLY BROKEN STICK

"Where are we going?" Elizabeth asked as she followed Hugo along the dirt path.

The trees of Wildgrove Park darkened the light of the full moon. Small rays of moonlight broke through openings. The spring air was thick with humidity.

A bead of sweat rolled down Elizabeth's face as she struggled to see the rutted path. Each step was slower and more deliberate than the last. She carefully planted her heel before fully committing to the step.

"Hugo, I can barely see anything. And I'm wearing heels. Where are we going?"

"Not much further. Just around the bend." He paused and stretched out his hand, waiting for Elizabeth to catch up.

She took his hand, and he guided her along the path. Hugo stopped in front of a small alcove. A billowy, white renaissance chemise dress and an emerald green overdress hung from a tree branch.

"Hugo. Is that... Is that my Ren Fest dress?" Elizabeth asked. "What's it doing here?"

Hugo backed away from Elizabeth, continuing down the path. "Put it on. I'll be right back."

"Hugo! I'm not putting this thing on in the middle of the woods at night."

"It'll be fine. There's no one around. Trust me." His voice trailed off as he disappeared down the path.

"Hugo Dodds!"

He was gone. Elizabeth surveyed around, checking the path multiple times. She examined the trees. There was no one around. She grabbed the white chemise dress. "Unbelievable."

She gave a quick sigh and unzipped her black dress. She gave one more look around. An owl hooted faintly in the distance. She carefully shimmied out of the black dress, so it didn't touch the ground.

A bead of sweat rolled down to the small of her back. She flung the black dress over a shoulder, trying to cover up her half naked body. She removed the chemise from its hanger and replaced it with the black one.

Her head disappeared into the billowy dress as she struggled to put it on before finally emerging through the opening. She straightened out the long hem, then pulled out any hair still trapped beneath. Elizabeth slipped her arms through and tied the corset-like overdress. She gave one final adjustment and stood there. The soft glow of whitish-blue moonlight that made it through the trees splashed across her face. Elizabeth checked down the path.

"Hugo?"

No response.

"I have the dress on," Elizabeth shouted.

Still nothing.

"HUGO?"

A noise, the clamoring of metal against metal, echoed in the woods. A figure bouncing in the pale moonlight galloped down the dirt path. He approached, closer and closer. Elizabeth's eyes widened.

"Hugo, this isn't funny!"

A figured approached with the distinct outline of a knight's helmet. A long stick dragged along the dirt path between the figure's legs as he galloped closer. His speed increased.

"Whoa, Sir Galahad. Whoa," Hugo commanded the wooden horse before coming to a stop.

He stumbled from the momentum and almost ran into Elizabeth. He heaved off the knight's helmet and sent it tumbling to the ground. It crashed and clanged from the impact. Hugo gave a quick glance.

"I hope I didn't damage it," he said before looking back at Elizabeth.

Elizabeth snickered. "What are you doing?"

"My lady," Hugo proclaimed as he dismounted the imaginary horse. He carefully placed the stick on the ground. "I have traveled far and wide. Faced many tribulations. Conquered many foes." He swung his arms around in magnanimous poses with each grand gesture.

Her breath shortened, and her heart raced. Her eyes brimmed with tears. "What's happening?"

"I have searched a lifetime for a lady more fair than thou, and I have found none. You are the light that doth maketh the sun envious. You are the joy that maketh me—" Hugo paused. He pulled an object from his pants pocket and concealed it within his fist. He knelt down, opened his fist, and presented a maroon velvet box to her.

Elizabeth cupped her mouth. Tears of joy fell down her face.

"I'm going to stop with the Renaissance Festival talk now."

Elizabeth laughed behind her hands.

"You are the joy of my life. I have loved you since the day we met in elementary school. I could not imagine a world without you. We have been through so much together. Happy times. Sad times. But through it all, we were together. I want to spend the rest of our lives together. Elizabeth Clark, willest thou doeth the honor of being my wife?"

Hugo opened the box. A diamond ring sparkled in the glow of a solitary ray of moonlight that made it through the tree branches.

"Yes," Elizabeth said, unable to hold back the tears. "Yes, I will doeth this honor."

Elizabeth presented her left hand. Hugo removed the ring and slowly placed it on her finger. Hugo locked with Elizabeth, and he sprung up. There was a small audible rip of cloth from his pants. He paid no attention to it. His hands cupped her face. His fingers traced along her jaw and neck before resting on the back of her head. Her heart raced, and her breath shortened. He leaned in, kissing her lips softly, gently—each kiss more passionate than the last.

Elizabeth wrapped her arms around his shoulders. She took in his scent, a mixture of mint, vanilla, and cedar cologne. The smell lingered, as Elizabeth etched it into her memory. Their bodies pressed against each other. He pushed forward. She leaned back. Their heartbeats synchronized. The world was silent.

Eternity passed.

They stopped for a moment of air, foreheads resting against each other. Their eyes were closed, searing the moment into memory. Their breathing labored.

Hugo broke the silence. "I think I tore my pants."

They laughed, opened and locked eyes. Her hazel eyes forever lost in the desire of his icy blue eyes.

"We can get them fixed," Elizabeth said, trying not to lose herself to tears of joy. They both laughed.

"I love you, Elizabeth."

"I love you too, Hu—"

～

THE MEMORY of that night faded and plucked Hugo back to reality as Max violently pulled on the leash, impatient to continue down the path. His heart raced, breathing intensified, and his head throbbed. He stumbled before looking around. The world spun for a moment.

Max gave out a loud session of barks before tugging again on the leash.

"Max, stop. *Sit!*" Hugo commanded.

Max ignored all commands, attempting to chase whatever caught her attention. Hugo shortened the leash, trying to gain control over the rambunctious puppy. Max relented, standing at attention, chest out, nose pointed, and tail wagging. Watching. Guarding.

Hugo gathered his composure, looking back to the alcove that years before held Elizabeth's emerald green dress—the tree now barren of leaves. Its gray branches twisted up to the partially clouded skies. Brown and yellow leaves piled over its roots. Hugo's back shivered from the chilly wind as it whisked the pile deeper into the woods, like discarded memories of a past long forgotten. Hugo gave out a quick breath and continued walking as Max pulled ahead.

He paused. The outline of a familiar black wool hat emerged from around the bend—its curved point was unmistakable. The purple hair bounced with every gleeful step. An unzipped black leather jacket covered a white blouse. The black and purple plaid dress sashayed with her every movement. Black tights matched the thick-soled boots, and a pumpkin shaped bag bounced off her hip.

Hugo couldn't help but stare. Each step was an eternity. His eyes widened. A lump formed in his throat.

Please don't talk to me.

He stood waiting. Frozen. Enraptured. Max tugged to greet the stranger, but Hugo held her back. He could hurry past her, never having to say more than a simple greeting. His body stood paralyzed by her sight. His heart beat faster and faster—his eyes mesmerized by her purple lips.

'You might enjoy yourself,' Oliver Raskin's words from a week ago echoed through his mind.

"Well, hello, Hugo Dodds," Alice said as she approached, stopping within an arm's length of Hugo. With a mischievous smile, she pulled on the strap of her purse.

"Fancy meeting you here."

"I saw you going for a walk and decided to follow to see what mischief the two of you were up to," Alice retorted with a sly smile. "You sure do take a lot of them."

"Are you spying on me?" Hugo asked with a chuckle.

"Do you want me to?" She tilted her head and batted her emerald green eyes.

Hugo paused. "Not what I asked."

"But is it what you wanted to hear?" Alice swayed back and forth.

Words failed Hugo.

Alice squatted down in front of Max, rubbing her chin and ears. "How's my good girl doing today?"

Max's tail thrashed violently against Hugo's leg.

"She's being her usual pain in the butt self," Hugo replied.

"Aww," Alice said. "She's not a pain in the butt, are you?"

Max smiled as Alice continued to scratch her head.

"Do you have any pets?" Hugo asked.

"Umm. Sort of." She stood up, inching her way closer to Hugo, and smiled.

His back tightened from nervous anticipation at her close proximity. He wanted her to move closer and yet step away.

"At least, he thinks he's a dog."

"Thinks he's a dog?" Hugo asked. "A cat that thinks he's a dog?"

"No. No... No cat," Alice replied. "He grew up around dogs on a horse farm. He acts like a dog at times. Part horse, part dog."

"Ah. A horse."

"Something like that."

"Never took you as a rider, but I guess if it fits..." He winked at her.

"Fits what?" Alice inquired, turning a curious ear toward Hugo.

"Well, you dress as a witch, so I guess riding comes with the territory." Hugo chuckled.

"More than you know." Alice winked back.

"I'm sorry about Johanna the other day. She's not the nicest of people to get along with. She tends to keep to herself."

"I'm used to it," Alice replied.

"But you really do like dressing like it's Halloween, don't you?"

"It's who I am."

"Well, it's definitely a style that most people in town are not used to seeing."

"Trust me, I know. I've had quite a few looks the past couple of days."

"I like it, but you know others might think you really are a witch." Hugo laughed.

"What if I secretly am a witch?" Alice asked, causing Hugo to pause for a moment. "Or maybe I just like to dress the part?"

"Well, if you were a witch, I'd say you have to be who you are. You can't change it for something you're not."

Hugo caught Alice trying to hide her blushing grin by burying her head into her shoulder. She hid only for a moment before looking back at him. Her emerald green eyes locked with his icy blues. Emotions stirred within Hugo, and his stomach twisted in knots.

"Thank you," she replied. "That means a lot to me."

"Although," Hugo added, "I wouldn't wear a black and purple dress to the high school football game next week."

"Oh?" Alice asked. "Why not?"

"They might burn you at the stake for wearing the colors of their biggest rival."

"Well, I'll keep that fashion tip in mind." Alice paused and smirked. "I don't want to be burnt at the stake, now do I?"

Hugo smiled back. "Umm, we were heading in that direction, but do you mind if we join you?"

"Not at all. I could always use someone to talk to."

The three of them continued on down the path.

Hugo asked, "So, what do you do for work?"

"I'm in beverage distribution."

"Bartender?"

"No," she chuckled. "I oversee bottling and distribution."

"Ah, I see. That's cool. I hope they give you free samples."

"Of course. What about you? I never see you leave, except when you walk your dog. Do you work from home?"

"I'm a professional dog walker. I only have one client, and she doesn't pay me."

"Seriously?"

"No, I'm joking. I actually do nothing."

"Nothing?"

Hugo stopped and dropped his eyes toward the rut filled path, trying to find the words. Alice stopped as well, her puzzled expression now a concerned look. Hugo paused for a moment before looking at Alice.

"I used to be in finance. That was... until Elizabeth died. They gave me a week to grieve. Only a week. Then they expected me to go about life like nothing happened. Like how? How can I grieve for an entire lifetime lost in only a week?"

"That's horrible. I couldn't imagine the emotions you were going through in that week."

"I lasted a day. We were in a meeting to discuss budgets or some nonsense. People were arguing. I sat there listening. After a few minutes, I slammed my fist on the table and yelled, 'WHEN WE ALL DIE, NONE OF THIS WILL MATTER, SO WHO CARES?' Everyone sat there in stunned silence. I stood up, went to clean out my desk, and then I left."

"I'm so sorry you had to go through that." She hugged Hugo.

He smelled a hint of lavender from her clothes. The embrace of a woman stirred even more feelings within Hugo—feelings he locked away to be forgotten. Never to be embraced again. Thoughts stirred in his mind. Thoughts he tried to suppress, but the emotions were too strong. He wanted more.

"That's okay. I'm fine."

"I thought we agreed to not use that phrase," Alice scolded as she pulled back.

He wanted the hug to continue.

Hugo chuckled. "You caught me. I am most certainly not fine. I'm lucky that I have the luxury of not needing to work."

"Oh?"

"I still have half of Elizabeth's life insurance money. Plus, money left over from when her parents passed. I paid off the house. Sold my car. Kept hers. Got Max to keep me company. And every day, I wait for answers about what to do next. Hopefully, I get them before the money runs out."

"What will you do if it does?"

"I don't know. Work for the Raskins, I guess. Maybe then I'll actually fill up my fridge, since I won't have to use that as an excuse to visit them." He laughed.

They continued their journey. Alice occasionally picked up leaves, sticks, or other objects of nature found on the ground. One spot caught her attention. She stopped and carefully sifted through the brown, discarded leaves.

Hugo waited for her. Max investigated what Alice was doing, but was impatient to continue their walk. Alice kept digging to find the most prized ones. She picked up a few, placed them in her bag, and then they continued down the path.

"So, do you like collecting nature things?" Hugo asked.

"Sort of. I like to make things with them, but only the perfect ones."

"They all look the same to me. Dried up, shriveled leaves and broken sticks are all around us, so you have plenty to choose from."

"I can tell which are the perfect ones."

"And how can you tell which ones are perfect?" Hugo asked, his voice raised in a higher sarcastic pitch.

"Take this one, for example." Alice squatted down to grab a stick that was as long as her hand.

The grayish-brown stick snapped in the middle; the two halves barely held together by the bark. "This is a perfect stick."

"That's a broken stick," Hugo replied.

"Only to the untrained eye. Look." She pulled out a small roll of gaffer's tape from her bag. She wrapped the tape around the stick, mending the two pieces back together. "This stick has been damaged, yes, but with a little mending at the right parts, it will be as good as new." She ripped the tape off from the roll and gave it one final press.

"That looks like a stick with tape on it."

She placed the stick and tape back into her bag. She smirked at Hugo and continued down the path. Hugo took off after her. Max followed behind briefly before charging ahead. She tugged and pulled at the leash to get Hugo to move faster. After a brief game of leash tug-of-war, Max relented and took a more leisurely pace at the head of their newly formed pack.

"So, there is this thing coming up. A big fall, pumpkin, Halloween type festival the town puts on every year. You'd really love it," Hugo said.

"Oh, yeah?" Alice asked with a raised inflection.

"Well, I was thinking, since you are new in town—"

"I'd love to."

"You don't even know what I was going to ask."

"I didn't have to."

"Great, so they're looking for volunteers to run some of the food booths—"

Alice's pouty look, as if that wasn't the question she expected, stopped Hugo in his tracks.

"I'm joking."

"I don't think you are." She playfully stormed off ahead of Hugo.

He and Max hurried to catch up to her.

"I was going to ask if you wanted to accompany me to the festival."

Alice paused and turned back to Hugo with a beaming smile. "Are you asking me out on a date, Hugo Dodds?" She bit her lower lip in anticipation of his answer.

Hugo froze. His mind raced, trying to find an excuse to claim it wasn't a date. He wanted to say those words: *It's not a date.*

Those words failed him.

"Well, um, it doesn't have to be a date if you don't want it to be," he replied. "But it can be, if you want it to be."

"I already said yes," she replied.

"Yes to which question?"

"Yes to both," Alice answered with a smirk.

Hugo stood there in dumbfounded relief. "Great. So. It's a date."

"I guess so."

"Besides, I need someone to stop everyone from asking how I'm doing."

"Deal." Alice leaned her head back and smiled. "But on the condition that I can be as witchy as I want to be."

"Always," Hugo was quick to reply. "You have to be you."

Alice blushed. "Then it's a date!"

Hugo smiled. They continued along the path, with Max leading the way.

CHAPTER 8
IN THE CARDS

"You're not!" A hint of expected shock and amazement was in the mirror reflection's voice. "I thought we talked about this."

"It'll be fine," Alice assured the mirror. She pulled off the black container cap, pursing her lips in anticipation, as she applied the purple lipstick. She stood there, head titled, trying to find the words to justify her actions. "Besides, it's a harmless little date. It's nothing."

"That's how these things start," Alice's mirror reflection was quick to retort. "Need I remind you of Sam?"

Alice clenched her lips, pressing against each other, careful not to ruin the freshly applied layer. "Don't say that name." Alice glared at her reflection.

Her mirror reflection crossed her arms and rolled her eyes. "It started as a harmless little date. A little flirting over dinner. Teasing. Laughing. Kissing. Taking baths together..." her voice trailed off. "Then bam, we're uprooted to the middle of nowhere. Are you prepared to do that again?"

Alice slammed the lipstick tube down on the rim of the porcelain basin. The tube slipped from her hand, rolling down into the basin.

"Hugo is not Sam!" Anger washed over her face. "He isn't a witch like Sam... who was trying to exploit me... Take advantage of me... *Use me!*"

Alice's reflection paused on the hurt in Alice's voice. She enjoyed the playful back-and-forth banter, but even she knew her limits. She uncrossed her arms, rubbing her face before admitting defeat. "I'm sure he won't be. Just be careful. Hey. It's only the two of us, and I'm worried about you. No you, no me. You know?"

Alice lowered her head and in a soft tone whispered, "Thank you."

"Let's have a look at you," Alice's reflection said. "Do one of those twirly things. Let me check out the goods."

Alice took a few steps back and spun around. Her purple hair twirled in the air. She wore a tight black top that accentuated her silhouette. Billowy, mesh, long sleeves exposed her shoulders and arms and connected the top to her high neck collar. A black leather miniskirt hugged the curves of her hips. Fishnet stockings wrapped around her long legs, leading toward a pair of black Doc Martens. Alice's reflection struggled to find the right words. She examined her up and down. Her mouth gaped open.

"How do I look?" Alice asked, finishing another twirl.

"I'd sleep with you," Alice's reflection commented.

Alice stopped, hands on her hips. A disapproving stare on her face. "That's not what I asked."

Alice's reflection winked. "No. But that's what you *wanted* to ask."

Knocks on the door echoed up the stairs to the bathroom. Response knocks, the sound of wood smacking against the closed door, echoed through the bathroom.

"I know. I know," Alice shouted to her overprotective guardian on the other side of the door.

Alice's reflection leaned against the edge of the mirror, framing her Cheshire Cat like grin between both of her hands. "It's looovvver boy."

Alice scrambled to pick up the makeup tubes, stuffing them into a worn, black canvas pouch, which she then tossed onto a shelf. She opened the bathroom door.

"Stay!" Alice commanded to something out of the reflection's view.

"Don't do anything I wouldn't do tonight," Alice's reflection shouted. "Wait! Do everything I would do. Either way, have fun. Enjoy yourself!"

HUGO DODDS PACED AROUND the gray, hexagonal, gazebo like porch. The soles of his black Chelsea boots echoed with every step atop the boards. He glanced over toward his house. He paused, reflecting if he was making a mistake.

He paced around to the front of the porch and peered over at Johanna's house across the street. The yellow house was darkened with the curtains drawn. The sun was setting. People and families marched in an unorganized procession toward the fall festival in the center of town.

A few acknowledged Hugo standing on the porch. He gave a half nod and waved in response. He spun around, hiding himself further on the back of the porch as he awaited Alice's arrival, and knocked on the black door again.

Knocking came from inside the house with someone speaking in an indecipherable language. He tried to look through the black sheer curtain draped across the door's window. He couldn't see any movement inside. Then he heard the noise of metal against metal as the lock unlatched, and the door opened. Hugo gave an audible gasp, his mouth gaping.

Alice stood in the doorway smiling. He struggled to find words. His eyes traced the curves of her body from her black top to the leather skirt, and finally to her fishnet stockings. Hugo wanted to find the words, needed to find the right words, but her beauty stole them.

He finally offered a simple, "Wow."

"Hello, Hugo," she said, brushing her hair behind her ears. "I'll be right out. Just a moment." She closed the door behind her.

Hugo stepped back, tugging at his black leather jacket. He brushed his fingers over his short beard, making sure it was properly groomed. Then he ran his fingers through his wavy, long, coifed hair, attempting to put every hair back into place. He waited for her return.

She exited the door, wearing her black tailcoat and signature hat.

"You look great," his words returned to him.

She blushed. He noticed her eyes trace his wavy hair before locking onto his icy blue eyes. She paused only for a moment before continuing to examine his neatly trimmed beard. His black leather jacket tight around his chest, accenting his slightly muscular build. The light colored jeans that hugged his legs. The black leather boots.

Alice was silent. A sly smile betrayed her closely guarded thoughts. She bit her lip before manifesting, "You too."

Hugo smiled at the thought that those two words were all she could say at that moment.

"We should get going." Hugo motioned down the porch steps. "The line for the turkey legs is going to be super long if we don't hurry."

Alice expanded her smile before responding with a hint of sarcasm, "Oh, wouldn't want to miss out on a turkey leg."

"Best in the state!" Hugo responded before leading her down the stairs.

Alice took up position on the left of the sidewalk.

Hugo was quick to interrupt. "Sorry, I have to be on that side."

"Oh?" Alice seemed startled.

"It's a chivalry thing. A personal thing. I have to be between you and the cars," Hugo explained as he stepped to Alice's side.

She smiled. "I appreciate a chivalrous man."

"All those years going to the renaissance festival, I guess they rubbed off on me." They joined the procession leading toward the center of town.

JOHANNA NEWES SAT in her high-back antique chair, watching the procession down the street from behind a small opening in her curtains. Her brunette hair was pulled neatly back into a ponytail. A grandfather clock ticked in the background. Her living room was dimly lit as to not alert anyone to her presence.

A wretched, blasphemous holiday, Johanna thought.

She noticed movement across the street and saw a familiar figure. She pulled back the lace curtain to get a better view. He was unmistakable. She also recognized a familiar pointed hat.

"How could you, Hugo?" she whispered as she tapped against her pinned cloak clasp.

Hugo and Alice proceeded down the street. Johanna sprung up from her chair and turned off the antique lamp on the side table to darken the room.

THE TOWN CENTER was a flurry of revelry and joyous people. Throngs of people mingled through the brightly colored tents and food trucks that lined the streets. Kids ran around in a menagerie of Halloween costumes. The smells of fried food and expensive beer saturated the air. A melody of carnival music blared from mobile rides that beckoned, calling young children to partake—for a fee, of course.

A Ferris wheel, taller than the buildings, gave riders a magnificent view of the town. Faux jack-o'-lanterns adorned the tops of the ornate streetlamps, struggling to fight back against the darkness of the night sky. Hugo and Alice wove their way through the crowd, clutching their prized turkey legs.

"Look, Mommy, she's a witch like me," a young child's voice caught Alice's attention.

She bent down, looked the child in the eyes, and smiled at her witch costume.

"Well, hello, fellow witch. Are you causing mischief and mayhem, like me?"

The child giggled as Alice asked the question. She reached behind the child's ear and conjured a small candy bar. She paused, seeking confirmation from the mother before handing over the treat. The child's eyes widened at receiving a gift of chocolate.

"Thank you," the child replied before showing her mom.

Alice stood up.

"I love the costume," the mom replied before they scurried away.

"Oh, it's not a costume," Hugo stated before he winked at Alice and nudged her shoulder. "Do you always carry around small candy bars in your pocket?" he joked.

Alice lightly smacked Hugo across his chest. The back of her hand slid across the smooth leather. "Jealous you didn't get one?"

"Actually, yeah."

"Too bad. Fresh out," Alice replied. "Have to save the rest for trick-or-treaters. So, what's on the agenda, Hugo Dodds?"

"Well, we have to stop by the fortune teller; that's always fun. They have a bobbing for apples booth—catch as many as you can in one minute to win prizes. Maybe ride the Ferris wheel." There was joy in Hugo's voice, a joy he hadn't felt in a long time. "Oh, and we have to try the homemade cider. What do you want to do first?"

Alice took a bite of her turkey leg. She wiped the juices from her chin, careful to not get them all over her coat. "This is a good turkey leg."

"Told you. Best in the state." Hugo took a bite.

"The fortune teller sounds fun."

"Great. She pulls three tarot cards. You'll love it. It's all for fun."

"Hugo? Hugo Dodds?" a familiar male voice shouted over the noise.

Hugo recognized that voice from a few weeks ago. He stopped, dropping his head, fretting over the interaction to come. Biting his lower lip, Hugo hoped the person who mentioned his name would disappear. He turned around to see George and Julia approaching.

"We didn't think we'd see you here. How are you doing?" George asked.

"He's doing just fine, thank you," Alice intersected. "I don't believe we've met. Alice Primrose, Hugo's date." Her elbow nudged Hugo's arm.

"Oh, a date?" Julia said. "Well, we'll leave you two alone. It was lovely to meet you."

"Great to see you, Hugo," George added as he and Julia hurried away.

"Date obligations fulfilled." She winked at Hugo and took another bite of her turkey leg.

They finished their turkey legs and worked their way through the crowd toward a red canopy tent. An older woman sat at a makeshift table. Her wild, gray hair was tucked under a maroon headscarf. Fake gold coins dangled from the scarf. She wore a multi-colored, tie-dyed, billowing dress that could have been the required uniform for a hippie commune.

Various rocks and bright crystals adorned the black velvet tablecloth. An opaque crystal ball, roughly the size of a softball, rested atop a black pedestal. A scuffed up, plastic bucket sat in one corner with a sign that read: *Donations for the Newbury Grove Annual New Year's Eve Celebration.*

"Step right up. Step right up. Learn the mysteries of your future yet to be. Let Madame Sophia tell you your fortune," she barked to attract potential customers.

Hugo and Alice approached.

"Ah, the happy couple. Care to know what love has in store for you?"

"Oh, we're not a couple," Hugo replied. He quickly shot a glance over to Alice, hoping he didn't say anything to upset her.

"Not yet, anyway," Alice was quick to respond, giving Hugo a mischievous grin and a wink. "Maybe it's in the cards."

Hugo placed two, twenty-dollar bills into the bucket. They sat down on a pair of plastic foldable chairs.

Madame Sophia shuffled the deck, careful to not let any cards slip out prematurely. The corners tapped against each other as they rapidly found their new positions. She offered the deck to Alice, inviting her to cut. Alice split the deck into three roughly even piles.

"Fate has been cast." Madame Sophia gathered up the deck. She flipped over the first card. The Tower Card. "I see a sudden upheaval in your past. A change. For good or for worse, but a change nonetheless."

Alice shifted in her seat.

She flipped over the second card, placing it in the center of the black velvet cloth. The Nine of Swords. "Great trauma, anxiety, hopelessness—probably brought on by this great upheaval—washes over you."

Alice fixated on the cards. Her cheeky grin was gone. She shifted even more on the hard plastic chair. "I don't think we should continue."

"Come on," Hugo said. "We have to find out what happens next."

Madame Sophia flipped over the concluding card. The Two of Cups. "A union. Possibly love or marriage..." her voice trailed off. She paused for a moment to inspect the cards. "Ah, it all makes sense now. A great upheaval in your past led to the feeling of great hopelessness, but if you persevere, you will find the connection, the partnership you seek."

Alice's eyes lingered on that last card.

"Did you stack the deck? This must be your love connection deck, right?" Hugo asked, teasing at the possibility it was all a setup.

Madame Sophia picked up the cards and shuffled yet again. "I do not stack my deck. I merely interpret what's before me."

The cards snapped into place. She shuffled a few more times before offering them to Hugo. He cut the deck a few cards from the top.

"Fate has been cast," she said as she took the deck once more.

She flipped over the first card, placing it near the middle of the table. The Five of Cups. "A great loss, grief—"

"We're done," Hugo exclaimed. He bumped into the table as he stood up from the chair.

Madame Sophia secured the crystal ball as it rocked back and forth.

Alice grabbed his arm, beckoning him to sit down. "I made it through mine; you can make it through yours," she said, looking up at him. "Besides, we need to figure out what happens next." Alice smiled as she released her grip.

Hugo locked onto her eyes—begging, hoping, pleading for the support to continue. She gave a small nod. He sat back down in the chair. He extended his hand, beckoning for hers. She interlocked her fingers with his as their hands cupped together. She gave a quick squeeze, letting it linger before releasing.

Madame Sophia flipped over the next card. The Two of Swords. "It looks like you'll have to make a difficult decision. One that could be very painful."

Hugo's eyes fixated on the first card. The words echoed through his mind. Grief. Loss.

She flipped over the concluding card, placing it at the end of the row. The Four of Wands. "This is very good."

"It is?"

Sophia's fingers guided Hugo's eyes across the three cards. "A great, painful loss in your past," she explained as she moved onto the other two cards. "You will be forced to make a difficult decision. If you make the correct decision, then you will find a joyful celebration in your personal life. These are the cards as I interpret them."

Alice squeezed Hugo's hand. His solemn face froze at the sight of the cards. Madame Sophia snatched the cards up and shuffled them back into her deck. She turned her attention back toward Hugo, staring at the empty space on the table. A blank expression on his face.

"So, I'd save up for that ring if I were you."

Alice and Hugo snapped their gazes at Madame Sophia before looking at each other. Alice let go of Hugo's hand.

"I'm sorry. Why a ring?" Hugo asked.

"Based on both of your readings," Madame Sophia responded. "I see potential love in your future."

Alice and Hugo scrambled to find something to say next. Anything. They locked eyes. Knowing glances turned to half smiles.

"Thank you for the reading," Alice said. "It's been very—"

"Enlightening," Hugo finished.

They both stood; Hugo was careful to not knock over the contents of the table, and they exited the tent.

"So," Alice said. "You going to save up for that ring?"

Hugo lowered his head and chuckled. "The night's still young. There are plenty of chances for you to change your mind..."

Hugo's voice trailed off as his shoulder slammed into a smaller, more diminutive body. Hugo grabbed the other person's shoulder to stabilize them both. A dance of two people colliding, trying to not fall over onto the pavement.

"I'm sorry. My fault. I wasn't looking," he explained. His eyes locked with the unsuspecting soul. "Johanna, I wasn't expecting you to show up."

"Johanna. What a wonderful surprise to see you," Alice said in a low, sarcastic tone. Alice's eyes fixated on Johnna from beneath the brim of her hat.

Johanna Newes brushed back her displaced ponytail. She tugged at her trench coat like jacket, giving two taps to the ringed cloak clasp before composing herself. "Sorry to run into you, Hugo. I wasn't paying attention to where I was going."

"I'm sure it was an accident," Alice added.

Hugo arched his eyebrows as he gave her an inquisitive look.

He turned his attention back to Johanna. "Are you okay?"

"Fine," Johanna replied. "No harm done."

"I thought you didn't enjoy coming to this event," Hugo said.

"I thought, why not head down and see what all the fuss was about?" Johanna replied.

Hugo motioned off into the distance. "We were going to try our hands at bobbing for apples, if you'd like to join us."

Alice gave Hugo a stern tap against his side, startling him. "Don't you mean giving our heads a try at it? Besides, I'm sure Johanna has other things she wants to do."

"Thank you for the invite. Bobbing for apples does seem—" Johanna paused. "Fun."

Alice kicked Hugo's boot. He took the hint that three was a crowd.

"You know," Hugo added. "Actually, I promised to take Alice on the, um, Ferris wheel."

"I'm afraid of heights, and I need someone to hold my hand," Alice chimed in.

Johanna gave a half smile. She tapped the clasp twice. "I understand. Have fun."

She stepped away before turning back. "Oh, Hugo, wasn't the Ferris wheel Elizabeth's favorite ride here?"

A solemn look masked Hugo's face. He went to pinch his ring, but Alice's hand intercepted him. She interlocked her fingers with his, holding tight.

"Enjoy, you two," Johanna added before disappearing into the crowd.

Hugo stood there motionless. Alice placed her hand on his chest, below his shoulder. She rubbed his muscular chest over the black leather.

"Hey," she said. Hugo locked eyes with Alice. "Come on. I bet I can get more apples than you."

He smiled. "You're on."

CHAPTER 9
THE TRIAL

The kettle whistled throughout the kitchen. Steam poured out and then disappeared like a ghostly apparition. Johanna Newes tempered the blue gas flame and removed the kettle from the stove burner. She poured the hot water into a burnt orange teapot. The tea steeped within an internal strainer. Johanna placed the kettle back down on the stove. She grabbed the teapot and proceeded into her living room.

A brass floor lamp with a navy hood was the only source of light in the room. Gold tassels hung down, concealing the light bulb underneath. The grandfather clock stood like a sentinel guarding the entrance to the kitchen. Its tick was the only sound echoing off the barren walls. A darkened lamp rested on a black stained oak side table next to the front window. The navy curtains blocked out the sights transpiring outside.

The gold wingback chair, filled with elegant flora designs, moved to the middle of the room. A side table waited next to it with a white teacup and saucer situated atop. The muted floral pattern matched the wingback chair. Johanna set the teapot down next to the cup and saucer. She snapped toward the window; the noise outside drew her attention. She heard them—the voices of excitement from the ghouls and monsters and creatures that roamed the night.

Trick or treat. Beggar's night.

What a wretched excuse to celebrate something so profane, she thought. *So blasphemous.*

She hurried over to the front door to verify the porch light was off. It was. She double tapped the cloak clasp pinned to her lapel. She then cupped her hands together and bowed her head as if she was giving a silent prayer. After a moment, she focused on an antique, carved oak display stand resting along the wall facing the wingback chair.

Elizabeth's picture frame, the one given to her by Hugo, rested in the back corner of the table. Johanna stood up straight with her shoulders pulled back and arms at her side. She marched toward it with brief steps as if she were in a funeral procession.

Twisting legs rose from the ground to the flat top of the display table. A shelf beneath connected the four legs together. Built into the table were two rectangular drawers, intricately carved with images of a tree branch and oak leaf patterns. A chiseled wolf's head served as a handle. An engraved oak leaf, with a brass key in its center, separated the two drawers. Johanna turned the key until a mechanical bolt unlocked. She gripped under the wolf's jaw and pulled open the right drawer.

She removed a box from inside and placed it atop the table. It was a plain, black jewelry box with a tarnished metal hook clasp. She pulled on her hair tie behind her head. It slipped down and off the ponytail before she tossed the hair tie onto the table. Her brunette hair flowed behind her shoulders. She took a deep breath, holding it for a moment, and then drew out her exhale.

She unlocked the metal hook clasp methodically. A mixture of hesitation and determination. The clasp was free of its lock. She gave two rapid taps of her cloak clasp and moved her hands to the lid.

Holding both sides, she opened the lid of the box. Her eyes looked away from the item inside, but she knew she had to face it.

Especially on this night.

She opened the left drawer and removed a black twisting stick. She held the anti-magick wand in her right hand and examined the twisted patterns leading to the point. It was twice as long as her hand. The thicker end rested on her palm. Her thumb followed the ridges of the twisting wood. She rotated the stick, her thumb now pressed against the flat bottom side of the wand. She held the wand above the box, ready to strike at the item held within. Her hand shook, and her arm tensed.

Do it, you coward, she thought. She reeled back with the wand higher in the air. Her arm now vibrated her shoulder and upper body. *End it now. End the suffering. Do it!*

Her nostrils flared. Anger in her eyes. Malice in her heart. Poised, she was ready to strike with hell's fury at the item held within the black box. She gritted her teeth. Tears welled in her eyes. She held it for as long as she could.

Her arm lurched forward, but missed the intended target. She slammed the wand down onto the table. Her open hand held it in place. Johanna hunched over the table; her hair now covered her face. Tears flowed down her cheeks.

"I can't do it," she cried. "I can't do it. I want it to end. Please make it end. Why did you do this to me? Why?"

She threw the wand back into the drawer, slamming it shut, and then buried her face into her hands and bawled. She removed one hand from her face. Johanna traced the circular pattern of the cloak clasp with her fingers. She snuffled twice and regained her composure. She pulled her hair back behind her shoulders.

Johanna extracted a jeweled amulet held within the black box. A golden disc, worn with age. Interlocking links of gold passed through a metal loop at the top of the disc. Johanna cradled the disc in her hands. She circled the amulet with her thumb, feeling each precision cut into the eight burnt orange gems that encircled a golden jewel in the center. It was heavy—heavy with the burdens of multiple life-times lived.

Johanna focused on Elizabeth's photograph. Her bright smile and hazel eyes. Elizabeth's auburn hair, which matched the golden leaves in the background, reminded her of Abigail.

"ABIGAIL!" Johanna shouted. "Abigail, are you in here?" Johanna entered the wooden barn. The smell of hay and animals lingered in the poorly filtered building. The room was dark and foreboding. "Abigail. This isn't funny." Her hand stretched out for the wood pillars of the empty livestock pins. Johanna took small steps as she moved through the straw covered dirt floor. "Abigail, are you in here?"

The room went dark as two hands cupped her eyes. A woman's voice whispered, soft like it was telling a secret only they knew, "I've taken your sight. What will you give me in exchange for your sight back?"

Johanna spun around. Her dark brown eyes locked with Abigail's hazel-colored ones. Johanna's heart beat against her rib cage. Her breathing intensified. Johanna brushed Abigail's auburn hair behind her ear. She leaned forward and whispered softly into Abigail's ear, "I give you my heart so that I may look upon thee with mine own eyes and not suffer a day longer."

Johanna wrapped her arms around Abigail's body. Johanna's hands carefully traced her spine down her black petticoat until it found the small of her back. She pressed her hands, drawing Abigail in closer. Abigail held her breath and closed her eyes in anticipation. Johanna leaned in and kissed her soft lips. Abigail's hands worked their way up to the back of Johanna's head, fingers intertwined with her brunette hair. Johanna stopped momentarily for a quick breath and then gave her a small kiss again.

They touched foreheads, both gasping for air.

"I have missed this," Johanna said. "What about William?"

"Out in the fields. He's far from here," Abigail replied. She pulled back. "I have something for you." She pulled out a ringed silver cloak clasp from her apron pocket. She showed Johanna the intricate, fili-gree design that interwove around the flat surface.

"What is this?"

"This is an old family heirloom." Abigail flipped it over. The words 'For My Eternal Love' were engraved into the silver ring. "I want you to have this. Since I've taken your heart, you can keep this close by knowing that my love for you will always be eternal."

Abigail pinned the cloak clasp to her black petticoat below her left shoulder. Johanna touched the silver ring. Her fingers traced along the interwoven lines. Their eyes locked again. Abigail gave a slight nod.

Johanna grabbed Abigail's waist and tossed her onto the hay of the animal stall. She climbed on top of her. Johanna undid the buttons running down her chest. Abigail's hands tried to find their way up Johanna's long, flowing skirt and became tangled in the folds of the fabric. She hurried to expose Johanna's body underneath. Johanna paused and locked eyes with Abigail once more.

"I love you," she said.

Abigail paused her pursuit. "I love you too," she replied. "I—"

"What is happening here?" A man's voice interrupted.

Johanna rolled off of Abigail, covering up her exposed legs.

"William," Abigail shouted. Her hands shook as she buttoned back up. "I thought you were working in the fields?"

"I came back for the fork. What in God's name is happening here?"

"We, uhh..." Johanna tried to think of words, any words. They locked their desperate eyes, hoping either would find the right answer. Johanna concentrated on William and continued, "We—"

"She bewitched me," Abigail yelled.

Johanna snapped her head back toward Abigail. Her eyes

widened, and she held her breath. The taste of straw in her mouth erased the taste of Abigail's lips.

A week later, Johanna was on trial for witchcraft, accused of bewitching her true love, Abigail. Her secret love. She was the furthest thing from being a witch. She had heard the stories—rumors that a witch had taken up residence in the woods surrounding their small town.

She never believed them. She thought the townsfolk were merely superstitious and worried about what was out there in the dark woods.

The knock of the judge's gavel echoed through the makeshift courtroom. She stood on a raised wood platform and held the rails to her side. Her stomach pressed against the rail in front of her. Murmurs and whispers filled the air. The gavel echoed again. At the front of the room, the judge sat at a long table with a half dozen of the other town elders.

"This court shall come to order," the judge's voice echoed through the largest chamber of the Town Common House. The room fell silent. "Johanna Newes. You are hereby accused of practicing witchcraft by William Anderson. How do you plead?"

Johanna scanned the room; her eyes widened at the horror set before her. Their eyes focused on her, judging her. Afraid of her. Condemning her. She tried to clear the lump in her throat. She held back tears in her eyes. Her eyes finally rested on their eventual target: Abigail. Her head held low.

"How does the defendant plead?" the judge asked again.

"Not guilty," Johanna responded with a crack in her voice, trying to find the strength to defend herself.

The crowd's whispers and murmurs filled the air. The gavel struck thrice more.

"Order. Order."

The room fell silent.

A man at the table rose and proclaimed, "The court calls on William Anderson."

A man in his mid-thirties stood up and marched to a chair set before the table, holding his hat.

"Do you, William Anderson, proclaim before God that you shall tell the truth and only the truth?"

"I shall," he responded and sat down.

"Please recant for the court what you witnessed the accused of doing," the judge commanded.

William shifted in his seat as he gathered the words needed. His eyes focused on Johanna's horrified expression. "Your honor, I returned to the barn to get my pitchfork to help work in the fields. That's where I found her. She was laying on top of my wife, Abigail, trying to—"

He hesitated, his eyes dropping to the floor. "I found her trying to remove the clothes from Abigail and have her way with her."

Gasps and rising murmurs broke out in the courtroom. The judge beat the gavel to regain control. "Order. Order," his words flowed out to fight against the crowd noises. "There will be order in my courtroom."

The room fell silent again.

"I must have disrupted her spell because Abigail looked at me and pleaded that Johanna bewitched her." William leapt to his feet, pointing his hat at Johanna. His eyes blazoned with anger. "I knew she was a witch. She lives alone, unmarried. She is the witch who lives in the woods. She'll bewitch all of your wives too. Maybe even your husbands as well."

The crowd erupted in noise once again. The gavel knocked against the wood to silence them.

"Thank you, Mr. Anderson. You're dismissed."

He strode back into the crowd and sat down next to Abigail. Her gaze was still forward. Her bonnet shielded her eyes from Johanna's terrified face. Tears streamed down her face.

"The court now calls on Abigail Anderson," an elder's voice commanded.

Abigail sat there for a moment and then stood. Her head

remained low, unable to look at Johanna. She trudged toward the chair and addressed the town elders.

"Abigail Anderson, do you proclaim before God that you shall tell the truth and only the truth?"

"Tell them the truth, Abigail. Tell them," Johanna blurted out.

"Witchcraft," a voice yelled as the crowd erupted into noise once again.

"Order. Order," the judge yelled.

Abigail raised her head. Her eyes reddened. Her lips pressed firmly together. Johanna saw the deluge of emotions on her face. Her eyes locked with Abigail's. She wondered if Abigail wanted to tell the truth, or even if she did, she would lie as to not suffer the same fate.

"I do." Abigail's words were barely audible. She sat in the chair, lowering her gaze back to the floor.

"Please inform the court of what transpired that day," an elder's voice instructed.

Abigail sat in silence, her gaze unmoved from the spot on the floor.

"Please inform the court of what transpired that day," the elder repeated.

Abigail remained silent.

"I won't ask again," the elder threatened.

Abigail raised her head and locked eyes with Johanna. A tear rolled down her face. She mouthed the words, "I'm sorry."

Tears flowed down Johanna's face. She nodded her head and mouthed back, "It's okay."

Abigail closed her eyes and slumped forward. She folded her hands in prayer. "I was in the barn. Johanna entered. She bewitched me with a kiss. She threw me onto the hay and then—" Abigail paused for what felt like an eternity. "Johanna tried to have her way with me."

Chants of "hang the witch" erupted throughout the room. The judge banged his gavel, and the room fell silent once again. The men at the table conferred with each other. They paused for a moment to glance over at Johanna.

The judge stood and leered at Johanna. "Johanna Newes, you are hereby found guilty of practicing witchcraft. The sentence is that you shall be hung by the neck until dead."

Johanna fell to her knees. She buried her head into her left arm, crying. She clutched the silver cloak clasp with her right hand. Abigail stood and ran out of the courtroom.

"Your honor," a booming voice said from the back of the room. "They may hang witches in Salem, but I have a more efficient way of dealing with them."

The judge stood and surveyed the back of the room. "Come here and identify yourself before the court," the judge ordered.

A burly man took a final sip of tea and set the cup down on a table in the back. He approached the front of the room. All eyes focused on him. The leather soles of his brown boots tapped against the wooden floorboards and echoed throughout the room.

He wore a green coat. Gold buttons running down the center held it closed. He wore an oversized leather tricorn hat. The leather was tanned and brown with age. He removed the hat as he approached the front of the room.

"Your honor, please allow me to introduce myself. I am Thaddeus Price, witch-finder appointed by his majesty, King William the Third. I have been tracking witches to this area for some time. It seems you have found one."

He approached the town elders. Thaddeus produced a piece of paper from his coat pocket and handed it to the judge. The elders examined the paper.

"Okay, witch-finder, what do you propose we do?"

Thaddeus turned to address the crowd. "We burn the witch."

Johanna let out a cry of sheer terror. The crowd burst into confusion and horror.

"You're mad," an elder shouted. "Mad and barbaric. We are a civilized society."

"I assure you I am neither mad nor barbaric, unlike the rest of you," Thaddeus proclaimed. "Fire. Drowning. Hanging. None of these work on a true witch. Witches can use their black magick to survive after your means of death. I have something that's a little more... permanent."

"What do you have in mind?" the judge asked.

He yanked a chain from his coat pocket. A golden disk twisted in the air at the end of the chain. Eight orange gems encircled a yellow jewel in the center. He held the amulet aloft for the crowd to see. "Behold the amulet of witch's fire. Anyone wearing this while facing the setting sun shall have their insides set ablaze in extreme agony. This is the only way to be certain a witch is truly dead."

His words mesmerized the crowd. Their eyes focused on the jeweled amulet dangling from his hefty hand. Thaddeus lowered the amulet. He withdrew a black, twisting wand from his other coat pocket as if he was unsheathing a sword. He twirled it around and stretched it high into the sky for all to see.

"This is an anti-magick wand, used to dampen the witch's powers and cause her great pain." He charged over toward Johanna. She cowered in fear to the back of the podium. "See, even now, she recoils at the sight of the wand without me having to use it." Thaddeus beamed at Johanna with a devilish, knowing grin on his face.

They paraded Johanna through the town shortly after being given her fate. The citizens shouted obscenities at her and threw rotten vegetables, accusing her of killing their crops. They proclaimed she was the one responsible for the children falling sick. They cursed her very existence. She had done none of this.

She was no witch.

Johanna tripped and fell. The town guards picked her up by her arms and dragged her. She screamed and kicked and pleaded as they pulled her closer to her fate. Her protests fell on ears out for vengeance. A frothed up vengeance for no other purpose than to preserve her true love from suffering a similar fate.

"There! That tree will do," Thaddeus commanded. "Face her to the setting sun."

The guards picked up Johanna and threw her against the oak tree. She struggled, but they were too strong for her. They bound her hands behind the tree. Thaddeus sauntered toward her like a stalking predator. He smiled as Johanna's eyes widened with fear and desperation. He placed the amulet around her neck.

"Please," Johanna pleaded with him. "I'm not a witch."

"I know," he whispered back. "But take solace in the fact that your sacrifice will help me find the true witch. No hard feelings." He took a step back to admire his handiwork with a devilish grin.

Johanna squirmed and pulled at her ropes, each tug fiercer than the last. "Please," she cried out to the crowd. "Please stop this. I don't want to die."

The sky turned bloodred as the sun descended behind a line of trees. The amulet glowed as the last of the dying light shone on the town. An intense heat exploded through Johanna's chest like a fire burning within.

"Please. Please stop this," she wailed in agonizing pain. "I'm not a witch."

Johanna did not erupt into fire, as there were no flames. An imaginary force wasn't burning away at her body, but her soul. She writhed under her constraints. Her hands turned red and the ropes tightened, while she lashed and pulled to break free. She let out a final screech that echoed through the town. The women shielded the children's eyes at the horror of Johanna's torment. Thaddeus grinned with a low, wicked laugh. Johanna's face scrunched and contorted in agony before falling silent. She hung lifeless against the tree.

THERE WAS a knock at Johanna's front door.

She turned around to see where the noise came from. The knock sounded again. She heard muffled words on the other side. She stood still, holding her breath, not wanting to alert them that someone was in the house that evening. The knocks stopped.

Johanna breathed a sigh of relief. She retreated to the wingback chairs. She lifted the teapot and poured the hot liquid into her cup. She sat down, picked up the cup, and took a sip. *I hate this wretched night.*

CHAPTER 10
TREATS WITH TRICKS

"Do you think we'll get many trick-or-treaters?" Elizabeth asked. Her feet shuffled out the front door and onto the front porch. The light next to the door was the only light in the growing darkness. Her body was frail and weak, but she still wore a brave smile. A red scarf wrapped around her head hid her missing hair.

"Watch your step." Hugo clutched her arm below her shoulder. His grip steadied her as they moved toward a waiting chair.

She braced herself on the arm before easing into the chair.

"Do you want a blanket?"

"Then they wouldn't see my costume. Isn't it great?" Elizabeth pointed to her dress. She wore a full length, crushed red velvet gown marked with a spiderweb lace running down to the bottom of the skirt. A black petticoat overlaid the red gown. The puffy shoulders hid her frail, bony shoulders. She wore a black choker with an attached collar that framed her face in matching red.

"Do you want the teeth?" Hugo asked.

"Yes."

Hugo handed her a pair of plastic vampire teeth. She slowly put them in, trying to not cause a coughing fit. She smiled, exposing her new vampire fangs.

"Don't move," Hugo said with a morose smile, knowing this would be the last time she would greet trick-or-treaters. "I want to remember this moment forever, my vampire queen."

HUGO STOOD on his porch in his black pants and shoes. He wore the same white button up shirt from his last Halloween costume. The billowy sleeves ended in French cuffs. Over the shirt, he wore a double breasted, bloodred velvet vest. A black satin cape was draped over his shoulders. The interior lining matched his vest. He held his plastic vampire teeth in his hands before putting them back into his pants pocket.

He gazed at the empty porch chair which, only a year prior, held his wife safe and sound. He clutched a bucket of candy in his left hand. His right drifted toward his wedding ring. His fingers almost clamped down when a voice broke the silence.

"I dated a vampire once."

He spun around to see Alice half sitting on her porch rail.

"Oh, yeah?" he asked, unsure if it was actually true. He moved toward his rail to be as close as possible to her.

"It didn't work out between us. He sucked," Alice finished. Her head tilted toward Hugo with a knowing smirk on her face.

"Wooooooow," Hugo drew out the word, trying not to laugh. "That was suckingly bad."

"I thought you'd like it." She winked at him.

She wore a traditional, plain black witch's costume with a V-neck cut that exposed the top of her chest. The dress was snug to her body, accentuating her curves before turning into a skirt above her hips and ending at her knees. There was a tattered hem on her sleeves and skirt. She wore the stereotypical witch's hat; the tip pointed high into the sky. A contrast to her normally curved headwear.

"You know, on Halloween, it's customary to dress up in a costume. You're not supposed to wear your everyday clothes," Hugo playfully teased.

She gave a pouty look, hopping off the rail. "You don't like my costume?" She twirled around, spinning the skirt in the air.

He wanted to respond with yet another teasing comment, but held himself back. He focused only on her as she twirled around. The skirt hung in the air. Time slowed. He couldn't pull himself away. Their eyes locked once again as she came to a stop. He wanted her to continue.

"It's very bewitching," Hugo replied.

Alice grabbed the skirt with both hands, curtsied, and smiled.

"Trick or treat," a child's voice interrupted.

A young beggar stood on his porch steps wearing a plastic Frankenstein mask. Hugo pulled out a bite sized chocolate bar from his supply.

"There you go." Hugo dropped it into the child's waiting candy bucket.

The young Frankenstein bounded down the stairs, crossing across the yard, then raced up Alice's porch steps. Jack-o'-lanterns on either side guarded each step. The candles inside flickered to combat the growing darkness of the night sky.

"Trick or treat," he offered to Alice.

She squatted down to meet him face-to-face. "My, what a scary Frankenstein's monster. Did he only give you one piece of candy?"

He nodded.

"Well, at this house, I give out two pieces." She took two pieces of candy from her black plastic cauldron set on the porch and dropped them into his waiting bucket. "Now go forth and cause mischief and mayhem. Fly, my monster, fly." She smiled as the child ran down her porch steps onto his next destination.

"It's not a competition, you know," Hugo said.

Alice rose with a knowing grin on her face. "I know."

"So, I have to ask, why do you like Halloween so much? I mean, it can't only be the whole witch thing, right?"

"No, it's not just about the witch thing." Alice paused, trying to find the words. "Halloween, or Samhain as it's traditionally called, is about remembrance. A day of reflection on those we've lost. It's said that on this night, the veil is thin, and the spirits of our ancestors walk among us once more. I guess that's why I like it so much. I want to believe it's true."

"If only..." Hugo's words trailed off. He glanced back at the empty chair.

More kids descended on their porches. Hugo and Alice handed out candy as fast as the kids appeared from out of the darkness. Their supplies grew low.

"Why the vampire costume?" Alice asked.

"It was from last year. We usually do... did a couple's costume. She wanted to be a vampire king and queen. I didn't get a new one this year," Hugo said, his voice lowered. "I didn't want to let her down."

"It suits you," Alice said. Hugo gave her an inquisitive glance. "I'm a huge *fang* of the look."

"Okay, how many of those puns do you have?"

"Enough to get me to dawn, but I wouldn't *count* on it."

"Could have been better," Hugo said as he handed out more candy. He thought of a response. "What sound does a witch's car make?"

"What?" Alice asked, excited at continuing their little game.

"Broom. Broom. Broom," Hugo answered.

She hid her mouth behind her hand, trying to hold in her laughter. Her eyes focused on Hugo and his impish grin.

The night wore on. Visitors continued to beg the question, "Trick or treat?" Hugo and Alice handed out their pieces of question, wanting to avoid any sorts of tricks that evening. They asked Hugo the question once more.

"Here you go." He grabbed for a piece of candy, but only felt the smooth plastic bottom. He peeked inside and found nothing. "I'm sorry. Looks like I'm out."

The kids hung their heads low in disappointment. Alice noticed their sad faces.

"Are you sure?" one of them asked.

Alice raised her right hand above her waist. She gave a quick snap of her fingers. She lowered her hand so no one could accuse her of what had transpired.

"Yeah, I'm sorry," Hugo said. "Fresh out."

He turned the bucket over. Handfuls of candy fell onto the porch. The kids gleefully picked up what they could. Hugo peeked back into the bucket, dumbfounded at what happened.

"Maybe you should look harder," Alice said.

"This was empty," Hugo exclaimed.

"Doesn't look like it to me," she replied with a wink.

The kids gathered their candy and left his porch.

"Well, I'm all tapped out," Hugo said.

She investigated her bucket. "Yeah, me too. It was a good night."

"It was a great night."

His eyes locked onto Alice. He gave a thought to invite himself over. As the trick-or-treaters' night ended, he wanted their night to continue, but an unseen force kept pulling him inside. He tried to speak, but the words failed in that moment. *Would she accept? Would she even want me to come over?* These questions raced through his mind. He needed to ask, but in that moment, he couldn't.

Hugo grabbed the front door. "Well, have a good evening." He opened it.

"Hugo," Alice shouted.

He stopped and fixated on her. She shifted uneasily as she gave a few taps to the bottom of her plastic cauldron. She pouted her lips. He felt like she wanted to tell him something, or ask him something, but she was holding back.

"You too."

"Enjoy Samhain," he said and disappeared inside.

Hugo stood in the entryway and closed the door behind him. He placed the bucket on the entryway table. It knocked over a pile of mail to the floor. Max came running down the stairs to greet him. Her tail wagged, beating against the wall in excitement.

"Come on, Max," Hugo commanded. "Let's go outside." He strode through the house to the kitchen.

Max went bounding down the back stairs, surveying her little kingdom to find the perfect spot. Hugo stood on the porch, looking over at Alice's house. The purple house. He thought of her purple hair. The way the black witch's costume hugged the curves of her body and how the skirt floated in the air. Her playful jokes. Alice sitting on the railing. Her emerald green eyes. All these emotions flooded him. He cupped his hands around his mouth, fingers up like he was praying, his thumbs pressed against his lower jaw.

Do it. Have some guts and do it. His eyes followed Max as she continued her adventures around the yard. She investigated smells all over—the shed, the unkept bushes, the hibernating grass. She circled and circled to find the best spot.

He turned toward the purple house. His eyes focused on the large bay window. *What do you have to lose? Go have some fun.*

"Come on, Max," Hugo yelled. "Let's go get a treat."

Max ran into the house. Hugo shut the door and locked it. He opened the refrigerator and surveyed the chilled wine bottles. He grabbed the closest one, but released it after spotting another bottle. The black and gray checkerboard label with the playing card, four card suits, and the crown. He pulled out the mysterious new brand and shut the door.

He hurried back down the hallway and placed the bottle on the entryway table. He ran up the stairs. His foot caught the edge of the step. He extended out his arm to brace himself before launching back up the stairs. He was on a mission, and nothing would stop him.

Moments later, he bounded down the stairs, no longer dressed as a vampire, with the same enthusiasm as Max had earlier. He wore dark jeans and a black, long sleeve Henley shirt. Sitting at the base of the steps, he put on his black shoes. He opened the closet door and removed his black leather jacket. Max came running at the prospect of going on another walk.

"No walk tonight," Hugo said as he stood. He removed his black leather jacket from the closet and slipped it on.

Her tail still wagged.

"Computer, lights off."

The lights in the house turned off as an electronic beep confirmed the command.

Hugo snatched the neck of the bottle between his middle and ring fingers and yanked it off the table to pass it to his other hand. He opened the front door. He glanced back at Max, who had a gleeful smile on her face. Her tail wagged. She still loved the prospect that they were leaving for a walk.

"Don't wait up, buddy," Hugo said.

Max's tail stopped wagging, and she sat down as he exited and shut the door behind him.

CHAPTER II
SAMHAIN

H ugo jogged down his porch steps, carrying the bottle of wine, and strode over to the purple house next door. He paused at the base of the porch steps. He felt a presence; eyes watched his every move. He turned around and saw nothing. There was still a sense that someone or something watched him. He peered over at Johanna's house across the street. The dark blinds were drawn shut. No light. No movement. Nothing. Perhaps it was only his imagination or something else.

Hugo turned his attention back to Alice's house, looking up at the black front door. The lights in the jack-o'-lanterns dimmed as the candles slowly melted from existence. Plastic candles flickered in the windows. His palms were sweaty. The bottle felt like it was going to slip from his hands. He grabbed onto the neck and held the bottom to ensure its safety. A sense of nervousness and dread and excitement all at once coursed through his body. He couldn't wait any longer. He trekked up the steps.

Hugo stood before the black door, clutching the bottle of wine in one hand and hesitating to knock with the other. He tried to peer through the window set into the center of the doorframe. The sheer black curtain obstructed his view into the house, but an unmistakable silhouette moved inside.

Determined not to cower away, he knocked. The sound of creaking floorboards, however faint, grew slightly louder as a figure approached the door. The lock mechanism turned, and the door cracked open. Alice peered around the side and gave a smile as soon as she recognized who was standing at the door.

"To what do I owe the pleasure?" Alice asked, brushing her violet hair behind her right ear.

"I thought that since Halloween was your favorite holiday, you shouldn't spend the evening by yourself," Hugo replied as he presented the wine bottle. "This is a new brand I've been waiting to try. I thought maybe we could share the bottle."

Alice opened the door fully and stood in the threshold. She had exchanged her trick or treat witch costume for all black athletic lounge clothing. She clearly hadn't been expecting visitors on this dark evening. Alice took the bottle and examined the logo; her eyes lingered on the heart, crown, and upside down spade.

"Red-Hearted Queen? I saw this in the store, but haven't tried it yet. Thank you. Please come in." She stepped into the hallway.

Hugo accepted the invitation and followed. He placed his jacket on a coat rack by the door and his shoes respectfully next to it. The house was designed similarly to Hugo's, only reversed. A winding staircase led upstairs. A door nestled beneath the stairs. The hallway led into the kitchen with a dining room in between. An entryway led to the living room off to the side.

Multiple ornate antique console tables lined the hallway walls. Black candelabras adorned the tables. The candles dripped with wax as they dimly lit the hallways with dancing, flickering light. Purple and white crystals filled in the space around the candelabras.

"Please feel free to make yourself at home," Alice invited as she moved down the hallway and disappeared into the kitchen.

Hugo entered the living room. His eyes widened with amazement as the sight overwhelmed him. Every square inch was covered with some sort of object. Black candle sconces, old pictures of relatives, animals, stages of the moon, and other various spooky images decorated the walls.

A fireplace centered on the wall to the adjoining hallway. Its warmth and glow illuminated the room. Lit candles filled the mantle, more for show than light. The wax of various shades of purple, black, red, and white dripped down the front of the mantle like gnarled fingers stretching for the dark hardwood below.

A grandfather clock continually ticked away on the far wall next to a hutch containing various oddities. Fully stocked, dark oaken bookshelves lined the remaining wall spaces in the room. Crystals, pumpkins of various sizes, and plants filled in every available space. The smell of sage and incense burning lingered in the room. Hugo felt overwhelmed and intrigued at the same time.

Dark red curtains with gold trim draped the windows opposite the fireplace. A matching velvet Victorian couch sat below the windows. Dark wood trim offset the red velvet. Pillows of various sizes lined every inch of the couch. A small, round table separated the couch from a black, high-back leather chair. The leather was weathered in various shades of black from use and held secrets to stories that took place over its lifetime. Colorful Tiffany lamps boxed in all the furniture pieces.

An elaborate hourglass stood alone on the round table. It drew in Hugo's attention. Sand slowly fell through the glass opening into the larger chamber below. Three twisting pillars held up the hourglass. A wood ring sat in the center of one pillar. Hugo touched the ring, and it moved. He twisted the ring up, and the sand appeared to slow down. He rotated the ring down a few times, and the sand fell faster. Curiosity got the better of Hugo, and he spun the ring all the way to the top of the pillar. The sand nearly stopped falling.

"Neat," Hugo said. He turned his attention to the decorations on the wall.

Alice entered the room carrying two wineglasses with the opened bottle.

"I take it you're not a minimalist, are you?"

"Quite the opposite." Alice set the wineglasses on a coffee table in front of the couch. "I'm a maximalist."

"A maximalist?"

"I want to bring the space to life with variety and history and creativity. It's... it's just who I am."

"I like it," said Hugo. "There's always something interesting to look at."

"That's the idea," Alice said as she poured the wine into the glasses. She handed one to Hugo. "To Halloween," said Alice as she presented her glass in a toast.

"To Samhain," Hugo responded as he clinked her wineglass.

"It's pronounced Sauin," she replied with a wink before taking a sip of wine.

Hugo smiled, smelled the inside of the glass, and took a sip as well. A strange, bitter taste washed over his tongue. "Bold, fruity, and a hint of something... I don't know what."

Alice scrunched her face and took another sip. "There is definitely something else in this. I'm not certain, but it's... different."

She paused for a moment before walking over to the leather chair. The chair was large enough that she could sit with her legs crossed. Hugo moved the pillows aside and took a seat on the couch. The velvety cushions felt soft despite the aged appearance.

"We had a good number of trick-or-treaters tonight," Hugo said before taking another sip.

"Did you come over here just to make small talk?" Alice quickly replied before leaning back in the chair.

"Um, well..." Hugo mustered before taking another sip. "No, I thought—"

Alice grinned. "Wow. You're out of practice, aren't you?"

"In a lot of things," Hugo replied. "I haven't done much since Elizabeth died."

"Grief can be hard to overcome."

Hugo peered at the burning log in the fireplace and then back at

Alice. "We used to drink wine by firelight all the time and just talk," Hugo explained before pausing. "It feels good to do it again."

He finished his glass and poured more from the bottle.

"What was she like?" Alice asked.

"She loved life. She was a ray of sunshine. Elizabeth was my everything," Hugo replied. "She would have loved your decorations. History was her passion. She would have examined every picture you have on the wall. Probably tell you about the era."

"Sounds like she knew what her passion was and followed it," Alice said before drinking the rest of her glass. "All historians have a favorite time period. What was hers?"

"She loved the renaissance the most," replied Hugo. "She used to drag me to the Renaissance Festival every year. It wasn't my thing, but I went anyway. For her. She always dressed up in costumes. She was in heaven. I enjoyed watching the jousting, though. This year, I didn't go. I couldn't bring myself to go."

"You loved her. I can tell," Alice said.

"She was my everything, and now she's gone. The worst part was that all I could do was watch. Watch the love of my life fight for hers. She hid the pain, but I saw it in her eyes. She always felt guilty about her parent's deaths. I never understood it. Not until I watched her die, and there wasn't anything I could do. We were a team, a partnership, and she had to fight that battle alone."

"She wasn't alone. You were there for her. That's all she could have asked for—you by her side."

Hugo focused on the stillness of the reddish-purple liquid held in his hands. "I would've given anything to fix her, like a magic wand or something I could've waved to heal her... If only they were real."

"What if they were?"

Hugo huffed. "If only." After taking another sip, he set his glass down. He twisted his ring, gave it two turns, and stopped. Hugo wasn't here to discuss his past with Alice. He wanted to discuss their future. Picking up the glass again, he took another sip. "So, what brings you to a small town like Newbury Grove?"

Alice sat upright in her chair. She refilled her glass and gulped down half of it. "Have you ever trusted someone... someone you were so certain supported you... only to have them betray you?"

"Can't say that I have."

"I did. Her name was Sam. I trusted her so much that I revealed a secret. A secret that only a few knew. Sam betrayed me. Turned on me."

"Turned on you?"

"The relationship," Alice paused, lowering her eyes to the floor. Hugo could sense she was holding back. "I had to get away. I had to leave. We argued. She was talking to the wrong people. I couldn't trust Sam any longer. I was terrified. I searched for a place I could hide away. That's when I found Newbury Grove. So far, this place has been welcoming—well, mostly. I hope it stays that way." She glanced up.

"Don't worry about Johanna. She's grumpy to everybody."

"She's not the one I'm most worried about." Alice locked eyes with Hugo.

He lost himself in her emerald greens. Hugo sensed a hint of fear behind her eyes. Their gazes lingered. He fought back feelings of jumping across and tearing at each other's clothes. Burning desires swelled from deep within. He wanted her in that moment and was certain she wanted him. The unforeseen force of his past held him back.

Alice bit her lower lip. She held her breath for a long pause before exhaling. Hugo's heart beat faster, and his head swirled. It felt like an eternity, yet it was only a few fleeting moments. He wanted it to last forever and hoped she did as well.

Hugo was the first to look away. He took a few more sips. Those few sips of wine mustered enough courage within Hugo to spit into his hand.

"I promise that I, Hugo Dodds, do solemnly spit swear, sealed with a kiss, will never turn on you, Alice Primrose, for being who you are," he proclaimed as he extended his right hand. "On the condition that you accept me for all of my faults."

Alice giggled before spitting and extending her right hand to proclaim, "I promise that I, Alice Primrose, do solemnly spit swear, sealed with a kiss, will never turn on you, Hugo Dodds, and accept you for who you are."

They shook hands.

"Sealed with a kiss." Hugo raised his glass for a toast.

"Sealed with a kiss," Alice responded as she clinked his glass.

A slight shiver pulsated through her arm as he dragged his fingers across her palm and let go of her hand. They sipped more wine before letting out a laugh.

"There is definitely something different in that wine." Hugo pointed to the wine goblet. "We should find out. It's driving me crazy."

"I'm something of a wine expert," Alice explained.

"Oh! You're a 'wine connoisseur,'" Hugo sarcastically replied with a smirk.

"I'm a little more than a 'connoisseur,'" she retorted.

"Elizabeth loved wine. She got me into it. I was more of a bourbon man, but it grew on me. Now"—he hesitated as he glanced down at his goblet—"it's all I drink." He finished the remaining wine.

Alice placed her glass on the side table. She paused for a moment. She tapped her fingers on her knees. Her foot twitched. She bit her top lip as if to hold herself back from speaking. She glanced around the room, focusing on many areas before locking eyes with Hugo. "If I show you something, do you promise not to freak out?"

"That doesn't sound ominous at all."

"I need you to promise."

"Well, now I'm both intrigued and worried."

"I'm serious."

"I swore an oath to you, didn't I? I promise."

"Come with me." She smiled and extended her hand.

"Where?"

"Trust me."

Hugo set his glass down on the coffee table, rose, and took her hand. She led him down the hallway to the wooden door below the staircase. She grabbed the brass knob and pushed the door open. It led to a set of twisting stairs descending into the darkened basement. Small chips of paint flaked and peeled off the stairs, giving them a withered appearance.

"Elizabeth and I watched enough crime shows for me to know I shouldn't go down these stairs with you." Hugo chuckled.

"Trust me, what I have down there isn't criminal," Alice reassured him. "But it should be." She gave a Cheshire like grin.

They entered the darkness. The stairs creaked as they slowly proceeded down. Their feet gingerly touched the next step as they built trust in its ability to hold. It was dark. The faint smell of herbs only eased the smell of dampness and mildew.

Alice grabbed for the light pull string. The basement partially illuminated with the warm glow of the incandescent light. It was dull and empty. Scant cardboard boxes littered the grayish floors. The walls were barren. A few cracks traversed along the channel grooves of the cinderblocks, damaged with age. A wood door with ornate iron fixtures was the only distinctive feature along the back wall.

Hugo paused, questioning the dimensions and layout of the basement, realizing the door should go outside. He couldn't remember a basement entrance in the house's backyard.

"Where does the door go?"

"Let me show you," Alice said. She grabbed the cast iron handle, hesitated, and let go.

"What's wrong?"

Alice focused again on Hugo. Her face no longer beamed with delight. "I need to know if I can trust you. I need to know if you trust me."

"Of course. I already said you could," replied Hugo.

"I need to know."

"You can trust me. What do you have in there?" Hugo took a step closer to the door. His body tightened, unsure of what was about to happen. He positioned his right foot to make an expeditious retreat backward, just in case.

"What's behind this door is nothing like you could've imagined." Alice gripped the handle a second time. She pushed forward, revealing a secret room.

Hugo moved closer to peer through the doorway. The smell of grapes, earth, and mustiness lingered in the air. The room was dark. Only the outlines of what appeared to be wooden barrels along the wall were visible in the incandescent glow. Alice entered through the doorway. Hugo followed.

YULE

Light In The Darkness

CHAPTER 12
THE CELLAR

Alice gave a quick snap of her fingers. Candlesticks, placed throughout the room in wall sconces, flickered to life. They revealed the massive size of the room. To Hugo, the room appeared larger than both houses combined. Green vine plants hung from the thick wooden trusses that lined the ceiling. Stacked wooden barrels rested along the back walls. Filled wine bottles rested on a rack.

Wine making equipment adorned one side of the room organized in methodical fashion. Five wooden round tubs sat on elevated platforms. The tubs were wide enough for multiple people to stand in them. Their ringed barreled like appearance awaited their next supply of grapes. A wooden valve, placed on the bottom of the tubs, emptied into wooden channels that flowed into two wine presses resting below.

A workstation table was set up directly across from the vats on the other side of the room against the wall. Above the table, a set of shelves organized a wondrous number of things. Hugo's eyes traveled to each one. Glass jars filled with items from nature. Vials filled with liquids. Wood boxes of all shapes and sizes.

An apothecary box drawer set against the back of the table pressed against the wall. Aged parchment sleeves labeled the multiple pull out drawers with the various ingredients listed inside. A black cauldron, larger than a grapefruit, yet smaller than a volleyball, sat in the center of the table. A muddler next to it waited for the next ingredient. An hourglass, identical to the one in the living room, stood in a corner of the table.

"What is this place?"

"This is where I make wine," Alice replied.

"How does it even exist? Are we in your backyard?"

"It's a special room."

"How special?"

"You could say it's magical."

"What's with all this stuff in the jars and the drawers? Why a cauldron?" His eyes lingered on it before focusing back toward Alice. "I know that you like dressing like a witch, but—"

"I don't dress like a witch to make a fashion statement. I dress like a witch because I am one," Alice explained. She paused for a moment. With a wide-eyed gaze, she dropped her arms to her side. "Does that scare you?"

Hugo glanced at the ground to gather his thoughts. He took a step, not toward the door, but further into the room to continue his exploration. Overwhelmed by this new reality in his life, he paused, then locked eyes with Alice. She interlocked her hands, holding them close to her body, and stood up straight with her shoulders pulled back. Alice slightly swayed back and forth. Her emerald green eyes glared back at him warily.

"Not at all," Hugo answered. "I told you. I accept you for who you are."

Alice blushed with a beaming smile. She released her hands, and her shoulders relaxed. The swaying stopped. "Good," she replied. "Let me show you why I'm a wine expert."

Alice strutted to the hourglass and rotated the ring to the middle of the pillar. She turned around. Her shoulders arched back, and her head tilted up. She pulled back her sleeves and snapped her fingers, like a conductor commanding the attention of her orchestra. The room was alive with activity. Boxes of grapes rose into position. Grape crushers, large metal plates with wooden handles, bounced into position and stood at the ready next to the wooden vats. The room waited with bated breath, eager for the next move.

Alice paused. She outstretched her hand and closed her eyes. She exhaled a long, slow breath before taking a quick gasp. Her hands gestured back and forth as she conducted the symphony unfolding in the room. Each move was more affirmative than the last.

The boxes dumped the grapes into the large vats. The grape crushers followed. They danced, sloshing back and forth. The wet sound of grapes being crushed under the metal plates filled the air. Purplish-red juices flowed out of the wooden valve, pulling bits and pieces of grape skin like a flash flood down the channels. The grape must flowed toward the wooden barrel-like presses below. The next batch of grapes rose; their boxes dumped their contents into the vats. The stomping dance continued.

Alice turned and proceeded to her workstation. She grabbed a wine bottle filled with water and emptied the contents into the black cauldron. Alice leaned over, placing her lips below the cauldron. She whispered words in a language Hugo could not comprehend. A secretive language that intrigued, tantalized, and excited him. A small flame appeared below the cauldron. There was no kindling or fire source. The flame appeared to linger in the air. The table was untouched from the flame. Small bubbles danced inside the cauldron.

Alice pulled down a thick, brown leather grimoire from a shelf. She cradled the book in her hands as she lowered it onto a wooden bookrest. Her fingers dragged over the spine and across the scuffed, weathered binding. She traced the arcane symbol of two equilateral triangles touching, one upside down, that was pressed and branded into the front cover. She flipped open the book to a random section and perused the clandestine pages.

"Let's see. What shall we make?" Alice glanced over to Hugo. She gave a wink and then returned her eyes back to the ancient book. "We have *Luck*. That's very popular. Gives the drinker extraordinary luck for the next two hours, or whenever they sober up."

Hugo moved closer to Alice. He leaned against the table, trying to get a better look. Their shoulders touched; his left shoulder to Alice's right. She bit her lips, smiling.

"Maybe you won't need that," Alice said in a hushed tone as she continued flipping through pages. "This one is called *The Fountain of Youth*. Each glass makes you look five years younger."

"For how long?" Hugo asked.

Alice thought for a moment. "Well, until sunrise the next day."

Alice flipped through more pages. Their appearance was tanned and stained with time. She stopped on a page. "Here we go. Perfect beginner's spell for you to learn. It's called *Air Walk*. This prevents you from crashing to the ground. Very popular for those who've drunk too much." Alice chuckled. "One sip, and it's like you're floating in the air."

Alice pulled open drawers of her apothecary box to examine the contents inside. She called out each ingredient as she withdrew them from their cubbyholes. "Let's see. A leaf blown by the breeze. A pinch of dirt. A bird's feather. A sprig of peppermint." She placed them one by one into a granite mortar bowl on the table. "Grab that pestle there, and start smashing those together." She motioned to the club shaped object laying on the table, about as long as Hugo's hand.

"So, is this why you collect nature things?" Hugo asked.

"I told you. Only the perfect ones."

Hugo grabbed the pestle and was about to grind the ingredients into a fine powder.

"Wait!" Alice exclaimed, stopping Hugo. "Let me see that."

Hugo handed over the objects. "What's wrong?" His eyes widened as if he had somehow messed up.

Alice removed the objects from the bowl and picked up a cloth. She wiped both of them in a clockwise rotation over and over and over, as if she was never satisfied with each pass. "Sorry. I normally have mortars and pestles dedicated to each spell. I don't want to contaminate them with the wrong ingredients. That's my secret."

She finally finished as if satisfied on some level that the ingredients would not be contaminated. Alice gave one final examination with her fingertips for good measure. She placed the ingredients back into the bowl and handed them to Hugo. "Good as new."

"What happened to them?" Hugo asked as he resumed his assigned duties. The stone against stone sound resonated in the mortar bowl and echoed throughout the stone wine cellar. The crackling of the leaf. The smashing of the peppermint sprig. The mortar bowl grunted with every strike of the pestle.

"They disappeared during the move," Alice began as she rearranged items on the workstation. Each one seemingly moved at random and with less thought than the last. "Or before the move. I... I don't know. It was all such a blur. No doubt Sam took them."

She opened and immediately shut a few of the drawers. She slammed her hands down. Her fingers attempted to dig into the wood table. Her face glared off into emptiness. Hugo recognized that look. The anger hidden behind lying eyes. Her body was no doubt tense and ready to burst out in frustration. He knew it far too well. How natural that anger felt, like breathing or simply existing.

"I'm sorry you had to go through that."

She turned to him and smiled. "It's okay. I'm fine."

"No, you're not," he responded immediately.

"No, I'm not." She bowed her head. Her purple hair partially obscured her face. Her shoulders slumped, and she released her death grip on the table. Alice let out a sigh of relief.

Hugo stopped his work. He placed his hand on top of hers. "Hey. Look at me."

She turned and locked eyes with him. Her emerald green eyes watered as they held back tears. His icy blues struggled to reassure her. Their gaze disappeared into an eternal bliss.

"It's okay to not be okay."

A solitary tear left a trail as it moved down her soft, pale face. Alice sniffled and wiped it away with her free hand. She turned her other to clutch Hugo's hand.

"It is okay to not be okay," she said, laughing away any more tears.

He let go of her hand, while hers remained on the table, now empty.

"I think the powder's ready," Hugo said, looking into the mortar.

Alice composed herself, preening her hair back into place. She rested her chin on Hugo's shoulder to peer into the mortar. "Good enough."

Hugo felt the vibration of her words, but that sensation was fleeting. He yearned for more.

She took the mortar and dumped the contents into the bubbling cauldron. She carefully pulled her hair back behind her ears and bent down over the cauldron. Her purple lips moved back and forth as she recited more words of the unknown language. He didn't understand what she was saying, but he didn't care. Hugo focused on her soft lips. She could have spoken English in that moment, and her words would have been indecipherable.

She finished and then blew over the cauldron. The bubbles stopped, and flame dispersed. She picked up the cauldron, cupping the bottom with her hands as if it were now cold to the touch. Alice carried the cauldron to the wine presses and poured in the liquid. After returning it back to the table, she grabbed two vials of powder. One was labeled *Brewing Sugar*, and the other was *Brewing Yeast*. She headed back to the presses and added in a small bit of the contents.

"You know, I can do magic too," Hugo said.

"Oh, yeah?" Alice turned her attention back toward him. "How so?"

He pulled out his phone from his pocket. "I can turn my house lights on and off with this. Also, I speak commands to the house, and it does stuff." He smiled and winked at Alice.

"Yours is magic that ends with a *C*. A simple parlor trick. Stage magic," Alice retorted with a sly smile. "Mine is magick ending with a *K*. I'm empowered by my own arcane abilities. The difference between me and your phone is that I don't require a Wi-Fi connection." She winked.

"Oh yeah, well, can you play music with your magick?" Hugo asked.

"No, that's what a speaker system is for," Alice said as she sauntered over to the wine rack.

She pulled out a few more of the dark green bottles. She carefully reviewed and selected each one to be sampled that evening.

Alice handed them to Hugo before placing the vials back on the shelf. She gathered the hourglass resting at the back of the table. She spun the ring to the bottom. The sand fell faster and faster.

"Come on," she commanded. "You don't want to be left inside. It won't feel pleasant."

Hugo quickly followed.

Alice snapped her fingers, and the room went dark. She shut the door to her wine cellar. "That hourglass will speed up the fermentation time. Everything is automated and will finish the process. Within a few hours, the wine will be ready to drink."

"I don't think my phone can do that," Hugo replied.

Alice laughed while Hugo clutched the wine bottles. They headed back up the basement stairs.

THEY SAT NEXT to each other on the red velvet couch. Three more empty bottles littered the coffee table—remnants of their night together. Hugo grabbed a fourth. Alice snapped her fingers, sending the cork shooting out of the bottle's neck and bouncing off the ceiling. He poured the wine into their waiting goblets. They clanged the glasses together, and each took a sip. Hugo's face recoiled as he took a drink before portraying a look of ecstasy. He set the glass down on the table and then leaned back into the couch.

"That one really packed a punch at the end."

Alice picked up the bottle. "I call this one *Contortion* because it contorts your face with a bittersweet surprise. Less on the magical side and more of a personal flavor choice."

She set the bottle back down. She took one more sip, placed the glass on the table, and joined Hugo by leaning back into the couch.

"You should sell these. You'd make a fortune," Hugo said.

"I do. Sort of."

"Where?"

"Through Ez, my friend and mentor. She sells it in her nightclub. It's a magick users only club."

"So, non-magical people like me can't get in, huh?"

"I'd sneak you in."

"Have you tried to sell it in stores? I may know a few people who could help you out."

Alice gazed up at her ceiling and let out a sigh. "That's my dream. To have my own wine sold in stores."

"Do it."

Alice blinked at Hugo. "It's not that simple."

"Why not?"

"Have you seen how I make it?"

"So. No one needs to know how it's made, as long as it's good."

Alice huffed. "I don't think Ez would like that very much. Besides, I don't exactly have a massive supply of grapes to produce extra bottles. I practically tap out the local supply as it is now."

"Well, if it's your passion, you should follow it. I'll be your biggest supporter."

Alice smiled. "Thank you."

They leaned closer to each other, their shoulders touching. His fingertips glided over her exposed forearm. He wrapped them around her wrist, but didn't squeeze. His thumb massaged the back of her hand. She closed her eyes. The hairs stood at attention with his every stroke. Shivers shot up her arm. She curled her toes as goosebumps magically appeared.

Alice couldn't decipher what invisible words Hugo was drawing on the back of her hand. Words in a dark language that she couldn't read, but which her body would fully understand. She bit her lower lip. Her breathing paused. A smolder built inside her.

Alice turned her head toward Hugo. Their eyes locked. An unseen force pulled her closer to him. Her heart raced. The smolder spread across her being. Hugo leaned toward her. They touched; his forehead against hers. The inner smolder now raged out of control. Emotions set ablaze with desire. His breath danced across her lips. Each exhale torturously teased her. She wanted nothing more than for him to kiss her. She closed her eyes again, waiting for him to make the move.

The waiting was excruciating.

It was exquisite.

"How much have we drank?" Hugo asked.

His words pulsed through her as she shivered.

"Too much." Her voice was soft and low.

"Then why aren't I feeling it?"

The grandfather clock chimed once. Hugo pulled away. A wave of disappointment doused the inner smolder. Alice's body longed for him to touch her again. Her eyes opened and drooped with inner pain.

"It's only nine? It was a few minutes before nine when I came over. That can't be right. Where are the other eight chimes?"

Alice focused on the side table. The elaborate hourglass moved from where she had placed it earlier in the evening. "Hugo, did you touch this hourglass?"

"Maybe." He paused. "Why?"

"And did you turn this ring all the way up?"

"I feel like I shouldn't answer."

"Oh, that's not good."

Hugo sat up on the couch with a distraught look on his face. "It's never good when a witch says it's not good."

"How many bottles did we drink?" Alice asked, even though she already knew the answer.

Hugo counted the bottles on the table. "These three, plus that one I brought over."

"Oh. Well." Alice paused. She locked onto Hugo's eyes. "Things are about to get really interesting, really fast."

"How interesting?"

"I need you to listen to me. You need to stay perfectly still. The hourglass slowed down time. Like a lot. The opposite of what we did downstairs. We might have been moving around fine, but our bodies have not yet processed all the wine we drank tonight. I need to normalize time again, but when I do..." Her voice trailed off.

Hugo's eyes widened. "Oh, no."

Alice counted the bottles again. The three bottles they brought up, plus the one he brought over. "It'll be like drinking all four bottles at once," Alice explained.

Hugo's face turned pale. Alice felt the fear in his eyes.

"Oh, no." His voice lowered with dread.

"This happened to me once before. Only once. I'm going to turn the ring. I need you to be perfectly still."

Alice picked up the hourglass. The sand sped up with each partial turn of the ring as it descended toward the middle of the pedestal. The ticking of the grandfather clock started back up. Eight more chimes followed.

"Alice, I don't feel so good." Hugo stood up and stumbled over the coffee table.

"Don't move. Sit back down."

Alice went for his hand, but he pulled it away, clutching his stomach. He stumbled around the room and fell over on to the hardwood floor.

"Hugo!" Alice shouted before he passed out.

Hugo woke up naked in his bed. He had no recollection of how he got there. Distorted images flashed in his memory.

Was I dreaming? The thought raced through his mind. Daylight struggled to break through the drawn curtains. His head no longer throbbed. His eyes focused on the imperfections of the ceiling.

The disheveled bedding was scattered over his body. He felt the weight of an arm draped over his chest. A woman's leg interlocked between his. The warm breath exhaled on his bare shoulder in long, drawn out cadences. He felt skin against skin. Body against body. He wasn't the only one naked in the bed. He hadn't felt this sensation in months. It felt good. It felt normal.

His left middle finger slowly traced an invisible line from her shoulder, over the elbow, down the forearm, before circling in her palm. She stirred from her slumber. Her leg stretched and rubbed against his like two pieces of kindling trying to reignite a raging fire.

He then followed a familiar path from her hip, over the curve of her butt cheek, and down the back of her thigh, right above her knee. She let out a long, relaxing moan before kissing his ear. Her tongue, ever so softly and gently, traced the inner labyrinths hidden deep within. Hugo's eyes rolled into the back of his head. This was bliss.

A familiar voice whispered softly into his ear, a secret only allowed between the two of them, "Good morning."

Her body fell with his chest as Hugo drew out an exhale.

"Good morning, Elizabeth," Hugo whispered in response, turning his head to see a tuft of messy purple hair laying on his shoulder.

Alice lifted her head, her eyebrows scrunched together with a confused expression. "Who's Elizabeth?"

Hugo jolted. His head was buried in the crevice between the cushion and the back of his couch. Hugo's heart raced, and his head pounded.

His shirt dripped in sweat. He flipped to his back. His chest rose and fell with each labored breath.

The room was dizzying, like waves rocking on a ship at sea. Max's head rested on the edge of the couch, staring into Hugo's ear. Her tail wagged. She let out a low whimper to express her need to go outside. She begged for attention. Her tail wagging increased in intensity. She whimpered again. Hugo sat up, running his hands over his face and through his damp hair. He was still in the same clothes from last night.

Max backed away from the couch in a whirlwind of circles, excited at the prospect of finally going outside. She let out a loud bark that pierced Hugo's ears.

A small apothecary bottle sat on his coffee table with twine tied around the neck. The words *Drink Me. -Alice* were written in black ink across the attached tanned note tag. Hugo picked up the clear, cylindrical bottle. The blue liquid swished inside. He removed the cork stop and paused only for a momentary concern. The throbbing removed all doubt, and he downed the drink in one chug. It tasted of blueberries and oak.

Max ran out the back door, barking and running through the yard. Hugo stumbled behind. He held onto the guard rails as he descended the steps one at a time. He slumped into the plastic chair, waiting for Max to finish. His breathing slowed, and the pounding headache ceased. He no longer felt the sweat running down his back. His shirt, however, was still damp. His vision cleared. The overcast, gray clouds on the fall day felt blinding.

"There he is," a familiar voice said over the fence. "Feeling better?"

"Yeah," he drew out his response. "What was in that?"

"One of my potions," Alice said. "The cure for hangovers."

Hugo stood up and meandered over to the fence to greet her. Each step felt more secure than the last. "You could sell it and make a fortune."

"I already do," Alice replied.

Hugo paused. He struggled to remember the events of last night. "What... what happened?"

"Well. You got really drunk, really fast, and then passed out on my floor. I helped carry you to your couch, with a wee-bit of my magick... with a *K*, by the way." She winked at Hugo.

Hugo dropped his head, ashamed of his actions. In a hushed tone, he said, "I'm... I'm sorry for ruining your evening."

"Don't be. That was the most fun I've had in a long time."

"Still, I didn't mean to cause a mess."

His eyes locked with her emerald greens. His eyebrows begged for forgiveness. Hugo hoped she noticed the hurt in his eyes.

Alice's smirk turned into a half smile. "How about you make it up to me?"

"Absolutely," Hugo replied.

"Do you want to meet my horse?"

Hugo's eyes widened with curiosity. "Sure."

"Midnight. Tonight. In the woods," Alice said.

Hugo raised his eyebrows. "Where in the woods?"

"Oh, you'll know," Alice replied as she stepped away from the fence and disappeared back into the house. "Get plenty of rest. You're going to need it."

CHAPTER 13
ALICE'S HORSE

The waning crescent moon cast little light. Clouds canvased the sky, attempting to suppress what little star light tried to penetrate the inky darkness. Shadows of tree trunks stood as the watchful sentinels of Wildgrove Park. Their trunks squealed as they shifted ever so slightly in the chilly fall air. Overhead limbs stretched out over the path, ready to strike at those who dared venture into the woods at night. Their skeletal like hands swayed back and forth. Snake-like trails crisscrossed the landscape as the tree roots waited to enthrall the feet of unsuspecting victims.

Hugo stepped in short strides along the path. Confidence made with each step, yet respectful of the traps set out by the guardians of the forest. The smell of musty, rotting leaves permeated the air as each step released their aromatic flavors into the sky. The sound of a screeching animal in the distance echoed off the dark tree trunks. Then he heard a stick snap. Hugo paused.

His heart slammed against his ribs. He gulped for air, trying to prevent it from exploding through his chest. Attentively glancing over one shoulder and then the other, Hugo surveyed his surroundings, looking for the familiar shadow of a stalking coyote. Sticking his hand into his pants pocket to grab his phone, he pondered using the phone's flashlight, but he let go. He buried his hands back into his jacket pockets. As far as he could tell, he was alone in the woods.

He continued along the path.

What if this is some sacrificial ritual? The thought pervaded Hugo's head. *She must really be pissed at me.* A mischievous grin painted across his face. His stride grew bolder. Hugo had journeyed through these woods so many times that he knew every imperfection in the dirt path by heart. He gathered speed. He charged forth at a quickened pace, then he stopped.

A small alcove broke the ranks of the lined trees. A familiar alcove. Their alcove.

He removed his hands from their hiding spot. His right hand clutched the left. The index and thumb twisted the black onyx ring. He gazed into the small clearing. The world faded away. A spectral image of a green and white renaissance dress floating in the air burned into Hugo's imagination. The ring spun faster. His heart pounded, and his breath came shorter.

"Hugo!" Elizabeth's voice echoed through the forest.

Hugo released the ring and clenched his hands into fists. Squatting down, he squeezed his eyes closed and shut out the world. He wheezed at the air, desperately trying to normalize his heartbeat with every breath. He remained balled up for a moment. His eyes snapped open. The green and white apparition was gone. He rose; his legs were relieved of pressure.

He checked back down the path where he came. A fleeting thought about leaving entered his mind. He focused down the path yet traveled. He thrust his hands into his jacket's silky lined pockets. With his eyebrows bent with determination and his chest puffed out, he continued down the path.

A white light broke through the darkness. The faint glow grew with every one of Hugo's steps. He slowed as he approached. The twisting shadows receded into the darkness, revealing grayish-brown tree trunks that circled a large clearing. Hugo paused. A shadowy outline of a figure stood in front of the light. The unmistakable silhouette of her rounded, pointy hat. The unmistakable curves of her body. He let the image sear into his memory.

Hugo emerged from behind the trees. His eyes adjusted to the light emanating from a rock on the ground. The shadowy outline disappeared with every step until Alice emerged in the light. Her head was tilted, and the brim of her hat obscured her emerald green eyes.

She leaned against a broomstick floating horizontally in the air with her feet crossed. Her right hand clutched the back of a padded, brown, saddle-style bicycle seat attached above the bristles. Interwoven streaks of purple and red were amongst the black broomcorn.

She leaned into her outstretched left arm; her hand stabilized her along the thick brown handle. Streaks of black markings and tan oval knots broke up the color along the smooth handle. It rose slightly toward the end and then jutted down, giving the appearance of a charging thoroughbred's head.

Alice uncrossed her feet and raised her head. "You're late."

"Well…" Hugo's voice trailed off as he removed his hands from his jacket. He rocked back and forth on the balls of his feet. A sly smirk appeared on his face. "The thought did cross my mind that you brought me out here to be used in some ritual sacrifice."

"The night's still young," Alice replied. The tails of her waistcoat hoodie nearly dragged along the ground as she stood up. Her Cheshire grin matched his smirk. "Besides, I would have done it in my basement. Saves time and effort on the cleanup."

Hugo chuckled.

Alice gave two taps to the padded brown seat. "Hugo Dodds, I'd like you to meet my horse."

"So, I'm guessing that was you," Hugo proclaimed.

"Was me?" She played with the brim of her hat, adjusting it a few times.

"That night in the yard a couple weeks ago. I saw something flying through the sky. That was you," Hugo explained. "Right?"

Alice's eyes widened. She hesitated and finally mustered, "Did it frighten you?"

"No," Hugo replied. "Not at all."

The smile returned to Alice's face. "Great," Alice said. "Hop on up. You're going to learn how to fly." She gave a final tap of the seat.

Hugo approached the broom. It hovered in the air, rose and fell ever so slightly, like a boat bobbing on calm waters. Hugo touched the smooth, polished handle. The broom jerked forward at the unfamiliar touch.

"Easy, boy. Easy," Alice's calm voice whispered, grabbing the broomstick before turning her attention back to Hugo. "He's not used to other people touching, let alone riding him."

"So, it thinks it's a horse?"

"Well, sort of," Alice explained. "Kind of. It's a branch from a hickory tree that grew up on a horse farm. The tree was around a lot of horses and farm dogs. It observed and took on their personalities—"

"The tree thought it was a horse?" Hugo interrupted.

"And a dog," Alice emphasized. She petted the head of the broomstick. Her fingers glided down the angled part of the handle toward the end.

"The tree thought it was a horse and a dog?"

Alice tilted her head toward Hugo. "He is a very loyal horse dog."

"And you're petting it?"

"Clearly," Alice said with a confused expression as she turned her attention back to the broomstick.

Her fingers circled to the underside, scratching its would be chin. She focused on the broom's would be face.

"But it's a stick?"

"Yes."

"But it's a stick!"

Alice leered toward Hugo. Her eyebrows arched as they narrowed, and her eyes widened. "Do you want to ride him or not?"

"Does he have a name?"

A befuddled look overcame Alice's face. "I've always called him broom."

"Every horse and every dog has to have a name. You have to name him." Hugo stood there, hands on his hips, with an impish grin. "He needs a name."

Alice rose and crossed her arms. She shifted her weight to one side and tilted her head in the opposite direction. She paused. "Tell you what," Alice said. "You survive this, and you can name him."

Perking up, Hugo asked, "Survive?"

Alice glanced toward the broom and gave a wink. "He can be a little... temperamental. Like I said, he's a loyal horse dog."

Hugo approached the broom, hand outstretched, ready to grab the handle.

Alice stopped him. "No. No. Not like that. You have to introduce yourself first. Gain his trust."

Hugo gave a discerning look and then moved around to the front of the broom. "Umm... Hi, broom." He gave a half-assed wave. "I'm Hugo."

"Pet him!" Alice instructed. "Pet him like you're scratching Max between the eyes."

Hugo placed his hands on his hips and leered at Alice. She smiled and nodded toward the broom. Hugo touched the end of the handle with two fingers. He lightly traced the handle along its nose, to the forehead, and around the neck before circling back on the underside chin. The broom waved up and down as it reacted to his touch. He petted the broom again, noticing every bump and little imperfections along the wooden handle. The broom gingerly moved forward, nudging Hugo in the stomach.

"I think someone likes you," Alice said. "Ready to take a ride?"

Hugo nodded, and Alice led Hugo toward the seat. He placed a palm on the stick, slowly closing his fingers into a tight grip. Swinging his left leg over the broomstick, he straddled the seat between both legs. He sat back. The broom held its position in the air as it received Hugo's weight.

"Now the basics—" Alice began.

The broom lurched forward and bucked toward the sky like a horse throwing a rider. Hugo let go of the handle and fell backward. The rich, earthy smell of damp leaves wafted over Hugo's nose as he hit the ground with a thud. His limbs sprawled out in every direction. He was momentarily stunned. The broom flew into a loop-the-loop before stopping above Hugo.

"Broom! We talked about this. Be nice to Hugo," Alice scolded.

The broom turned around and nudged into Alice. She held his chin and scratched his head.

"It's okay. It's okay. But! Be nice."

She leaned over, looking at Hugo's face staring up into the night sky. Her head obscured Hugo's view of the crescent moon.

"Are you done horsing around?" She extended her hand to help him up.

"Funny," Hugo replied, accepting the gesture.

He stood up, wiping away the wet leaves. He hesitated for a moment before delicately wrapping his fingers around the hickory branch. Hugo clutched the stick with his other hand for stabilization, not wanting to fall for its tricks again. He swung his leg over the seat and sat back.

"Now what?"

"Lean forward when you want him to go," Alice said, mimicking the movements. "Lean back when you want him to stop. Lean into the turns. Lift up to go up. Push down to go down."

"Seems simple enough," Hugo replied.

"The most important thing to remember is you're working as a team. Together. You aren't controlling him. You're guiding him. You have to be on the lookout for where to go, and he'll do the rest," Alice finished her instructions. "When you're ready, lift your feet and lean forward."

Hugo repositioned his hands, lightly tapping the handle with his fingers to find the right spot. He squeezed, but too tight. He leaned forward with his eyes focused. His heart raced. He paused and smiled at Alice. "I know what I'm going to name him," Hugo said.

"Oh?"

"Galahad," he replied before kicking up his feet. "Yah, Gally. Yah!"

The broom shot forward, increasing speed as it lurched toward a tree.

"Pull up," Alice's voice was frantic. "Pull up!"

Hugo pulled back on the broomstick and climbed into the sky. Branches of trees clawed out in their attempt to contain and snare the pair. The branches snapped off after striking Hugo's leather jacket. He leaned left and right, zigzagging his way through the myriad of ash, oak, and sycamore tree limbs. Hugo leaned forward, hugging the handle as closely as possible. Their pace quickened. Hugo focused on a small opening that appeared ahead. Their escape.

He gently pulled the handle closer to his chest, rising further into the sky. His heart beat faster and faster with every second. The whacks and snaps of tree branches quickened. A sharp pain hit his cheek from some unforeseen object. He tucked his head closer to the chest. The opening approached.

They burst through the tree lines. The chilled air rushed past his reddened face. The crescent moon bathed them in a faint, bluish-white light as they continued their climb to freedom.

Hugo leaned back, slowed down, and allowed himself a moment of reflection. The soft yellowish glow of the town center appeared off in the distance. The unmistakable peak of St. Jude's steeple. The bell tower of city hall. Small luminescent orbs dotted the landscape from porch lights left on to turn back the darkness.

The night air was quiet, peaceful. Hugo released his grip, sliding his hands back along the broomstick. He sat up to take it all in. His eyes closed, allowing himself to savor a moment of joy. He leaned back and tugged on the wooden handle.

The broom bolted higher in the sky. The inertia caught Hugo by surprise, and he fell further backward. They climbed higher. The invisible hand of gravity latched on to Hugo's shoulders. He slid back along the smooth leather of the bicycle seat. His hands could no longer hold on. The broom shot higher into the sky. Hugo's eyes widened, and he let out a barbaric yawp at the sudden realization that he was no longer ascending with the broom.

Hugo tumbled through the air, but the dark sky hid its secret.

"Hugo!" Alice shouted.

The trees swayed back and forth, obscuring his view of her.

His body tumbled over and over in a dizzying display. Streaks of purple energy shot out and fought back against the darkness from the woods below him. Energy crackled as the purple sparks hit their targets below. He wondered if she was trying to clear a path to save him. He hoped.

The broom vanished in the night sky. His body continued its descent toward certain doom. Hugo was shouting, but couldn't hear himself over his fear. The treetops grew closer and closer.

The barren limbs continued to sway back and forth. They stretched as far into the sky as they could, waiting to snatch their prey. He could not see Alice below, only more streaks of purple energy. Hugo closed his eyes, not wanting to see his impending doom.

Elizabeth. The name coursed through his mind. His final thought.

"Hugo!" Alice shouted into the sky.

His eyes snapped open. Her voice echoed off of the waiting trees. *Alice!* He couldn't muster the name, only the thought.

Hugo was only a few feet away from the trees. Their limbs quickened with anticipation in the chilled wind. A wood branch rose and smacked Hugo in the face. Not a tree limb, but the familiar sight of brown with streaks of black and ovals of tan.

Hugo wrapped his arms and legs around the broomstick. The inertia caused him to slide off the side. Galahad barrel-rolled with Hugo's limp body, desperately attempting to stabilize their momentum. Hugo found the bicycle seat. He slowly rose, grabbing the handle with a firm grip. His eyes focused on the treetops zipping past at great speed. He leaned in.

Hugo kicked the broomcorn bristles. "Fly, Galahad! Fly!"

Hugo and the broom circled around the top of Wildgrove Park at a great speed. He pulled back on the handle, rising higher into the sky. He leaned forward, resting his chin on the smooth hickory. The wind rushed across his face. The chill in the air was of no concern.

They climbed higher and higher, almost perpendicular to the ground. He raised his right hand and gave a two-finger salute toward the crescent moon. With a wink, he grabbed the handle and descended.

Their vertical descent gained speed. They fell with purpose toward the trees below. Barren limbs awaited the duo.

"Not yet," Hugo commanded.

They continued their rapid descent.

"Not yet."

They were within yards of the trees. Their limbs quickened their pace with the breeze.

"Not yet!"

Galahad pushed against Hugo's hands, but Hugo resisted altering their course.

They were within feet of the trees.

"Now!" Hugo shouted, rearing back on the broom handle.

They pulled out of their tailspin and sailed along the treetops. They circled around, reducing speed, before descending back into the clearing to a waiting Alice.

Hugo's heart raced with exhilaration. His cheeks were red with wind burn. A smile... a long-forgotten smile... played across his face. He tried to catch his breath. The thrills of the night's activities were still fresh in his mind. He placed his feet on the ground and leaned back into the seat.

"Good boy," Hugo reassured Galahad as he patted him on the handle. "You did good."

"What the fuck was that?" Alice yelled as she was now deep into the thicket of the trees. She trudged back.

"That?" Hugo pointed to the sky before nonchalantly leaning back in the seat. "That is what we in the business call expert flying. Natural skills."

Alice rushed over to Hugo and shoved him in the chest. He rocked back and forth, nearly falling off the broom if not for his left foot propping him up.

Alice hugged him, burying her head in between his neck and shoulder. "You scared the shit out of me." Alice's muffled voice tickled Hugo.

He wrapped his arms around her, weaving his right hand into her vibrant purple hair, gently massaging the back of her head. They held together, interwoven as one, for what felt like an eternity. Hugo had not experienced this in months. He didn't want it to end. He leaned in closer to Alice and whispered, "Maybe I'll teach you to fly like that someday."

Alice relinquished her hold on Hugo and gave him another shove.

He chuckled at Alice's frustration. "I'm kidding."

"Gally, dump him," Alice commanded.

"Wait, wait..." Hugo's voice trailed off as Galahad bucked up into the sky, dumping Hugo back onto the cold, damp ground.

The thud resonated through his back. The earthy, musty smell wafted over his nose.

"Help."

RAVENHILL DRIVE WAS SILENT. The houses darkened as their occupants slumbered for the evening. The glow of their porch lights dimmed as the riders approached their houses from the back to reduce the possibility of being seen by any potential onlookers. They flew between the two houses before coming to a stop in between them. Alice's feet greeted the ground as Galahad softly came to a full stop.

Hugo sat as far back on the seat as he could. His arms wrapped around Alice's waist, head resting where her shoulder met the bottom of her neck. The faint hint of rosemary and sage perfume enticed his senses. He didn't want to let go. He lingered as long as possible before finally releasing his hug. His fingers slowly traced around her waist. He felt the smooth polyester fibers of the coat against her body. Alice slightly arched her back.

She shivered.

He smiled.

Hugo swung his leg over Galahad. Alice followed. She bit her lip and brushed her hair behind her ears. They stood, eyes locked, inches from each other. He lost himself in the stare of her emerald green eyes. She locked onto his icy blues.

An unseen force pulled him closer and closer to her. Hugo's desires burned in that moment. He wanted to act, but something held him back. Neither dared to utter the dark secrets of their intentions in that moment.

"Thank you," he finally broke the silence. "Thank you for a fun evening. I haven't experienced this in months."

She smiled. He turned and headed back toward his door.

Alice called out his name in a panic, "Hugo!"

Her words stopped him in his tracks. He reluctantly turned around.

"The night's still young. Would you like to come inside?"

She adjusted her hat by pushing it back. Her face perfectly illuminated in the moonlight. The glow of her purple hair. Her lips narrowed. Her eyebrows arched. A look of uncertainty.

Hugo froze. His heart raced, and his eyes widened with anticipation. He tried to find the words he wanted to say. The words he needed to say. All the years of speaking failed him at that moment. He couldn't verbalize his heart's desires. His heart's wants. His heart's needs. He wanted Alice in that moment, but something held him back.

"I had a great time tonight," Hugo said.

Alice lowered her head, pulling her hat back down. The brim hid her face from Hugo.

Hugo's shoulders slumped. His wide-eyed expression narrowed to contain the tears that swelled. "I want to, but I don't think I can."

Alice raised her head; her eyes narrowed and brow scrunched. Hugo's stomach sank from the hurt in her eyes. "What are we? Just friends or something more?"

"I want us to be something more," he replied.

In that instant, he wanted to bend her backward and kiss her the way he used to kiss Elizabeth. *Elizabeth.* Her name echoed through his mind, haunting him, tormenting him. He sank into the ground, unable to move, held in place, so he wouldn't act on his emotions. "I... I need more time."

Alice nodded. "Okay. I can give you time. All the time you need." She wiped away a tear and smiled. Hugo knew that smile—the smile to mask the pain.

"Thank you."

Hugo fought back the tears swelling in his eyes. He stuffed his hands in his jacket pockets and turned. His head hung low like he had committed an atrocity. He knew, in that moment, he had messed up. He knew with every fiber in his being he should turn around and rush toward her in ecstasy.

An invisible string pulled him, compelled him back inside. He tried to escape, to run toward her embrace. That invisible string lurched him forward into the sanctity of his house.

"Have a good night," she said.

He turned back. Alice stood upright, perhaps hoping he would reconsider, as he ascended his porch steps.

"You too, Alice. It was fun." He disappeared inside the faded, tumbledown home.

CHAPTER 14

WORKING HIS MAGIC ON HER

"I fucked up, Max," Hugo said as he paced his living room. "I really fucked up."

Max lay in front of the fireplace; her eyes watched Hugo's movements. As he paced, Hugo examined his phone with the determination of an artist scrutinizing their work. He swiped and gestured as if directing part of the screen to new locations. He stopped.

Hugo examined the phone one last time before he turned his back to the couch and plopped down. He tossed it onto the seat next to him and, in the same motion, covered his face as he leaned back into the couch cushions.

"I'm an idiot. I ruined it. I ruined everything. Why didn't I go in with her that night?"

The spattering of rain crashed into the window behind him.

"I bet she hates me now. I'm sure avoiding her for a few days hasn't helped."

Max furled her eyebrows one last time at Hugo's nonsensical blabbering before closing her eyes.

He leaned forward and glanced over at the phone. He picked it up and scrolled through the playlist again. Every song had to be perfect and in the correct order. The phone bounced once as he dropped it back down. "I should go over there."

Max opened her eyes and gave Hugo an uncaring glance before she closed them once more.

Hugo jumped up and peered out the window. Dark, gray clouds blanketed the sky. They moved and swirled with the trepidation of ruin. It was a hard rain—cold, dark, unrelenting. Water saturated the yellowish-green autumn ground. Alice's black SUV remained parked in front of her house.

She's still home. Now's your chance.

Hugo scanned the dust covered pictures on the mantel. He stopped at his wedding picture. Elizabeth's radiant smile. His joyous grin. The candid moment captured on paper of them lost in each other. Elizabeth in her white wedding gown. He in the black tux with a blue tie. Their wedding colors. Their high school colors. The colors of the first time they fell in love with each other. The memories flooded back.

Maybe it was for the best.

Emotion swirled through him. He contemplated sitting back on the couch as the rain pattered against the window. The sound of the storm grew more intense. The crash of rain became more violent against the window.

Hugo glanced over at his phone. Without time for doubt, he snatched it up and stuffed it into his pants pocket. Hugo strode over to the mantel and turned the wedding picture around.

"I'm sorry," he said as he moved toward the front door.

He took his black leather jacket out of the closet. In a dizzying motion, Hugo flung the jacket around him and put his arms through the sleeves.

"Max, I'll see you later."

∽

"LEAVE HIM," Alice's reflection said. "He clearly doesn't want you. Leave him."

Alice leaned back against the side bathroom wall. She tilted her head and leered at the mirror with disapproving eyes.

"Don't give me that look," Alice's reflection retorted. "You know I'm right. He's been avoiding you for what... a couple of days now? You're too good for him. It's for the best, actually."

Alice was silent. Her reflection was perplexed and matched Alice's silence. The mirror searched carefully for its next words. Anything to convince Alice. Her reflection leaned forward as close to the glass as possible and locked onto Alice's eyes. "You're never going to compete with his dead wife," the mirror said.

Alice scowled in response.

"You know I'm right," the mirror pleaded.

Alice stood up and turned her back. "He'll come around," she replied. "When he's ready."

"How long are you willing to wait?"

"As long as it takes."

"And if he doesn't..."

Alice paused before offering a reply. "Then I'll continue to wait."

Alice's reflection buried her face into her palms, trying to find anything to help plead her case. Her reflection paused, then raised her head until only her jaw remained buried in her cupped hands. "Why?" the reflection asked in a muffled voice before dropping her hands. "What makes him so special?"

Alice lowered her head only for a moment and then turned. Tears welled in her eyes. She locked onto her reflection to reveal her inner, unrelenting truth. "He accepts me for who I am. No one has ever accepted me. They only wanted what I could do for them."

Alice and her reflection wiped away their tears on the sleeves of their shirts.

There was a knock at Alice's front door. The sound reverberated up the hallway walls and into her bedroom. Alice snapped toward the mirror. A shocked expression appeared on both of their faces.

Galahad rushed through the open bathroom door. Excited, it bounced around in the air. More knocks reverberated through the walls. Galahad bounced and spun all around the bathroom.

Alice comforted the excited hickory horse-dog. "I know, boy. I know," she said as she touched the slanted front of Galahad's broom handle.

She scratched its chin and down the top of Galahad's head, trying to soothe the excited flying broomstick. "You wait up here. I'll go see who it is. You be good."

Alice glanced back toward the mirror. The shocked expression on her reflection's face was now a beaming smile. Her reflection tilted her head toward the exit, beckoning her to leave. Alice rushed through the bedroom, closing the door behind her, before pausing at the top of the stairs to compose herself.

A third set of knocks greeted Alice as she descended toward the door. A dark figure appeared through the black veil curtain. She paused.

Alice wiped her face once more. She ran her fingers through her hair to hide any clue of her bathroom therapy session. She took a deep breath. Her heart skipped a beat. She pulled back the curtain to see a rain drenched Hugo standing on the other side. She giggled and opened the door.

"Hugo!" Alice said. "You're soaked."

The short walk over had drenched Hugo. His hair was dripping wet. Beads of water flowed down the smooth leather of his jacket. His shoes were soaked. Hugo stood there like a love scorned puppy. A somber frown on his face. "I'm sorry."

"For what?"

"For leaving you the other night," he replied.

"You don't have to apologize. I—" Alice paused. "I should apologize to you. I shouldn't have put you in that situation if you're not comfortable yet."

"No. I want to make it up to you."

"This is now twice you're having to make things up to me," Alice replied with a smirk. "One more, and I'll think it's a habit with you."

Hugo chuckled. "Can I come in?"

"Of course," she replied. "Get out of the rain."

Alice shut the door after he entered. Water pooled on the hard-wood entryway.

"I'm making a mess," Hugo said.

Alice snapped her fingers. The water evaporated from the floor and his jacket. His hair was still damp.

"I like the wet hair look on you," she said with a smile.

Hugo rummaged his fingers through his hair, creating a messy hairdo. "How does it look now?"

"Perfect," Alice replied with a grin that betrayed her excitement. "What can I do for you?"

"I thought maybe we could spend the day together or something," Hugo said. "If you didn't have other plans."

Alice paused, unsure of what to say next. She immediately erased all other plans the moment he wanted to spend the day with her. "I was going to make some more wine—"

"I can help," he interrupted as he took off his jacket and placed it on her coat rack.

"Yeah. I can always use... help," Alice replied. "Head downstairs. I need to finish something upstairs first."

He strutted toward the basement door. "Don't keep me waiting too long," he said before he disappeared into the darkness.

Alice bit her lip with a delightful grin as she wiped away a single tear.

THE CANDLELIGHT from the wall sconces danced and flickered off the stone walls, which gave the dark, damp place a welcoming warmth. The room was dimly lit, yet everything was visible in the low light. Hugo carried a cardboard box of destemmed grapes up a small set of wooden steps leading to the top of the platform. He dumped the contents into the wooden vats. They disappeared into the dark, purplish, liquid wine must. The stompers worked their unseen magick to liquify the grapes. He set the box down and turned toward Alice at her workbench.

Alice worked her witchy magick as she brewed a potion. Her shadow danced across the wall in the flickering light. He traced the arch in her back as she bent over to speak her dark, forbidden language into the bubbling cauldron.

His heart skipped a beat as he took in a breath and held it. Her every curve enthralled his eyes. Time disappeared. He couldn't look away. He was enraptured by her beauty.

Have I been holding my breath for eternity?

He didn't know.

Hugo relinquished the breath to ask a question, "Have you ever made wine the old-fashioned way?"

Alice paused her work and turned around. She leaned back against the edge of the workbench. Her hands placed on her hips accentuated her curves. Hugo held that breath once more.

She tilted her head. "The old-fashioned way? No one's ever asked me that."

"Yeah." Hugo peered into the vat closest to him. "You know. Stomping the grapes. With your feet."

"Why would I do that when I have the stompers do it for me?"

Hugo locked onto her emerald green eyes. He never took his eyes off of her as he descended the platform steps with the confidence and swagger of a tango dance enticing his partner. Each phrase lingered as he took the next step.

"You know. For fun."

"For fun?" Alice smirked.

"Yeah." He grinned back. "Fun."

She paused and crossed her arms. "Would you like to make wine the old-fashioned way, Hugo Dodds?"

He arrived at the bottom of the platform steps. His gaze was unrelenting. Hugo pulled his shoulders back, tightening his shirt against his muscular chest. "Sounds like fun to me."

She stood upright and beguiled him with her swaying hips as she moved closer. She was inches away. He could feel her aura. Her presence. He wanted it to last.

"It can be messy," Alice pleaded in a hushed tone.

"I'm not afraid to get a little messy," he answered as he matched her volume.

She pulled away, never breaking eye contact with him. "You might want to put on some shorts. It'd be a shame to stain those pants of yours."

The belt buckle echoed against the stone floor after Hugo unzipped and dropped his pants. Alice watched him remove his socks, toss the clothing aside with his foot, and stand there in the cold, damp cellar, with his boxer briefs and black, long sleeve T-shirt. She smiled at him and bit her lip.

"I'm okay like this," he replied. "That is, if you don't mind."

Her leggings dropped to the floor with a snap of her fingers. Alice stood there in the chilly dampness of the cellar in her gray, long sleeve shirt and black underwear that exposed enough skin to indulge Hugo's desires. She moved closer.

"Not at all." Their bodies barely touched as she leaned to whisper into his ear. Her breath teased Hugo with tantalizing delight, as if she was enrapturing him under one of her spells. "I like it when it's messy."

"I have a feeling it could get very messy," he whispered back to regain control.

Alice stood there in silence and closed her eyes. She took a deep breath and exhaled slowly. Hugo backed away and took her left hand with his. Firm, yet gentle. He cupped her fingers and steadied her hand with his thumb against her knuckles. Alice opened her eyes.

He led her up the steps to the top of the wooden platform to the waiting vat. One step at a time. He was cautious, methodical, and teasing. He dared not rush her, lest she slip and fall. His eyes locked and focused on hers. She gazed at his icy blues. He guided her with the fingertips of his other hand placed on her back. They slipped down to the small of her back with each step. She let out a small moan as his fingers glided along her spine.

They made their way to the top of the platform. She snapped her fingers with her free hand. The stompers lifted and exited the vat. They took their normal resting place, free of any liquid. Hugo firmly placed his hand on the small of her back. He led her toward the wooden vat.

He slid his hand across her back to let the fingers graze over the shirt. He grabbed onto her upper arm to support her as she stepped over the vat wall and into the murky liquid. Hugo let go of Alice and joined her as they sloshed around in the frothy wine must. His toes dug into slippery chunks of smashed grapes. Bits of grapes squeezed under his feet. An odd, slimy sensation.

"I feel silly," Alice said.

"That's okay," he replied. "We can be silly together."

Alice pulled her hair back behind her ears. "Now what?"

"Now, I'm going to work my magic," he replied. "That's magic with a *C*, by the way."

Alice did not hide her smile as she let out a giddy laugh.

"Phone," Hugo called out to his phone resting on the work-bench across the cellar. "Play my *WORK MY MAGIC ON ALICE* playlist."

"Now playing your playlist," the phone replied in its automated female voice.

The sultry sounds of Nina Simone's "I Put a Spell on You" echoed off the stone walls.

"Really?" she replied. "I should be offended by this."

"But, honestly, are you?" he replied with a cunning smile.

"No, not really. It's cute."

"Just cute?"

"It's adorable."

Hugo moved closer. He placed his hands around her waist. He

teased her with small taps as he worked his fingers down to the tops of her hips. She placed her hands on his shoulders.

She leaned in closer toward his ear and asked a loaded question, to which he felt she already knew the answer. "Now what?"

"Now we stomp the grapes."

They began their waltzing dance across the wooden vat. The soft grape skin gave way under each slow step. The liquid and soft grapes oozed under their feet and between their toes. They moved with purpose as to not slip and fall into the liquid. Hugo wanted to wrap his hands around her back and pull her closer. He strained at the thought, but he needed to wait. They danced around as the music swelled to a finish, never taking their eyes off each other. The liquid wine must sashayed with every seductive step.

A sultry cover of "Wicked Game" played next.

"I want to thank you," Hugo said.

"For what?"

"For these past few weeks. For helping me to remember excitement again. To remember joy. To remember living again."

Alice choked up. "You're welcome, Hugo. I want to thank you too. Thank you for accepting me. For not freaking out... over who I am."

"Your secret is safe with me."

Alice smiled. The liquid poured down the chute and into the press below as they continued their dance.

The Cure's "Lovesong" played next.

"I need you to know one thing," Hugo said. "Elizabeth will always be part of my life."

Alice peered right into his icy blue eyes. Her face was no longer giddy with excitement. "I would never replace her. I don't want to replace her. She is a part of your life just as much as magick is a part of mine."

A tear rolled down Hugo's face as he smiled. Alice wiped away the tear.

She added, "I would never ask you to forget her. Ever."

Hugo moved his hands around Alice's back. He felt a shiver

course through her body as he pulled her closer. Alice slid her arms under his and wrapped them around his back. She buried her head into his shoulder. She exhaled in the comfort of his chest, and Hugo rested his head on hers. They continued their dance, now interlocked as one.

A slow, almost spell-like cover version of "Witchcraft" played next.

"I *really* should be offended by this one," Alice said.

"You like it," Hugo retorted.

His fingers lightly tapped on her back as they worked their way down and stopped short of the end of her shirt. A heat surged inside of him. He wanted to continue further; to reach under her shirt and work his way further down along the softness of her skin. He wanted so much more in that moment.

"I like it," Alice replied.

"And I like you, Alice Primrose."

Alice pulled back at the words he spoke. Their slow dance through the liquid grapes stopped. The music faded into the background. His breath caught in his chest, worried he said something wrong. She glared at him, blinking.

He waited for a response. Each passing moment felt like his calculated risk was imploding before his eyes. Her lip quivered. Each breath was shorter than his last until he was no longer breathing. A flood of emotions overtook his body.

She responded before their magical moment disappeared into ruin, "I like you too, Hugo Dodds."

"May I kiss—" his words trailed as she nodded profusely.

Hugo slid his hands around the back of her neck to cup her head. His fingers wove into her purple hair. He leaned in to kiss her soft, purple lips. Slow and soft at first before pushing forward with more intensity—fire and passion. He tugged ever so slightly on her purple hair. Their tongues introduced themselves to each other and quickly found familiar forbidden desires.

A pulse rippled through his body. He melted away, lost in the thought of pure bliss—bliss he hadn't felt in ages. He lost track of time and space and what was real. His mind and soul were ablaze with ecstasy. He wanted to live in that moment for eternity.

He pulled his hand away from her hair. In that moment, they stopped kissing, stopping to catch their breaths. His chest rose and fell, breathing deeply to quell the fire within his soul. It was too late. He wanted more. He needed more.

They leaned against each other, forehead to forehead. Hugo had not felt the fulfilling embrace of another soul in months. The embrace deluged the dry, cavernous hole in his soul with the flood waters of bliss. They locked eyes. Desire blazed within him. They matched each other breath for breath.

In a hushed tone, whispering a secret only they would know, Hugo asked, "Should we go upstairs?"

Alice let go of Hugo and snapped her fingers. A bottle flew across the room. She snatched it out of midair. With another snap, the cork jumped out and ricocheted off the ceiling. She downed a gulp straight from the neck of the bottle. She slammed the bottle against Hugo's chest.

"Drink," she commanded.

Hugo did as he was told. He drank the magical elixir held within the green bottle. "What now?"

Alice snapped her fingers. The bottle flew out of Hugo's hand and landed on the wooden platform. She grabbed Hugo's arms and turned him around, so his back faced the open room. With a shove of pure magical force emanating from Alice's hands, Hugo stumbled backward.

He tripped over the vat wall and fell onto what he thought would be the stone floor. Instead, it was as if gentle hands cradled and placed him on a cushioned cloud. He glided across the room like being on ice. A familiar sensation from his days of playing youth hockey.

Drops of reddish, purple liquid fell onto the stone floor from Hugo's wine must stained feet. He realized he was no longer touching anything solid. Instead, he was floating in the air. He smiled with ecstasy and anticipation.

He glanced over to where he once stood. Alice's eyes locked onto him with a sense of passion, desire, and hunger. She trudged through the wine must. Each step sloshed more liquid down the chute into the press below. Not even the vat wall could break her stride. She strutted into the air as if the platform had extended itself above the stone flooring. Alice's pace quickened as she moved closer.

Hugo stood up. An invisible force held him in the air. He removed his shirt and tossed it to the floor below. His toned chest was bare to the cold, damp air. He rushed toward Alice. She leapt into his waiting arms. The grape juices dripped down Hugo's backside as she wrapped her legs around his waist. They kissed again with renewed passion and hunger for more.

Hugo held Alice closely to his chest as he dropped to his knees. He worked his hands down her back and under her shirt. She softly bit his bottom lip as each of Hugo's fingertips traced their way up her spine. His hands worked to remove her shirt. She pulled away and threw up her arms to allow him to remove another barrier to their delight. He removed her shirt and cast it aside.

His firm yet gentle hands laid her down on the soft, invisible floor. Fingertips dug sensual paths down her back. They caught the elastic band to pull down the last barrier between them. He relished the moment as she writhed in anticipation, trying to wiggle her way out faster. She pressed her lips together as she was now fully exposed to the cold air. He grabbed the elastic band of his underwear and flung them off.

He lay on top of her, on top of her soft body. He gazed into her emerald green eyes. Hugo gently kissed her sweet purple lips. He moved his hands down her body until they rested on the curves of her hips. He pulled her closer. As close as they could be. She wrapped her arms and legs around Hugo in ecstasy. They breathed as one. They moved as one. They became one.

Hugo pulled up his pants and gazed at the spot in the air where they had been moments before. He was now on solid ground. He allowed himself to smile.

"That is definitely a first for me," Hugo said.

"Me too," Alice replied. "Come here. I need your help."

Hugo sauntered over to the semi-clothed Alice Primrose toiling away at her workbench.

"What are you working on?" Hugo peered over her shoulder.

She hunched over, carefully reading from a spell scroll that was set out. Her fingers held her current place in the spell. The cauldron was ready to receive her next ingredient. "Next, two items coming together as one. Open the third drawer from the right in the top row, and hand me the stick inside." Alice pointed to the apothecary drawers.

Hugo did as instructed. He pulled out the stick with black gaffer tape wrapped around the middle. "Hey, it's our stick. Our perfectly broken stick."

"Throw it in," Alice said, never taking her eyes away from the spell.

Hugo tossed the stick into the cauldron. It sunk below the bubbling water inside.

"Next, grab that bottle of powder." She motioned with her free hand to a bottle sitting on a shelf. She never broke her gaze or moved her fingers.

"This one?" Hugo placed the bottle in Alice's view.

"Dump it in. The entire bottle."

Hugo poured the powder into the cauldron.

"Spit into the cauldron," Alice instructed.

"What's with you and spitting?"

"The spell calls for us to both spit into the cauldron. It's like we are kissing... in the cauldron. Now spit."

Hugo hovered over the cauldron.

"Stick your head in and do it," Alice interrupted.

Hugo stuck as much of his head into the cauldron as he could, but he never took his eyes off of Alice. He spit into the bubbling liquid.

"Now my turn."

Alice picked up the spell scroll and kept her eyes focused on it. She stuck her face into the cauldron, but kept one eye focused on the spell. Setting the spell back down on the table, she bent over the cauldron and recited ancient, arcane words.

Hugo stood and watched as she worked her magick. He loved to watch her work, invoking her arcane abilities and speaking a language he didn't understand. He smiled.

Alice pulled away and wrapped up the scroll. She placed it into an open rectangular box on the backside of the workbench. She closed the lid and locked it shut with a clasp on the front. With a snap of her fingers, a stone in the wall of the wine cellar above her apothecary drawers opened to reveal a hidden compartment. She placed the box inside and snapped her fingers again to close it.

"What was that?" Hugo asked.

"That's why I'm here." Alice picked up the cauldron and carried it over to the winepress. The reddish, purple wine must bubbled as the green liquid poured in from the cauldron. "This is a very special potion."

She turned back to Hugo, holding the now empty cauldron. A few strands of purple hair draped over her face, nearly obscuring her left eye. She held an impish smile with her eyebrows furled in a sultry expression of lust, passion, and love. Like she was holding a secret. A secret that only the two of them knew.

Alice never broke her gaze from Hugo. She moved closer. Small steps at a time. Hugo was anguished in how long she took walking toward him. He could tell Alice relished in her seductive waltz, each step slow and languished. Her hips swayed to entice and tease his senses for more.

She continued, "You must always maintain your focus on the

spell scroll, or else you forget what was written as soon as you look away. Many have tried to copy it, but it never worked. Some have died trying to obtain it. It's very sought after in the magical world. I have the only known copy remaining. As far as everyone else is concerned, it's lost forever."

"What's so special about it?" Hugo asked.

"It's called The Lovers' Kiss," Alice said as she moved closer to Hugo.

An unseen force pulled them together. He wanted to indulge in their passions, their desires, for another round.

"How seductive," Hugo said in a low voice. "What does it do?"

"Its properties are lost to time. No one knows exactly what it does. Few have attempted to make it. Everyone has failed. It can only be made after an expression of love between two individuals," she said before leaning in closer. She whispered into his ear, "Wouldn't it be great to find out together?"

The hairs on Hugo's neck stood up as her warm words rushed over him. She kissed his ear, her tongue exploring the hidden inner labyrinths deep within, ever so gently, softly. Hugo closed his eyes and lost himself. All thoughts and emotions left him. Only a singular thought flowed through his body. How much he wanted her again at that moment.

She pulled back. Hugo opened his eyes to see her smile a Cheshire grin back at him. He laughed. He thought about taking her hand once again and indulging themselves for another session up in the air.

Hugo took the cauldron from Alice and placed it on the ground. He wrapped his arms behind her hips. He placed his hands on the small of her back and pulled her closer. Their mouths nearly touched in a physical embrace. He teased her and made her wait. She smiled a sultry expression. The anticipation filled the minuscule void between the two.

Hugo leaned in closer and asked into her ear, "So, why are you here because of it?"

"Sam," Alice responded as she pulled away.

The sultry expression vanished, and resentment replaced it. She picked up the cauldron. Hugo's cheerful expression disappeared, realizing he blew the moment.

"I told Sam about the potion; she wanted us to make it together. I refused. Sam grew angry and furious. I still wouldn't make it. She started talking, and people found out because she blabbed. The wrong people."

Alice flung the cauldron on to the workstation. It rocked back and forth, nearly tipping over, before coming to a full stop.

"One night, some people came looking for me... for it," Alice continued. "Luckily, Galahad alerted me. We got out of there and raced to Ez. She helped me hide and lay low. We moved around from place to place. Sometimes, I never knew where I was. Then, one day, Ez said she found a perfect place for me to hide. A small town, far from my home. I could hide out there and build a new life."

"I'm so, so sorry," Hugo said.

Alice focused her eyes down on the empty cauldron. "It's okay," she said. "I'm fine."

Hugo rushed over and grabbed under her chin with his index finger. He gently pulled up to look her directly in the eyes. "Hey, what did I tell you? It's okay to not be okay."

"Thank you." Alice closed her eyes as Hugo moved his index finger from under her chin and across her lips before finally pulling it away.

"So, want to speed this thing up and give it a try and see what happens?" Hugo picked up the hourglass from the workbench.

"That's where people get it wrong," Alice replied. Hugo placed the hourglass back down. "You can't rush it. You have to let it age naturally."

"So, how long are we talking? Weeks?"

"Months."

"Well, I'm sure it will be worth the wait."

CHAPTER 15
ALWAYS TESTED

Max raced Hugo up Alice's stairs—a race Hugo did not know he was running. Max squeezed between Hugo and the wall, shoving him to the side.

"Max!" he shouted. "Stop being so impatient."

She was now in the lead and poised to win the race. With a few more gallops, she arrived at the top of the stairs. Victory was hers. Max turned toward Hugo and basked in her victory. Her tail smacked against the wall as she patiently waited for him to finish their unknown race.

There was a knock at Alice's bedroom door. Max whirled around. Her ears perked back, and her nose snarled.

Another knock.

She let out an ear-piercing bark that echoed throughout the hallway.

Another knock.

She hunched low and backed toward the stairs. Her hind feet were on the edge of the step. She barked twice more. Two more knocks replied back.

Hugo climbed to the top of the stairs and scratched her backside. She sprang into action and leapt toward the door. She let out a flurry of barks. The knocks replied in kind from the other side.

"Max, will you stop!" Hugo shouted as he covered his ears. "You're going to blow out my ears one day."

He grabbed her collar and pulled her away from the door. Hugo knocked three times. Three knocks replied. He opened the door.

Galahad greeted them on the other side. Max, surprised by this unfamiliar object floating in the sky, let out another series of ear-piercing barks. She hunched low in a ready state of fight-or-flight. Her tail was between her legs. She bared her teeth and drew back her ears.

Galahad bounced with excitement at a new friend. It moved closer to introduce itself. Max did not reciprocate the friendship. With each bark, she moved further and further away from the floating hickory stick. She slipped behind Hugo and peered from behind his legs.

"Are you afraid of Galahad, Max?" Hugo asked. "First, the vacuum and now a broomstick. I think you're afraid of cleaning objects."

Galahad nudged forth. Max flailed her paws on the hardwood surface as she tried to escape the horror of yet another cleaning object trying to get her.

Hugo entered the bedroom and whistled. "Both of you. In!"

They did as they were told, and Hugo shut the door.

Max ran and dove under the bed to hide from the floating object. Galahad followed by sticking its handle under as well. Max whimpered.

"Be good, you two," he commanded as he entered the bathroom.

His hand combed through the darkness to find the light switch before resting on the plastic knob. With a flick of his fingers, he fought back against the darkness of the bathroom.

The aroma of linen, rosemary, and lavender washed over him.

Unlit candles, with their trail of melted wax like gnarled fingers, were scattered throughout the room. Each towel was folded neatly and in its proper place. A far contrast to the mildew smell of his somewhat decently cleaned bathroom. He made a mental note to clean out the bathroom trash can when he got a chance. He strolled to the toilet and lifted the seat.

"Now I see what she sees in you," a familiar voice echoed, causing Hugo to pause. "Don't stop on my account."

"Are you offering to help?"

"If only I could."

Hugo turned around, perplexed. The room was empty. "Alice?"

"She's still downstairs, lover boy," the voice responded.

"Is this some kind of trick?"

"Well, sort of..." her voice trailed off.

Hugo crept toward the mirror, each step soft and surefooted on the tile bathroom floor. He peered into the mirror and saw not his reflection, but Alice's, staring back at him. Her reflection winked and blew him a kiss.

"Are you spying on me now?" Hugo asked with a sly smile.

"Not exactly. I'm her inner thoughts. Her feelings. Her... personal therapy session. I'm her reflection."

"Like her *literal* reflection?"

"Yep. I know all. I see all. I feel *all*! Like that little soiree the two of you had the other night." She leaned closer as if to whisper a secret. "Do you want to know what she really thought?" Alice's reflection winked at Hugo.

"That, um, feels rather, um..." His words failed him in that moment. The tantalizing thought of knowing Alice's innermost personal thoughts and feelings was an opportunity too good to pass up. Still... He paused and gathered himself. "That feels like an invasion of her privacy."

"Good," Alice's reflection stated as she leaned away from the mirror. "You passed the test."

"So, I'm being tested now?"

"You're always tested, Hugo Dodds." She crossed her arms with a stern look. "Never fail one of hers."

"Good to know."

Three distinct knocks rattled up the staircase walls and into the bedroom. Max emerged from her hiding spot and started barking once more. Galahad flew out and into the bathroom, excited at the prospect of yet another new visitor. Three more knocks in rapid succession. There was a delay before they rattled the door again. Galahad knocked three times on the bedroom door as if to answer the call back to the known visitor.

"You better go answer the door, lover boy."

The knocks rattled the walls once again. Hugo headed back through the bedroom, failing to complete his initial purpose for coming upstairs. Max waited impatiently at the door. Galahad bounced around, ready to greet the visitor. Hugo cracked open the door.

"You stay," he commanded Galahad. It slumped low in disappointment. "Look. I'd let you downstairs if I could. It's not up to me, but I'll talk to her." Galahad perked back up.

Hugo and Max entered the hallway, closing the door behind them.

"I'll get it," Hugo said as he descended the stairs.

Max followed close behind. She tried to squeeze past Hugo, but he was prepared for her this time. He descended to the base of the steps.

"It's probably Ez," Alice shouted up through the open basement door. "She's great. You'll love her."

Hugo grabbed the ornate, diamond shaped doorknob. Max tried to worm her way around to see who was knocking at the door.

"Get back," Hugo commanded Max.

She didn't listen. She fought her way through, anxiously awaiting the door to open. Hugo positioned his body between her and the wall.

"Back!"

He opened the door. The crisp, cold late-November air rushed inside. Standing on the porch was an older woman in a fashionably warm coat. Short of stature, but standing tall with personality. Her hair made up into a beehive style.

"You wouldn't believe the night I had," her voice trailed as she was greeted not by Alice, but by an unknown man. "You're not Alice."

She took a step back and checked she didn't approach the wrong purple house.

"Nope. I'm not Alice," he replied. "Hugo Dodds. I take it you're Ez. Alice has told me so much about you."

He extended out to shake her hand. His body blocked Max from trying to peek out the door. Her tail wagged and beat against the wall.

She lingered on the hand in front of her before glaring up at Hugo. Esmerelda raised a discerning eyebrow and shook his hand. "Charmed," she said. "Aren't you going to invite an old woman in from the cold?"

Hugo backed away from the door. "Ah, yes. Please come on in."

Esmeralda Honeydew entered the purple house, and Hugo closed the door. She removed her coat.

"I can take that for you," Hugo offered.

"Thank you," she replied as she handed it over.

He placed it on the coat rack, next to Alice's tailcoat. Max sat next to her, pressing her head against Esmerelda's body. Max's tail wagged, knocking the shoes on the floor back and forth.

"Hello." She patted Max on the head. She rubbed the underside of Max's chin; her tail wagged faster and faster to display her excitement.

"Max, leave her alone," Hugo commanded. She didn't listen.

"He's fine," Esmerelda replied. "He just wants scratches."

"Her name is Maxine, but we..." His voice trailed off. "I call her Max for short."

"Well, she's a good girl, aren't you?" Esmerelda scratched behind Max's ears.

"I'll be right up," Alice shouted from the basement.

Three distinct knocks came from upstairs.

Esmerelda focused her attention up the stairs and shouted, "I hear you, good buddy!"

The knocks stopped.

Alice ran up the stairs and greeted her friend. "Ez! I hope you didn't have any trouble on the way over."

"Nothing I couldn't handle, kiddo," she replied as she gave Alice a hug. She backed away and pointed at Hugo with her thumb.

"Oh, that's Hugo," Alice said. "Hugo, this is Esmerelda Honeydew."

"We met," she replied. "Maybe we can go somewhere and talk business?"

"Oh, sure," Alice answered. "I have everything ready downstairs."

"Well, let's go take a look." Esmerelda stepped through the basement doorway.

Alice followed, closing the door shut behind her.

"I don't think she likes me, Max," Hugo said, looking down at her. Her tail swept back and forth at the excitement. "No, she definitely likes you."

THE BASEMENT WAS WELL LIT. Empty grape boxes were strewn about the floor. The door leading to the wine cellar was open. The candle wall sconces held back the darkness. Esmerelda closed the door as they entered the cold, damp cellar.

Alice strode over to the wine rack with a spring in her step. The bottles were neatly organized based on their magical properties. They lay ready for packaging and transportation to The Coven Club. Alice stood next to the rack with her head held high and a smile on her face. She arched her back and puffed out her chest. Alice was proud of her work.

"Okay, so we have bottles of Luck... obviously," Alice said as she recited the wine labels. "We also have Courage, Insight, Happiness, Fertility—be careful who you give that to—Protection, Air Walk, and my personal favorite, Contortion."

Esmerelda examined the wine racks. She surveyed each bottle, reading the labels. "This is all of them?"

"Yep. All 576 bottles are ready for boxing. Forty-eight crates of wine in total delivered as promised," Alice replied.

Esmerelda shook her head. "Impressive. Impressive indeed. Especially given the circumstances."

"Hugo helped me. We did this together."

Esmerelda turned around and scolded Alice with a narrow-eyed glare, as if she were in trouble. Any sense of pride faded from Alice's face.

"Did he?"

"He is a very good and capable assistant," Alice replied.

Esmerelda continued her examination of the bottles. She pulled one out of the rack. A bottle marked "Insight" in black calligraphy lettering set against a faux weathered label. She snapped her fingers. The cork flew out with an audible *pop* before it landed on the ground. She smelled the wine. She took a sip and sloshed the liquid around in her mouth before drinking it.

"Pretty good," she said.

"This whole batch has been excellent so far."

Esmerelda snapped her fingers once more. The cork returned to her hand. She popped it back into place. With a tap, the cork descended back into the bottle's neck.

"You did good, kiddo. You did good."

"Thank you. That means a lot," Alice replied. "And thank you for everything you've done."

"Any time, kiddo. Any time," Esmerelda said. "But I want you to do something for me."

"Sure. Anything."

"Leave him."

"Leave him?" Alice questioned. "I can't leave him. He lives next door."

"You shouldn't have shown him any of this in the first place. Now he knows you're a witch. We have ways of dealing with him if you want us to," she offered.

"What?" A shocked expression fell over Alice's face. "I don't want him taken care of."

"I'm only saying it's an option," Esmerelda responded.

"Look. He's a really great guy. He accepts me for who I am. He's bonded with Galahad—"

"Who's Galahad?" Esmerelda asked.

"My broom. Hugo named him."

"You let him name *your* broomstick?"

"Yes. He named it before he flew on it."

Esmerelda nearly dropped the wine bottle onto the stone floor. "He *flew* on your broom?"

"And fell off and almost died."

"He almost *died*?" Esmerelda buried her head into her free hand. "Alice, you have to stop being this impulsive to anyone who shows the slightest bit of interest in you. We can't keep doing this."

Alice's eyes locked onto the wooden vats elevated above the floor. She paused, thinking about the night a few weeks ago. That fantastic night of sexual pleasure and relief. The night that even now sent a tantalizing chill through her body, right down to her soul. She glanced back at Esmerelda. She prepared for the onslaught that was about to occur. "We made love."

"You *what?*" Esmerelda said with a rising anger.

"Hugo was helping me make wine. He wanted to make some using the old-fashioned stomping technique. He leaned in to kiss me. One thing led to another and—"

"Alice!" Esmerelda pressed her fingers against her forehead.

"I think I lo—" Alice stopped herself from saying the full word. "I really like him."

"Well, I certainly hope so, kiddo. I hope so," Esmerelda responded.

Alice dropped her eyes to the ground to hide her disappointment.

"Does he know about the spell?" Esmerelda asked.

Alice focused on her workstation. Her eyes locked on the hidden drawer in the stone wall. "He wouldn't know what to do with it if he did," Alice replied.

"Let's keep it that way," she said as she shoved the bottle back onto the rack. "If you are going to continue to see him, you're on your own if anything happens. There is no moving. There is no hiding. There is nothing. I can't afford it again."

Alice's hands trembled. Her lips quivered. She thought back to the night in the backyard. Coming to Hugo's defense at the Raskin's market. Hugo inviting her to the festival. Hugo making love to her. How Hugo made her feel like it was okay to be who she was.

I made the right choice.

Alice composed herself, stood tall, shoulders back, chest puffed out. "I'm willing to risk it."

"I hope you're right, kiddo," Esmerelda said. "I hope you're right, for your sake."

LATER THAT NIGHT, Hugo and Alice gathered in her living room. Max slept in front of the crackling fire. They sat on her red velvet couch; each occasionally took a sip from their wineglass. "You know, watching this on a TV isn't the same experience," Hugo said.

"People watch fireplaces on TV?" Alice asked.

"Oh yeah," Hugo replied. "Big industry. You have different fireplace types. You can have different music playing in the background. Not to mention holiday themes."

"Where's the coziness of that fire?"

"It's all part of the magic," Hugo said before he took a sip of wine. "That's magic with a *C*, by the way."

"Well, I prefer the real thing."

Alice took a sip of wine and then placed her glass on the coffee table. She snuggled against Hugo. He placed his arm around her to comfort her. He played with her vibrant purple hair.

"You should let Galahad down here to enjoy this."

"I keep him up there so people won't see him."

"You have this house well-guarded. I think he'll be okay every once in a while."

Alice repositioned her head so she could hear the beating of his heart. "I could think about it."

"Although, I guess a broomstick and a fireplace don't necessarily go together." They laughed. "Everything go okay with Ez today?"

There was a pause. Alice closed her eyes. "Why do you like me?"

Hugo took a sip before answering. "Is this another test? I was warned by you... well, your reflection... that there are always tests."

"No test." She opened her eyes. Her head slid down his chest as she repositioned herself to lay in his lap. She wanted a better view of his eyes. "I want to know. Why do you like me?"

"Well..." Hugo failed to continue in that moment. "You're optimistic. Compassionate. You're fun to be around."

"It feels like you're holding back. Tell me."

"Sexy..."

"That goes without saying."

Hugo sipped his wine, then set his glass down on the end table. "Honestly?"

She locked onto his eyes. "Always."

"You accept me with all of my faults. You know I'm broken, and you accept it."

A tear fell down her face, and Hugo wiped it away.

"Why do you like me?"

She blinked a few times to hold back the tears welling in her eyes. "Because you defend me. I'm broken too, and yet you still accept it.

You accept me for who I am, and you don't use that to your advantage."

Hugo smiled. "That's us. Two perfectly broken people." He bent down and kissed her on the forehead. "So, how do you change the channel on this fireplace?"

CHAPTER 16
THE UNUSUAL TABLE

Red ribbons adorned the tops of green wreaths that decorated every lamp post. Orangish-white lights illuminated the town center. Holiday shoppers entered and exited the stores carrying brightly colored packages and bags. A light snow fell on the area, enough to cover the ground and provide a festive touch to the surrounding buildings. A stark contrast to the foreboding, nighttime sky above as the clouds swirled and stewed, and the snow fell.

Hugo and Alice strolled in unison down the sidewalk. Their pair of steps left temporary impressions in the blanket of snow. She wrapped her arm around his torso, leaning into him. Her head and brimmed wool hat rested on his shoulder. Hugo was between her and the traffic on the streets. His arm wrapped around Alice's body, drawing her closer to him. They received the occasional odd glance, but were mostly greeted by smiling, welcoming faces.

They continued through the town center until they arrived at their destination, Antonio's Italian Ristorante. They hesitated outside the door and below the red, green, and white awning. Their colors matched the festive atmosphere in the town.

"Are you sure about this?" Alice asked. She lifted her head and found his eyes. "You don't have to if you don't want to. We can always go someplace else."

His gaze focused on the table in the window's corner. Empty. Waiting. He responded, "I'm sure."

He paused for a moment to gather the courage. He wanted to continue.

He smiled at Alice to remove the worry from her face. The fear faded as she smiled back. He opened the door, motioned with his head, and held it.

"Ladies first," he said as he waved her to go in.

Alice entered with a smile, her nose turned up to the sky. He followed behind.

Antonio's Italian Ristorante bustled with activity. People ate dinner as the night settled. Hugo and Alice approached the host standing at a podium.

"Hello, and welcome back to Antonio's Italian Ristorante. How many will be joining you tonight?" the host asked.

"Umm, just the two of us. Reservation under Dodds," Hugo replied. "The usual table this time, please."

"Right this way," the host said as he grabbed two menus.

The host guided them along a familiar path—a path Hugo had taken many times before. They weaved around a few tables, merely momentary obstacles, to their fated seats. The host placed the menus across from each other. The white linen tablecloth, nearly immaculate, draped over the round table. Neatly folded black napkins. A red Venetian candle jar rested in the center. The light flickered back and forth inside. The snowy setting outside was a backdrop for their evening through the corner windows.

"Enjoy," the host said before departing.

Hugo helped remove Alice's tailcoat and set it down on his seat. He held the seat while she sat down.

"Such a gentleman," she said.

"Well, I try to be," he replied as she helped push in her chair.

Alice removed her hat and handed it to Hugo. He took them over to one of the many coat racks placed throughout the restaurant. He took off his black wool winter coat and placed it next to hers. He returned and sat in his usual seat, the one in the corner of the window.

They watched through the window as the freshly falling snow enshrouded the landscape like their own personal snow globe. The white blanket covered the parked cars and sidewalks with a fine layer of powder. The perfect snowy canvas imprinted with the foot-prints of people passing by outside. The orange glow of the town lights splashed across the low hanging blanket of clouds swirling above. The restaurant was crowded, but to Hugo, they were the only two in this intimate setting.

"It's very beautiful," Alice said.

"It's why we always tried to get this table," Hugo replied. "It offers the best possible views both outside and inside."

He found Alice's eyes, focusing on her wide-eyed gaze. He smiled, and she returned the gesture. The purple hair. Her emerald green eyes. It drove him wild. He wanted to launch himself across this table into her waiting arms. He hadn't felt this emotional since—

"Welcome back, buddy boy," a familiar Italian accented voice interrupted. The strong smell of cheap cologne filled his nostrils. "How you doin'?"

Hugo shook his hand. "Good to see you, Antonio. Packed house tonight."

"We manage. We manage," he said before turning his attention to Alice. "I saw you walk in with a pretty girl, but I didn't think she'd be this stunning up close. Antonio Moretti. A pleasure to meet you." He extended out his hand toward her.

She shook his hand. "Alice Primrose. A pleasure as well. Hugo here told me that this was the best Italian restaurant in the state."

"The world," Antonio replied. "The world. Don't forget, they know about our meatballs back in Italy."

Alice gave Hugo a discerning glance. She jokingly scolded him, "You didn't tell me this is world famous."

"Must have slipped my mind," he replied with a deadpan expression.

"Hugo here is the best guy I know, and I know a lot of people." Antonio patted him on the back with his thick hand. "Don't let him fool ya. Hugo Dodds can be quite the scoundrel, if you know what I mean." He winked at Hugo and completed his familiar wingman routine.

"Oh, I know," Alice answered back. "I found out firsthand how much of a scoundrel he can be."

She winked at Hugo, and he blushed with embarrassment. Hugo rubbed his forehead as if he was invoking some magical ritual that would cause him to disappear from the room. It failed.

"What can I get you two to drink?"

"What's tonight's wine special?" Alice asked. "Hugo is something of a wine connoisseur, and I'm sure he'd tell you all the great things about it."

Alice placed an elbow on the table. She rested her chin in her palm and smiled a mischievous grin toward Hugo. She winked. Hugo rolled his eyes, and she blew him a kiss.

"Oh, a connoisseur?" Antonio remarked. "How about the best bottle for our resident wine connoisseur?"

Hugo jolted from the heft of Antonio's hand as he lightly smacked Hugo on the back. Antonio meandered away from the table.

"Connoisseur? *Really?*" Hugo playfully asked.

She winked at him. "A bit of pre-dinner flirting, my dear."

"You know, you could get on the wine list here. Think about it. Locally brewed wine. Here at Antonio's."

Alice dropped her gaze. She unfurled the black napkin and set it on her lap. "Oh, I don't know about that."

"Why not? You do make some good wine. Even if you took the extra special bits out. Between this place and the Raskin's Market, you'd make a fortune. It's what you want, isn't it?"

"I don't know. I already got a good thing going," Alice replied. "I mean I want to, but I don't want to ruin it with Ez."

"Think about it. Talk to her." Hugo grabbed the menu. "Besides, I'm sure you could work it into the deal so we can get free food all the time."

Alice paused and shot a disparaging glance at Hugo.

He buried his face behind the menu.

"Free food?"

He lowered the menu, meeting her eye to eye. "Well—" he started. "You would brew the wine. I, the local wine connoisseur, would approve of said wine. We should get our meals comped because we'd be here all the time, anyway."

He winked back. She cut off his gaze with her menu.

A waitress approached the table. She carried two empty wine-glasses and a greenish-black bottle. She set the glasses down in front of them and presented the bottle, holding it so the label was clearly displayed.

"A new offering, compliments of Antonio himself," the waitress said.

Their eyes locked on the familiar black and gray label and the elegant white lettering. The gold crown. The playing card suits. The heart on top.

"A bottle of *Red-Hearted Queen*."

Alice and Hugo locked eyes with each other. They arched their eyebrows with widened eyes and lips curled up. Hugo slightly shrugged his shoulders. Alice shrugged her shoulders with a slight head tilt in response. He assumed she had the same reservations he did about this particular brand. Hugo turned his attention to the waitress.

"That'll be fine," he said.

The waitress set the bottle on the table. She produced a winged corkscrew from her apron pocket and placed it atop the neck of the bottle. The wings lifted as she twisted it deeper into the soft wood cork. Each twist brought back memories of the bitter taste.

"There is definitely something else in this." The memory rushed back of Alice's initial assessment when taking that first sip. The memory of the bitter taste. Nothing like he'd ever tasted before in wine.

I should turn this down, but I can't offend Antonio. Suck it up and drink it.

The waitress pushed down on the handles, and a small pop broke the silence at the table. The cork was free from its hiding spot. Hugo watched every motion intently.

She removed the corkscrew and poured wine into both glasses. "I'll give you two a few minutes to look over the menu."

They gave each other unknowing glances.

"Well, Mr. Connoisseur," Alice egged him on. "Try it out."

Hugo grabbed the stem of the wineglass. He examined the reddish-purple liquid inside. He spun the glass around, releasing the aromatic flavors held within. He raised the glass to his nose, taking in all the smells.

"Fruity. Earthy. A hint of oak," Hugo said.

"So far, so good," Alice replied.

Hugo took a sip. He sloshed the liquid back and forth in his mouth. His taste buds savored the liquid before he gulped it down. His face contorted, not out of disgust, but frustration. There was a distinct taste, but he could not figure it out.

"There is a hint of something," Hugo said. "I still don't know what."

Alice grabbed her glass. She swirled it around and sniffed the inside before taking a sip. She made a face as the liquid washed over her taste buds. She swirled it around in her mouth before taking a drink. Her head tilted. Hugo thought she was searching for the answer about the mysterious ingredient.

"I don't know what that is," she replied. "There's something in this wine. I can't place it."

Hugo took another sip. "I think yours is better."

Alice smiled and raised her glass. "A toast."

Hugo followed suit. "A toast to what?"

"A beautiful evening with a handsome guy, whom I'm proud to see have the courage to be at this table tonight."

He glanced down at the black onyx ring on his hand. His head swirled, and his stomach twisted in knots. His body shivered as though his soul rattled. A jolt ran up his spine.

"Aren't the decorations beautiful?" Elizabeth said to Hugo. "I love the falling snow at Christmas time."

Hugo lurched back in his seat, shocked to see Elizabeth's face. Her hazel eyes. Her auburn hair. Her infectious smile. She now sat at the table in place of Alice.

"Is everything okay, Hugo?"

"You're not here," Hugo said. "You're not supposed to be here. Where is she?"

"Where is who?" Elizabeth asked.

"Alice." He raised his voice. "Where is Alice?"

"I don't know who you're talking about."

There was an eerie silence. No commotion from the various diners. No staff walking about. Only silence. He scanned the restaurant and found it barren. Tables and chairs were empty. The host was no longer at his familiar position, ready to greet anyone walking through the door. Antonio was nowhere to be found. He frantically searched, trying to find Alice. There was only the two of them. He set the glass down on the table. His face was pale—any sense of joy and excitement now gone.

"She was right there. Right where you're sitting," he yelled as he turned his attention back to Elizabeth. "Where did she go?"

"Hugo, you're scaring me," Elizabeth said with a frightened tone. She set her glass down.

"This isn't how it happened," Hugo said.

"How what happened?" Elizabeth asked as Hugo leapt from his chair. "Where are you going?"

"I have to get out of here," he exclaimed.

He ran through the empty restaurant, weaving around the tables.

He followed the familiar path to the exit. He tried to open the door, but it wouldn't budge. He tried again. It was unrelenting. He pulled and jostled at the door, but nothing happened.

"You can't leave, Hugo," Elizabeth said. "You can't abandon me." She rose from the table. Her arms were rigid at her side while her shoulders raised. Her head tilted, and her normally hazel eyes glowed red. "You can't leave, Hugo. You're here with me. Forever. Like you promised."

She crept toward Hugo. The table and chairs pushed aside, screeching across the floor as she rambled into them. Her eyes grew brighter as she approached.

"Stay with me, Hugo," she pleaded. "Stay with me forever. Like you promised."

He pulled at the door, but it wouldn't budge. He pulled again and again. It wouldn't give way. He slammed his shoulder into the glass, trying to break free. Over and over. Each time, he bounced further and further away as it felt like the glass was growing stronger.

The top of the door bled wine from the outside. The reddish-purple liquid covered up the picturesque winter landscape he was trying to escape to. He recoiled in fear, letting out a scream.

He grabbed a chair and gave thought to smashing the nearest window. He reared back, ready to strike with all his might. He stopped. Each window bled wine now. The wine covered windows cut off the outside world. The restaurant grew dim.

Elizabeth crept closer and closer. Each step lingered to allow the fear to set in. The lights from the Venetian candle jars faded as she passed. Her face decayed and sunk with each step. Her skin shriveled, giving her a skeleton like appearance. Her ghastly hand outstretched. The skeleton like fingers clawed at the air, beckoning Hugo.

"You said you'd love me forever, Hugo," Elizabeth cried out in a dark, agonized tone. It almost echoed on every word as it filled Hugo's ears. "You said we'd be together. Forever. And now we will."

The light faded. The restaurant grew darker.

Hugo slammed the chair into the glass window only for it to bounce off. He tried again. The window grew stronger with every blow. He threw the chair across the ground to impede her progress, but she pushed it aside. She never wavered.

He screamed in frustration as he pulled at the door in one last desperate attempt. Her hand brushed against his face. The terror set in—the realization that there was no escape.

"You're mine, Hugo Dodds," Elizabeth said in a deep voice conjured from a place of darkness Hugo dared to not venture. "You're mine. Now and forever."

Her hand engulfed his face. A cold sensation ripped through his body toward his soul. Everything became dark as the world faded away. There was nothing, only darkness. A rush of emotions overcame Hugo—loneliness, isolation, desperation, sadness, horror, fear. He swirled in a vortex of pain and suffering in this empty void.

"Forever," Elizabeth's ghoulish voice said through the darkness. "We're here forever."

He tried to scream, but there was nothing. There was only the void. His eternal fate.

"Hugo," a familiar voice cried out.

He recognized that voice. Alice. Her voice felt like an anchor in this whirlwind of bleakness. He wasn't in a bleak void. He was seated at his usual table in Antonio's Italian Ristorante with his dinner date, Alice Primrose. Everything rushed back to him. Streaks of light fought back against the darkness.

"Hugo," Alice said.

She snapped her fingers in front of his face. He shook his head, gasping for air as the world—the real world—came back to him.

"Are you okay? You kind of zoned out there for a moment."

He still held onto the wineglass they had toasted moments before. Sweat dripped down his back. He breathed heavily in and out. He set the drink down and rubbed his temples, trying to calm his nerves.

"I'm sorry," Hugo said in a dizzying attempt to gather his thoughts. "I... I don't know what happened. We were... We were toasting and then, all of a sudden, it was like I had a living nightmare. Everyone was gone. You were gone. Elizabeth was there, but it was like she was some sort of ghoul. She tried to claw at me and... and I couldn't escape. Everything went dark. And then I heard your voice. And I snapped out of it."

Alice set her glass down on the table far away from her. "I think we've had enough of this *Red-Hearted Queen*."

"It was so real and terrifying." Hugo gazed numbly at a spot on the table.

Alice grabbed Hugo's hands across the table. She locked onto his eyes. "It's okay. Breathe with me," Alice assured him.

She breathed in deeply, and he matched her. She held it for a moment before letting out a drawn-out breath. He followed. They repeated it a few more times.

"Do you feel better?"

He nodded.

"How's the wine tasting tonight?" the waitress asked as she returned to the table. "Are we ready to order?"

Alice broke her gaze with Hugo. "There's a funny taste to this wine." Alice pointed to the bottle. "I think we're done with it."

"Oh! I can get you another bottle," the waitress replied.

"No!" Hugo piped up. "Water. Water would be fine."

"I'll be right back." The waitress grabbed the bottle and walked away from the table.

"We can leave if you want," Alice said.

Hugo shook his head. "No. I promised you the best Italian food in Newbury Grove. We're going to have the best Italian food in Newbury Grove. I'm not going to let one nightmare ruin the whole evening."

"Don't you mean the world-famous Italian food of Newbury Grove?" Alice asked.

They let out a chuckle. They found each other's eyes once more.

Hugo became lost in her emerald greens. Alice gazed into his icy blues. They smiled before picking up their menus.

"So," Alice said. "What do you recommend?"

"The meatballs are excellent," Hugo said with a wink. "They're world famous."

"Back at your usual table?" a shrill voice interrupted.

Alice cringed and buried herself behind the menu. Hugo closed his eyes, dropped the menu, and soothed an imaginary headache. They both turned to see Johanna wrapping a burnt orange scarf around her neck.

"Good evening, Johanna," Hugo replied. "How was your meal?"

"Adequate," she answered. Johanna neatly tucked the burnt orange scarf into the black overcoat that accentuated her tall, lanky frame. She removed a pair of black leather gloves from her pockets. She slipped them on and gave two taps to the cloak clasp pinned to her coat lapel.

"You should have tried the meatballs," Alice retorted.

"I did," Johanna responded. "As I said, adequate."

Johanna leered at Alice. Her eyes grew narrower with each passing moment. Alice matched her gaze. Their eyes locked into an unrelenting, unseen combat of who would blink first. The tension was too much for Hugo.

"That's a shame," Hugo interjected. "They're world famous. Maybe it was a bad batch."

"Maybe I'm loyal to my own meatballs," Johanna replied as she gave a few taps to her cloak clasp.

"Maybe you can give Hugo some of yours to try. Like a taste test," Alice interjected. "A competition for world's best meatball. It's going to be hard to dethrone a meatball that's famous in Italy."

"Maybe." Johanna gave Alice a scornful look. "Enjoy your evening." She turned and headed to the exit.

"Don't let the door hit you on the way out." Alice held up her left hand and readied to snap her fingers.

"Don't!" Hugo said in a hushed tone.

"She's not worth it," Alice replied as she picked up her menu. "So, about those meatballs."

"Hmm," Hugo replied. "You gave me an idea."

"Good or bad?"

Hugo grinned at Alice.

CHAPTER 17
CHRISTMAS COOKIE EXCHANGE

"You know I'm not a kitchen witch, right?" Alice asked.

"There's a difference in witches?" Hugo responded as he sifted through her kitchen cabinets looking for mixing bowls, measuring cups, and other utensils.

"Of course there are. We have our own areas of expertise. It's like our profession," Alice answered. "There are apothecary witches, like me, who brew potions. Then you have kitchen witches who specialize in baking. Green herbal witches grow things. Medicinal witches. Coven witches like Ez who keep knowledge and secrets. Cosmic—"

"Cosmic?" Hugo gave Alice a puzzled look.

"They specialize in astrology and tarot and stuff like that," Alice answered. "Then there are the eclectics who dabble in a bit of everything, but master none of it."

"So, what is this? Like a major in college or something?"

"No! Not like a major." She paused and thought for a moment. "Yeah. Actually, kind of like a major. You pick an area you want to focus in and study it. I picked apothecary brewing, which is why I make my magical wine. I didn't choose baking."

"I'm not asking you to make magical cookies. They're regular, old Christmas cookies. How hard can it be? We follow the recipes and boom. Cookies. No magick."

"No magick?" Alice asked with a discerning look on her face.

Hugo placed the gathered items on the island in the center of the kitchen. "No. We're giving them to Johanna. Elizabeth did this every year. This might help fix whatever icy relationship the two of you have."

"She started it," Alice retorted.

"I know, but a little kindness goes a long way. It's the holiday season, after all."

"Fine," Alice relented. "I'll help bake them. For Christmas' sake." She moved to the island and plopped her hands on the wooden countertop. Her head tilted to the side.

"Fair warning, though," she continued. "I'm not the best baker in the world."

"Neither am I. We can be the worst bakers in the world together."

"There is this whole store dedicated to baked goods in the town center. What is it called? The name escapes me." Alice held up a finger to her chin and gazed at the ceiling. "Oh yeah! They call it a bakery because, you know, they bake stuff. Like baked goods. And cookies."

Hugo moved around the island and hugged Alice. His hands moved up and down her back. Alice quivered the further down his hands traveled. They inched closer and closer to the small of her back with each passing rub.

"Where is your Christmas spirit? You don't buy cookies in a cookie exchange. That's the whole point."

"I have plenty of Christmas spirit, thank you very much. I don't have a lot of baking spirit."

"Well, I'll cover you in that area." Hugo released her and strode to the pantry. He removed a bag of flower and sugar. He proceeded to the refrigerator to gather eggs, a box of baking soda, and other ingre-

dients. He carefully placed each item on the island in their desig-
nated places.

"You know, if you want the best cookies, we should ask Holly,"
Alice offered.

Hugo paused. "Who's Holly?"

"Holly. Holly Claus. Santa's wife. She's a kitchen witch," Alice
replied with a confused look. "You don't know who Holly is?"

"First, I've never heard of Holly Claus, only Mrs. Claus," Hugo
answered. "Second, there is no Santa Claus or Mrs. Claus."

Alice stood there with crossed arms. Her face was solemn, and
her eyes were piercing. Hugo's smile faded to worry.

"How dare you?"

"You... you don't still believe, do you?" Hugo asked.

"First, the Clauses are the nicest people I've ever met." Alice
raised a finger to illustrate her point.

"You're joking, right?"

Any figurative pretense of staring daggers seemed to manifest
thoughts of Alice literally throwing kitchen knives. Alice snapped her
fingers, and the refrigerator, cabinet, and pantry doors flung open.
Hugo ducked behind the island as all the items he previously placed
on the wooden countertop flew past his head and found their way
back to their original storage homes. The doors slammed shut with
another snap of Alice's fingers.

"Second, you're being very insulting right now, especially this
close to Christmas. Third, the Clauses make frequent visits to Ez's
place throughout the year. I've known them for a while. Fourth,
Holly's shortbread cookies are the best. She gives me a batch every
year for Christmas. They are the best you'll ever taste if—and right
now that's a big if—I'm feeling in the Christmas giving mood."

"Perfect." Hugo rose from the sanctity of his hiding spot. "So,
you're already familiar with cookie exchanges."

Alice stormed out of the kitchen.

"Alice!" Hugo shouted as he followed her into the hallway. "Alice,
wait."

Her footsteps echoed down the hallway as she stormed off. Fresh, lush evergreen garland adorned the hallway. The smell of cinnamon and pine permeated throughout the house. Red and green candles were lit in their black candelabras atop the antique tables.

Max and Galahad rushed into the hallway from the living room, excited to see the commotion. Max's tail swung low, back and forth. Galahad hovered at eye level. It surveyed the hallway, looking for any signs of trouble, only to be excited at the sight of Alice and Hugo.

"I'm sorry."

She stopped and held an arm back, wiggling her fingers. He accepted her unspoken invitation and grabbed her hand. She turned around to face him. He batted his eyes in his attempt at an apology. Max nudged Alice's free hand.

"Look, I'm sorry if I offended you. I was joking around."

"It hurt, Hugo," Alice replied. "It didn't feel like joking around."

Hugo's playful expression turned morose.

"She's not that hurt," a familiar voice yelled from upstairs.

"We don't need input from you," Alice yelled back.

In a rhythmic, sarcastic response, the voice replied, "I know what she really wants."

"Enough from the peanut gallery," Alice replied as she snapped her fingers.

The bedroom door slammed shut, and the voice upstairs became muffled.

"This is important to me," Hugo said. "Because it was important to Elizabeth. I want to make sure it continues. And I think it will go a long way to help patch things up. I've known Johanna for a while. I don't want things to be awkward, especially if—"

"If what?" Alice asked.

"If whatever this is continues."

Alice pulled back her hand and placed both hands on her hips. She gave him another glare of impending doom. She asked, "So, what is this then?"

Hugo sighed. He carefully considered his next words, knowing full well the importance they carried. "This has been... heaven," he replied.

Alice narrowed her eyes in a discerning, puzzled gaze. He touched both of Alice's hands. She allowed him to hold and lift them.

"This past month and a half has meant more to me than anything you could understand. I want things to continue on our journey. I don't want a neighborhood war to break out between two of the few people I still care about," Hugo said.

Alice glanced down at the floor and then back toward Hugo. His mouth curled into a half smile. His eyes somber, yet hopeful. She glanced away again for a moment. She found his eyes once more and smiled.

"Okay. Okay. I'll do this, but only for you," she replied.

She pulled her hands away from Hugo and snapped her fingers. All the items in the kitchen returned to the places Hugo had assigned them.

Hugo wrapped his arms around Alice and pulled her closer. Alice blushed as their bodies pressed against each other. Her heart beat against his chest. He kissed her on the forehead.

"Perfect," Hugo said as joy returned to his face.

He let go of her and marched to the kitchen, leaving her behind. Max followed. Galahad floated past Alice. It stopped and turned to face her.

"Oh, come on," Alice said as she plodded past. "You can help too."

Galahad circled around in excitement and followed everyone into the kitchen.

Alice stood next to Hugo. Their shoulders touched. She leaned into him. He soaked it all in—her presence, her breath, her aura. A sensation coursed through Hugo's body. He smiled and winked at her. She placed her hand on top of his.

She tilted her head toward him and whispered into his ear, "Where do we start?"

A shiver ran down his back.

"First," Hugo began as he analyzed the recipe. "We mix all the ingredients in the bowl."

They read through the list and divided the items. Their hands smacked against each other as they took turns adding their assigned items to a large, glass mixing bowl.

"I didn't realize baking was a contact sport," Alice said.

Hugo leaned closer and whispered, "That's what makes it fun together." He gave a wink and then stood up straight. "Now we mix." He focused on Alice, waiting for her to act.

"With what?" Alice surveyed the table.

"Do your thing. Mix it together," he replied with a swirling motion of his finger.

"You said no magick."

"Well, I assumed that's how you mixed stuff."

She bent down and opened a cabinet door. She pulled out a handheld mixer and stood back up. She dangled it in front of him. "You know what they say about someone who assumes. It makes an ass out of you—"

"I thought you liked my ass?" he interrupted.

"Right now, that's questionable," she replied as she shoved the mixer against Hugo's chest.

He chuckled and took the mixer. He plugged it in and stirred the bowl, transforming the ingredients into dough. "Take the flour and spread some on the table."

Alice spread out the flour.

"Now, sprinkle a little more on the dough," he instructed.

"Sprinkle a little more?" Alice dipped her fingers into the bag of flour.

"Yeah."

"Like this?" She flung a puff of the white powder toward Hugo's face.

He stopped the mixer in shock. She put an elbow on the table and rested her face in her palm. She gave an impish smile toward her handiwork.

A surprise smile overcame him. Hugo set the mixer down and pushed the bowl toward the middle of the table. He mirrored her pose. Elbow on the table. Flour covered face resting in the palm of his hand. A knowing expression. He licked the flour around his lips. She winked at him.

"Why, Ms. Primrose, I do believe you're flirting with me."

"If I was flirting, you'd know it."

"Oh yeah?"

"If I was flirting, I might have dumped some flour on your head like this." She snapped her fingers with her open hand.

A cloud of flour extruded from the bag toward Hugo. His hair and face were now covered in the white powder. Galahad bounced through the air in excitement. Max barked at Galahad's movements.

Hugo stood up. "Well, Ms. Primrose. You picked the wrong person to have a food fight with."

He peeled off a small clump of dough from within the bowl and flung it toward Alice. She snapped her fingers. The little lump of dough stopped in midair.

"No magick," Hugo shouted.

"That's not fair," Alice responded.

"Exactly."

He grabbed the bowl and chased Alice. She ran away, circling around the island. Alice snatched the bag of flour and proceeded to fling bits of powder toward Hugo. He gave chase.

He flung small bits of dough back as he became like a ghostly apparition. They circled the island, giddy with glee. Alice allowed Hugo to catch up to her. He wrapped his free arm around her.

"And now, Ms. Primrose, the champion of food fighting shall reclaim his crown." He raised the bowl to dump the contents on her head.

"Gally, save me!" Alice playfully called as she pretended to struggle in Hugo's grip.

Galahad flew across the table to her aid by poking at Hugo's ribs.

"Easy, Gally. Easy," Hugo said. Each poke was less playful than the last. Hugo set the bowl on the tabletop. A sharp pain emanated from his side from Galahad's latest glancing blow. "That one hurt. Max, help!"

Max rushed to Hugo's side, not to help him, but to save Alice. She jumped up and pushed against Hugo, giving a loud bark with each shove.

"Traitor!" Hugo called out. "You're supposed to help me."

Max continued to shove the pair. With the combination of Galahad's pokes and Max's shoving, the pair wobbled.

Hugo and Alice fell to the floor. He was able to twist them around so he hit the floor and Alice landed on top, straddling him. They laid on the floor face-to-face. Her purple hair engulfed his head. Their noses nearly touched. They lost themselves in each other's eyes. Lost in a dark, secret language they only knew. They smiled and chuckled.

Alice moved in and kissed Hugo. Her soft lips pressed against his flour covered ones. Each kiss was longer and deeper than the last. He moved his hands to the back of her head. His fingers intertwined in her purple hair. His other hand wrapped around her waist, attempting to pull her closer than was possible.

He curled his fingers along her back. As they continued kissing, Hugo was set ablaze with passion. After a few minutes, he pulled his hand away from her hair, and they stopped kissing. They locked onto each other and breathed deeply together. Hugo yearned for more.

"So, I guess we'll have to start over then, huh?" Hugo stated.

JOHANNA SAT in her high-back chair looking out her living room window. The drab and dreary gray December sky blotted out the setting sun. A light blanket of fresh snow on the ground covered the slumbering yellowish grass beneath. Desolate trees lined the street. A few cars passed by the window. She sipped her cup of tea. Her eyes always kept a watchful vigilance over her neighborhood street, as was her daily ritual. She glanced up and down the street, but her eyes focused on the real threat. The black door of the purple house across the street.

She took another sip of her steaming Earl Grey tea.

There was motion. The black door opened. Johanna set the tea cup down in the saucer dish she held with her other hand. She placed them both on the stand next to the window. She sat up straight with her eyes focused. They widened as Alice emerged from the door and jogged down the steps. Alice continued across the street. Alice held a small, red box in her hands. Johanna held her breath. Alice continued past her parked, black SUV.

This is it, Johanna thought as she stood up and pulled the curtains shut. She hurried over to the display table that held her dark tools, the ones that would help her exact her revenge.

JOSIAH NEWES PUSHED his way through the crowd. He tried desperately to save his daughter bound and tied to the tree.

"Please. Please stop this," Johanna cried out. "I'm not a witch." She screamed. Her body went limp, head buried into her chest. Only the ropes kept her body upright.

"Behold," Thaddeus proclaimed. He removed his oversized tricorn hat, lifting it high into the air. "The amulet of witch's fire claims yet another witch!"

The crowd erupted in cheers of jubilation.

Josiah pushed further toward the center. "No! No! Not my daughter," he yelled as he finally broke free of the crowd. "Not my Johanna. She's no witch."

He rushed to her side. He removed the restraints, catching her limp body as it fell into his arms. He was an older gentleman, not particularly muscular, but he was able to lift her body and carry it. The crowd hissed and booed as he picked up her lifeless body.

"My friends. My friends. Our deed is done," Thaddeus yelled to silence the crowd. He turned his attention to Josiah. He smiled a wicked grin. "Besides, we are not mad barbarians. Let him take her to give her a proper burial."

Josiah carried her body to a horse-drawn cart. He struggled to place her onto the back of the cart. His grip nearly slipped. He lifted his knee to help push her lifeless body as it rolled onto the wooden platform. Josiah ran to the front, climbed aboard, and whipped the horse to ride off. Thaddeus smiled and placed his hat back on his head.

The horse pulled the cart as fast as it could. Josiah jostled with every rut and bump in the road. He whipped the reins, begging the horse to run faster. It felt like an eternity. The road went on and on with no end. He glanced back to Johanna's lifeless body. It rocked back and forth. Faster and faster, they went down the path until they arrived at a walking path hidden off the main road.

Josiah pulled back on the reins; the cart struggled to come to a full stop without wanting to plow through the horse. He leapt down from the seat and grabbed Johanna's body. He ran with her down the dirt walking path. Deeper and deeper, he ventured into the woods. Her body was heavy. The amulet waved around her neck. His grip slipped as he stumbled over tree roots. He nearly fell, but he was able to hold himself upright. His lungs burned. He wanted to stop, but he kept going deeper into the woods.

There was a cabin in a clearing of the woods. He ran up to the door and kicked it. He waited. It opened outward. Standing in the doorway was an elderly woman. She wore a black dress covered in dirt. Her gray, curly hair was matted and tangled in knots. Her face was unwashed. Her skin was old and leathery from working the fields in too much sun.

"What happened?" she asked in a panic.

"They burned my daughter," Josiah replied as he carried Johanna's body into the cabin.

"Set her on the table. Quickly!" the old woman exclaimed. She rushed to a shelf of bottles and jars, grabbing a few in a hurried pace. "How long ago?"

"Not long."

"She's dying. We don't have much time." She went to her fire-place. A black cauldron of bubbling water hung above the fire. She removed the cauldron and handed it to Josiah. "Empty this outside. I need to start fresh."

He rushed to the door and dumped the contents onto the ground. He brought the cauldron back. She hovered over Johanna's body. She worked to remove her black petticoat. Each button resisted. She pulled and tugged before all eight buttons were undone. The white undershirt was now fully exposed with a black, charred burn mark.

Josiah covered his mouth to prevent himself from throwing up. Tears gathered in his eyes. "What have they done to my daughter?"

The woman tore at the undershirt. A similar black burn mark festered out in spiderweb like patterns across Johanna's chest. Their black veins grew and clawed their way outward across her breasts right before their eyes.

"We might be too late," she said. "I don't have enough time to make a potion."

"Please, Willow," Josiah begged through his tears. "She's all I have left. Please. We have to try something. I can't lose her. I can't lose anyone else."

Willow examined the amulet of witch's fire. Her fingers ran over the ridges of the jewels. She touched Johanna's face. She nodded to Josiah. "I can try something. It's not perfect. I can use magick on the device that did this to bring her back. But if I do this, she'll forever be tied to the fate of this amulet. As long as this amulet exists, so will she."

"Do it," Josiah said. A solitary tear flowed down his face. "Anything to bring her back. She's all I have. Please."

Willow pulled out a leatherbound grimoire. She flipped through the pages until she found the needed entry. She held the amulet of witch's fire with her right hand. She placed her left hand over Johann's heart and recited an incantation. The language and words were foreign to Josiah. The spiderweb mark slowly retreated into the black mark until both disappeared. As she finished, Johanna sprang up and gasped for air.

THE MEMORY of the gasp jolted Johanna back to reality. She wanted the satisfaction of finishing *that* memory, but it was for another time. She prepared herself for what was to come. Johanna turned the brass key in the center leaf. The locks clicked. Johanna double tapped her pinned cloak clasp before opening the left drawer. She withdrew the black, twisted wand held within.

There was a knock at the door.

Johanna turned and proceeded toward it, not in a hurry, but cautious. She held the anti-magick wand out in front, ready to strike. The tip pointed toward the door. Her steps carefully placed. Her eyes shifted from the door to the window and then back to the door. Always cautious. Always vigilant.

Another knock echoed through the entryway and living room. Johanna went to grab the doorknob, but stopped short.

"Who is it?" Johanna called out.

A muffled voice spoke, "It's Alice. From across the street. We have a gift for you."

Johanna paused and thought, *We? No. That's her trick. Her trick to get you.* Johanna gripped the wand tighter. The ridges indented into her hand. She moved to the side of the door. Sure of her aim, the tip of the wand was ready.

Johanna used her other hand to unlock the deadbolt and then gripped the doorknob.

"Just a moment," she yelled back. She took a deep breath and rotated the silver knob. Johanna exhaled and then yanked the door open.

Her eyes widened as standing in the doorway was not Alice, but Hugo looking toward someone out of her view. She pulled the wand back and stuffed it into her pocket.

"Hugo," Johanna said in shocked amazement. She opened the door further and stood in the threshold. "What a nice surprise."

"We brought you something," Hugo said.

"Merry Christmas, Johanna," Alice followed.

She handed Johanna the small, red box. Johanna laid her eyes on the box, trying to decide if she should take it or not.

The pause lingered.

"It's homemade sugar cookies," Hugo said. "Not as elaborate as Elizabeth used to make, but we thought we'd continue the tradition in her memory."

"It took us three attempts to make them. We kept getting... interrupted," Alice said. "We made them with that extra Christmas magick." Alice winked at Hugo.

Johanna stood there, caught off guard by the gesture. "I..." Johanna began as she took the box. "I don't know what to say."

Hugo smiled. "It's been a tough year for both of us. I thought maybe a little cookie exchange could help to make the season bright."

"I wasn't expecting this." Johanna raised her eyes from the box to Hugo. "I don't have anything to give you."

"Don't worry about it," Hugo said. "Keeping Elizabeth's tradition alive is good enough for us."

Alice added, "It was all Hugo's idea."

"Thank you. Thank you for honoring her memory. I hope you continue to do so."

"The Raskins are coming over to my house for Christmas dinner. We'd be honored if you joined us," Hugo said.

Johanna's mouth dropped. First, cookies, and now an invitation for Christmas dinner. She never expected a Christmas invitation. She was at a loss for words. She focused on the box of cookies. The fleeting thought of accepting crossed her mind. Johanna glimpsed Alice's pointed hat, and the words came flooding back. "I appreciate the gesture, but I already have plans on Christmas. I'm seeing some friends. Out of town."

"That's okay," Hugo responded. "Maybe next year."

"I really do appreciate everything," Johanna said. "Thank you."

"You're welcome. Merry Christmas," Hugo said.

He winked at Alice and blew her a kiss. They turned, locked hands, and strolled back toward the purple house.

Johanna watched them cross the street before shutting the front door. She opened the cardboard box to peer at the yellowish cookies held within. She removed one and took a bite. The sugary goodness melted in her mouth. She was taken aback by how good they tasted. Almost as good as the ones Elizabeth used to make, but still not quite.

Johanna set the box down on the table next to her tea cup as she proceeded to return the wand to its drawer. She went to the window, drew open the curtains, and returned to her duties as she sat in her wingback chair. She opened the box and took out the half-eaten cookie to take another bite.

CHAPTER 18
YULETIDE BLESSINGS

"Wake up," Alice whispered into Hugo's ear as he slept on the side of his body. The hairs on his arms stood up as the gush of wind and her warm breath washed over their ridges. "Hugo. Wake up."

He stretched out his legs and tugged at the bedsheets before recalling them back to make himself into a ball. He grunted a refusal at her beckoning siren call.

"It's Christmas morning," she whispered before kissing his cheek.

He pulled the bedsheets over his head to ward off any further attempts to wake him from his winter slumber. Alice poked Hugo over the bedsheets.

"Wake up!" she pleaded as she shook his body. "It's Christmas morning. It finally came. Wake up!" She rocked him back and forth with enough energy to wake the dead.

Maxine let out a soul piercing bark.

"Ahhh," Hugo shouted as he flew off the covers to see Max's head resting on the mattress. "Not so close to the ears."

She wiggled her tail and spun around in circles with excitement.

Galahad mimicked her every move, while circling around Alice's bedroom. It stopped when Maxine stopped.

"I see how it is," Hugo said to the excited pup. "Betrayed by my own dog. Traitor."

He rolled over. The face of a purple haired witch gleamed down at him. Her eyes were wide with anticipation, and she had a giddy smile on her face. Her arms were tucked closely to her body as she was ready to spring up from the bed. She was a wound ball of energy ready to set loose on the goodies that awaited them downstairs. She could hardly restrain her excitement.

"I'm guessing it's Christmas morning," Hugo said.

"It's Christmas morning!" Alice yelled as she rolled backward off the bed.

Alice made a mad dash for the bedroom door, nearly tripping on her purple pajama pant leg before she caught herself. The door flew open with a snap of her finger, and she disappeared into the hallway. Maxine and Galahad followed, leaving Hugo alone in the room.

"She really likes Christmas," Alice's reflection said from the bathroom. Hugo was mostly alone in the room. "I should have warned you."

"Thanks for the heads up," he replied.

"You're welcome."

Hugo grabbed his black onyx ring. He spun it around a few times. The ghosts of his Christmas past flew by in an instant.

He whispered in a hushed breath, "Merry Christmas, Elizabeth. I hope you're having a good one. I know I am."

He rolled out of bed. He stretched out his shoulders and neck, then entered the bathroom and turned on the lights. Alice's mirror reflection stared back with a befuddled gaze.

"Merry Christmas," Hugo said.

Alice's reflection was at a loss for words, which was unusual for her. She broke the silence after a moment, "No one has ever wished me Merry Christmas before."

"Glad I could be the first," he replied. "I meant it. Merry

Christmas."

"Merry Christmas, Hugo," she replied. "She's waiting for you."

Hugo nodded with a smile and left the bathroom.

"Hugo!" Alice's reflection beckoned him to return.

He popped his head back through the door.

"She loves you, you know?"

"Of course. I do too."

"Then tell her."

Hugo lowered his head in thought before nodding back.

Alice's reflection smiled. "Go on," she said. "Go join her."

"On or off?" He pointed to the light switch.

"Leave it on."

Hugo gave her a wink and disappeared back behind the wall.

The sound of Christmas merriment grew louder with each step as Hugo descended the stairs. The nails on Max's feet clacked against the hardwood floor. Alice's giddy excitement as she riffled through wrapped packages. The sound of Christmas music. Nothing modern, but old classics as Alice preferred. Hugo didn't even recognize some as they were in a Gaelic tongue. The smells of cinnamon, dried oranges, and pine greeted Hugo as he moved into the entryway of the living room.

He stood there and took in the sensations of the moment. The Yule log crackled in the fireplace. Melting wax candles of green and gold adorned the mantle between hanging stockings at both ends. Their bubbly, gnarled, icicle like drippings nearly clawed their way to the floor, like ghostly apparitions of Christmas past wanting to join in the festivities of present day. A large red candle stood in the center; it was large enough to burn for a week. This was the Christmas candle—the symbol of the returning light through the darkest of nights.

The decorated Christmas tree, nearly as tall as the ceiling, was nestled snugly in the back corner of the living room on the other side of the red velvet couch. Streams of gold and silver lined the walls. Greenery of holly, pine cones, and wreathes decorated the room on every surface. They competed for space alongside Alice's usual assortment of maximalist possessions. Some nearly fell off, but Hugo knew there was enough magick in the living room to keep them in place.

This felt right to Hugo. This felt like home. He burnt the sensations of that morning into his memory.

Max was busy snooping and smelling every present. Galahad followed Max, mimicking her every movement. Alice removed her presents from beneath the tree. She sorted the brightly colored packages in order of the ones that she wanted to open first, alternating between large and small. Alice raised her head away from her duties toward Hugo standing in the entryway.

He pointed to the greenery that hung above his head. "I'm standing under mistletoe."

"Well, you know what that means," Alice said with a mischievous grin.

He returned the grin with a come-hither stare. She stood and approached him. She ran her fingers through her hair, pulling it back behind her ears. She pouted her lips. A smolder in her eyes. He stood up tall with his chest out. Alice stopped short and blew him a kiss.

"First. Presents," Alice said as she tiptoed back to her bounty laid out on the ground.

Hugo didn't feel disappointed. He chuckled and added this moment to his slideshow of memories.

Hugo joined Alice on the floor. Max wormed her way into his lap.

"Okay. Okay. Merry Christmas to you too," he said.

Galahad followed suit and laid across Alice's lap. Hugo and Alice both smiled at each other for a moment. It felt like an eternity passing in an instant. They laughed and rubbed their respective pets.

"Give me. Give me," Hugo said.

They tore into their presents. They opened their presents one at a time and explained the special meaning behind the gift. Alice snapped up a large package in purple paper with silver ribbon.

"Wait!" Hugo said. Startled, she paused. "Open that one last."

"Well, now I want to open it even more." Alice turned the neatly wrapped gift to examine all sides. It was the only one wrapped in purple paper.

"It's special."

"That's really not helping this situation."

"Go ahead," Hugo said with a giddy glee.

Alice's eyes widened. She wildly ripped the paper as if it was of no importance to her. She dug through the contents inside. The purple paper gave way to a black cardboard box. She flung open the lid. Her jaw dropped as if all the excitement left her body.

Hugo recoiled slightly out of fear that he misjudged his special gift. Alice cupped her mouth. She leaned in closer to examine the contents.

"Do you..." Hugo began. "Do you like them?"

Alice pulled out a stone mortar and pestle. *Alice Primrose* was engraved in purple letters along the side of the bowl and the pestle. She pulled out six more, each engraved with her name in a different color.

"I thought no one could take them from you if they had your name on 'em," Hugo explained. "And I got different colors, so you can coordinate them to individual spells."

Alice's eyes glistened. A solitary tear ran down her face; she quickly wiped it away. "I love them," she mustered in a hushed tone.

"For a moment, I thought—"

"This is the best Christmas present I've ever received. Thank you."

Hugo smiled. "I'm glad you like it."

Alice placed them back in the box. She shoved Galahad off her lap before diving under the tree. She reemerged with a small, rectangular package about the size of her hand. She handed it to Hugo.

"Open," she commanded. "I was going to wait, but now seems appropriate."

Hugo carefully removed the tape from the folded corners. Unlike

Alice, he wanted to take his time and savor opening his special gift. He removed the paper to reveal a flat, white box designed to hold jewelry.

The air flowed up inside the box as it rushed to fill in the space when the two sides separated. Purple tissue paper stood between him and his special Christmas gift. He peeled back a corner. He relished the anticipation of what could be inside.

"Hurry up and open it," Alice blurted.

"I'm savoring this moment."

"Savor faster."

Hugo pulled back the paper to reveal an antique, brass door key. The toothy end was offset with two open circles merging to form a heart shape. Odd marks were etched into the key shaft. He examined it closer. It was surprisingly heavy for its diminutive size. It wasn't like any key he had seen before. It was well worn and weathered—it had clearly been used a few times.

Hugo was a little confused. "Is this a key to your wine cellar?"

"Better," she replied. She motioned to the front door. "That door, when shut, can only be opened from the outside with a special key. There are three of them. I have one. Ez has another. And now you."

Hugo's eyes snapped to Alice, wide with shock. He was at a loss for words.

"I hope you like it."

"I'll..." he started as he shoved it into his pajama pocket. "I'll guard it with my life. Thank you."

"You don't have to be that dramatic," Alice said before she tore into a new package. "It's just a key." She winked at him.

"Oh, it's more than *just* a key."

They finished opening their gifts.

"I have a gift for Max." Alice handed Hugo a small round package.

Hugo ripped open the paper to reveal a plush, black cauldron dog toy with a bubbly green top and cloth flames sewn to the bottom. He squeaked it a few times. Max nearly knocked Hugo over as she attempted to take it from him. He relinquished it, and she sprinted throughout the house, squeaking away at her newly acquired toy. Her toenails clacked across the hardwood floor.

"Every witch needs her own cauldron. I called Nick and asked him to make it special," Alice said.

"Nick?"

"Santa Claus."

"Oh. Right," he replied as he dug under the tree. "And I have a gift for Gally."

Galahad bounced around the room with delight.

"Look at you, Hugo," Alice said with a smile. "A gift for a broomstick."

"Honestly, it's a gift for all three of us."

Alice ripped into the package as soon as he passed it over. Galahad waited with bated breath at the big reveal. Alice opened the box to find a mountable footrest.

"It's so I... I mean, we... can catch ourselves before falling off. And so our feet aren't dangling. Lightweight so it won't weigh Gally down. It connects right to the seat. I had it specially made."

Alice removed the footrest from the package. Galahad touched it to more closely examine the Christmas gift. He flew out of the second entryway, down the hall, back through the living room, and down the hallway once more. He increased his speed with every pass.

"Okay. Okay. Okay!" Alice shouted to calm him down. "Come here, and I'll put it on for you."

Galahad flew to Alice, bobbing up and down with the patience of an overstimulated child.

"I think he likes it," Hugo said.

"Stay still," Alice commanded.

Galahad did as instructed. She attached the footrest to the bolts under the seat and tightened the nuts.

"There. Now go show it off."

Galahad continued his circuit. Max, excited with the squeaking of a new toy, followed Galahad. The two of them raced around the house.

"Kids!" Alice said as she turned back to Hugo. "So excited at Christmas time."

Hugo laughed. "Merry Christmas, Alice Primrose."

"Merry Christmas, Hugo Dodds."

They leaned in closer and kissed. This was the only Christmas gift Hugo really wanted. He pulled Alice closer to him, but she pulled away.

"I almost forgot."

"What?"

"Gifts from Santa!" She stood up and rushed over to the mantle. She dug into her purple and black colored stocking.

"Did you do this?"

"Shush," Alice said as she covered her mouth with her free index finger. "Go check yours."

Hugo begrudgingly stood and schlepped over to his stocking. He was willing to play along with her little game. Alice pulled out a small cookie box, neatly wrapped with a purple ribbon. With a tug, the ribbon released the box from its protective hold. She opened the flap to reveal the delectable delights hidden within. Alice let out a giddy joyful sound before removing one of the cookies and taking a bite. She moaned with excitement. A moan Hugo sort of recognized from somewhere else.

"Everything okay over there?"

Alice removed the half bitten cookie and shoved it into Hugo's mouth. "Eat it," Alice ordered.

Time stood still. For a brief moment, Hugo could see sound and hear colors. With each bite of the cookie, the world came alive with invigorating energy. He knew joy. He knew happiness. He knew fulfillment. He knew peace.

Alice's aura radiated with a multicolored glow he had never seen before. He chewed and chewed. Each bite brought him new sensations. Shivers ran down his back, and his arms tingled. His hair stood up. He wanted to run a marathon. Every muscle twinged. His body was alive and full of energy. For a moment, he thought he was having a stroke. He swallowed the cookie, and everything returned to normal.

"What was that?" Hugo asked, feeling like he needed to catch his breath.

"That"—Alice began as she wiped away the remaining cookie crumbs from her chin—"was one of Holly Claus' special cookies infused with the joy of Christmas magick. She sends at least one every year."

"Do you have any more?"

"Nope. Just the one. The rest are chocolate chip." Alice pulled out another cookie and shoved it into her mouth. Mumbling though a mouthful of cookie, she added, "Check yours."

Hugo delved into his. He could feel a square, wooden object down at the bottom of his traditional red stocking with white fuzzy trim. He pulled out the object to reveal a black onyx colored wooden box. The same color as his wedding ring.

The box was masterfully crafted. Chamfered edging all the way around. Perfectly stained wood. Seamless in design. A nearly perfect cube, except for a groove in the middle of one side to indicate where to open the box. Hugo hadn't even noticed it was cut in half until he lifted the lid.

Inside, a neatly folded piece of paper hid a circular indentation. It had a slightly raised middle as if it was designed to hold something in place. A similar indentation was on the inside of the lid.

"What is it?" Alice asked.

"I don't know, but I think it's a storage box." He unfolded the paper.

Hugo,

Difficult tasks can be accomplished with a little help.

—Nicholas "Santa" Claus

His eyes read the words over and over. He examined the box and the indentation. He studied the perfectly round shape. Smooth to the touch. This was a box made by a master craftsman. So intricate in design that he couldn't even see where the wooden hinges attached the two halves together. His left thumb circled the indentation. He caught a glimpse of the ring on his hand. He now understood the purpose of the box.

His heartbeat quickened. A bead of sweat rolled down his back. He was short of breath. Memories flooded back. Elizabeth's name echoed through his mind like he was haunted by the ghosts of Christmas past. The room spun. Alice's grandfather clock chimed on the hour. Each strike of the bell rang through Hugo's soul. A voice grew louder after every strike.

The voice chanted his name, "Hugo."

It was unmistakable. His name. Another strike of the chime.

"Hugo Dodds."

That voice. That familiar voice.

"Don't forget me, Hugo Dodds." It sounded like Elizabeth.

Each strike of the chime chipped away at the happiness that was healing the broken wounds in his soul.

His eyes closed, and he focused on the day. The events that led him to this very moment. The memory he burned in his mind of Alice blowing him a kiss under the mistletoe. The opening of special gifts. He felt the weight of the key in his pocket. The chimes stopped, and the voice vanished.

Hugo opened his eyes and found Alice. She was slowly pulling her index finger from her mouth as she lapped up the melted streaks of chocolate. She paused for a moment, like a kid caught with her hand in the cookie jar before pulling her finger out with a loud pop.

"What?" she asked.

Hugo focused on her emerald green eyes, trying to center himself. Restore himself. His breathing slowed. His heartbeat returned to normal. He focused on those emerald eyes.

"You okay?" Alice asked. "You're starting to worry me."

Hugo glanced down to the box. "Can I ask you for one more Christmas present?"

"It's kind of late for that."

"For this one, you don't have to get me anything," he said before focusing on her eyes once again. "I need you to help me with something."

Alice squinted her eyes in a puzzled gaze. She placed the cookie box back into her stocking. "Sure. What is it?"

"I need you to help me remove my ring."

Alice gawked at Hugo, frozen by what he was asking. "Are... are you sure?"

His gaze never wandered from Alice's eyes. "I've never been more certain of something in my life."

Alice approached Hugo. Each step was soft and slow as if she was giving him time to reconsider, but his mind was already made up.

"You don't have to take it off if you don't want to."

"No." He held out his left hand. "I want to. I need to. I'm ready."

Alice grabbed the black onyx ring. She twisted it a few turns as Hugo had done countless times.

Tears formed in his eyes. He had played this moment in his mind over and over. He stopped himself every time he thought of removing the ring. He never had the strength to do it himself. He clutched the note tightly with his other hand. He took in two large breaths to fight back the tears he knew were coming.

Alice whispered, "Are you ready?"

He tried to conjure the words, but they failed him. He simply nodded his head. Alice twisted the ring. It caught on the meaty part of his finger, not wanting to leave the place where it had rested for so many years. She twisted the ring even more, like she was pulling off a cork from a corkscrew.

The ring refused to give up. Hugo wanted to look away, but forced himself to watch. With a few more twists, the ring gave way, and Alice removed it from Hugo's finger. She held the ring in her hand.

Hugo collapsed his hands together. He examined the smooth skin that molded itself to the shape of the ring. He twisted at the now invisible ring. Tears rolled down his face. He locked eyes with Alice.

He tried to speak, but could only whisper, "Thank you."

She dove at Hugo and wrapped her arms around him. They buried their heads into each other's shoulders and cried together.

Alice pulled back first and wiped her tears. "Let me see the box."

Hugo handed it to her, and she placed the ring inside. It fit perfectly into the indented circle. She closed the lid, sealing the ring safely within.

"I know the best place for this."

Hugo wiped the tears from his eyes. "Where?"

Alice marched over to one of her bookshelves filled with macabre odds and ends. Crystals, flowers frozen in time, a set of keys, a quill, and pictures of her long-gone relatives. She moved a small crystal ball out of the way and set the black box in its place.

"This is where I keep some of my ancestral remembrances. Things from the past that keep my ancestor's memories alive. It will be safe here. I hope you don't mind."

"No. Not at all. That seems like the perfect spot," Hugo replied with a smile.

He joined Alice and hugged her from behind. He gave her a small kiss on the cheek and then placed his chin on her shoulder. He focused on the black box now resting on the shelf.

"Merry Christmas, Alice Primrose."

She touched her head to his. "Merry Christmas, Hugo Dodds," she replied. "I hope it was a special one."

"It was. It most certainly was."

CHAPTER 19
AULD LANG SYNE

The bleak nighttime air was cold and stung Alice and Hugo as they strolled down the sidewalk. The exterior lights of Newbury Grove High School fought back against the winter darkness. Large, black tarps covered a portion of the entrance to the two-story building. The brick facade was weathered, chipped, and worn with age. Years of environmental torment damaged the hardened exterior. Scaffolding rose from the ground where, before the holidays, workers valiantly fought back against the structural decay.

A large banner hung over the entrance and welcomed guests to the *Annual Newbury Grove New Year's Eve Celebration*. It thrashed back and forth in the winter wind. It clanged against the steel of the scaffolding, held tightly by its straps. Various people of all ages braved the winter cold for the warmth of the communal celebration.

Hugo Dodds and Alice Primrose were amongst those who entered the high school. Hugo grabbed the door from someone who held it open for them. With a grand gesture to welcome Alice, Hugo invited her into the building for a walk down his memory lane.

"It's over here." Hugo guided Alice to a glass showcase.

The showcase was filled with various photographs, trophies, and awards the students had won over the years. Most importantly, the showcase was filled with memories. Hugo's eyes fixated on the sports trophies. He scanned for one photo in particular, but he was unable to find it.

"Are you sure you're in here?" Alice teased.

"They moved it," Hugo said. "Every time I stopped in to visit Elizabeth, I always double checked to make sure it was still here. They moved it, probably to make room for new stuff."

He scanned every photo of various athletic championship teams. Their trophies were right in front to display their winning achievements. Each photo he passed raised a concern that the school had erased the memory of his achievement. He hurried past each one before stopping. He double tapped the glass.

"This is it," he exclaimed. "Right here."

Alice took a closer look. "I don't see you," she replied.

"What?" Hugo said in disbelief. "I'm right there. The one in the back. Second from the left. Regional Hockey Champions." Hugo pointed to a picture of his high school hockey team.

Three rows of elevated teenage hockey players faced the camera with solemn expressions. A staple of all team photographs. They were adorned in their black and royal blue jerseys with an emblazoned, screaming blue jay on the front—the high school mascot.

"Why does everyone have this real, mean, *serious* look?"

"That's what you do," Hugo stated, shocked this wasn't common knowledge. "You've got to look mean and serious for the opponents."

"That can't be you," Alice exclaimed with a teasing, Cheshire cat like smile. "He looks way cooler."

Hugo chuckled. "That's me, all right."

"Look at that hair!" Alice said. "So moppy and long and wild. I *love* it."

Hugo tugged on his black leather jacket and puffed up his chest. He ran his fingers through his neatly combed, coifed hair. "You have to have the flow going if you're a hockey player."

"You should grow it out that long again," Alice said as her gaze found Hugo. "It's a good look on you." She winked.

He smiled and took her hand in his. They held hands as they proceeded toward the sound of music and merriment echoing down the hallway. They readied themselves for the approaching new year.

There, at the end of the glass showcase, was a memorial for the school's fallen teacher. Her auburn colored hair flowed in curls behind her shoulders. Her hazel eyes glistened with happiness. Her smile was beaming. Elizabeth.

Her official school photo was memorialized in the glass case. A sign above read, "Gone, but not forgotten." It was surrounded by notes from her students. Some notes mentioned how much Elizabeth was loved as a teacher. Other notes were sealed and meant only for heavenly eyes. Hugo lingered on the photograph. He'd seen it before, but only briefly.

"Are you doing okay?" Alice asked.

Hugo didn't respond. He was committing the entire memorial to memory.

"We can leave if you want to," she added.

"No," Hugo replied. "I'm okay."

"I thought we agreed to not use that phrase," Alice responded. "Is it too much?"

He turned to Alice and grabbed both of her hands. He held them high as he moved closer. "I'm doing unbelievably well. I should be thanking you."

"Thanking me?" Alice said with a shocked look on her face. "Why?"

"I was lost and numb and confused. I was broken, shattered into a million pieces. Then this purple haired witch moved in next to me, and my life changed. I... I started to feel things again. I felt happy." Tears welled in his eyes. "I wanted to be like my old self again, but I couldn't. I didn't know how. I wanted to find joy, but I only found torment. And then... and then you gave that to me. I was in a bad place before I met you."

"You're making me cry." Alice pulled one hand back and wiped away tears flowing down her face. She grabbed his hand again.

Hugo motioned to Elizabeth's picture with his head, not wanting to let go of Alice. "I loved Elizabeth. I will always keep her in my heart and mind and never forget her. But my heart is big enough for more than just her," Hugo said.

Alice smiled through her tears at the anticipation of what was coming next.

"I love you, Alice Primrose."

Alice let out a small, joyful, laugh through her tears. "I love you too, Hugo Dodds."

They hugged, burying their heads into each other's shoulders to hide their tears. They held each other for an eternity before pulling back. Hugo leaned in and kissed Alice on her soft, sweet lips. They were lost in bliss.

Hugo knocked off Alice's hat during their embrace. He picked it up off the floor and returned it to her head. "I need my purple haired witch looking the part before we go in there." Hugo adjusted it a few times to get it right.

"You're not embarrassed to be seen out in public with a witch?" Alice asked with a wide smile.

"Embarrassed? No," Hugo replied with a wink. "I want them to be jealous."

They locked hands and ventured down the hallway.

THE GYMNASIUM WAS DECORATED with brightly colored banners welcoming in the new year. A table of refreshments was set up in front of the recessed bleachers. A few bartenders handed out drinks for a nominal fee. All proceeds went toward repairs of the high school, of course. A net of balloons hung above the revelers. Music blared through a set of speakers set up at the far end. The DJ played a mixture of pop classics.

The revelers packed the gymnasium as it was filled with excitement for the festivities. Some wore party hats. Many had brightly colored glasses in the shape of the digits for the new year. People congregated on the sides of the gym, discussing their various holiday exploits. Others danced to the melodic beats closer to the speakers. Children ran around, in and out of the crowds, playing various games of tag and keep away. Some of their parents chased them, not to play along, but in an attempt to wrangle them in from causing too much of a disturbance.

Johanna stood in the corner opposite the entrance and rolled her eyes at the sight of the children playing. Not that children were being children, but a resentment toward the parents for letting them run roughshod around the other revelers. More and more people flowed into the gymnasium. The excitement of the people partaking in the evening. The New Year's Eve event had gone off without a hitch. Smoothly. Uneventful. The way she liked it. She allowed herself a rare moment to smile at the happiness of the evening.

That smile, however, was short lived. Her eyes dropped to the empty space next to her. The space that should have been occupied by Elizabeth Dodds, the one who enlisted her to help with the annual festivities many years ago. Her smile dissipated as fast as it had appeared. She gave two taps to the cloak clasp pinned below her left shoulder.

She bowed her head in thought. *You'd really love this. Everything is going perfectly. I miss you, my friend. I wish you were here to see this.*

Johanna caught sight of Hugo and Alice, hand in hand, as they entered the gymnasium. Her face turned solemn and then furious. Everything had been perfect until now. He had to walk into this gymnasium, this event, with *her*. His betrayal was like a slap in the face to Elizabeth's memory.

Hugo and Alice stopped and talked with many people. They laughed. Johanna's eyes narrowed as she focused on the woman with the purple hair. Alice's witch like appearance sent shots of adrenaline coursing through Johanna's veins. That woman ruined this perfect evening with her presence.

Johanna turned back to the empty spot. "I'm sorry," Johanna whispered in a low voice. "I'm sorry you had to see that. He should be more faithful."

Johanna focused her eyes on the couple. Hugo was introducing Alice to various people. They talked and laughed before moving on. They meandered their way to see the Raskins before moving on to the next group. Johanna watched their every movement. Hugo and Alice worked their way through the room. Johanna needed to get closer.

She left her self-appointed spot, dodging children and ignoring other revelers, who attempted to make conversation with her. As Johanna moved closer, she never lost sight of her targets: the betrayer and the seducer.

She tapped Hugo on the shoulder to interrupt his conversation with someone. He turned around with excitement.

"Johanna!" Hugo exclaimed. "How are you doing?" He tugged on Alice's tailcoat to get her attention.

She turned around with a half-hearted smile. "Hello, Johanna. Did you have a good Christmas? Did you like the cookies?"

"Christmas was adequate. The cookies were good. Perhaps not as great as Elizabeth's, but they were good," Johanna replied.

"I'm happy you enjoyed them," Hugo said.

"I'm surprised to see you two here," Johanna said.

Hugo chuckled and replied, "I'm surprised to see you too. Glad you could make it."

"Well, I've committed to this every year, and I don't want to break my commitment," she replied. "You should never break a commitment."

Hugo's smile disappeared for a moment. He seemed lost in thought. He glimpsed Alice's purple hair, and the smile returned.

"Everything is great," Alice said. "Everyone is so nice and welcoming and... and this is a fun evening."

"I'm glad you're having fun," Johanna said. "I'm going to go back to my commitments now. I just wanted to say hi."

Someone shouted Hugo's name, and he waved with his left hand. Johanna paused. All feeling left her body. Her face turned morose. She felt sickly, horrified. She tapped her cloak clasp, but held it tightly. Its elegant, crisscrossed filigree dug into her hand and left a temporary impression. She couldn't believe what she was seeing. Hugo's wedding ring was gone.

"Are you okay, Johanna?" Hugo asked.

Johanna was fixated on the ringless finger. She traced the hand's every move.

"Johanna?" Hugo asked again.

She snapped out of her trance. "You took off your ring."

"Uh, yeah," Hugo replied as he pinched his ringless finger. He felt the bare skin, then let go. "It... It was time. Alice and I are in a relationship now, and it felt like it was time."

"We love each other." Alice smiled at Hugo. "And tonight, we'll ring in the New Year with a kiss at midnight."

"I see," Johanna said as she backed away. "I'm sorry. I just remembered... I need to go do something."

"Take care," Alice said as Johanna scurried off.

The evening passed. Johanna stood in her spot off to the side. The occasional volunteer asked Johanna a question, but she blew them off. She wasn't paying attention. Her focus was on Hugo and Alice. She checked the time on her watch. Midnight drew closer. She glanced to the empty spot next to her. Thoughts raced in her mind. Anything she could do to stop that kiss from happening at midnight.

"I'll do something," she whispered to Elizabeth's invisible ghost. "I promise you. I'll do something."

She scanned the room for anything that could cause a distraction or put an immediate end to the festivities. Anything to prevent midnight from coming. Johanna focused on a middle-aged gentleman moving from group to group. He was holding a drink and shared a laugh. He was making sure everyone had a great time.

Frank! Johanna thought. Frank was the head of the New Year's Eve committee. His power and, most importantly, his access to the building gave her an idea. She moved through the crowd as fast as possible. Time was against her.

"I'm sorry to barge in, Frank," she said as she approached him. "But I need the keys to the maintenance room."

"Johanna! Having a great time?" Frank asked.

"It's been a great evening up until now," she replied. "An extension cord went out. I need to get a replacement. I don't have keys."

Frank removed the keys from his pocket and handed them to Johanna. "I'll get them from you at the end of the night," Frank said. "Hurry up. You don't want to miss the balloon drop."

"I know," Johanna replied. "I know."

She took the keys and left the gymnasium. She hastened through the hallway and passed the showcase. Elizabeth's memorial gave her a momentary pause. She lost herself in Elizabeth's smile and her auburn hair. She was reminded of their tea parties together and happier times. She thought of how much Elizabeth reminded her of Abigail. *Her Abigail*, and how much her betrayal shattered her soul. Johanna pulled away from the picture and ran down the hall.

She arrived at the electrical maintenance room and checked the time. She only had a few minutes before midnight. She tried the keys one by one. There were too many. She inserted one, but it wouldn't budge. She tried another, but nothing. With each passing key, she breathed heavier and heavier. The clock raced. It was going to win, and Elizabeth's betrayal would be complete.

She tried one more key, and there was a click. The key worked. Johanna laughed with momentary relief. She scanned the area to see if anyone was watching. She was alone in her deeds. She opened the door and slipped inside.

~

ALICE ALLOWED HERSELF TO SMILE. This evening was perfect. Hugo seemed happy. He smiled as he interacted with everyone. He shared stories of Elizabeth's past and talked of Alice's future. As he greeted everyone, Hugo immediately introduced her—not as his neighbor or an acquaintance, but as his girlfriend. Everyone welcomed her. She received the occasional odd stare. Those who still had not quite reconciled with her purple hair and witchy appearance, but she didn't care. She felt welcomed, and that's all she wanted.

Alice grabbed Hugo's arm and pulled him onto the dance floor.

"I don't like to dance. I'm not very good," Hugo pleaded as he reluctantly followed her through the crowd.

"I don't care. It's the effort that counts," Alice replied. She, on the other hand, loved dancing.

They moved and danced to the pulsating music.

Alice sashayed her hips and made certain Hugo saw her moving her hips. She gave him a wink, a smile, and occasionally brushed up against him. She hoped it tormented him in all the right ways. He grinned after every teasing glance.

As the music slowed, they held each other close and swayed with the beats of the music. Alice smiled with tears in her eye.

"Hey. Everything okay?" Hugo asked.

"Everything is perfect," Alice replied.

"All right! We are seconds away from midnight," the DJ said over the speakers. Cheers and whistles echoed throughout the gymnasium. "Grab that drink, grab that special someone, and let's count it down!"

The scoreboard counted each second down from sixty. More and more cheers erupted the closer it got to midnight.

Alice looked Hugo in the eyes and said, "Thank you for everything. I love you, Hugo Dodds."

"I love you too, Alice Primrose."

"Thirty seconds!" the DJ shouted.

The scoreboard went off, and the gymnasium went dark. Commotion rose as people were audibly confused.

"Everyone, stay calm," Frank shouted. "Stay calm. We lost power."

The revelers verbally expressed their disappointment as midnight drew closer.

"I can fix this," Alice whispered to Hugo.

"Are you sure?" Hugo asked. "Aren't you afraid someone will notice?"

"It's dark. No one will see me."

"Do it," Hugo said. "Give the evening some of that Alice Primrose magick."

Alice drew in close to Hugo. She raised her hand between the two of them to hide it from prying eyes. She closed her eyes and drew in the might of her arcane abilities. Alice snapped her fingers. The room illuminated back to life. The crowd clapped. The scoreboard resumed its countdown with only seconds to midnight.

"Oh. Oh! It's almost time," the DJ shouted. "Five... four... three... two... one. Happy New Year!"

Cheers of "Happy New Year" erupted. The colorful menagerie of balloons rained on the crowd below. Some drank from champagne flutes. Some kissed their significant others.

In the center of the room, Hugo and Alice embraced with a kiss to welcome in the New Year. Alice melted from the burning passion that flowed through her. She was lost in her bliss. She was welcomed into a community. She was lost in the arms of someone who loved her, not for what she could do, but because of who she was. She was Alice Primrose. She was a witch, and Hugo Dodds loved her for it.

Alice pulled back from Hugo, and their eyes met. "Happy New Year," she said.

"Happy Witchy New Year," Hugo replied with a wink. They hugged once again.

As Alice rested her head on Hugo's shoulder in their embrace, she noticed Johanna enter the gymnasium from the darkened hallway. Johanna glanced back to the darkness and then at the light inside the gymnasium. Johanna's mouth dropped into disbelief and shock.

Johanna focused her scornful eyes on Alice. An unnerving and unsettling expression was on her face. Johanna snarled at her before she turned around and stormed out.

Alice thought for a moment that Johanna must be involved in the power outage somehow. She wasn't sure why though or why she looked so angry the power was restored. Her heart sank. All feelings of happiness and joy disappeared. They were replaced with a solitary thought, *Does she know?* She stood there and held Hugo tighter.

CHAPTER 20

THE NEIGHBORHOOD WATCH

Johanna Newes sat in her wingback chair with her eyes focused on the black door across the street. She sat, watching, waiting, plotting her next move. The room was silent except for the ticking clock. She sat upright and rigid, like a predator ready to spring into action. She took a sip from the tea cup she held in her hand. The saucer plate was in the other hand. The hot Earl Grey tea rushed over her lips, but she never broke sight of the door. She placed the cup down on the saucer and leaned forward in the chair. *I know what you did. I've got you now,* she thought, never breaking her gaze.

The door opened. Johanna placed the saucer on the table next to the window before grabbing the arms of her chair. "Right on schedule," Johanna said.

Max pulled Hugo onto the porch. The excited golden retriever tugged and pulled at the leash, nearly dragging Hugo down the stairs. Johanna watched him say something to the dog, but she couldn't really tell. His free hand pointed at a spot next to him. Max lowered her head and sat next to Hugo. The dog glanced up at him, awaiting her next command.

"Get going," Johanna muttered.

Her fingers dug into the arms of the chair. She leaned forward in anticipation. Ready to leap into action. Hugo and Max jaunted down the steps and took off on their daily walk. Johanna sprung from the chair. She gave two taps to the cloak clasp pinned to her sweater. She rushed to the antique display table and turned the brass key.

"I ABSOLUTELY LOVE THIS TABLE," Elizabeth said as she rubbed her hand across the smooth tabletop. "Where did you get it?"

"An old friend," Johanna replied. "A very old friend."

Johanna smiled as Elizabeth inspected every inch of the display table. Her fingers ran across the smooth yet weathered surface. Elizabeth's auburn hair flowed down her back, and her hazel eyes focused on each detail. It reminded her of an old friend. An old friend she had not seen in so many years, but thought about every day. Johanna's true love. Her betrayer. Her Abigail.

"What period is this from?" Elizabeth asked before interrupting herself. "Wait, don't tell me."

She examined the intricate details closer. The fine carving of the wolf head handle. The oak leaf with a keyhole in the middle. Elizabeth tried to pull on the handle, but it was locked. She pointed to the keyhole and turned back to Johanna sitting in one of her two wing-back chairs.

Johanna shook her head. Elizabeth frowned in disappointment.

"Lost ages ago," Johanna replied.

"I'm going to guess, based on the age, the elaborate carving, the weathering, that this dates back to the early 1700s?"

Johanna shook her head, smiling. "Late 1600s."

Elizabeth shrugged. "Close enough. What's a decade or two?"

She proceeded over to a similar chair to the one Johanna sat in. A small table holding a teapot, tea cups with saucers, and a plate of cookies, separated them. Johanna provided the tea; Elizabeth the cookies.

Elizabeth topped off her cup before sitting down. She took a sip. "I love the antiques in your house. Hugo never wants to buy any. He says they make modern furniture for a reason. I think he doesn't want to pay for it." They chuckled.

"Well, they can be expensive and come at a great cost," Johanna replied before taking another sip. "I prefer the antiques. It keeps memories of the past alive."

"Where did you get these chairs? I think I can convince Hugo to at least get some antique chairs."

"I can't remember," Johanna said as she set her tea cup down on the table. She tapped her cloak clasp twice before placing her hand on the arm rest. "I only remember something about an old lady. Funny, isn't it? So many people come and go into our lives. They help to shape us. But as soon as they leave, we start to forget about them. Like they're being erased from history. It's like they die all over again. Only our memories can keep them alive. And if we forget them, well, that's the cruelest thing we could do." Johanna fixated on the hardwood floor. Her face solemn and expressionless.

"That's why I love history," Elizabeth replied with a smile as she touched Johanna's hand. "It keeps their memories alive."

Johanna locked onto Elizabeth's hazel eyes and smiled. "That it does. That it does."

"What about that broach? Where did you get it?"

"This?" Johanna pulled her hand away from Elizabeth and tapped it twice. "This was a gift from an old lover. We're no longer together."

The memories of that fateful day in the barn rushed back to her. The bliss of true love broken by the horrors of betrayal and agony.

"I'm sorry," Elizabeth replied.

Johanna shook her head. "Don't worry. It was a long time ago. We had a falling out, but I never stopped loving her. I wear it as a reminder of lost love."

"Well, she made a terrible mistake," Elizabeth consoled her. "Sounds like you still love her."

"I do. When you find that one love, it's hard to let go."

"That's true. I don't think Hugo will ever stop loving me."

"He better not," Johanna replied. "Or he'll have to deal with my wrath." They chuckled.

JOHANNA SHOOK her head to clear the thoughts of the past. She needed to focus on the here and the now. On her mission. She turned the brass key, and the locking mechanism clicked. Johanna pulled open the left drawer and withdrew the black, twisting wand.

She rushed over to the coat rack and held the wand in her mouth. She put her arms through the long, black wool coat. She wrapped her burnt orange scarf around her neck and tucked it under the coat before buttoning up. She pulled her ponytail out from under the scarf and let it drape down her back.

She took the wand, stuffed it into her coat pocket, and pulled out leather gloves. Her heart raced. Her hands shook with anticipation as she tried to put them on. She took a deep breath and held it for a moment. She drew out her exhale to calm her nerves before slipping on the gloves and stepping outside.

The winter sky was gray and bleak. The chilled wind whipped down the street as it stung Johanna's face. A hardened mixture of snow that melted before freezing again covered the ground. Johanna tried to speed walk across the street, but was cautious with every step. She mustn't fail in her mission, and she dared not fall on a patch of ice. She glanced where Hugo had walked off with Max. They were gone.

She stepped up onto the sidewalk and stood at the precipice of Alice's house. She checked around to see if there were any curious onlookers. The street was empty, except for desolate and barren trees. She focused on the overbearing purple house. The curtains were drawn closed. There was no movement. She had the element of surprise.

She stood up tall with her shoulders drawn back. She tapped her chest twice, feeling the cloak clasp underneath. *No turning back now*, she thought. She waited a moment before taking that first step up the walkway.

The walkway was surprisingly clear, but not surprising to Johanna. She knew who really lived here, and she would fix it. Johanna hesitated before ascending the porch steps.

Still no movement. Each step up was methodical. She didn't want to walk into some sort of trap or alert her presence early. She stepped onto the top of the porch. *This needs a careful approach*, she thought. *Check the windows.*

She approached the covered windows. She tried to look through, but saw nothing. No movement. She moved to the door, but couldn't see anything through the sheer, black veil that covered the door window. She moved closer to the glass. There was no discernable movement inside.

She gripped the twisted wand inside her coat pocket. She wrapped her fingers around the ornate, diamond shaped doorknob. She twisted it a few times. It was locked.

No! Why did he lock it?

She tried again with more force. The doorknob didn't budge. She wouldn't waste this opportunity. She knocked.

She could hear commotion. A rattling of a wall. Someone approached the door. This was it. She readied herself; she stood upright and tightened her grip on the wand. Her breathing quickened as the footsteps approached the door. The ornate knob spun, and the door opened.

"I told you that you'd forget the key," Alice said as she appeared in the doorway. Alice gasped. She leaned against the wall and closed the door against her as much as possible to hide the contents of her home. "Johanna. Well, this is a surprise. What can I help you with?"

Johanna flicked the wand inside her coat pocket. Nothing

happened. She tried a few more times, expecting bolts of energy to fly toward Alice, rendering her inert. Nothing. She thought about withdrawing the stick, but didn't want to give Alice the opportunity to retaliate. No. The element of surprise was all she had, and the surprise hadn't worked. She tried again, but it failed.

"Umm..." Johanna said, trying to think of any excuse as to why she would be at this house at this moment. "I wanted to see if Hugo was here."

Alice glared at Johanna with skeptical eyes. Johanna was known as the neighborhood watch because she always watched the comings and goings of Ravenhill Drive. If anyone knew Hugo had left, it definitely would have been Johanna, but she needed some excuse. Alice pulled the door closer to her body, almost crushing herself between the door and the wall.

"You just missed him. I'll let him know you stopped by when he gets back." Alice slid back into the house, ready to shut the door.

"Crazy night at the New Year's Eve party, huh?" Johanna asked.

"What do you mean?"

"Well. The... um... power outage," Johanna replied.

Alice maintained contact with the door and the wall, ready to close it. "It was only for a moment," Alice said. "It's no big deal."

"Well, when you're running the event, it can be a big deal," Johanna replied with a half-hearted laugh.

"I guess so," Alice answered. "Well, it resolved itself quickly, which was good. Everyone seemed to have a good time. I know I did."

"I was going to check with Hugo to see if he heard anything."

"Why would Hugo know anything?" Alice asked.

"Well, he knows people. I thought maybe he heard something about it over the past few days."

"It was only a small blip in power. I'm sure it's fine. Now if you'll excuse me, I have to get back to what I was doing. I'll let Hugo know you stopped by."

Johanna tried once more with the wand. Nothing. She slumped her shoulders and let go.

"Well, thank you," Johanna said.

Alice shut the door. Johanna heard the audible click of the lock.

Was I wrong? No. I know what I saw. Did the wand lose its power? Her face turned a ghostly shade of pale. She held her breath out of fear.

Will it still work on the amulet?

She turned away, but something in the doorframe caught her eye. She stopped and examined it. There were small, rune-like carvings in the black wood trim. So obscure that she never would have noticed them if not for standing so close. She ran her fingers over the engravings. They were meticulous and deliberate. Someone had placed them there.

She rolled her eyes in disappointment after realizing why the wand didn't work. She charged down the steps, heading back home. Her eyes were enraged. Her lips and nose snarled. *I need to try from the inside.*

OSTARA

A Time of Rebirth

CHAPTER 21
THE NIGHTMARE BATCH

Birds chirped from barren trees—the first sign of spring on the bright, crisp, early March day. The town center bustled with activity of those who emerged from their self-imposed winter isolation as the days warmed, and the light grew longer. People came and went from the various shops. Some took advantage of the nice weather and partook in a midday stroll.

Alice and Hugo emerged from the bakery. He carried a sack of acquired baked goods of Alice's choosing. Hugo positioned himself between Alice and the street. They passed by the window of Antonio's Italian Ristorante—their normal dinner date spot.

"All I was saying earlier is that we don't have to sit at that table if it makes you feel uncomfortable," Hugo said.

"And why would it make me uncomfortable?" Alice replied.

"Well..." Hugo paused. "Since it was Elizabeth's usual table, I don't want you to feel obligated to sit there."

"What if I want to sit there?"

"I... I don't know. I thought maybe you felt pressured into sitting there."

"I like sitting there. Why can't it be our table too?"

"Well," Hugo said. "Yeah. I guess. We can always switch seats if you want, in case it feels awkward."

Alice turned around and stepped in front of Hugo to stop him. She peered intently into his icy blue eyes and leaned in. The smell of his cedar and vanilla infused cologne tantalized her senses. A tingle ran down her back. Many thoughts of pleasure and ecstasy overwhelmed Alice, none of which were why she decided to confront Hugo directly to his face.

Later, she thought before giving him a sly smile.

Hugo took a step back. His eyes widened as Alice leaned closer.

"Do you know why I like to sit there?" she asked.

"Umm. No. I guess I don't."

Her smile grew and her voice hushed to keep the answer only between them. "I'm guessing you don't know why Elizabeth liked to sit there, either."

Hugo blankly stared back. Alice refused to blink. The tension built between them. Hugo shifted in his stance. Her smile grew. He relented and blinked a few times. The tension faded away as he glanced down.

"I guess I don't."

"You have much to learn, Hugo Dodds. That seat not only gives me a great view of you against the backdrop of the town, but it has a great view of the moon as well. And as you know, I —" Alice's words trailed off as they urged him to finish the sentence.

He replied in a somewhat sarcastic tone. "I know. I know. You never miss a beautiful moon."

"Well"—Alice tilted her head back with her Cheshirish grin—"maybe you do know something, after all."

Hugo clutched his ring finger. He let go as soon as he found the finger barren. Her eyes narrowed, and she raised her right eyebrow. Alice tilted her head and placed a hand on her hips.

Hugo shrugged his shoulders and lifted his left hand for her to see the empty finger. "Habit."

She gave him a wink and continued walking. Her eyes lingered on Hugo for as long as possible.

"Watch out!" Hugo yelled.

He grasped Alice's arm, but could not stop her from colliding face-to-face with a passerby. They reeled back at the force of meeting head-on and covered their face with their hands.

"I'm so sorry," Alice offered as she assessed the damage done with her fingers. Nothing was bleeding or broken, merely numbed from the collision. "That was entirely my fault."

"I think I'm okay," the woman said. "It was an accident. It happens."

Alice raised her head and held her breath. Her eyes widened, and her body tensed. The world slowed. Emotions swirled, and she was filled with anxiety and loneliness and heart ache. Alice stepped back. Her mouth quivered at the sight of a woman with golden blonde hair that emerged from beneath a red knit cap.

"How did you find me?" Alice asked in a low, hushed tone. "They told me you wouldn't be able to find me."

She raised her right hand. A glow of purple energy formed in her palm as it raised waist high. The arcane bolt was ready to strike at its target—her ex-lover and betrayer—Sam. The purple energy dissipated as Hugo grabbed her arm and forced it down to interrupt the magick spell.

"Excuse me?" the woman asked as she lowered her hands.

"You're not Sam." Alice took in the stranger with a red knit cap all too similar to the one Sam wore. Alice gasped at the thought that she had nearly attacked an innocent bystander. "I'm... I'm sorry. I thought you were someone else."

She squatted down and buried her head into her arms. Her hat once again shielded her from the outside world as it had the last time she had a panic attack. Her breathing labored as she tried to soothe her frayed nerves. Her mind clouded as the world spun out of control.

"Is she okay?" the woman asked.

Hugo squatted next to Alice. He braced a hand against her back.

"She'll be fine. Are you okay?" Hugo asked the woman in the red knit cap.

"I think I'm okay. I'm sorry if I..." her words trailed off. "Does she need help?"

Alice rocked back and forth to the rhythmic beats of her labored breaths. She pulled her arms closer and tapped her shoulders. A technique she learned to help calm herself in the middle of one of her attacks.

"I think she needs a moment. I got it," Hugo replied. "I'm sorry again."

"It's okay. I hope she feels better," the woman said as she continued down the sidewalk.

Hugo grabbed her far shoulder, pulling her in for a hug. He held her until she felt safe again. His hand moved across her black tailcoat in a swirling pattern. The back rub helped soothe her frayed nerves.

"Hey," Hugo whispered into her ear. "It's okay. That wasn't Sam. It's okay." He continued rubbing her back.

"I was going to attack her," Alice sobbed as tears rolled down her cheek into the arms of her coat. "I could have hurt her. I could have hurt her really badly."

"You didn't do anything," Hugo answered. "It's okay. I got you."

"Thank you," Alice sobbed. She stopped tapping her shoulders. "I love you."

"I love you too." He paused. "What do you say we head back home and we try one of those cupcakes?"

Alice lifted her head. Her mascara left trails of inky, black streaks down her face that followed her tears. Hugo pulled some napkins out of the bag and offered them to Alice. He moved closer to shield her face.

He leaned in and whispered, "I think I can shield you if you want to take care of that."

Alice realized he hadn't offered the napkins to wipe away the mascara. He was offering protection from any onlookers so she could take care of the mascara her way. She buried her head back into her arms. Her hat once again hid her face. Hugo removed his leather jacket and used it to shield her.

Alice snapped her fingers. The inky, black trail disappeared. Hugo pulled his jacket away.

"How do I look?" she asked.

"Perfect," Hugo replied. "As usual."

She chuckled. They stood up. Hugo put on his jacket and grabbed the bag of baked goods from the sidewalk. He took Alice's hand with the other, and they continued their journey home together.

LATER IN THE DAY, Alice stood at her workstation in the wine cellar. She pressed various ingredients with one of the mortar and pestle sets Hugo gave her for Christmas. A few taps of the pestle, and then she dumped the contents into the bubbling water of her cauldron. She removed another item from the apothecary cabinet and crushed it as well. Her movements were robotic and low energy, missing her usual zeal and zest.

Alice stopped and gazed at the wall in front of her. Her eyes lingered on a single spot. Her mind went blank and her face expressionless. The blankness was broken by flashes of her encounter. A scenario she feared the most, only to realize in her moment of panic she could have harmed someone innocent. Her hands shook. She closed her eyes and inhaled to calm herself.

The door to the wine cellar opened. Alice snapped out of her meditative state to see who had entered her sanctuary, ready to strike at any would be intruder. Hugo entered carrying two cups of tea. She relaxed and felt a bit of shame that she was ready to attack him as he entered.

"I thought you might need this." Hugo set the cup on her workbench.

The warm liquid soothed her as she took a sip. "Thank you," Alice replied.

"I'd ask you how you're doing, but I already know," Hugo said. "Besides, I don't want to break our promise."

Alice chuckled. "You just ask in a roundabout way, huh?"

"Oh, no! She's learned my secret," Hugo said before taking another sip. "Do you want to talk about it?"

Alice shook her head.

Alice's station was unkept. The items were strewn about the table and not in their usual places. Drawers were left open. Ingredients were left in piles. This wasn't Alice's usual way of working.

"Do you want any help?" Hugo asked.

"No, I'm fine. I just..." Alice started. "I need some alone time to clear my head."

The stompers sat idle in the vats. Boxes of grapes piled up on top of the wooden platforms.

"Are you sure?" he asked one more time.

"I'm certain."

"Well, if you need any help, I'll be upstairs. Yell if you need anything." He took his cup of tea and left the wine cellar.

Alice's eyes glazed over as she stood at the work station, taking small sips in between empty thoughts.

A FEW DAYS LATER, Alice descended the steps leading from her bedroom with her usual zest. She bounded into the living room to find Hugo sitting on the couch with Max and Galahad close by. Her hair bounced off her shoulders, and she had a smile on her face.

"It's supposed to be a clear night. A little chilly, but what do you say we go for a ride?" Alice asked. "Gally! You want to go for a ride tonight, boy?"

Galahad flew about the living room before bobbing up and down in front of Alice with excitement. It nudged her with light taps, anticipating that they were ready to depart now. Alice laughed off Galahad's attempts to fly at that very moment.

"Okay. Okay," she said. "We can't go until tonight. You know the rules."

"I think a ride would be great. It's been far too long," Hugo said. He sat up and moved toward Alice. He brushed Galahad aside. "Excuse me, buddy. I hope you don't mind me cutting in," he said and kissed her on the nose. "Glad to see you feeling better."

"Thanks. Tonight is going to be great. Full moon. Clear skies." She grabbed Hugo's shirt and pulled him closer. "A great guy. It'll be perfect." She returned the kiss.

Her cell phone rang.

"It can wait," Hugo said.

She recognized the ringtone. "It's Ez, I need to get it," Alice replied with a hint of disappointment. "But hold that thought." She stepped over to the phone sitting on an end table in the living room and answered. "Hello, Ez."

"I thought you said this wasn't going to interrupt your work?" Ez's voice came from the other end of the phone.

The smile and joy on Alice's face were now gone, replaced with a pale expression of loss and confusion. Hugo matched her worried expression.

Alice's voice caught in her throat. She tried to speak, but words didn't flow. After what seemed like forever, she finally responded, "I don't know what you mean."

"I'm talking about the last batch you sent. It was completely ruined. What did you do? What did *he* do?" Her voice emanated from the phone.

Hugo moved closer to Alice.

"He didn't do anything," Alice replied.

Hugo stopped in his tracks. "What's wrong?"

Alice put up a finger to silence him.

"What happened?" Alice asked into the phone.

"Every one of my customers got sick. They were throwing up. Some floated up to the ceiling. One man belched fire. Fire, Alice! Almost burnt my expensive new bar top."

Alice stood there motionless. Her free hand shook. She wanted to curl up into a ball. She couldn't believe the words she was hearing. "I... I don't know what happened."

"You need to fix this and soon. Also, if this is an indication of how your relationship will go, I'll have to find someone else."

Alice buried her head into her free hand. "I'm... I'm sorry, Ez. I'm so, so sorry. It wasn't him. It was me."

"Kiddo, look, if this was anyone else, it would be over. I'm giving you another chance to prove this relationship won't affect anything. Got it?"

"Ez, please let me explain," Alice pleaded.

"Fix it," Ez cut her off. "Or it's over."

The call dropped. Alice threw the phone into the black, wingback chair and buried her face into her hands. Her purple hair enveloped her face.

Hugo took a few steps closer, but still kept some distance. "What is it? Everything okay?"

She lifted her head. Tears welled in Alice's eyes as they turned a shade of reddish-pink. Her lips curled inwards in a last-ditch effort to stop her from completely crying. "No. No, it's not okay. The last batch was bad."

"Like stale?" Hugo asked.

"Like every bit of potion I brewed was messed up. It nearly burnt down her bar."

"It's not your fault," Hugo assured her.

"I never mess up. Never," Alice said.

She stormed past Hugo and made her way to the basement door. He followed.

"Where are you going?"

Alice opened the basement door. "She said I need to fix it. If I don't, I lose everything I've built. My next order isn't coming for a few weeks. I don't know what to do. I can't fix it!" Alice stepped into the darkness and slammed the door shut behind her.

CHAPTER 22

FIX IT TOGETHER

Hugo paced back and forth in the living room. The soles of his shoes echoed against the hardwood with every step. Max lay on the Victorian couch, unfazed by Hugo's impatient pacing. He pulled out his phone to check the time. It had been a few hours since he called Carol Raskin—a few hours since he called in the biggest favor of his life. He knew full well the Raskins would deliver. He wasn't sure of how long it would take them.

He pinched his ring finger, expecting to find the familiar black onyx ring, but only found it barren. His habit was so ingrained into his soul it was second nature. He turned toward the bookshelf. He focused on the black box sitting amongst the other items. He thought about touching the ring once more. *No. Focus.*

He entered the hallway and pulled back the curtain on the door to peer outside. Nothing. His waiting continued.

Galahad floated in front of the basement door. It waited for the door to open. Hugo wanted it to open too. Any time now, that door would open, and Hugo would give her the great news.

Galahad tapped the door. Nothing. It tapped a few more times. Still nothing.

"It'll be okay, buddy," Hugo said.

Galahad glanced toward Hugo for a moment before turning back to the door. Hugo headed over to Galahad and petted it on the head.

"She needs some alone time. It'll be okay." Hugo hoped those words were true.

The sound of a delivery truck rumbling down the street could be heard through the door.

"They're here," Hugo said as he rushed to pull back the curtain.

A white box truck came to a stop in front of Alice's house. He reached for the doorknob, but stopped. He glanced back to Galahad.

"Gally, come here, boy," Hugo said. Max jumped off the couch and pranced toward Hugo. "Not you, Max. Stay back. Gally, I need you to go upstairs."

Galahad kept its focus on the basement door.

"Gally, I need you to go upstairs for a moment," Hugo said as he scurried over to Galahad. He touched the end of the broomstick handle and guided it to focus on himself, instead of the door. "I need you to go upstairs. Please. Just for a moment."

There was a knock at the front door. Max barked at the intruder. Galahad rushed past Hugo and knocked against the front door.

"No, no, no, no! Upstairs. Go upstairs!" Hugo shouted.

He tried to force the broomstick away from the door. Max's bark echoed throughout the entryway. Her nose pressed up against the door, and she waited for her moment to pounce.

"Max, back away. Get back."

There was another knock at the door.

"Get back!" Hugo commanded.

They didn't listen. He tried to brush them aside.

Another knock at the door. Hugo opened it slightly and squeezed his head through the gap, careful to not let anyone see into Alice's house.

"Can I help you?" Hugo asked.

A deliveryman stood on the porch examining his digital delivery pad. "I have a shipment here for a Dodds. Hugo Dodds."

"That's me," Hugo answered.

He squeezed his way through the gap to not reveal too much. Max tried to stick her head through the opening, but Hugo pushed it back. The end of Galahad's broomstick poked out from behind the door, but Hugo was quick to shut it behind him.

"Dogs. Her bark is louder than her bite, and she'd kiss you to death before attacking."

"Sign here, please." The deliveryman handed over the digital pad.

Hugo drew his name with his index finger and handed it back.

"Where do you want them?"

"Right here is fine. I'll take them in," Hugo replied.

"You sure?"

"Yeah. Right here will be fine." He pointed to the porch.

"Suit yourself. That's a lot of grapes. What are you doing with this much, anyway?"

Hugo paused, trying to think of any answer other than making magical wine. "Fruit salad," Hugo replied. "We make a lot of fruit salad. Grapes are our favorite."

"To each their own," the deliveryman said as he trudged down the porch steps. "It'll take me a moment to unload all of this. You sure you don't want me to take it in for you?"

"No, I can get it."

THE LIGHTS FLICKERED in the wine cellar. The room was darker than usual as the lights from the wall sconces were dimmed. Alice sat hunched over on a stool in front of her workstation. Her head hung low. She flipped through the pages of her spell book.

She reviewed each and every spell she made that day. She read each line multiple times. *How could I have messed up? I never mess up.* She was far too distracted from her encounter that day. She slammed the book shut.

Alice focused on the spot where Hugo had placed a cup of tea.

She buried her head into her hands. He had tried to help her, but she had turned him away. The one person who tried to help her, she turned away. She remembered the blank stares. The empty thoughts. She was far too distracted, and that encounter messed everything up.

She got up from the workstation and meandered toward the wooden platform. She lumbered up the steps to the top. A few discarded, empty boxes littered the area. She checked the vats. There was nothing of use inside. She screamed and kicked one of the boxes into the corner.

"Damn you, Sam!" she yelled.

She picked up the other box and threw it across the cellar. It landed with a thud and partially collapsed in on itself. She screamed again.

There was a knock at the wine cellar door.

"Go away!" Alice yelled. "I want to be alone."

The door opened, and Hugo entered with a box of grapes. "Then I suppose you don't want these?"

Alice stood there in shock at the box Hugo held in his hands. "Where did you get those?"

"I worked my magic and called in a few favors," he replied as he set the grapes down on the floor. "There's more where this came from. A lot more. I'll need your help to bring them in."

Alice rushed down the steps and examined the box. She couldn't believe it. She looked up at Hugo with tears in her eyes. She wanted to say so many things. She tried, but words failed her. She could only conjure an almost inaudible, "Thank you." She buried her head into Hugo's chest.

He wrapped his arms around her, rubbing her back and shoulders with his palm. "You're welcome."

"I... I don't know what to say. No one has ever done something like this for me," Alice said through tears. "Thank you."

Hugo pulled back from Alice. He looked her right in the eyes. "Hey. You helped me. I helped you. This is how it works," he said.

"We'll fix it. Together. Okay? You can boss me around and tell me what to do."

Alice nodded as she wiped away tears rolling down her face. "But I always boss you around." They chuckled. "How much did you get?"

"Your entire front porch is covered in grapes. And some of the walkway. Most of the walkway."

"Why didn't you have them bring 'em inside?"

"Gally wouldn't listen and go upstairs. I had to... improvise."

Alice gave Hugo a discerning look. "See, this is why I keep him upstairs."

They left the wine cellar together and went upstairs to get their new bountiful harvest.

A WEEK LATER, Alice hid in her bedroom, not wanting Hugo to hear the conversation. She sat on the edge of the bed and picked up her phone to call Esmerelda. She waited with bated breath after each dial tone. Each one more tortuous than the last.

A woman's voice could be heard though the phone, "Go ahead."

"Ez! It's Alice. How was the delivery?"

"Kiddo, this is your best batch yet. I've had nothing but compliments... compliments from everyone."

Alice breathed a sigh of relief over those words. "Fantastic news. You have no idea how worried I was."

"No need to worry, kiddo. Your job is secured," Ez replied. "I'm sorry I yelled at you before. Emotions were running high after that night. I shouldn't have said those things. You did good. You did *great*."

"See! I told you it would be fine," Alice's reflection yelled from the bathroom.

Alice covered the phone with her hands. "Thank you for that commentary."

"You're welcome," her reflection responded.

"Who's that?" Ez asked.

"It's my reflection," Alice answered. She paused while deciding to tell Ez the truth about the new batch. "We did a great job."

"*We?*" Esmerelda asked. "You and your reflection?"

"No. Hugo and I. We did it as a team," she replied.

"You made this with Hugo?"

"I couldn't have done it without him," Alice said. There was a pause that lingered far too long. "Ez? You still there?"

"I'm here. Maybe I underestimated him."

Without missing a beat, Alice replied, "You have. He's a really great guy. I love him, and he loves me. I had one of my panic attacks before I made that previous batch. He tried to help me, but I wouldn't allow him to. I was distracted. Far too distracted. I should have stopped, but I didn't."

There was another pause. "Sounds like you found someone special. Good for you, kiddo."

"We each found someone special," Alice added.

"That you did. That you did. Don't lose it, kiddo. Not like I did."

"I won't."

"Take care of yourself. Talk to you later," Ez said before hanging up.

"See!" Alice's reflection said. "What did I tell you?"

"You were right." Alice fell back and splayed across the bed. She exhaled a long breath she had been holding all day.

"I'm always right," her reflection replied. "Always."

"Debatable," Alice said, staring off into the black canopy above.

CHAPTER 23
THE RING

Alice pinched the brim of her hat and adjusted it a few times before settling on the right position. She turned her attention upstairs and tapped the railing. Her eyes focused on the winding staircase, waiting for Hugo to emerge from the bedroom. Alice dreaded this day, the one-year anniversary of Elizabeth's death, for Hugo's sake.

"Everything okay? It's getting late," she yelled up. "We should get going."

"Yeah," Hugo replied. "I'll be right down."

A concerned Galahad brushed up against Alice in the entryway as she pulled on her black and purple tailcoat.

"It's okay, Gally," Alice said as she secured the last buttons. "You need to stay upstairs until we get back, okay?"

Galahad met Alice face-to-face. It did small bobs up and down, expressing its own separation anxiety about Alice leaving without it.

"Don't give me that look," she said as she brushed down the slant of the broomstick handle. "When we get back, I'll take you for a ride. Okay?"

Galahad weaved back and forth in excitement before begrudgingly heading up the stairs past Hugo coming down. It shut the bedroom door.

Hugo jogged down the steps. He was dressed in all black; dress pants and a long sleeve button up shirt complemented his black leather jacket and boots. He dressed like he was going to a funeral or at least reliving one.

"I think I've delayed long enough. Max is up there in her cage. Max and Gally can keep each other company." Hugo adjusted his jacket while walking past Alice. "Your reflection was not happy we were leaving Max up there with her. Something about the noise from her barking."

"Ignore her. She complains all the time," Alice replied. "Are you driving or do you want me to?"

"I'll drive," Hugo replied as he frantically searched the console table, moving items and then putting them back. "Have you seen my keys?"

"Where's the last place you put them?"

"I don't know. That's why I'm looking for them."

"Do you want me to drive?"

"No. I want to drive. I need to. I just need to find these stupid keys." Hugo went into the living room. "You didn't move them, did you?"

"Why would I move them?"

"I don't know. I can't find them." He rearranged things in a futile attempt to locate them.

Alice rolled her eyes. If there was one thing she disliked the most in the world, that was her things being rearranged from their perfect spots. She thought for a moment and then went into the kitchen. There, hanging by the back door, was Max's leash. She removed the leash to find the keys dangling underneath.

"Found them!" she shouted.

Hugo rushed into the hallway. "Where were they?"

She emerged from the kitchen. "The last place you put them. Hanging beneath Max's leash." She handed the keys to Hugo. "Do you need to talk about something?"

"No. I'm fine." He stuffed the keys into his pants pocket. "I'm fine."

"Don't you use that 'I'm fine' with me," Alice scolded Hugo. "We don't do fine."

Hugo brushed his hair back a few times. "I'm fine, really."

"Are you sure?"

"I'm fine. It's just—"

"You can't fool me. You're not fine," Alice replied.

Hugo lowered his head and sighed. "I'm good. I'm just... nervous. I'm feeling a lot of things right now. Today is dredging up a lot of emotions, and I don't know how to process it."

Alice hugged Hugo. "It's okay. Someone smart once told me it's okay to not be okay. This is a big day for you. I'm proud of you for going."

"I know. I haven't been back there since we buried her. I was okay with it, but now I feel like I've done something terrible, and I don't know what to do," Hugo said with a voice that held back tears.

Alice pulled back from Hugo and grabbed his shoulders. Her emerald green eyes locked with his icy blues. "Look at me," Alice commanded. "You've done nothing wrong. I know this is a very emotional day. It will be okay. I'm here for you. We'll do this together."

Hugo nodded. He took in a deep breath. "I think I'm ready. It'll be good to visit with Elizabeth again."

Alice kissed Hugo on the cheek. They turned and proceeded to the front door.

Hugo stopped. "I need to get something."

He headed back down the hallway.

"What are you getting?" Alice said with a worried look.

"I'm not going to put it on. I just want it with me," he replied as he entered the living room.

Alice frantically followed Hugo and stood at the living room entrance. Hugo hurried over to Alice's memory shrine and picked up the black box that held his wedding ring. He opened the box, expecting to find his black, onyx ring. It was empty. He snapped his attention to Alice with a panicked expression.

"Where's the ring?" Hugo asked.

"I'm sure it's safe," Alice replied.

He showed Alice the empty box. "It's not here. Where's the ring?" He frantically checked the box again, hoping he had overlooked it in his panic.

"Maybe it fell out. Did you look at it recently?" Alice asked.

Hugo dropped to the floor, peering under the bookshelf. The area was dark and held onto its secrets. "I haven't touched it since Christmas."

He pulled out his phone and turned on the flashlight. He scanned the entire area, but his search was fruitless. He crawled along the floor, checking each and every bookshelf. He stood back up. Dust and dog hair now covered his black dress pants.

"Look at my pants," he said before trying to swipe them clean.

Alice snapped her fingers, and the pants cleaned themselves. He turned his attention back to the memory shrine. He moved things out of place.

"Why is there so much stuff here?"

Alice grew annoyed. She could tolerate a lot, but she drew the line at messing with her things. "Let me help you." She moved to get Hugo away from her ancestral items. She put things back where they belonged.

Hugo checked under the couch. Nothing. He haphazardly threw the pillows and cushions across the room. He shoved his hand into the crevice of the couch, desperately trying to find his wedding ring.

Alice rolled her eyes at the mess he was making. She snapped her fingers. The cushions and pillows flew back into their rightful places. A cushion pinned Hugo's hand against the back of the couch.

"Maybe you should forget the ring," Alice suggested.

Hugo withdrew his hand and leered at Alice with anger. "You'd like that, wouldn't you?"

"Like what?"

"You'd like me to forget this whole thing," Hugo yelled, flailing his arms about. "You'd like me to forget her."

"How dare you?" Alice placed her hands on her hips. "I'm going to chalk this up to this being an emotional day."

"*Where's the ring?*" Hugo shouted.

Alice lowered her head to hide her eyes beneath the wide-brimmed hat. She bit her lip, preventing her from saying anything she would soon regret.

Hugo clapped his hands together before placing them on his hips. "So, you do know, don't you?"

"You don't need the ring, Hugo," Alice replied.

"You don't know what I need," Hugo shouted in a fury Alice never heard before. Her body tightened. "You don't know how difficult this is for me. I want one thing. One thing that will help me, and you took it from me. Hand it over."

"No," Alice was quick to reply. "You don't need it. Even though it was gone, you kept reaching for it. Don't think I didn't notice."

Hugo threw his hands into the air. He stormed to the front door.

"Hugo!" Alice shouted as he opened it. "Let's talk about this."

The walls of the house shook as he slammed the door behind him. Alice ran after him.

The springtime air was breezy and slightly warm for this time of year. The sky grew a colorful orange and yellow as sunset approached. Hugo charged down the front steps. Alice was quick to follow him out the door. He let out an audible huff as he strode off the steps onto the walkway. He cut across the grass toward his silver car parked in front of his house.

"Hugo!" she shouted. "Hugo, let's talk about this."

He continued toward his car. "What's there to talk about?"

"I tried to help you."

He stopped and turned back. "How is this helping me? Huh? How?"

"I..." she struggled to get the words out. "I didn't want to see you hurt again."

"This. This hurts worse." He pointed at her with both hands open, like he was accusing her of a grievous crime. He stood there for a moment. "How do I know you didn't plant that box on Christmas? That note?"

"I wouldn't dare," Alice replied. Her expression changed to hurt, and tears formed in her eyes.

"How do I know that with all of your magic... Wait, I'm sorry, *magick with a K*... that you haven't put some spell on me, and you're slowly making me forget about her. And you're"—he struggled to find the next words—"you're changing everything. Maybe I never wanted to change a thing or move on."

"How dare you?" Alice asked in a soft tone. "After all we've been through, this is how you act?"

Hugo licked his lips and peered off into the distance for a moment. He focused back on Alice. "I've got to go."

He pulled his keys from his pocket and continued into the car. He slammed the door shut behind him and started the engine.

"Hugo, wait!" Alice yelled.

The car pulled away. She ran after it. In the heat of the moment, with all the emotions coursing through her body, she raised both of her hands. "Hugo, *wait!*"

She snapped her fingers. An explosion of purple arcane magick erupted from under the hood. The car rolled to a dead stop. Alice cupped her hands in shock at what she had done.

Hugo exited the car and glared at Alice. His eyes widened with unmistakable furious anger. He stood there motionless, silent, and in disbelief at Alice.

"I'm sorry," she said through her hands. She slowly dropped them. "I'm so, so sorry. I... I just acted."

"Fix it," Hugo said in a low command. "*Fix it now!*"

Alice snapped her fingers again. The car revved back to life.

"We'll talk when I get back," Hugo said. He grabbed the car door, slammed it behind him, and sped off down the road.

Alice was left there in the middle of the street, crying and alone.

CHAPTER 24
WITCH-FINDER NEIGHBOR

Johanna sipped her tea as she leaned back in the chair. She held the white porcelain cup with both hands. She breathed in the steam rising from the hot liquid. The hints of lavender and honey filled her with calmness. She almost let herself feel peace. She took another sip. The sweetness of the honey excited her taste buds. Her daily ritual was nearly completed.

Johanna watched the activity of Ravenhill Drive through her window. The street silent—the way she liked it. The evening sky grew darker. Splashes of oranges, yellows, purples, and reds filled the air as it drew closer to sunset. She took another sip. Johanna took her role as self-appointed neighborhood watch very seriously. She expected peace and quiet on her street. She would not tolerate shenanigans. She would not tolerate the abomination of a purple house across the street.

Her eyes focused on the purple wood siding of the Folk Victorian home. The gray porch. The black door. Johanna wanted nothing more than to take Alice down. She wanted her gone from the neighborhood. She wanted her gone from Hugo's life. She wanted things the way they were before.

There was movement at the door. Johanna sat up in the chair. Her eyes focused on what was about to transpire. Hugo Dodds emerged from the house. She glared at him. The thought that he could betray Elizabeth with not just anyone, but *her*, permeated through Johanna's mind. Hugo marched off toward his silver car parked in front of his house.

She emerged from the black door. Alice Primrose—the bane of Ravenhill Drive—the one who disrupted everything. Johanna's eyes focused on her every movement. Johanna could tell they were arguing. Their arms flailed about. Furious expressions on their faces. She only wished she could hear what was being said.

Hugo continued his march to his car. He entered, started the engine, and took off. Alice followed him. She raised both hands and snapped her fingers. An explosion of purple arcane magick erupted from under the hood of the car.

The tea sloshed back and forth as Johanna's hands shook. Her nostrils flared. She set the cup down on the table next to her. The porcelain clanking against the saucer dish was the only noise in the room besides the tick of the clock. Johanna knew. She always knew. She could never prove it, but this was all the proof she needed. Her neighbor, her nemesis, was a witch.

Johanna rose from her chair. She strode with purpose over to her display table. She turned the key, releasing the drawers. She pulled out the wood box and set it on the table top. She opened the box to reveal the amulet of witch's fire. She withdrew the black, twisting anti-magick wand from the other drawer. She examined both items. Malice manifested in her thoughts. This was the day she had waited for. The day she prepared for. The day she knew would come for centuries. This was the day she would get her vengeance.

ALICE CLOSED the front door and leaned against it. Her hair covered her face, and she buried her head in her hands, sobbing. She hadn't wanted to upset Hugo. She only wanted to help him. She wiped away a tear with her index finger and sniffled twice. Her eyes were blood-shot red. Galahad knocked furiously on the door upstairs.

"It's okay, Gally," Alice yelled up. "It's okay." The knocking stopped.

Alice removed her hat and tailcoat, placing them back on the coat rack. She went into her living room. In a room full of oddities and macabre curiosities, she felt empty. She trudged over to a bookshelf. She removed a book with purple leather binding and opened the cover. The book was not a book at all. It was hollow; a secret compartment inside held a special item.

She removed the black onyx ring and examined it. It felt cold to the touch, smooth, yet well-worn with age. This one little item held so much power over Hugo. It handcuffed him to a life he couldn't let go of. It was Alice who finally removed it and freed him... or so Alice thought. She put the book back and headed to the couch.

Before she could sit down, there was a knock at the door. *Hugo!*

She pocketed the ring and moved to answer the door. She turned the diamond shaped knob and flung it open. She was surprised, not by Hugo, but a new visitor. A visitor who had only stopped over once before.

"Johanna," Alice said. "I'm not in the mood for any more insults." She shut the door, but Johanna braced it with her foot.

"I'm not here for any insults," Johanna said. "I saw your argument, and I thought maybe you could use some girl talk. You know."

Alice glared at her, curious as to why she came over now. "Why?"

"Look, I know we've had our issues in the past. I also know how lonely it can be without someone to talk to. I thought maybe you needed an ear to listen."

Alice held the door. She blinked a few times, trying to clear any remaining tears.

"You can tell me to leave at any time," Johanna offered.

Alice opened the door to let her in.

"Thank you," Johanna said as she entered.

Alice shut the door behind her. She noticed Johanna scrutinizing her home or at least the items visible in the entryway. Johanna leaned over to examine her console table. The purple and white crystals scattered across them. The black candelabras holding melted candles. Johanna recoiled at the sight, drawing her hands and arms closer to her as if to not touch anything by accident.

Johanna peeked into the living room. Alice watched her check out the red, velvet couch. The black high-back chair. The gold trimmed red drapes. The various plants and other oddities visible from the hallway. Johanna kept her arms and hands close to her chest, but Alice could tell she wanted to explore.

Knocking came from upstairs. They both snapped to view the stairs, shocked at the sounds from above.

"What's upstairs?" Johanna asked.

Alice wanted to yell up to Gally to knock it off, but that would draw too many questions from Johanna. She struggled to think of something. Anything. Then she remembered. Galahad was not alone.

"Max," Alice said. "Hugo put her up in her cage. She must be excited and knocking against the cage."

"Ah," Johanna replied. "Of course."

"Would you like something to drink?"

"Tea. That is, if you have some."

"I can put on a pot." Alice retreated into the kitchen.

She strode over to a kettle resting on the counter. She picked it up and moved to the sink to fill it with water before placing it on the stove. The blue gas flame of the burner ignited to life with a snap of her finger.

Alice stepped back into the hallway. Johanna was gone.

"Do you prefer anything in your tea?" Alice called out, trying to find her.

"Just plain, thank you," Johanna replied from the living room. "You have a very interesting collection."

"Thank you," Alice said as she peeked into the living room.

Johanna was examining the various oddities. "I'm a bit of a maximalist. I like to fill in all the space."

Johanna smiled at Alice. "You've done that very well. Every inch covered."

Alice returned to the kitchen. She didn't have time to wait for the water to boil on its own. She snapped her fingers. Steam poured out of the spout, and the black kettle whistled. She picked it up and grabbed a few tea bags from her tea cabinet. She threw them into a purple, ceramic teapot followed by the steaming water.

Alice heard Johanna moving down the hallway, but then she stopped. There was a rattle. *The basement doorknob.* Alice popped into the kitchen entryway. Johanna's hand was firmly wrapped around the knob, ready to open the basement door.

"Please don't go down there," Alice said. "It's a mess. Nothing is down there except old boxes." Alice retreated back into the kitchen.

"You have a very interesting home."

"Thank you," Alice replied.

She wanted to get back to Johanna as fast as possible, so she would have to rely on a little magick. She snapped her fingers. Two cups flew out of the cabinet and landed on the counter. The teapot rose and poured the steeping tea into the waiting cups.

"A lot of interesting stuff."

"I've collected a few things over the years." Alice picked up one of the black and orange tea cups.

"I've collected a few items myself," Johanna said. "Items that you might find interesting."

Alice emerged from the kitchen carrying the cup. "Oh yeah? Like what?"

Johanna produced the black, twisting anti-magick wand hidden within her shoulder bag. "Interesting things like this." She held it aloft for Alice to see.

Alice stopped in her tracks, and a sinking feeling filled her gut. Her breath froze in her chest. Her heart raced at the sight. "Where did you get that?"

"So, you do know what this is," Johanna said with a wicked grin. "Standard issue for all appointed Witch-Finders."

"I thought they didn't have any more of those," Alice proclaimed. Her hands shook. Drops of tea spilled over the lip of the cup and onto the floor.

"I took this off of a dead man who did unspeakable acts to me. He sentenced me to a life of hell," Johanna said. "And now, you will feel what I felt."

Alice dropped the tea cup. It fell to the hardwood floor and shattered into tiny pieces. The liquid splattered all over. She raised her hand, ready to snap her fingers. She was about to make a motion to disarm Johanna when a black bolt of energy struck her chest.

It was like fire and electricity coursing through her body. Every muscle contracted at once. Alice was awash in great agony. She let out a scream, at least, she assumed she did. She was in far too much pain to hear herself. Her body reverberated from the shock.

Johanna moved toward Alice's prostrate body. Slowly. One foot in front of the other like stalking prey going in for the kill. She kept pointing the wand at Alice. Johanna flicked her wrist, and another bolt shot her. Alice's agony echoed throughout the house. It felt as if her whole body was exploding.

Knocks on the upstairs bedroom door reverberated throughout the house. "GALLY!" Alice yelled. "HELP!"

"Who's Gally?" Johanna demanded.

She backed away and glanced up the stairs. Johanna was careful to keep a watchful eye on Alice. Another bolt shot from the wand. Alice shrieked.

"Who's Gally?"

The knocks grew louder. Max barked at the commotion.

"Help me!" Alice screamed.

The knocks grew louder and louder. Max's bark was nearly drowned out by the sound of wood against wood. It echoed and then stopped. Johanna tried to look up the stairs while never losing sight of Alice.

The sound of wood shattering emanated from upstairs as the bedroom door exploded from a collision. Galahad raced down the stairs, bouncing off the walls as it turned in the tight corners toward Alice below. Johanna shot at the charging broomstick, but missed. The broom smacked Johanna against her chin in a glancing blow. She spun around, knocking over a candelabra on the console table.

Galahad flew into the living room. It circled around and charged back at Johanna. She ducked behind the wall as Galahad flew past and back up the stairs. Alice rose to one knee. Johanna flicked her wrist and sent another black bolt to meet Alice. She screamed yet again as she collapsed to the floor.

Johanna fired another bolt back toward Galahad. It flew up the stairs as the bolt dissipated in an inky cloud against the wall. She waited for it to return, furiously looking up and then back to Alice.

The hardwood floor felt cold against Alice's face. She could barely move. She wanted the pain to end. Alice mustered enough willpower to reach into her pocket. She pulled out the black onyx ring. Her fingers collapsed around it as she drew her hand close to her heart.

"Find Hugo," Alice yelled. "You have to go find Hugo at the cemetery."

The sound of glass shattering came from the bedroom upstairs. Galahad was gone, off to find Hugo Dodds.

Johanna shocked Alice again. She released the ring in the excruciating pain. It rolled across the hardwood floor, into the living room through the other entryway. It wavered and fell over in the middle of the room.

Alice laid helpless on the floor, crying in pain. In agony. In torment. Her mind raced for anything that could help her in that moment, but could only offer a solitary thought. *Why?*

Johanna moved and stood over her body. She grabbed Alice's shoulder and flipped her over onto her back. Johanna was careful to never let the wand point away from Alice. She squatted down, inches from her. Johanna traced the wand along Alice's face.

"Do you feel that?" Johanna asked.

A line of fire burned across Alice's skin as it followed the tip of the wand, yet, there was no flame. Tears ran down Alice's face, but they could not quell the burning sensation. She wanted to scream, but the numerous hits temporarily paralyzed her.

"That's the feeling of fear. Of dread. Of hopelessness. Centuries ago, that's what I felt. I want those feelings to be seared into your memory as they were into mine."

Alice's eyes widened. She tried to snap her fingers. To call forth her powers of arcane magick. Nothing happened. In that moment, she was powerless to act.

Johanna stood up. The wand remained pointed at Alice. "Grab your keys," Johanna commanded. "We're going for a drive."

CHAPTER 25
THE GRAVE

The warm spring breeze became chilly as the sun sank in the sky. Trees waved back and forth; their budding leaves emerging from their winter slumber. It was quiet. Solemn. Peaceful. The quiet was only disrupted by the occasional bird chirp.

Hugo turned his car onto a paved path that led into Newbury Grove Memorial Park. The path wove itself through the cemetery along the rolling hills like a ceremonial black carpet affair. The tree branches played the role of welcoming hands that greeted any new and potential future residents. Small offshoots diverged to various parts of the cemetery.

Each pathway was guarded by gray and black tombstones, silently observing anyone who dared enter the hallowed grounds miles out of town. Hugo kept his eyes focused on one particular path. A path he had not traveled since the previous spring.

The car slowed as it approached a bend in the back of the cemetery. Hugo put the car into park and shut off the engine. He sat in silence for what felt like a lifetime lived years ago. His hands gripped the steering wheel. His knuckles turned white. He focused on his empty ring finger, barren of his prized black onyx ring. The ring he should have kept on. The ring he should have brought to see his wife.

He took deep breaths, holding each before he exhaled. He looked through the passenger window toward a tree. A mighty oak tree tasked with standing guard. It waited. Watched. Judged. Hugo exited the car.

He tugged at his leather jacket. He brushed his hair, making sure every piece was in its proper place. He combed his beard, so it was presentable. He stood there for a moment and gathered the courage to continue.

I should have kept the ring on. She kept the ring from me on purpose.

He pinched his ring finger only to find it barren. His fingers unfurled, and he clenched them into fists. He kept his eyes on the solitary oak tree and took a step onto the grass. He navigated between the headstones, careful to not actually step on the graves. The granite stone markers might as well have been blank. He didn't bother to read any of them. His eyes focused on the correct one.

He stopped in front of the mighty oak tree. Its branches swayed in the spring breeze to welcome him back. He nodded to acknowledge a job well done protecting the grave site—Elizabeth's grave.

The gray, granite headstone was rectangular with a slight curve on the top. The front was smooth, but the sides were naturally rough. In the center of the curve was an oval portrait—an engraved portrait of his beautiful smiling wife.

White roses were carved into the stone on both sides of her face. Hugo's eyes fell on the words below the portrait—Elizabeth P. Dodds, Beloved Daughter and Wife. His eyes lingered on the date— March 30. It had been a year, yet it felt like an instant.

Hugo knelt down in front of the headstone. His eyes focused on the portrait. He wiped away dirt and debris that gathered in the crevasses of the laser etching. He stared into her eyes and fought back tears.

"I'm sorry," Hugo said. "I'm sorry I didn't come back sooner. I wanted to stop by, but I—"

He lowered his head, and a flood of emotions washed over him. The grief he had worked so hard to overcome broke through the barrier. Everything rushed back. The restaurant when he found out the cancer came back. Their last trick or treat together. The hospital visits. The church. His mind flooded with emotions. Tears flowed down his face.

"I should have been back sooner. Everyone tried to tell me to move on, but I couldn't. How could I? There hasn't been a day that went by that I didn't think of you. Your smile. Your warmth. Your smell. I wanted it all again. I've begged for it," Hugo sobbed. "I miss you. I miss you so much."

He wiped away the tears rolling down his face.

"I got a dog. I named her Maxine, like you wanted. I call her Max. Consider it a compromise," he let out a chuckle as his tears rolled past. "She's a real pain in the butt. You would love her. I'm sure she would have loved you more than me."

Hugo paused.

"Everyone misses you. I get reminded about it all the time. People tell me how great you were. How you're missed. How you're loved. The Raskins are watching after me. They always make sure I'm taken care of. Well, I think they're mostly making sure Max is okay."

He allowed a slight smile before his face fell solemn. He scanned the cemetery to ensure he was alone. There were only the ghosts of past lives in the cemetery that evening. He licked his lips. He moved his jaw, readying himself to tell her his secret. Shame washed over him.

"I..." he started before admitting his betrayal. "I met someone. She's new in town. She moved in next door. She's unique. She has a purple house filled with stuff. You would've loved it."

He paused.

"She's a witch. Like a really for real witch. And she has a flying broom. And does magick. That's magick with a *K*. There's a difference. She reminds me of that constantly. Oh! And there's this magick mirror who tries to flirt with me all the time. And wine! She makes wine. This magical wine. We made wine together. She turned me into a true wine connoisseur, like you always wanted to do."

There was a hint of joy in Hugo's words.

"She let me fly her broom. I named it Galahad. Just like—"

Hugo's words became quieter.

"Just like the horse I rode on when I proposed. And I almost died!"

His voice picked up again.

"I fell off the broom, and it saved me. It scooped me up before I crashed into the trees. And we flew around, going faster and faster. It was fantastic. He's... He's a good buddy."

The tears stopped.

"For the past few months, she has made me feel so much joy and happiness. Feelings I haven't felt in a long time, and I think I blew it."

The joy faded from his face.

"We got into an argument and... and I said things out of frustration. I shouldn't have said them. I lashed out at the one person who actually made me feel happy again. And... and I ruined it."

The breeze picked up. The tree branches cracked and strained at the movement. The sky grew darker as it turned a shade of purple, yellow, and red. Hugo bowed his head. He struggled for the words.

"I love her," he told Elizabeth. "She loves me too. I want it to work. I want to move on, but I can't. I thought I did. I tried, but you were always there in the back of my mind. Then today happened. I can't let you go. How could I? How can I let you go?"

He grabbed the headstone with both hands.

"What should I do?"

He leaned his forehead against her portrait. Tears flowed down his face.

"Please tell me."

There was only silence.

Something struck Hugo, and pain erupted in his right ribs. The force knocked him over onto the ground. He clutched his side and clenched his teeth. His face contorted in agony. He couldn't hold it any longer and let out a cry of pain. He rose to see what hit him. There, floating in the air, was Galahad.

"Gally!" Hugo yelled. "What the hell?" He gathered himself. He stood up and brushed off his jacket and pants.

"She couldn't do it herself? So, she sent you to finish the job, huh?"

Galahad floated there. Unmoved from the question, he waited.

"Well, what do you want?"

Galahad crept closer to Hugo. It bumped against his chest.

Hugo backed away. "What are you doing?"

It bumped against his chest twice more. Hugo leaned over and glared it in the face. His eyes changed from annoyance to concern at the hickory stick floating before him.

"Alice wouldn't have sent you without the cover of darkness," Hugo remarked. Fear washed over him. "What's wrong?"

It floated forward and lightly tapped under Hugo's chin. It backed up and turned around. The broom waited for Hugo to get on.

Hugo turned back toward the grave. "I..." Hugo spoke to Elizabeth. "I have to go."

Hugo grabbed the broom handle and swung his leg over the seat. He placed his feet on the footrest. He pulled up on the handle, and with a "yah," took off.

Hugo and Galahad flew over the farmland leading into town. They flew as fast as Galahad could. The wind rushed over Hugo's face, and his hair blew wildly. He didn't have the cover of darkness to hide. He needed to hide. He couldn't let anyone see him flying.

Hugo pulled up on the handle, ascending to dizzying heights. He tried to fly as high as he could. The church steeple was first to appear off in the distance. More and more buildings emerged on the horizon. With his eyes focused, he leaned forward.

To hell with it. He cut across the center of town, finding the fastest route to her house. He noticed some people look up as he streaked across the sky. He didn't care. He had one thought. One solitary purpose. Get to Alice.

Galahad flew down Ravenhill Drive toward the purple house. Hugo saw the front door open. He held his breath as panic set in. He leapt off onto the top of the porch and went charging through the door. He stopped himself before tripping on the knocked over entryway table; its contents spilled across the hallway floor.

"Alice!" Hugo shouted.

He continued down the hallway. He paused to examine the shattered tea cup on the ground. The black and orange pieces were scattered in a pool of liquid. He ran to the kitchen. There was nothing. He sprinted into the living room. It was there in the middle of the room —the distinct black onyx ring. He picked it up off the floor. He rolled it back and forth between the tips of his fingers, looking it over.

"Alice! Are you here?"

"Help!" Alice's voice came from upstairs.

Hugo placed the ring on the coffee table and charged to her voice. He grunted with every step as he dashed up the stairs. The sight of Alice's splintered bedroom door stopped him in his tracks. He touched the hole in the door—the hole big enough for a broomstick to fly through.

"Hello? Is someone there? Please help me," a familiar voice shouted from inside the room.

Hugo pushed opened the door to find the room vacant except for Max. She whined and barked in her cage.

"Wait a moment, Max," Hugo said as he rushed past.

"Please help!" Alice's voice came from the bathroom.

The bathroom was dark. Hugo turned on the lights, only to find it empty.

"It's you! You have to help," Alice's reflection exclaimed. "You have to help me."

"What happened?"

"I... I don't know," she said. She paced back and forth in her mirrored bathroom. Her hair was messy, and her hands cupped over her mouth, only removing them to talk. "There was a voice, then I heard an argument and shouting."

"What voice?"

"A woman's voice," she replied.

"Ez?"

"No. A voice I've never heard before. She was angry. I heard screaming and then..." her words trailed as she let out a scream of agony. She bent over, holding her stomach. "I'm in pain. You have to find me."

Tears flowed down her face. "Help me," she pleaded.

Hugo grabbed the sides of the mirror, pulling himself closer. He wanted to pull her through the glass to safety. He could only watch as she bent over in pain. In agony. Like Elizabeth.

"Where? Where is she?"

"I don't know. I don't see sights. Only feelings," Alice's reflection said. She fell to the floor, screaming in pain.

"What do you feel? Please tell me. I can help you, but you have to tell me where to find her first," he pleaded as the ornate mirror design indented into his hands.

"I feel fear. I feel a chill, a breeze. I feel..." The agony overtook her. "I feel... I feel... sacrifice."

"Sacrifice?" Hugo asked. His mind raced, trying to find what it could mean. *Sacrifice.* He ran through everything it could be. His eyes widened with the sudden realization of where she was. The place he once thought she was bringing him...

"I know where she is. She's in the woods!"

"Hurry!" Alice's reflection yelled.

Hugo ran out of the room, nearly tripping down the stairs as he tried to skip steps. Galahad waited for him in the entryway. He grabbed the broom handle and jumped onto the bicycle seat.

"To the woods!" Hugo commanded.

They flew out the door and into the sky.

CHAPTER 26
BURN THE WITCH

The town center came alive with activity as the sun set in the western sky. Shops closed up for the evening. Antonio's Italian Ristorante received dinner guests. The local pub welcomed new visitors. A handful of pedestrians were out for a walk on the lovely spring evening. Brilliant shades of purples, yellows, and oranges painted the sky. The scene was picturesque. Peaceful. A far cry from what transpired in the black SUV that exited the town.

Alice drove her SUV past the trail entrance of Wildgrove Park. She glanced over to her passenger. Johanna sat motionless. Her eyes focused on Alice's every move, while holding the twisted wand in her right hand. It pointed at Alice's side.

"Don't think about trying anything," Johanna said. "Keep your eyes forward. Both hands on the wheel."

Alice did as she was commanded. Her hands gripped the steering wheel in the top corners. Her eyes focused forward. "Where am I going?"

"There is a service road up the street. Turn into it. Nice and slow," Johanna said, her voice calm and steady.

They left the town of Newbury Grove behind. Alice drove down the road—woods to her right, farm fields on her left. A dirt path, barely wide enough for a vehicle, came into view.

"Turn there," Johanna instructed.

Alice slowed the SUV. She released her grip on the wheel, sliding her hands into new positions in preparation to make the turn. She glanced over toward Johanna. Her eyes never wavered from Alice. She pressed the brake, slowing the vehicle. Each finger wrapped around the molded vinyl wheel.

As the last finger tightened its grip, Alice made a sharp turn and accelerated the SUV. It jerked forward as it headed toward a tree. Alice's body slammed against the driver side door. She turned to see if Johanna was caught off guard, but a bolt from the wand struck her side. Every muscle convulsed at once as the pain overtook her.

"Stop the car!" Johanna yelled. Another black bolt shot out from the wand and struck Alice. "Stop the car now!"

Alice stomped on the brakes. The SUV jostled the occupants as it came to a full stop. Alice lurched forward and then slammed back against her seat.

"I can make this as painful for you as possible if you don't do as I say." Johanna's face was furious; her eyebrows were hunched. Fire burned in her eyes. "Do you understand me?"

Alice nodded.

Johanna raised the wand, pointing it at Alice's head. "I'm sorry. I didn't hear you."

Alice turned her gaze toward Johanna. The tip of the wand was mere inches from her eyes. Alice cleared her throat. Johanna's face wore a condescending expression, waiting for an answer she already knew.

"I understand," Alice replied in a low voice.

"Now that we understand each other, drive on. We can't be late." Johanna motioned down the road with her head.

A shadowy tunnel of barren trees lined the path. Their branches swayed in the breeze as they beckoned the pair to proceed further into the darkness. The SUV rolled forward and disappeared into the woods. Alice carefully navigated down the service road. The dirt path carved a winding procession to their final destination. They stopped at the end of the path; trees blocked any further progress deeper into the forest.

"Turn it off and open the door," Johanna commanded. "Slowly."

Alice did as instructed and gripped the handle to open the door.

"Slowly," Johanna reiterated.

The door creaked as Alice exited the vehicle. Johanna sprung out of the passenger side and shuffled around the front. She kept her ever-watchful eyes and wand trained on Alice's every movement.

Alice gave a quick glance around. There was no movement. She listened for any signs of life. She only heard the sound of the branches swaying in the breeze like the cackling of laughter at what awaited further in the woods.

"Walk," Johanna ordered. "We're late. Walk!"

Alice proceeded past the first line of trees. Their smaller tree trunks swayed in the breeze as if they were giddy with glee. Alice grabbed one to balance herself on the rugged terrain. She took a few more steps and then spun around.

She tried to produce arcane bolts of energy, but was met with that far too familiar searing pain as another black bolt hit her. Another and then another. She fell to her knees. Her body hunched over to deal with the pain.

Johanna approached her. She placed the tip of the wand under Alice's chin, lifting it so they met eye to eye.

Tears of pain welled in Alice's eyes. A helpless expression. "Why are you doing this?"

Johanna stood over her with the wand inches from Alice's face. "What I'm doing is showing you mercy. The same mercy afforded to me years ago. Now get up. Slowly."

Johanna backed away as Alice rose to her feet. Tears rolled down Alice's face.

"A few more feet. We need a good view of the sunset," Johanna said.

Alice was in visible agony from the lingering effects of the wand. She held her side where she had been hit and searched around, as if hoping for help to arrive. Any help. But there was nothing. It was only her, Johanna, and the cackling trees.

Johanna focused on the setting sun. The deeper shades of orange and red filled the sky.

"This will do," Johanna said. "Put your back to that tree."

Alice did as she was told.

Johanna produced a rope from her bag. She tied it around Alice's body multiple times. The rope constricted Alice's chest with each pass, binding her closer to the trunk of the tree. Johanna tied the ropes as tightly as she could. She then produced a smaller length of rope and bound Alice's hands together. She marched around to face Alice.

"What is this?" Alice asked. "Some sort of ritual sacrifice?" Those words brought back memories of her and Hugo many months ago when he had first learned to ride Galahad.

"You could say that," Johanna said as she dug into her bag.

Alice's eyes widened as the gold disk emerged. The yellow jewel surrounded by eight orange gems. Her face went blank and pale.

Johanna smiled. "Oh! You know what this is, don't you?"

"I... I thought it was a legend," Alice replied.

"Oh, it's real. Very real," Johanna said. "It has caused more destruction, pain, and misery than you will ever know."

Johanna approached Alice like a stalking predator savoring every step. Her smile grew wider as she drew closer. The fear grew on Alice's face. Johanna tried to place the amulet of witch's fire over Alice's head. Alice struggled, moving her head back and forth. She buried the back of her head into the tree so Johanna could not put it on.

Johanna jabbed her with the wand. Alice screamed in agony as her head lurched forward. Johanna slipped the gold chain over Alice's purple hair. The amulet dangled around her neck.

Alice sobbed. "Please. Please don't do this." Her tears rolled down her face and fell at her feet. "Why are you doing this?"

"Oh, I've been where you're standing. I know that fear. The frightening helplessness as people condemn you to die a gruesome, painful death you didn't deserve. And it is painful."

Johanna pointed toward the amulet with the wand. Alice glanced down before returning to Johanna.

Johanna continued, "I've lived more lifetimes than anyone should. I've lost more loved ones than you will ever know. I've felt more pain than humanly possible all because a witch bound me to the fate of that amulet. It was because of a witch like you that I was condemned to this lifetime of pain, torment, and suffering. I've made it my vow to never forget. Never forgive."

A DARKNESS FELL over the cabin. The late afternoon sun was now obscured by the engulfing trees. Smoke rose from the diminutive stone chimney, and a light flickered in the window. It seemed peaceful. Quiet. Unassuming. A hooded figured emerged from the shadows of the trees. Footsteps crushed the wet grass as the evening dew set in. The figure never broke stride as it approached the cabin.

Johanna pulled back the hood of her cloak as she stopped in front of the door. She stood for a moment to prepare herself for what was to come. She lingered on the door in front of her. A thin layer of moss had overtaken the wood. The brief thought of turning and running away entered her mind. She hesitated, but the anger of the past drove her forward. Johanna knocked three times.

"Who is it?" a once familiar voice said from inside.

"It's Johanna Newes. May I come in?"

The voice replied without hesitation, "Yes. Yes. Please enter."

Johanna lifted a latch and swung open the door. The cabin was small. It had been many years since Johanna first set foot in here, but it remained largely unchanged. The room smelled of musty dirt. The cabin was illuminated by a set of candles that floated in the air. Plants and cutting tools covered the very same table which had held her lifeless body. Shelves held jars and other assorted bottles. A fire smoldered in the hearth below a black cauldron.

An elderly woman sat in front of the fire within the confines of an armed chair. Time had not been pleasant to Willow the witch. Her fingers withered and gnarled with age. A cane rested to one side. She wore a shawl to warm her frail body. Her skin was even more weathered and wrinkled than when Johanna last saw her. Her hair was thinned and short to remove the tangled mess that had once adorned her head. She smiled at her visitor.

"Come closer, my dear," Willow said. Johanna approached, looking over the room to make sure they were alone. "It's been so long since I last saw you. You haven't aged a day."

Johanna's youthful appearance betrayed her true age. It had been over thirty years since that fateful day. Thirty years since she was condemned for practicing witchcraft. Thirty years since she was sentenced to hell for a crime she never committed.

"I need your help."

"I can try the best I can, but my bones are tired and weary. Magick becomes more difficult for me."

"I need you to fix me."

Willow closed her eyes and slumped in her chair. "That's something I cannot do."

Tears welled in Johanna's eyes. A fierce anger smoldered and wanted to erupt from deep within her soul. "Why not? I... I need your help. You're the only one who can fix me."

"The only way to save you was to tie you to that amulet. Your father knew that, but still insisted I bring you back."

"You lie!"

She pointed to the very spot Josiah had stood years ago. "He was right there. He looked me in the eye and begged me to bring you back because you were all he had left. There was a pain in his eyes. How could I say no?"

Johanna clenched her fists and buried her mouth behind them to hide the gnashing of her teeth. "You lie. You can fix me."

"I cannot."

"Do you know what I go through? How people question why I don't age? Why I can't answer them? Why I have to move to avoid questions before they condemn me yet again for being the horrific abomination that you are?"

"I'm so sorry. I truly am, but there is nothing I can do."

"You lie. This was your dark magic. You can fix me, but you *choose* not to."

"My dear, I can't. I don't have the knowledge or the spell to undo it. You are tied to that amulet. As long as it exists, you will remain frozen in time. I told that to him, and yet, he still wanted you to live. It will only end when that amulet is destroyed. A task I don't envy."

Tears flowed down Johanna's face. The thought that she was forever trapped to the very thing that turned her into this monstrous creation ripped apart her soul. The inner fire erupted in a barbaric, soul splitting scream.

"I'm sorry. There is nothing I can do."

Those words didn't ease Johanna's pain. Nothing would— nothing short of untethering herself from that amulet. Her pain must be shared. The person who condemned her to this fate must suffer. Like the monster who placed the amulet around her neck had suffered.

Johanna withdrew the anti-magick wand from her pocket. Johanna smiled through her tears as Willow's eyes grew wide with fright at the sight of the twisting wand.

"If I have to suffer, so will every witch or sorcerer or anyone who utters a word of magic." She pointed the wand at Willow, and a black bolt flew across the room.

It struck her on the side, knocking her from the chair. Her frail body slammed into the wood floor. Willow let out an agonizing scream. She tried to lift herself up, but couldn't. Her joints were too frail from old age to lift her vulnerable body off the ground. Johanna aimed the wand once more and struck her with another bolt of anti-magick. She repeated it, again and again, until Willow's body lay lifeless on the cabin floor.

"I've lived for over three hundred years. I've watched too many friends and loved ones die. Do you know how many people I've buried? How many people I've forgotten? I move every few years because people get curious when you don't age. They ask questions. Questions I *cannot* answer. *I am alone.* An eternal life alone is hell. I'm in constant suffering!" Johanna yelled. A cathartic release of tears flowed down her face.

"Johanna, I can heal you. You'll no longer be tied to this amulet. I promise. You... You won't be alone any longer. You'll be free to live life as who you want to be," Alice begged.

"I know the *real* cost of healing. I was condemned to this life of pain and suffering by a witch who tried to heal me once. What makes you think I want a witch to heal me again?"

"It'll be different this time. I can help you heal those wounds. Please, we can do it together."

"I came here thinking I was done with witches. I thought I found peace. Elizabeth's kindness and warmth helped to make me whole again. I loved her more than anyone since..." Johanna's voice trailed off. "I had to watch her die like everyone else. I don't want to forget her like the others. I can't forget her."

"I'm so sorry, Johanna," Alice offered. "She meant so much to so many people. I only wish I could have been there to help her."

"One day I looked out, and there's a purple house across the street. Then I found out you tried to replace the only friend I had left. You stole her husband. You stole her life. She was the only remaining thing I cared about in this world, and you tried to erase her," Johanna cried. Her nostrils flared, eyebrows crinkled, and her eyes glared. "I won't let him forget her, replace her with *you*."

"I'm not replacing her. He knows this," Alice pleaded. "I never tried to replace her. I tried to live up to her. Please, I can help you." Her voice caught in her throat.

Johanna stood silent. She moved behind Alice to get a better view of the setting sun. Alice struggled against the restraints. She tried snapping her fingers, but failed to produce anything. The wand had dampened her powers. The ropes pulled tighter against her chest and wrists as she squirmed. The sun descended, and the sky turned darker shades of oranges and reds.

CHAPTER 27
UPON A WOODEN STEED HE RIDES

Hugo leaned forward on the broomstick. His chin was inches from the hickory handle. His hair blew wildly, and his face had become wind burned. He pulled back on the handle, beckoning Galahad to climb higher and higher. They flew past the town center with blazing speed. The townsfolk gazed up at the sight of a person riding a broomstick flash by in an instant. Many seemed to questioned if that's what they actually saw before returning to their daily routines.

Hugo flew across Wildgrove Park. His eyes frantically searched for any signs of Alice beneath the treetops below. Their branches swayed back and forth to conceal their secrets. Hugo and Galahad climbed higher to see more. The number of trees expanded before them.

They flew past the clearing where months before he had learned to fly Galahad. They traced his normal walking path, searching for any signs of Alice. Hugo only saw the budding limbs of trees.

They stopped. Hugo sat up, scanning as much of the park as possible. His head moved from spot to spot, searching for any signs of movement. His breathing intensified—short, rapid breaths in and out. His nostrils flared, trying desperately to let in as much air as possible. His thoughts traced back to the last words he said to her— words that couldn't be unsaid and would haunt him for eternity.

Elizabeth, help me find her. Please help me find her, Hugo thought.

There was only silence.

"I don't see her," Hugo said to Galahad.

It spun around in slow circles, giving Hugo enough time to continue his search. His heart thumped against his chest; the rhythm increased with each passing second. He held his breath for a moment and closed his eyes.

THE RHYTHMIC BEATS of the heart monitor filled the room. It was dark. Only the soft glow of an overhead light above Elizabeth's bed illuminated the area. An oxygen tube was placed in her nose. Wires connected to heart monitor leads crisscrossed her body before disappearing under her hospital gown. She wore a purple knit hat on her head; her vibrant auburn hair was a distant memory. Her face was sunken and skeletal. Her breath grew shallower with every passing moment. Hugo held Elizabeth's frail hand as—

"NOT NOW." Hugo opened his eyes. "Focus. Find Alice." He was jolted back to the task at hand. He scanned the park one more time. Still nothing.

"Alice!" Hugo yelled.

Faint screams echoed in the distance to the west—a woman's scream of agony.

Galahad snapped around; the momentum nearly threw Hugo off balance. He gripped the hickory handle tighter. His shoes planted on the footrest. He leaned forward; his eyes locked in on the target. With a loud "Yah," they took off.

Galahad flew along the outside of Wildgrove Park. Newbury Grove faded into the background. The setting sun descended behind the tree lines. The pair dove, flying even with the tops of the tree. The trees were a dizzying blur on either side as they flew past. Hugo focused his eyes on the dirt service road that appeared.

"There," Hugo said. "Go down there."

Galahad banked sharply to the right. Hugo leaned into the turn to maintain balance. They flew into the tunnel of barren trees. Their branches cackled at what was about to transpire within the shadowy depths. They followed the winding road until Hugo saw it up ahead —Alice's black SUV.

They zipped past, weaving in and around the trees now standing guard over the dark ritual about to transpire. His eyes widened at the sight of Alice tied to a tree, struggling to break free. He recognized the woman standing behind her. Johanna.

"Alice!" Hugo shouted.

Johanna whipped around. Her eyes widened with the surprise of seeing Hugo approaching on a broomstick. She flicked her wrist, and a black bolt shot out of the twisting wand. It streaked across the sky, heading straight for the charging wooden steed.

Galahad pushed up to avoid the oncoming assault. The overbearing trees blocked any escape. A branch smacked Hugo in the face, causing him to fall backward and pull up on Galahad. Their momentum spun them around. The black bolt struck Galahad on its left side.

The surprise attack of the tree branch and the force of the bolt knocked Hugo off balance. His fingers released their grip of Galahad. He went tumbling through the air. The ground was hard and unforgiving. He grimaced at the impact as pain exploded through his ribs and side. He tried to gasp for air, but couldn't. He fought for breath a few more times before air filled his lungs once again.

Galahad spun through the air and crashed into the ground head first. It flipped end over end before coming to a stop on the ground. It lay there, motionless.

Johanna smiled at her deeds. She turned back toward Alice to witness the end of her handiwork. A forceful explosion of energy lifted her up. Johanna was slammed onto the ground, and the impact momentarily stunned her.

The wand flew through the air, bouncing off a tree and landing in the underbrush. Johanna tried to get up, but she couldn't move. She tried to squirm, but the unseen force held her in place.

Alice's eyes focused on Johanna. Her hand raised as far as she could in the restraints. Alice clenched her fist tighter. Johanna begged for Alice to release her as the force constricted her.

"Get the wand," Alice shouted. "Stab the necklace with it."

Hugo sprang up. The pain along his side caused him to grimace and stumble to one knee. He picked himself up and ran over to where the wand ricocheted. A pile of discarded sticks lay at the base of the tree. He grabbed at anything that appeared to be a wand.

"Is this it?" Hugo yelled. He held up a grayish stick in the sky.

"It's twisted and black," Alice shouted. "Hurry."

He searched through the brush. He discarded anything that wasn't twisted nor black. He ventured further beyond the tree. He flipped over discarded leaves. Their damp underside did not reveal the treasure he sought. He fell to his knees, hands outstretched. He picked up anything, everything he could touch.

"I can't find it," Hugo said.

The sun retreated beyond the horizon. The orange jewels glowed. The yellow jewel flickered.

"Hugo! Forget the wand," Alice shouted. "I need you to remove this necklace. I can't hold Johanna down and remove it at the same time."

Hugo continued his search. He brushed aside debris. He found nothing. He sat back on his feet to get a better view of the area. His eyes scanned everywhere. He lurched out with both hands to feel for the wand.

"Hugo!" Alice shouted once more.

Sticking out of the ground between a pile was the black wand.

The tip was lodged into the wet ground beneath decaying leaves. Hugo crawled over. His fingers wrapped around the twisted design. He pulled the wand like he was unsheathing a sword, ready to slay a monster.

"I found it," he said with a smile.

Hugo leapt to his feet, looking over toward Alice. Any sort of relief quickly faded. The sun disappeared beyond the horizon, and the sky turned bloodred. The amulet of witch's fire glowed. Alice let out a primal scream. Her face contorted in torment. Tears flowed down her face as her gaze met Hugo's.

Their eyes locked, not in longing or desire, but desperation. Her emerald green eyes begged for help. His icy blues were helpless but to witness the event unfolding before him. It felt like an eternity. The pain, the suffering, the torment. Her screams ripped through Hugo. His heart, his mind, and his soul shattered at what transpired.

Alice's screams stopped, and her body leaned forward. Her head hung lifeless above her chest. Hugo tried to scream. He tried to produce any sort of noise. His mind raced for what to do next.

~

HUGO HELD Elizabeth's frail hand...

~

HE WOULDN'T LET his emotions slip back into his torment. *Stab the necklace.* He raced through the trees toward her. Johanna writhed on the ground, gasping to catch her breath from the crushing force, as Hugo rushed past her.

He held up Alice's head, using his thumbs to pull back on her eyelids. Her emerald green eyes were vacant and lifeless. Tears rolled down his face. His muscles tightened, and his breath was short. "Alice, can you hear me?"

Alice's face turned a shade of blue.

Johanna stood up and took a step toward Hugo. She kept her distance. "You're too late," she exclaimed. "The witch is no more. The world should thank me."

Hugo guided Alice's head back to its resting position and turned to Johanna with malice in his eyes. His nose twitched. An internal fury built within him. He raised the wand high above his head.

Johanna's eyes focused on the twists. She grasped the faded silver cloak clasp on her lapel. She squeezed to the point that it imprinted into her hand. She mouthed the words, "Thank you."

Hugo crashed the wand into the center of the amulet. Black sparks of arcane magick emanated from the yellow jewel. The amulet disintegrated before his eyes. The orange gems fell out of the gold disk. They slowly dissolved before hitting the ground. The gold chain faded into memory. The amulet of witch's fire was no more.

Hugo watched Johanna's hands turned to dust. She was being erased from existence—her fate the same as the amulet's. The black wave of arcane energy slowly spread up her arms to her torso. Her eyes rolled into the back of her head. She gasped before smiling. Her legs and torso faded. The last remaining visage of Johanna Newes was her head turning to dust and floating away in the breeze.

Hugo pocketed the wand. He removed the restraints from Alice's hands and chest. He caught her as she fell limply into his arms. He lifted her lifeless body. His arms gripped under her knees and shoulders.

"Come on, buddy. I need you," Hugo yelled over to Galahad.

There was no response.

"Hey, we've got to go."

There was still no response.

"Gally, come on, buddy, I can't do this alone." A hint of fear and panic appeared in his voice.

Galahad lay motionless on the ground.

Hugo ran with Alice's body to the black SUV beyond the trees. His legs strained on the uneven terrain. He dodged around trees and other debris. Her body jostled in his arms. She grew heavier with each step. The strength came to him, and he continued forth. He had to get her to safety. He must get her to safety.

He slid Alice's knees down his arm, freeing his hand to open the passenger door. He struggled to set Alice inside. Her limp body caught against the door. He was careful not to hit her head when he placed her inside the car. He strapped the seatbelt over her so she wouldn't slump over.

He ran back through the trees to the lifeless broomstick. He stood for a moment, hoping it was only stunned. He bent down and brushed against it with his hand. It laid motionless.

"Please," Hugo pleaded. "Don't leave me too. I need you." He gripped the hickory handle and lifted it close to his chest.

The hickory broomstick, the horse dog Hugo had named Gala-had, was dead.

The sky grew darker, and shadows crept over the area. The trees cackled with excitement over what had transpired as they swayed in the breeze. Hugo stood up and rushed back to the SUV. He placed Galahad on the back seat. He climbed into the driver's seat and started the engine. The headlights fired up, fighting back against the oncoming darkness. He backed up and turned around. They sped away down the dirt path.

CHAPTER 28
THE LOVERS' KISS

Dusk fell on the area. The last vestiges of orange, red, and purple sunlight slowly faded from view, giving over to the darkness of night. The lights of the town center rose above the horizon like twinkling stars appearing in the night sky. The black SUV sped down the road leading into Newbury Grove.

Hugo's eyes focused on the road before him. He pushed the SUV to twice the normal speed limit. Hugo glanced over to check on her, only briefly, before returning his eyes to the road. Alice's lifeless body jostled with the movement of the car. Her head slumped over; her body was only held up by the seatbelt.

"Hold on, Alice," Hugo said in a mixture of fear and reassurance. "We're almost there."

Hugo's eyes only caught the town motto, 'Welcome To The Neighborhood' as the SUV zipped past the Newbury Grove welcome sign. He slowed down as they approached the town center. The Newbury Grove citizens went about their nightly activities.

He arrived at the intersection that led toward Ravenhill Drive. The tires screeched, rubber against asphalt, as Hugo whipped the car around the corner. He paid no attention to the stop sign, his mission far more important than any traffic laws. He picked up speed again before pressing the brakes once more to control the turn down their street.

Hugo could see their final destination. The purple house appeared from the darkness as they approached. He slammed on the brakes, stopping in front of the house. Their bodies lurched forward before snapping back against the seat rests. Hugo unbuckled himself and exited the vehicle. He ran around to the passenger door and removed Alice from the car.

Her head and arms dangled as he held her lifeless body. He struggled to hold on to her, changing his grip on her legs and torso. When he was satisfied, he gave a kick to the SUV door to shut it and hurried to the house. His muscles exploded in agony as he carried her across the yard.

He started the climb up the gray porch steps. Each step more odious than the last. He slightly rotated her body in an attempt to steady his balance. His foot caught on the ledge of a step. He tripped forward and let go of her legs, catching himself. He stood up, grabbed her legs again, and continued his ascent.

Hugo ran through the open black door. He ran into the living room and set her body on the red velvet couch. He grabbed the twisting pillars of the hourglass resting on the end table. He spun the ring to the top. The sands slowly fell. He placed it back on the end table and ran out of the living room.

He slammed the front door as he passed by on his way up the stairs. His leg muscles burned, but he fought through it and continued. He ran through Alice's bedroom to the bathroom held within. Max whined as he rushed past. He turned on the lights and grabbed the ornate gold frame of the mirror.

"You have to help me," Hugo said. "She's hurt, and I don't know what to do."

There was no response.

"You have to help me."

No response from the mirror.

"Are you there?" Hugo stood up taller.

He looked down to the floor on the inside of the mirror. Alice's mirror reflection lay motionless on the black and white checkerboard tile. Hugo's eyes widened with terror. He shook the mirror.

"Hey!" Hugo yelled. "Wake up. I need you."

There was no response. Her body face down. Lifeless like Alice downstairs.

"I need you. Please help." His hand slapped the wall.

No response.

As his heart raced and his breathing became labored, he stood there thinking. "What do I do?" he said in a low, hushed voice.

Esmerelda Honeydew. The name popped into his mind.

He hurried back downstairs. His hands braced against the walls; he leapt down a few steps and into the hallway. He scrambled to find Alice's oversized, rectangular black and purple purse. He unzipped the top and fumbled through the contents. He tossed aside various items, searching for Alice's phone. On the bottom, his prize awaited. He pulled out the phone and called Ez.

The ringing felt like an eternity. Each dial tone was more excruciating than the last. He heard a click.

"Hello?" Hugo yelled.

"You've reached Ez. I'm not able to come to the phone at the moment because I'm probably working behind the bar. You know what to do, kiddo," Ez's prerecorded voice said through the phone.

Hugo waited for the beep. "Ez! Ez, it's Hugo. Alice is in trouble. I need help. Please call back." He hung up the phone.

Then he stood in the hallway. He crept toward the living room entryway, not wanting to look at the red velvet couch. It felt eerily reminiscent to entering Hill Funeral Home's viewing room the year before.

~

HUGO ENTERED the viewing room with half steps. He tried to delay the inevitable as long as possible. If he didn't enter the room, then it wasn't real—not to him, anyway. The room was empty, except for Hugo and one other occupant.

The place smelled of lilies and lavender. White folding chairs were organized neatly into rows on either side of a center aisle way. A wooden lectern was placed in the front left. Floral arrangements were spread out in the front of the rectangular room. In the center, there was a tan wood coffin with one half open, revealing the occupant.

Hugo approached with half steps. His eyes focused, and his lips quivered. His eyes watered, but he held back tears as long as possible until a solitary tear fell. As he drew closer, he focused on her smiling face. The auburn wig placed on her head. She appeared to be at peace. No longer in pain. His Elizabeth...

"FOCUS!" Hugo yelled. "Focus. Help her."

He dialed Ez's number again. Once again, he got the voicemail.

"Please call me back, Ez! I need your help."

He placed Alice's phone in his pocket. He searched around for something, anything. He glanced down the hallway to the shattered tea cup. His eyes focused on the liquid on the floor.

Liquid. Drink. *Wine!*

Hugo flung open the door leading into the basement. The smell of mildew and dampness filled his nose. He leapt into the darkness. The stairs creaked as he hurried down. He braced himself against the wall, taking a risk with every hurried step. He lunged for a step below, and his foot slipped. He stumbled but grabbed ahold of the railing, preventing him from falling and smacking his head into the cinderblock wall. He picked himself up and continued.

He stretched into the darkness for the light pull string. His arm flailed into the air, searching, hoping. He felt the twine pull string.

His fingers wrapped around it and gave a tug. The light illuminated the empty basement. Hugo rushed over to the wooden door. He pushed on the cast iron handle revealing the dark room inside.

Hugo snapped his fingers. Nothing happened.

"Of course," he said. "Alice, we need to have a conversation about motion sensors."

"*A parlor trick. Stage magic,*" Alice's words from last Halloween filled his mind.

He pulled out Alice's phone and turned on the flashlight. He rushed over to the wine rack along the back wall. He pulled bottles, searching for anything that could help.

"Luck?" Hugo said. "Maybe." He placed the bottle under his arm, his hand holding the phone.

"Contortion? No." He pulled more and more bottles. "Courage. Insight. Happiness. None of these are going to work."

He continued. "Fertility. Not right now. Protection. Too late. Youth. I guess I'll try luck." He placed the phone into his pocket and ran back up the stairs.

He charged into the living room. Alice's body lay still on the velvet couch like a corpse in a casket. Her face had turned a pale blue. He knelt beside her, holding the bottle in one hand and gripping the top with the other. The cork buried flush into the bottle's neck.

"Fuck. Corkscrew."

He set the bottle on the coffee table, stood, and took off for the kitchen.

"She's a damn human corkscrew. What are the odds she has one?" he murmured to himself.

He yanked open the counter drawers and rifled through their contents. Silverware, kitchen towels, cooking utensils. A drawer full of coupons, batteries, and other various odds and ends. None held a corkscrew.

He flung open the cabinet doors. Plates and dishes. Coffee mugs. Glasses. Nothing resembling a corkscrew.

He opened the final cabinet door. Wineglasses hung upside

down. Resting in the corner below the hanging glasses was a lever corkscrew.

"Oh, thank God." Hugo exhaled. He grabbed the corkscrew and hurried back to the living room.

Hugo repositioned Alice's body, so her head was atop the arm rest. He placed the corkscrew overtop the bottle's neck. He squeezed and pushed down on the lever. The corkscrew descended into the soft wooden stopper. He pulled up and, with a small 'pop,' the cork was free.

He opened Alice's mouth. Her lips and jaw were cold to the touch. He poured in a small bit of wine—not much. He didn't want to drown her trying to resuscitate her. He closed her mouth and tilted her head back. He waited.

Nothing happened.

He tried a little more.

Nothing.

He picked up Alice's torso, hoping it would help her drink the liquid. He waited.

Nothing.

He placed her down. He ran back into the basement and wine cellar. He continued searching the bottles for anything to help. He found nothing. He let out a barbaric yawp. The same primal scream he imagined he let out in the church a year ago. He checked the phone. No calls. Zero bars. He rushed out of the cellar. One bar.

He dialed Ez again. "You've reached Ez. I'm not able to come to the phone at the moment because I'm probably working behind the bar. You know what to do, kiddo," Ez's prerecorded voice said once again.

Hugo hung up. He stood there; his emotions overwhelmed him. His eyes filled with tears. He could not hold back the deluge as tears fell down his face. He collapsed to his knees on the basement floor. His hand was the only thing keeping him upright. He could barely breathe through his sobbing. Fear washed over him at the realization that he couldn't help her. He couldn't help either of them. He hunched over and gasped for air with every sob.

"Why?" Hugo asked. "Why did this happen? Why did this happen again? Help me!"

His words pleaded out into the darkness for anyone or anything to listen. There was no response.

He raised his head. There, in the corner of the basement, below the stairs, rested an oak wine barrel. Not an ordinary wine barrel. Their wine barrel. The wine they made together. The one with the special potion that caused Alice to move and enter his life. The one Hugo insisted they make the traditional way. The one where Hugo and Alice shared their first kiss. Where they embraced for the first time. Where they made love for the first time. The Lovers' Kiss.

He had to try it.

He climbed to his feet and went back into the wine cellar to grab a glass. He hurried over to the barrel. He grabbed the wooden stopper in the top center. He wiggled it back and forth; it wouldn't give up the liquid held within. He continued working it until the stopper relented.

Hugo set the glass down and grabbed both sides of the barrel. He pulled with all of his might; his leg lodged under it to provide extra leverage. The barrel was unrelenting. The wooden brace below prevented any movement. He pulled with all of his might.

"Come on, you son of a bitch," Hugo yelled. His grip was slipping.

He leaned over the barrel. His hands moved along the metal hoop that lined both ends. He positioned his hands along the backside. His grip was tight. He inhaled deeply, then held his breath, clenching his teeth. He let out a primal scream, compelling the barrel to move.

He leaned backward, and the barrel rolled with him. The reddish, purple liquid poured out of the hole, splashing against his black leather jacket. He braced the barrel against his body, his right forearm holding it in place. He took the glass and filled it to the top. He rotated the barrel back to its previous position and returned the stopper. He rushed upstairs, careful not to spill any of the contents.

He hurried to Alice and knelt by her side. The wine sloshed back and forth in the glass. A few drops slipped over the edge, ran down Hugo's hands, and splashed against the dark wood floor. He set the glass down on the coffee table. He repositioned Alice once again. He grabbed the glass, parted Alice's lips, and held the glass above her.

He paused. He inspected the wine whirling around inside the glass.

"*I feel silly,*" Alice's voice came back to him.

"*That's okay,*" he remembered reassuring her. "*We can be silly together.*"

The wine spun from the movement of his hand as it traveled from the basement to above Alice's head.

"*Spit into the cauldron,*" Alice had commanded. He remembered never taking his eyes off of her emerald greens as he spit into the black cauldron.

"*What was that?*" he asked Alice.

"*A very special potion,*" Alice replied. He remembered the seductive expression on her face. The impish smile. Her sultry eyes. The purposely misplaced strands of purple hair. A secret that only the two of them knew.

Her words came back to him. "*The Lovers' Kiss.*" She winked.

"*What does it do?*"

"*No one knows. Its secrets are lost to time. Few have attempted it. Many have died to acquire it. Wouldn't it be great to find out together?*"

Together.

He took a drink, nearly half. He poured the rest into her mouth. The liquid splashed against her lips. Small drops dripped down the side of her cheek as it rushed over the edge of the glass. He closed her gaping mouth.

Hugo set the empty glass down. He picked up her body, hoping it would help in any way possible. His hands intertwined with her purple hair as he braced the back of her head. He waited for what felt like an eternity. He set her back down on the couch.

Hugo spun around and sat on the hardwood floor. His knees

pulled up to his chest. He spotted the familiar black, onyx ring he had placed on the coffee table earlier in the evening. He snapped it up. He held it in his right hand and examined the dark shine. Hugo positioned it over his left ring finger, allowing it to hover not even an inch away. He thought of putting it back on. Going back to his life of pain and misery and torment, torturing himself with things he could no longer change.

He held the ring in his fingers. His left ring finger moved closer. His eyes watered. He sniffled to hold back the tears. He pulled the ring away, collapsing his fingers around it. He placed his closed fist to his forehead and closed his eyes. A solitary tear fell down his face. He grabbed Alice's hand. He hoped. He prayed.

CHAPTER 29
THE COUPLE THAT BREWS TOGETHER

The rhythmic beats of the heart monitor filled the room. It was dark. Only the soft glow of an overhead light above Elizabeth's bed illuminated the area. An oxygen tube was placed in her nose. Wires connected to heart monitor leads crisscrossed her body before disappearing under her hospital gown.

She wore a purple knit hat on her head; her vibrant auburn hair was a distant memory. Her face was sunken and skeletal. Her breath grew shallower with every passing moment. Hugo held Elizabeth's frail hand resting on the soft, knit blanket that covered her failing body.

He leaned back in the hospital chair. The uncomfortable vinyl padding pressed against his back. His face and eyes were red. He bit his lower lip so he could feel something. He lingered on the flowers and balloons sent by the Raskins. Their brightly colored images were a stark contrast to the barren hospital walls. They were something to help brighten her mood, if even for a fleeting moment.

A nurse entered the room. Hugo glanced toward her, but quickly returned to Elizabeth. He paid no attention as she made her routine examination of the equipment. Hugo didn't care. There was nothing she could do that would change the outcome.

The nurse broke the silence, "Does she need last rites?"

Hugo slowly took his eyes off Elizabeth and onto the nurse sitting in a swivel chair. "I'm sorry. What did you say?" Hugo asked, not hearing her original question.

"Does she need anyone to perform last rites or anything?" the nurse asked again.

"Yeah, umm, no," Hugo struggled for the answer. "The... umm... the Priest stopped by earlier."

"Good," the nurse replied as she rose from the workstation. "She can hear you. If you talk to her, she should be able to hear you."

Hugo nodded his head and in a low voice said, "Thank you. I've been talking to her."

"It's tough," the nurse said. "I know what it's like sitting there—waiting, watching, feeling helpless. It's tough."

Hugo sat silently watching Elizabeth's shallow breaths.

"But at least she has you by her side," the nurse said. "I would like to think that matters more to her than anything in the world. I believe that."

"Thank you," Hugo said.

"Hopefully, it's not too much longer." The nurse left the room.

The rhythmic beeps of the heart monitor were once again the only sounds in the room. Hugo traced a heart on the back of her hand with his thumb. He traced the same heart pattern over and over. He looked away. He couldn't watch her suffer any longer. His resolve failed him in that moment. Tears flowed down his face. He pressed down on his lips as he tried to hold them back.

"My knight in shining armor," Elizabeth said in a low raspy voice. "Did you ride to me on Galahad?"

Hugo sat up in the chair. He leaned forward, grabbing her hand with both of his. He smiled and let out a chuckle to hide his tears. "Yeah. I rode him all over the world searching for a lady fairer than thou, but we found none," Hugo replied.

She smiled. "Galahad is a good horse."

"He was."

She coughed a death rattle. Her breathing became more labored, and she closed her eyes. "I want you to live, Hugo. I want you to live on," she barely managed in her raspy voice.

"I will," Hugo said. "I will."

"Promise me," she demanded.

"I promise you."

She gasped for air. Hugo leaned forward to rest his forehead on the bed rail. "I love you, Elizabeth."

"She loves you too," Elizabeth said. Hugo raised his head, confused by her answer. "Alice loves you."

"How do you know about Alice?"

"She loves you more than you know. Keep living, Hugo. Keep living."

"We had a fight. And I said things," Hugo said through tears. "Horrible things. Things I want to take back. But I can't. She got hurt. And I tried... I tried to save her. I don't think I did. So, now I've had to watch two women I love die, while I sat there helpless."

Hugo was a sobbing mess.

"Stop torturing yourself. You did all that you could. You couldn't stop it."

"I know. But it still hurts."

"You'll always have our memories. Live for her. Live for your futures. Please."

"I will. I will," he replied. "But how do I save her?"

"You already did. And she saved you."

"How?" Hugo asked.

Elizabeth fell silent. She took one final gasp of air and was gone. Hugo buried his head into his arms. Crying out into the darkness, her hand slipped from his.

~

A HAND BRUSHED against Hugo's cheek. The soft touch of a woman's hand. Her fingers traced along his beard and jawline. He raised his head. He was back in Alice's house. The collection of macabre oddities surrounded him. He felt something stirring. He wiped the tears from his face and spun around to both knees.

Alice was awake.

"Alice!" Hugo shouted. "Can you hear me?"

Her body squirmed. Air rushed into her lungs. She arched her back, flexing out her chest before falling back down onto the couch. She stretched out her arms, knocking over the wineglass, before pulling them back. She massaged her temples, grimacing with every deep finger massage. Alice rubbed her chest where the amulet had performed its dark deed. Her palm pressed deep into her sternum. She opened her eyes and beamed at Hugo.

"Hey," Alice mustered. "You found me."

"Always," Hugo replied.

Their eyes locked. Hugo smiled at Alice, relief in his eyes. She smiled back, but then surveyed the room as if she was unfamiliar with her surroundings.

"How did I get back here?" Alice asked.

"I brought you here after what happened," Hugo replied.

"I remember a great pain, and then it stopped. What happened?"

"After you went limp, I stabbed the necklace with the wand like you told me. It disintegrated. Then Johanna disappeared into dust, and I didn't know what to do. I broke every speeding law to get here. Your reflection couldn't help me. She was laying on the floor. I tried calling Ez, but I couldn't get ahold of her. I tried some wine, and that didn't work. Then I tried the one we made together. I think it worked because you're here now," Hugo finished.

He collapsed on top of her. His head buried into her neck. His arm grabbed the side of her shoulder. Alice wrapped her arms around him. Her fingers splayed out across his back. Her hands slowly rubbed the worn leather of his jacket in concentric circles. She cried. These were not tears of sadness, but joy.

"You saved me," Alice said.

"We saved each other."

They released from their embrace. Alice sat up and rotated toward him. Hugo sat back on his heels, now positioned between Alice's legs. He touched her knees. His hands slowly worked their way up her thighs. She slightly winced. He lost himself in her eyes. His icy blues matched with her emerald greens.

"I'm so sorry," he said. "I'm sorry for what I said and how I acted. I had no right. I understand you were trying to help me. I shouldn't have acted the way I did. I love you. I love you more than you know, Alice."

"I love you too, Hugo," her words fought through tears. "It's okay. I shouldn't have acted that way, either. I shouldn't have hid the ring. I should have trusted you."

Their gazes lingered. Their hearts raced. They desired each other in a way that transcended the physical.

Hugo rose. His hands cupped around her chin and traced the outline of her jaw. They continued behind her head. His fingers interlocked with her purple hair. He closed his eyes and leaned in. His lips pressed against hers. She wrapped her arms around his torso once more, kneading her fingers into his back as if she was molding and shaping him to her desires.

He kissed her softly. Her lips were still cold against his warm lips. They breathed heavily as if they gasped for air, but only found the wet embrace of each other. Their tongues danced in a forbidden tango. He pulled back on her hair ever so slightly. Not enough to hurt, but enough to excite her and send wild sensations through her body. Her eyes closed.

Time stopped. He was lost in the ecstasy of her embrace once again. Their hearts beat as one. They stopped, forehead against forehead, coming up for needed air. They opened their eyes and found each other once again in a lovers' gaze.

"It feels like I waited hours for you to come back," Hugo said.

Alice pulled back and glanced over to the end table where the hourglass stood. "Did you touch the hourglass again?"

"Yeah," Hugo replied. "What do you think stopped you from dying?"

Alice snapped back toward Hugo; her eyebrows crinkled. "Did you—" she started. "Did you speed it back up after giving me the wine?"

"No."

"Well, no wonder it felt like hours," Alice stated. "You should have sped it back up after giving me the wine."

"How was I supposed to know that?"

"You literally passed out on my floor because of it," Alice shouted as she fell back onto the velvet couch.

"You're welcome," Hugo responded.

Alice leaned forward. Her soft lips pressed against his to give him one more brief kiss. "I love you, Hugo," Alice said. "But you need to stop with your parlor tricks and learn how real magick works."

"That's it! Where's that necklace?" he joked as they broke into laughter.

Alice turned the ring in the hourglass back to the center. Alice's cell phone buzzed in Hugo's pocket and then fell silent.

"Hey," a familiar voice yelled from upstairs. "What's going on down there? I'm fine, by the way. No need to check on me."

"Should we go check on her?" Hugo asked.

"Let her wait a little longer," Alice answered, wrapping her arms around his shoulders.

She leaned in closer. An invisible force pulled them together. Closer. Eyes locked. Smiles wide across their faces. With desire in her eyes, Alice bit her lower lip. Hugo wanted Alice, and he knew she wanted him. A fleeting thought of picking her up once more and carrying her upstairs entered his mind. He could feel her warm breath on his lips.

"Where's Gally?" Alice asked.

Hugo's joyful expression faded into somberness. Alice's smile was a distant memory, replaced by panic and fear.

"What's wrong?"

"Alice..." Hugo struggled. "I'm so sorry. I think... I think Gally's dead."

Alice cleared a lump in her throat. Her breathing quickened. She shook her head in disbelief. "Where is he?"

"I'll go get him," Hugo said as he stood up.

He kissed Alice on the top of her head before leaving through the front door. Hugo sprinted down the front steps, heading to Alice's SUV. He grasped the back door handle. He paused for a moment, hoping, wishing, praying his buddy would be moving around, excited to see him.

He peered through the window and saw the brown broomstick. The slanted, charging head. The black streaks. The tan knots. The worn, brown, saddle style bicycle seat. The silver metal footrest he gave Alice as a present last Christmas. The black broomcorn with streaks of red and purple. His eyes welled up. There, laying motionless on the back seat, was the horse dog broomstick that flew him to find Alice.

He opened the door. He nudged the broomstick once more, but it didn't move.

"Oh, Gally. I'm so sorry." Tears fell down his face. He picked up the broomstick, cradled it in his arms, and held it close. The saddle seat pressed against his chest. "You were a good flying buddy. You rescued me when I fell. You looked after me. We flew all over, and you took me to find the best witch of all. I'll miss you." Hugo squeezed once more and carried Galahad into Alice's house.

Alice swung her legs off the couch and sat up as Hugo entered. "Oh, Gally," she cried. She stood up and rushed to Hugo.

He handed her the lifeless broomstick. Alice embraced the cold hickory handle. She rubbed her fingertips down the slant of its head and back up. Tears flowed down her face, falling to the hardwood floor. She wiped them away.

Tears welled in Hugo's eyes. "Can you fix him?"

Alice's grip on the hickory handle tightened. Weeping, Alice answered, "I can't."

Sniffling, Hugo wiped his nose with the back of his hand. "He was a good horse dog. A great horse dog. He pulled up and took the full brunt of it. He saved me. What was that?"

Sporadic gasps between her running tears, she managed, "It was an anti-magick wand. She used it to cause me great pain, but on Galahad—"

She paused before continuing, "On Gally, it stripped him of his magical abilities. I can't... I can't bring him back." She clutched Galahad close to her chest. Her head rested against its head.

Hugo pulled out the black, twisting wand from his jacket pocket. Alice's eyes drew toward the twisting point. Hugo grabbed both ends of the wand. His thumbs pushed up the center. His hands pulled the ends down. The wand bent, but it was unrelenting.

He pushed harder, and small cracks appeared. His nose flared. Anger burned in his eyes. A vengeful rage filled him. He pulled it closer to his chest, using it as leverage for his thumbs. There was a snap and then a crack before the wand shattered into pieces. Small bits of the center fell to the ground.

"There," Hugo said, holding the two ends in his curled fingers. "It can't hurt us anymore."

A half smile returned to Alice's face. "Thank you," she said. "Thank you for everything." She carried Galahad into her living room. Hugo followed.

"Hey," the voice yelled from upstairs. "Don't forget about me."

CHAPTER 30
THE NEIGHBORHOOD WITCH

There was a knock at the front door. Three distinct knocks echoed through the hallway. Alice left the kitchen to answer it. She already knew who waited on the other side. One knock, a slight pause, followed by two rapid knocks. Alice picked up her pace.

"I'm coming," she yelled. "I'm coming."

A shadow impatiently shuffled around on the other side of the black sheer curtain, surrounded by the sunny spring day. The knocks echoed once more before Alice gripped the knob.

She flung open the door. The warm spring air filled the hallway. Her eyes adjusted to the bright light. She found Esmerelda Honeydew waiting on the other side. Her head was tilted to the side, and she was frowning. She tapped the heels of her flats on the gray porch boards. One eyebrow arched.

"Hello, Ez."

"First of all," she said. "You called me last night and left some inaudible message."

"Oh, right," Alice replied. "The message. Sorry about that. I can explain. It was actually—"

"Then you didn't return my calls," she interrupted.

"Again, sorry," Alice pleaded. "I had a good reason."

"And then I had to drive all the way over here to make sure you're okay," Esmerelda scolded.

"I appreciate that. I really do."

"I'm glad you're okay, kiddo. Aren't you going to invite me in?"

"Oh yes," Alice said. "Please come in."

Esmerelda stepped inside. Alice closed the door, revealing multiple pairs of shoes. Alice noticed Esmerelda's discerning look over the extra shoes. Esmerelda removed her overcoat and placed it on the rack next to Hugo's black leather jacket. Two additional jackets were hung as well. One, a tan man's jacket. The other, a woman's overcoat. Esmerelda surveyed the empty living room. She glanced upstairs, waiting for her welcoming knocks of wood against wood. There was only silence.

"Everything okay, kiddo?"

"Fine," Alice responded as she disappeared back into the kitchen. "I'm making tea. Would you like some?"

"I never pass up a good cup of tea," she said. "I received an interesting news alert on my phone this morning."

"Oh, what was it about?" Alice grabbed the kettle to pour the steaming water into a purple, ceramic teapot. She felt as if she already knew the answer.

"It's a funny thing. I have news alerts set up for any sort of witchy activity that would be in the news."

"Oh." Alice cringed. The events of last night played out again in her mind. "Anything in particular you want to be alerted about?"

"You see, when you're helping to hide someone in a small town, you'll want to keep tabs on them. Like, oh, maybe setup news alerts from the local town paper with keywords like *witch*, or I don't know, *broomstick*."

Alice set the kettle down. Her shoulders slumped as she prepared herself for one of Ez's scoldings. "Those are some good keywords."

"To my surprise, I had an alert this morning from a certain small-town newspaper, which happens to be the very same town where a certain witch is hiding out. The article described how people saw someone flying through the air on what they thought was a broomstick."

Alice reappeared in the kitchen entryway. Her lips disappeared as they compressed into her mouth. "First of all, that wasn't me." She exclaimed, holding a finger in the air. She held up another. "Second of all, there is a very good explanation, which I will tell you... most of the details."

Esmerelda arched her eyebrows. Her eyes shot annoyed glances toward Alice.

"Every detail," Alice said before disappearing again behind the wall. She grabbed the purple, ceramic teapot and exited the kitchen.

Esmerelda gave a final glance back up the stairs before proceeding down the hallway. She took a seat at Alice's dining room table. She peeked through the bay window toward Hugo's house. Alice set the teapot down on a quilted black holder and checked to see what captured Ez's attention. The white paint was blinding in the sunny midday sky.

Alice smiled and took her seat. She snapped her fingers, and two black tea cups flew in from the kitchen toward the table. Three more followed and rested on the table in front of the other chairs.

Esmerelda's eyes widened. "Expecting more visitors?"

"No," Alice replied.

Ez snapped her fingers. The teapot rose from its position and hovered over her cup. The steaming, hot liquid poured out as the teapot tipped over. The teapot righted itself and sat back down on the holder once the cup was nearly full. Esmerelda picked up her cup, blew on the tea, and took a sip.

"Start talking," she said.

"Well"—Alice picked up the teapot—"that wasn't me." She poured herself a cup.

"Who was it?"

Alice took a sip, using the cup to hide her face. She peered over the rim toward Esmeralda. She licked her lips, wiping away drops of tea. "It was Hugo."

"Hugo?!?" she asked with a hint of anger. "Flying on your broomstick. During the day?"

"It was sunset," Alice replied.

Ez set her cup down. "Alice! We discussed this."

"He hurried to find me—"

"Find you?" Ez interrupted.

"So, the neighbor across the street—the one I told you was snooping around the house—she had an amulet of witch's fire. She tried to use it on me and would have succeeded if not for Hugo riding on Galahad, even though people saw him."

Esmerelda's face became solemn. She held her breath before asking, "Where is the amulet now?"

Alice took another sip. "Gone. Destroyed. Hugo destroyed it with an anti-magick wand."

Esmerelda breathed a sigh of relief. "At least she didn't use it on you."

Alice's eyes focused on the steam rising from the dark liquid held within her cup. She took a sip. "She did." Her eyes now focused on Esmerelda Honeydew, waiting for her reaction.

Esmerelda's eyes betrayed her stoic appearance with panic, fear, and anger. "Then how the hell are you sitting right here?"

Alice cleared her throat. "Well, Hugo brought me back here and then—" Her voice trailed off. She braced herself for the anger that would follow. She rotated her head, clearing any tension that had built up in her neck. "We had made a special batch of wine—"

"How special?" Esmerelda was quick to ask; her face furled as if she already knew the answer.

Alice hesitated. She took one more sip to hide behind the cup. She prepared for the wrath that was sure to follow. "We made some of The Lovers' Kiss."

"He knows? He knows about the spell? You told him? You gave up the very thing that brought you here in the first place?" Esmerelda asked.

Alice buried her chin into her chest, trying to sink away. She thought of the night she met Hugo in the backyard. How he was unafraid of her being a witch. She thought of him inviting her to the fall festival. She thought of Halloween night. She thought of Hugo opening up to her. The broom riding lessons. Christmas. The New Year's Eve party. Hugo consoling her on the sidewalk. Ordering the additional grapes. Flying to find her.

Alice sat up in her chair. Her shoulders were pulled back, and her head held high. Alice locked eyes with Esmerelda. "Hugo loves me more than you know—more than Sam ever did. He cares about me and wants to see me succeed. He embraces who I am and what I do. He never used to it his advantage. He never shied away. He wants me to be who I am."

The anger and frustration faded from Esmerelda's face. She leaned back into the chair, and her shoulders drooped. Her head tilted toward the side. "He must really love you."

A smile appeared on Alice's face. She set the cup down and blinked a few times to hide the swelling tears. "We love each other," she replied. "We've both helped each other. He's the only one I've ever considered making The Lovers' Kiss with. Without that potion, I wouldn't be sitting here in front of you today. He's the only one I'll ever make it with."

"Just be careful, kiddo."

"I'm always careful."

"Now, where's my buddy?"

Alice's smile faded. Her eyes closed as she bowed her head. She paused. The room fell silent only broken by the ticking of the clock in the living room.

"What's wrong?" Ez asked.

Alice glanced up to the ceiling before focusing on Ez. She wiped a tear from her eye. "He didn't make it. Johanna killed him with the anti-magick wand."

Ez took her eyes off Alice. She focused on a spot on the table, cupping her mouth and chin with her right hand. She sat in silence. Alice shifted in her seat. Ez extended across the table to grab Alice's hands and looked into her eyes. "I'm so... so sorry, kiddo."

Alice silently nodded. "He brought Hugo to me. If not for him, then Hugo wouldn't have found me in time."

"He was a good buddy."

"I know. The best buddy any witch could ask for."

The basement door opened, and Max came charging through. She ran over to greet the new visitor. Her tail wagged back and forth. She laid her head on Esmerelda's lap, begging for attention.

"I remember you." Ez patted her on the head. "Have you been a good girl?"

Hugo appeared from behind the door. "I've been trying to tell her that she could make a fortune selling that stuff in your store," he said down the stairs.

Esmerelda turned to the basement door. Her mouth agape, eyes wide, and eyebrows scrunched at the sudden disturbance. Hugo held the door as Carol and Oliver Raskin emerged from the basement as well.

"Even if it didn't have all of that magical stuff in it, we can make a fortune on the branding alone," Oliver said. "Only available at The Neighborhood Market, locally brewed wine by *The Neighborhood Witch*. I see the potential. *I see the potential.*"

"Always some gimmick with you," Carol replied.

"It's a great gimmick," Oliver stated.

"I'd have to agree with Oliver on this one," Hugo chimed in.

"See!" Oliver added. "But I'm also serious."

Esmerelda snapped back at Alice. "Who are these people?"

"They're... umm..." Alice stammered, trying to justify why strangers were in her home.

"Carol Raskin," she introduced herself with an outstretched hand.

Esmerelda turned and daintily shook her hand. "Charmed."

"Carol, this is Esmerelda Honeydew. She's my mentor and close friend," Alice said as she stood up.

"My friends call me Ez," she added.

"Well, Ez, it's a pleasure to meet you. This walking gimmick machine is my husband Oliver." Carol motioned back toward him.

"Pleased to meet you," he said with a nod.

Esmerelda glared at Alice; her eyes blinked rapidly. "So, does everyone know you're a witch? What happened to laying low?"

"After Hugo's little joy ride—" Oliver started.

"It wasn't a *joy ride*," Hugo interrupted.

"I agree with Hugo on that one," Alice added. "There was no joy in that ride."

Oliver continued, "We could claim that what people saw was a marketing stunt. Like one of those drones. Think of it. A witch mysteriously appears over Newbury Grove. Rumors spread—"

"Then we put up signs at the store. *Have you seen The Neighborhood Witch?* Anticipation builds. Then we have a big launch event," Carol finished his thought.

"I'd have my own wine in a store!" Alice smiled at the thought.

"If everyone *did* know she was a witch, then we could really move some wine," Oliver said. Everyone glared at him, eyes wide. Carol gave him an expression that screamed 'shut up' in the silence. "What? It's the truth."

Hugo strutted over and stood next to Alice. He slipped his hand behind hers. Alice interlocked her fingers with his.

"Ez, it's okay," he said, drawing her attention. "Carol and Oliver are like parents to me. They've looked after me... looked after us. With any potential rumors that could go around, we needed someone we could trust. I... I trust them. We trust them. It's okay, I promise you. Her secret is safe."

"It's not her being a witch I'm worried about," Ez replied.

"Esmerelda," Alice said, pulling her attention away from Hugo. Esmerelda's suspicious expression now dissolved into shock as Alice rarely spoke her full name. "You saw potential in me when no one else would, and I am forever grateful for that. They, especially Hugo, take me for the way I am. They accept me. They love me."

Hugo leaned in and rested his head on her shoulder. Alice rested her head on his. Esmerelda peered over to the Raskins. Oliver placed his hand on Carol's shoulder. They all smiled at her. Max laid her head on Ez's leg. Her tail wagged back and forth.

Esmerelda shook her head. "Non-magick wine?"

"Non-magick wine," Alice confirmed.

"It does solve the joy riding problem."

"It wasn't a joy..." Hugo's voice trailed off.

Alice kissed him on the cheek. "It was kind of a joy ride," she said with a wink.

Hugo gave Alice a shocked glance. "My side still hurts from where Gally slammed into it, not to mention when I crashed to the ground. You're welcome, by the way."

"Being front and center selling wine wouldn't exactly be laying low," Ez exclaimed, souring the mood.

Alice thought of a reply to counter Ez's doubts. The idea of having her own wine was too good to pass up. "No one needs to know it was me."

"You'd be the first person everyone would point to," Ez countered. "You're not exactly laying low as it is."

"Right, and I'd deny it," Alice answered. "I don't need my face on the bottle or a poster or anything. As long as it's my wine in the store, that's good enough for me."

"That's part of the mystique," Oliver added. "We don't know where it came from. If anyone questions it, we can say some vineyard wanted to use us as a test market."

Esmerelda was silent for a moment. "I hate to admit it," Ez started before picking up her cup. "I think Oliver has a good idea."

"See! She agrees with me," Oliver said with a giddy hint in his voice. "I know what I'm talking about."

"Just because she agrees with you doesn't mean you know what you're talking about," Carol added.

"So, I can sell my wine?" Alice asked.

"I was never going to stop you, kiddo. If it's what you want to do, I won't stop you. Just be careful."

Alice smiled and squeezed Hugo's hand.

"Now let's sit down and have some tea before it gets cold," Carol said as she moved toward the table.

They all sat down. With a snap of Alice's finger, the teapot rose and filled everyone's cup. The husband and wife grocers, the bar owner, the widower, and the neighborhood witch.

THE NEW NEIGHBORS

Hugo pulled back the sheer, black curtain and leered out the window. The distinct yellow running lights of a large semitruck pulled down Ravenhill Drive. The truck's wheels screeched and moaned under the weight of the truck coming to a full stop in front of Hugo's old home.

"Hey, babe," Hugo shouted.

"Yeah?" Alice peeked around the corner of the living room.

"So, the neighbors are moving in next door." Hugo stared out the window.

"So?"

"So? It's nearly midnight," Hugo answered. "And there is this huge semitruck that rolled down the street."

"I moved in at night," she reminded him.

"Well, you didn't have a semitruck."

"What difference does it make?"

"Well, I don't like it," Hugo said, continuing to peep outside the window.

Alice sauntered over and stood behind Hugo. She wrapped her arms around him. Her hands slowly crawled over his black T-shirt.

They worked their way across his chest and up his shoulders. She rubbed her hands into him a few times before coming to a rest. She placed her chin on his shoulder. She exhaled slowly, trying to entice him to do the same.

"Honey, you're nervous," she said. Her breath tickled as the words entered his ear.

"I'm not nervous."

She massaged the front of his shoulders with her fingers in small, concentric circles. "You are. We agreed to keep this house so you could finally let go of your old one. Now, you're nervous that it's actually happening. You need to let it go."

He brought his right hand up to his shoulder. He gave her hand a few taps before resting on top of it. He breathed in deeply. He exhaled, letting go of the sheer curtain with his other hand.

"You're right. No, you are right. I didn't think this day would come, and I'm freaking out."

"Of course I'm right," she said before kissing him on the cheek.

She slowly dragged her hands back across his chest. Her fingers lightly touched his abdomen below his ribs. They traced an invisible line around the side. Hugo closed his eyes, burning every sensual tracing into his memory. Her hands slid across his back. He arched out his chest. The sensation tickled him straight to his soul. She let go of Hugo.

Her hands hovered in the air for a moment before rushing back toward him. She slapped his butt and gave him a wink.

"Now go upstairs and finish getting dressed," Alice said as she retreated into the living room.

Hugo turned and went upstairs. The door to their bedroom was halfway open. The door was now whole. Replaced after Galahad, who over six months prior, had charged through it. Hugo entered the room. It was dimly lit from a bedside lamp next to the canopy bed. Max was curled up in the center of the bed. Her snores filled the room. She stopped at the noise of someone entering. She raised her head to see Hugo and wiggled the tip of her tail before she dug her head right back into the warmth of the bed comforter.

"You snore louder than me, buddy," Hugo said as he entered the bathroom.

He flipped on the light switch. He proceeded over to the porcelain sink and turned on the hot water, allowing it to run for a moment to heat up. He tested the water with a few swipes. He turned the other knob find the right mixture of hot and cold water.

Hugo cupped his hands, filling them with a small pool. He leaned over the sink and splashed the water on his face, working it into his beard. The water dripped down into the basin below. The steam from the hot water rose in the chilly air. He stood up and combed his beard with his fingers. He ran his wet fingers through his hair. He peered into the mirror to see his reflection to make sure his beard was perfectly groomed.

His reflection did not look back, nor was it alone. His reflection was locked in a battle of sexual conquest with Alice's reflection. Their lips pressed against each other's, battling for position. Their arms wrapped in a primal embrace. Their fingers tried to tear into each other's clothes. Her nails dug into his back and dragged along his shirt. He moaned as her fingers dug deeper into his back.

Hugo knocked on the side of the mirror. "Hey! Hey, you two. Knock it off. I need your help."

They stopped and pulled their heads away from each other. They glared at Hugo, annoyed at being interrupted.

"Go away," Hugo's reflection said.

"We're busy," Alice's reflection added.

They turned back toward each other. They pressed their lips together, jockeying for dominance. Their tongues combated in a seductive tango, lightly touching before retreating, then charging forth once again.

"Can you take like ten seconds to let me know if I look okay?" Hugo asked.

They pulled away from each other again. They shot Hugo annoyed glances. Each tilted their head and arched an eyebrow.

"You look fine," they each said before returning to each other.

Hugo's reflection dragged his hands down to the small of her back. She arched her back and moaned as his hands traveled further and further down. He jolted his hands down to grab her butt. He lifted her into the air and pinned her against the bathroom wall. She wrapped her legs around his torso, squeezing tightly to hold her grip. She moved her hands to the top of his shoulders. They stopped kissing only for a moment as they repositioned their bodies.

"I love you," his reflection said.

"I loved you first," Alice's reflection replied. They resumed their sexual conquest.

"Alice should really separate you two," Hugo protested.

Alice's reflection held up a hand and gave Hugo the finger. It was only for a moment before her hand found its way back to his reflection's shoulder. Hugo left the bathroom and turned off the lights.

"Finally," his reflection said.

Hugo paid no attention to it. He grabbed his black dress shirt off the bed and slipped it over his arms. He proceeded to button it as he jogged back downstairs. He removed his black leather jacket from the coat rack at the base of the steps.

"We really need a 'his and hers' mirror to separate those two," Hugo said as he slipped on the jacket.

"No, it'll make things worse," Alice replied. "We'll have to hear them pine for each other over and over all the time. It's for the best. Trust me."

She stood in the hallway wearing her signature brimmed, curved, pointed, wool hat. Her purple hair emerged from underneath it. She wore her black and purple, modern Victorian tailcoat. Black leather pants tucked neatly into her thick-soled boots. Hugo paused for a moment. He took her all in. His eyes traced the curves of her frame. He smiled.

"What?"

"Nothing," Hugo replied. "I wanted to burn this to memory."

Alice blushed and returned a smile. She moved closer and brushed a few of his hairs into place.

"I knew something was off," Hugo said. "They're so busy making out up there. They told me everything looked fine."

"Everything does look fine," she replied before kissing him on the forehead. "This is our one-year anniversary of meeting. Try to relax and enjoy it."

He wrapped his arms around her torso, drawing her closer. "I'm relaxed now," Hugo said. "What do you say we forget this whole thing and go upstairs and join in on the fun?"

"Later," Alice said as she touched his nose. "First, we ride. I'm not wasting a good moon."

She pulled away from Hugo and headed down the hallway toward the kitchen. She gave a whistle. An ash white broomstick entered from the living room. The handle was completely straight. The broomstick was broomcorn purple with streaks of bloodred and black. It had a large, brown, saddle style bicycle seat with an attached footrest. It followed Alice as it floated down the hallway. Hugo followed them.

Four movers, dressed in black coveralls, opened the doors to the semitruck trailer to reveal the treasures held within its cavernous hold. One pulled down a ramp. The screech of metal against metal sounded as one of them pulled it from a secret chamber. He bent down and dropped it. The loud clanging echoed through the silence of Ravenhill Drive. Two workers picked the other end up and secured it to the back of the trailer.

Boxes, crates, and covered furniture filled the back half of the trailer—all neatly packed and well organized. Two rectangular wooden crates were placed at the entryway of the trailer. They were longer than a person laying down and only a couple of feet high.

They were nondescript outside of a single red letter on each crate. A capital *K* on one. A capital *Q* on the other.

They were each placed on rolling dollies secured to the trailer by red straps. The movers removed the straps and threw them into a pile off to the side. They removed wood blocks that stopped the dolly wheels from moving and released the wheel brakes. In teams of two, they took positions at the ends of the crates. One held the bottom of the crate, while the other pushed the dolly handles. They carefully maneuvered the crates down the ramp.

Their four-person procession guided the crates up to the porch. They struggled to lift the crates. Each step creaked and moaned from the weight now bearing down on them. The crate with the red *Q* was first to go up the stairs.

The front mover, pulling up on the handle, struggled to get the wheels up each step. Each more odious than the last, as if the steps were fighting against the new occupants. The mover pushing the bottom of the crate heaved with all of his might. The other pulled with all of his. The wheels struggled to overcome the lip of the step. The step fought back.

One final push, and the wheels ventured up. During this entire process, not a sound was made from the movers. They worked in silence—unrelenting, unnerving. They opened the front door and proceeded inside with both crates.

ALICE AND HUGO entered the backyard followed by the broomstick. A crisp chill was in the autumn air. The full moon shone bright, illuminating the swaying treetops. Leaves rustled on the ground as they blew helplessly in the wind. They both took a deep breath and exhaled slowly, creating a stream of white fog. They continued for what felt like an eternity to Alice. She strained her abdomen to push it out further and further. He was the first to relent.

"I win," Alice said.

"You only won because I'm sure you're using magick of some sort," Hugo replied.

"I take great offense to that and my abilities to exhale," Alice retorted. "A bit of magick does help, though." She winked at Hugo.

"I knew it."

Alice grabbed the broomstick handle and swung her leg over. She sat back and gazed up to the moon above. The glowing bluish, white light greeted her like an old friend.

"What a great night for a ride," she said. "How I've missed this."

She ran her fingers along the top of the broom handle. The broom bounced up and down with excitement.

"Do you think it's ready?" Hugo swung his legs over and sat on the back of the seat.

He wrapped his arms around Alice's stomach, slowly drawing himself closer to her. She smiled and allowed herself a moment to enjoy the tantalizing sensation flowing through her body.

"He's ready," Alice said.

"What about them?" Hugo motioned toward the neighbors with his head.

Alice snapped her fingers. The surrounding area grew darker, blotting out the light in the backyard.

"They won't see us now," she replied.

Alice placed her feet on the metal footrests. She gripped the rough wooden handle. She could feel every cracked groove in the gnarled bark.

She sat there for a moment to take it all in before she leaned forward to yell out, "Yah!"

She pulled up on the broom handle and they took off into the night sky, flying toward the moon. As they cleared the backyard, a light turned on next door in the upstairs bedroom of Hugo Dodds' old house.

ALICE AND HUGO
WILL RETURN

ACKNOWLEDGMENTS

The characters, who would eventually become Alice and Hugo, have been with me since I was a teenager. They took on different names and forms, but their core personalities remained the same. Alice with her witchy magick, and Hugo with his fierce loyalty. They've always been there, but they became dormant in my imagination for a long period of time. Not forgotten, just dormant.

In October 2020, I visited a Maryland pumpkin patch with my brother. People were enjoying the season and looking for an excuse to leave the house during the height of the pandemic. I turned around and saw a woman posing for a picture seated among the pumpkins. I never saw her face, but she wore a black wide-brimmed hat. It was as if Alice Primrose herself was posing and a voice said, "Remember me?"

I want to start by thanking whoever was posing in the pumpkin patch that late October Saturday. The journey to get this book published began at that very moment.

To my brother. Thank you for recommending going that October Saturday. Without your suggestion, this book does not exist.

To my family and friends. Thank you for your encouragement along this journey. Thank you for the kind words and support. It truly means a lot.

To my beta readers. Thank you for your valuable insight and suggestions which helped me along my journey.

To my editor, Nichole Heydenburg. Thank you for being patient with me on my countless questions as a first-time author.

To my logo and cover designer, Fay Lane. Thank you for being accommodating, as I scrutinized over the minor details. The cover is outstanding.

To my book blurb editor, Kara Bernard. Thank you for helping me set the tone of the book before I started.

To my animated cover designer, Morgan Wright. Thank you for capturing the witchy essence of the cover.

To my character illustrator, Nicole Deal. Thank you for helping to bring these characters to life.

To my paternal great-aunts. Thank you for keeping that broken wine press in your garage all of those years. I think it seeped into my subconscious and gave me inspiration for Alice's wine cellar.

To my maternal great-grandmother, Ducky. Your short stature, youthful appearance, larger-than-life personality, and love of Halloween are still an inspiration years later. Also, thank you for introducing me to Pink Floyd.

To all of my writing teachers. Thank you for encouraging me to continue writing. I still am.

To the online #WritingCommunity. Thank you for answering my questions and providing daily distractions from writing. Now, stop scrolling and write something.

To my golden retriever, and the inspiration behind "Max", Chloi (pronounced Chloe). Thank you for dealing with my sleepless nights over the past two years as I finished this book. Thank you for waking me up during "The Witching Hour" at 3:30 a.m. to go outside. You provided the inspiration behind Hugo and Alice's meeting. You're the bestest buddy anyone could ask for.

Finally, thank you, Dear Reader. Thank you for taking the time to come along with me on this journey. This is just the beginning of Alice and Hugo's story. I hope you follow along in the future.

-Christopher M. Mason

ABOUT THE AUTHOR

Christopher M. Mason is an author and storyteller with a love of the gothic, paranormal, and fantasy. He grew up in Ohio and is a graduate of Wright State University, where he learned the art storytelling. *The Neighborhood Witch* is his first novel. Keep up to date with the Neighborhood Series and more by visiting his official website and social media.

www.christophermmason.com

CPSIA information can be obtained
at www.ICGtesting.com
Printed in the USA
BVHW032118140223
658502BV00002B/7